D0171461

Also by *New York Times* bestselling author
Beverly Barton and HQN Books

Worth Dying For

Watch for Beverly Barton's next
HQN title in fall 2007

BEVERLY
BARTON

DANGEROUS
DECEPTION

HQN™

To "The Children" and their playground monitor:
Kira Bazzel, Kim Kerr, Andrea Laurence,
Marilyn Puett and Danniele Worsham.

ISBN-13: 978-0-373-77067-0
ISBN-10:   0-373-77067-7

DANGEROUS DECEPTION

This edition published by arrangement with Harlequin Books S.A.

® and TM are trademarks of the publisher. Trademarks indicated with
® are registered in the United States Patent and Trademark Office, the
Canadian Trade Marks Office and in other countries.

www.HQNBooks.com

Printed in U.S.A.

PROLOGUE

I SWEAR I'LL FIND YOU.

Lausanne Raney ran the tip of her index finger over the blurry photograph, her touch gentle, almost reverent. Ten years ago, she had snapped this picture through the glass window that shielded the hospital nursery from the outside world. A thin barrier between her and her newborn daughter.

You have to know that I did what I thought was best for you. I was seventeen, with nobody who cared if I lived or died and not a cent to my name.

If she had it to do over again, would she still give her baby up for adoption? Pressing the snapshot to her breast, Lausanne clenched her teeth. She didn't cry anymore. She hadn't cried in years. Tears were useless. Self pity served no purpose.

Yes. The answer was yes. If circumstances were the same, then she'd still give away her child.

She'd known then, as she knew now, that allowing some childless couple to adopt her daughter had given the baby her only chance for a decent life.

Yeah, just look what a mess I've made of my life. If

*I'd kept you, I'd have screwed you up something awful.
I couldn't do that to you, sweet baby.*

Lausanne placed the photograph back in the small
box that contained only two other items. A tiny gold
cross attached to a necklace that had belonged to her
mother and Lausanne's GED certificate that she had
earned while serving five years in the state penitentiary.

But that was then. This is now. She had served her
time, paid her debt to society. And God help her, she had
learned her lesson. She couldn't trust anybody, couldn't
depend on anyone but herself, didn't dare risk falling in
love again. Her track record with men sucked. Her first
love had left her alone and pregnant. But that was
nothing compared to lover number two. He'd robbed a
convenience store while she waited in the car, oblivious
to what he was doing. But in the eyes of the law, she had
been his accomplice.

Lausanne closed the lid on the small box, then
crossed the bedroom of her two-room apartment in
Chattanooga, stood on tiptoe and slid the box onto the
top shelf in her tiny closet.

She wasn't going to live in a dump like this forever.
One day, she'd have a nice place, a new car and pretty
clothes. Someday. After she found out where her little
girl was. While she'd been in the pen, she'd made herself
two promises. One: When she got out, she'd work hard
and build a good life for herself. Two: She'd find out
where her daughter was and make sure she was well and
happy and with a good family.

Lausanne checked her appearance in the cracked

full-length mirror attached to the front of the closet door with rusty metal hinges. The entire outfit had cost her sixty bucks, but on her, the clothes looked more expensive. She had a knack for mixing and matching, for coordinating, for copying the styles she saw in magazines but using off-the-rack items from discount stores.

Today was step one in her plan to fulfill those promises to herself. Today she would begin a new job as a receptionist at Bedell, Inc. No more waitress jobs for her. And just as she'd been doing for the past six months when she'd been scratching by on minimum wage, part of each paycheck would go into a fund to hire a private agency to help her find her daughter.

CHAPTER ONE

SAWYER MCNAMARA, the CEO of the Dundee Private Security and Investigation Agency, handed the three agents congregated at the table in the conference room separate file folders. As he took his seat at the head of the table, he glanced at each person, his gaze lingering on Lucie Evans. As if sensing his intense scrutiny, Lucie looked up and glared at their boss.

"What?" she asked, her tone combative.

Sawyer shrugged. "Woke up on the wrong side of the bed, Evans?"

Bristling, Lucie frowned, then growled deep in her throat.

Nothing new there, Dom Shea thought. Any conversation between Sawyer and Lucie started and ended as a battle of wills. The two mixed like oil and water. And the entire Dundee staff couldn't figure out why Lucie was still a Dundee employee. Why hadn't she quit long ago? Or better yet, why hadn't Sawyer fired her? Who knew? Dom sure as hell didn't want to get in the middle of anything. He'd actually dated Lucie a few times. They'd had fun, but from the get-go, it had been apparent that there weren't any real sexual sparks between them, so they'd settled for being friends. Dom wasn't friends with Sawyer. He respected his boss. Liked the guy. Even admired him. But Sawyer McNamara kept a definite distance between himself and his agents.

"I'm sending y'all out on new assignments today," Sawyer said. "Read over the files I've given you, and if you have any questions, now's the time to ask. And if for any reason somebody wants to swap an assignment with another agent—think twice. I chose each of you specifically for the job I assigned to you."

They all understood that was Sawyer's way of saying, if you don't want the job I've assigned you, tough shit.

Dom opened the file folder—a rather thick dossier that included numerous copies of newspaper photos and articles as well as snapshots. The words Bedell, Inc. jumped off the pages at him. In the Southeast, the name Bedell was synonymous with old money. Generations of multi-millionaires accumulating wealth had made the current head of the family a billionaire. The original Edward Bedell, who'd settled in Tennessee before the War Between the States, had made his fortune with the railroad and later diversified. The current Edward Bedell's holdings covered a wide span of business interests worldwide—everything from real estate and construction to pharmaceutical sales and research. But the Bedell, Inc. headquarters was based in Chattanooga where the chairman of the board lived. Edward personally oversaw the day-to-day running of his family's corporation.

After flipping through the photos, Dom paused on a wedding picture from the Chattanooga Times Free Press dated six years ago. Audrey Bedell and Grayson Perkins. The golden couple. Studying the picture, Dom wasn't sure who was the prettiest, Audrey or her groom. Perkins had model perfect good looks that proclaimed him too gorgeous to be a man.

"You're sending me back to England!" Lucie pounded her fist on the table. Only once. But once was enough to shake the table and startle everyone in the room. Everyone except Sawyer, who narrowed his gaze smugly. The corners of his mouth tilted upward ever so slightly in a hint of a self-satisfied smile.

"Is there a problem with your taking this assignment in London?" Sawyer asked.

Squaring her shoulders and sitting up straight as a board, Lucie glowered at him, her henna brown eyes wide with indignation. "I spent the past two months in London and have had exactly five days downtime. From the initial report I read—" she tapped her index finger on the file folder "—I could easily be in London for another couple of months."

"Possibly longer," Sawyer replied.

Lucie gritted her teeth. "You could send Geoff Monday. He's a Brit and I'd think he'd jump at the chance to go home for a while."

"Geoff is busy on another assignment. Besides, you'll be guarding Mr. Smirnov's wife and children for the duration of his stay in London. He specifically requested a female agent. At present, that's you, Ms. Evans."

"Fine." Lucie gathered up the contents of the file, stuffed them back into the folder, then shot up out of her chair. "I'll check in with Daisy if I need anything." She jerked her shoulder bag off the back of the chair and marched straight to the door, then opened it and paused momentarily. After shooting Sawyer a bird, she left the office and slammed the door behind her.

Acting as if nothing had happened, as if one of his employees hadn't blatantly showed her disrespect, Sawyer glanced from Dom to Deke Bronson. "Finish looking over the files I gave you and if you have any questions—"

"No questions," Deke replied in a gut-deep, gravely voice that so perfectly matched his road-hard-and-put-away-wet appearance. "I think my assignment is pretty cut and dried. No need for any lengthy explanations."

Sawyer nodded. "Call me personally as soon as you get to California and speak to Berger. Putting his personal staff of bodyguards through the Dundee training sessions is a six-week deal, one that will make Dundee's a great deal of money. I'm sending you because you're the most intimidating-looking agent I have. Berger's hard ass staff will take one look at you and obey orders."

Expressionless, Bronson nodded.

After Deke left the room, Sawyer turned to Dom. "I assume you have questions."

"A few," Dom said. "First, am I handling this case alone or—"

"You'll go in alone...initially. If you need backup, I'll arrange it. And all of Dundee's resources will be available, as usual."

Dom tapped the file folder. "Why hasn't he called in the Chattanooga PD on this? If my daughter were missing—"

"That's just it," Sawyer said. "He's not one-hundred percent sure she's actually missing. It's just that no one has seen or heard from her in over a week."

"I'd call that missing."

"I agree…if Audrey Bedell Perkins was your average woman."

"Which she isn't."

"That's right," Sawyer agreed.

"So what does Daddy Moneybags think happened to his daughter? And what does her hubby think?"

"Bedell told me that at first he feared she'd been kidnapped, but there hasn't been either a ransom note or a phone call. He then assumed she'd gone off on one of her spur-of-the-moment trips."

Dom eyed his boss speculatively.

"Mrs. Perkins is not the faithful type. Occasionally, she goes on vacation with her latest lover."

"What does Mr. Perkins think about that?" Dom asked.

"I have no idea, but you'll get a chance to ask him when you interview members of the family."

"Not your typical all-American household."

Sawyer chuckled, the sound little more than a muted grunt. "Hardly."

Glancing at the file, Dom said, "Billionaire father, Edward. Spoiled-brat, thirty-year-old playgirl daughter, Audrey, who is missing. The fourth Mrs. Bedell, who is only a few years older than Bedell's daughters. Cara

Bedell, younger daughter and half sister to Audrey. And last but not least, the blue blood hubby, Grayson Perkins."

"You have a mystery to solve," Sawyer said. "If it begins to look like more than a rich bitch deliberately putting a few more gray hairs in Daddy's head, contact Lieutenant Desmond of the Chattanooga PD. He's the man you'll want on this case if things turn nasty."

Dom nodded. "You think somebody killed Audrey Perkins?"

"From the initial report we compiled on the lady, I think it's possible that there are quite a few people who would like to see her dead."

"HONESTLY, EDWARD, I don't see why you thought it necessary to hire a private detective to find Audrey." Patrice smoothed her hand over her neatly coiffed dark hair, styled and colored to perfection. Everything about Patrice Whitmore Bedell screamed *I'm rich.* "It's not as if she hasn't gone off on these little jaunts before."

Cara despised her stepmother. Tall, leggy, bosomy. And young. Far too young for her father. A gold-digging whore who had stroked the high and mighty Edward Bedell's sizeable ego and sucked his aging dick. Cara wondered how much of either the stroking or the sucking occurred now that Patrice was Mrs. Bedell.

Edward swirled the bourbon around in his glass, then glared at his wife. His fourth wife. Audrey's mother, wife number one, had been the love of their father's life. Unfortunately, Annaliese Bedell had died in a automobile accident when Audrey was barely two. Four years after his wife's death, he'd remarried. Wife number two had been Cara's mother and Edward had married Sandra Gilley only because she was pregnant. The marriage lasted until Cara was a year old, then ended in a bitter divorce. A couple of years later, her mother had committed suicide. Wife number three had come along when Audrey was twelve and Cara six, and that one had lasted ten years. Norah Lee had tried to be a mother to them. She'd failed miserably. And she'd also failed just as miserably in her three attempts to give Edward another child, praying each time to carry the child full term and praying just as hard that the baby would be a boy. She'd miscarried twice—both girls. And gave birth to a stillborn son.

Three years ago, Daddy dearest had brought home a new bride—the stepmother from hell. It hadn't mattered so much to Audrey because she and Grayson had their own home and didn't have to live under the same roof as *that* woman. Cara supposed that at twenty-four, she should have her own place, but some lingering hope deep inside her kept her here, at the Bedell mansion, close to a father who was usually indifferent to her. He'd provided for her, given her everything money could buy, but he'd never loved her. Not the way he loved Audrey. And more than anything on earth, she wanted her father to love her.

She had grown up in awe of her big sister, wanting desperately to be just like her. That, of course, had been impossible. Where Audrey was small-boned and slender, almost delicate in appearance, with a mane of fiery red hair and a temper to match, Cara was a rawboned, freckled, strawberry-blond. Audrey was the life of the party, the center of attention, a great beauty like her mother. Cara tended to be a wallflower, quiet and reserved and looked far more like their father.

"Audrey has never stayed away more than a week without letting me know where she was," Edward said in a low, steady voice. "She would never intentionally worry me...worry any of us. Gray and Cara both feel certain something is terribly wrong and that we should search for Audrey."

Edward downed the last drops of liquor then handed the glass to Jeremy, his minion. Or at least that's the way Cara had always thought of her father's servant-of-all trades—chauffeur, butler, personal assistant. Jeremy Loman possessed the appearance of a nonentity, being medium everything—from brown hair and eyes to average height and built. Not handsome. Not ugly. And he had the personality of a zombie, seldom speaking unless he was spoken to, standing guard over her father as if he had no other purpose in life.

"She's off with that lowlife scum Bobby Jack Cash and we all know it," Patrice said. "You're a fool to waste money on a detective from that expensive agency in Atlanta."

"It's *my* money," Edward told her. "And Audrey is *my* daughter."

"And my wife," a voice from the doorway said.

Everyone stilled instantly; then one by one, they turned and stared at Grayson Perkins IV. Cara's heart did a ridiculous little rat-a-tat-tat when she looked at her brother-in-law. It had always been that way for her, ever since she first laid eyes on him when she was thirteen and he twenty-one. Gray's mother had been on the board of some charity that Norah Lee had served on and the two became fast friends. Long after Norah Lee left the Bedell family, both Gray and his mother, Emeline, remained friendly acquaintances. Edward had hand-picked Gray for Audrey, deciding that his pedigree was far more important than the money his family lacked. The Perkins family contained predecessors who were Old South blue bloods, Confederate heroes and English aristocracy.

"Come in, my boy. Come in." Edward motioned to his son-in-law.

Gray hesitated for a split second; then, as handsome and debonair as any old Hollywood movie star, he sauntered into the living room. Gray was, without a doubt, the most beautiful creature on earth. Almost too pretty to be real. Tall, slender, elegant. With dark, curly hair, chocolate brown eyes and thick lashes any woman would envy. Every feature perfect.

Cara had been in love with Gray for as long as she could remember.

"If anyone cares what I think, I believe Edward is doing the right thing by hiring a detective to find Audrey," Gray said. "If she has run off with Bobby Jack, she could be in real trouble."

"Oh, Gray…" Cara wished she could wrap her arms around her brother-in-law and comfort him. She'd seen that forlorn look on his face too many times during the six years he'd been married to her sister. Audrey didn't deserve a man such as Gray. There were times when Cara wished Audrey was dead. And once or twice she'd even considered doing the deed herself.

"What time are you expecting the detective?" Gray asked.

"He's due in any time now," Edward said. "I expect him to arrive before lunch. He's driving in from Atlanta."

"I assume you've hired the very best money can buy."

"Naturally. I contacted the Dundee Agency." Edward eyed Gray inquisitively. "Why would you ask such a question?"

"It was merely rhetorical."

"Was it?"

"She's in love with him, you know," Gray said matter-of-factly.

"Who's in love with whom?" Edward asked.

Tears welled up in Grayson Perkins's big, beautiful brown eyes. He clenched his teeth tightly.

Oh, God, he's going to cry, Cara thought.

"Speak up, boy," Edward said. "You can't mean Audrey and that—"

"Yes, of course, that's who he means." Cara jumped in, wanting to spare Gray further inquisition. "Audrey is absolutely crazy about Bobby Jack Cash. She's made no secret of the fact that she's madly in love with him. She even asked Gray for a divorce."

"What!" Edward's face turned crimson.

"See," Patrice chimed in adamantly. "I knew it. Your

precious Audrey has run off with that scum and they're fucking their way through Europe or the Caribbean or—" A resounding slap across her cheek silenced Patrice instantly. She staggered for a millisecond as she cried out and clutched the left side of her face with her open palm. "You bastard." She glared menacingly at her husband, a man who, as far as Cara knew, had never before struck her.

Edward's nostrils flared and his eyes closed to mere slits as he balled his hand into a tight fist. "Don't you ever say anything so vulgar and crude about my daughter again. Do you understand me, woman?"

"I understand," Patrice said. "I understand a lot more than you think I do."

Dom had grown up on a ranch in Texas, lived in a big sprawling old house and shared a bedroom with his older brother Rafe. The Shea family hadn't been poor, but neither had they been rich. From the time he could walk, he could ride, and from the time he could ride, his Dad had put him to work, just as he had Rafe. Just as he did Pilar and Marta and Bianca when they got old enough. His mother, Camila, had been born and raised in Texas, but her parents had come from Mexico shortly after they married. Camila had raised her children in her Catholic faith, with great pride in both their Mexican and Irish heritages. Dom's parents had been strict, but loving, giving their children a solid foundation on which to build.

As he entered the foyer of the massive antebellum mansion on Lookout Mountain, he wondered if being this rich is what had turned Audrey Bedell Perkins into such a notorious first-class bitch. After reading the complete file on her, Dom had come to the conclusion that if she were a member of his family, he'd be glad she had run off and probably wouldn't want her to ever return. The lady spent her father's money as if it grew on trees. She cheated on her husband regularly and made new enemies everywhere she went. She was both envied and despised by the whole of Chattanooga's elite social circle.

"Good afternoon, sir," the stiff-upper-lip butler said as he showed Dom into the living room. "Mr. Edward has been expecting you."

Before they reached the half open double pocket doors leading from the foyer into the living room, Dom heard the sound of raised voices.

"Please, let's not do this," a female voice pleaded. "Gray shouldn't have to suffer this way and poor Daddy—"

"Poor Daddy," another female voice mimicked, none too kindly. "You're the one everyone feels sorry for. Poor, pitiful Cara. The ugly duckling. The daughter her daddy *doesn't* dote on, the sister Grayson doesn't even know exists."

"Shut the hell up," a male voice commanded.

"Mr. Shea, from the Dundee Agency, is here," the butler announced.

Silence.

Cold, hard stares focused on Dom as he entered the room. Then a large, tall man with a mane of thick white

hair still streaked with reddish-brown highlights came
forward, his big hand outstretched.

"I'm Edward Bedell. Come in, please."

Dom entered the living room, feeling somewhat like
an early Christian entering the coliseum in Rome. He
extended his arm and shook hands with Bedell. A firm,
cordial exchange. "Domingo Shea."

"I'm glad you're here, Mr. Shea. Your employer,
Sawyer McNamara, promised me his best man. Is that
what you are? Are you Dundee's best?"

"I'm one of their best," he replied. "My boss believes
I'm the best man for this job, otherwise he wouldn't
have sent me."

Edward Bedell nodded. "You know what I want—I
want my daughter found. And you also know that
money is no object. Whatever it takes, however much it
costs, find Audrey."

"Yes, sir. That's what I intend to do."

"I'll answer any questions, provide you with any
needed information. All you have to do is ask."

Dom glanced around the room. "You can start by in-
troducing me to your family. I assume they're your
family."

Bedell cleared his throat. "Yes, they're family." He
motioned to the leggy brunette with a set of topnotch
silicone boobs. When she came forward, he slipped his
arm around her waist. "This is Patrice…my wife."

Mrs. Bedell smiled at Dom. An I'm-not-happily-
married smile. A smile that made a silent but obvious
offer.

"Ma'am." Dom deliberately avoided direct eye contact with the lady. The last thing he wanted was to give the client's wife any wrong ideas.

"And this is my younger daughter, Cara." Bedell simply glanced at the tall, freckled, strawberry blonde who offered Dom a forced smile.

There was something sweet and downright wholesome about Cara Bedell's appearance. But knowing her background, considering the family she came from and the lifestyle she was accustomed to, Dom figured Ms. Bedell was neither as sweet nor as wholesome as she appeared.

"This gentleman is Audrey's husband, Grayson Perkins." Bedell looked directly at his son-in-law. "He's as concerned about Audrey as I am."

"We want Audrey found," Perkins said.

Dom studied the much-too-good-looking man. Pity Mother Nature wasted so much beauty on a guy. "Who was the last person to see Mrs. Perkins?" he asked.

Dead silence.

"I suppose I was," Perkins finally said. "We had breakfast together, then I left for the office at about the same time she left to go shopping."

"And that was when?"

"Ten days ago."

"And no one has heard from her since?"

"Not a word," Bedell said.

"Your daughter has done this before, hasn't she?" Dom asked. "She's just up and left town without telling anyone."

"Of course she has," Patrice Bedell said. "I tried to tell Edward that this time is no different from all the other times, but—"

"This time *is* different." Grayson Perkins's voice trembled when he spoke. "We suspect that she has gone off with a dangerous man, an ex-con named Bobby Jack Cash. He's the type who'd do anything for money."

In his peripheral vision, Dom noticed Cara Bedell ease steadily closer to her brother-in-law's side, a pained expression on her face.

"Do you have reason to believe that he might have forced her to go with him?" Dom asked.

"We don't know for sure that she left town with this Cash fellow," Bedell said.

"Of course we know," Patrice corrected. "She's missing. He's missing. They were lovers. What other conclusion could you draw?"

Dom glanced from one person to another, beginning and ending with Grayson Perkins. "I can think of one other conclusion."

"Just what would that be?" Bedell asked.

"Someone with a very strong motive killed Mrs. Perkins and Mr. Cash."

CHAPTER TWO

DOM RECEIVED THE INFO from Dundee headquarters around three o'clock. A routine check on Audrey Bedell Perkins's credit cards revealed that the lady had been traveling for the past ten days, racking up expensive hotel, limo, and restaurant bills, as well as bills from numerous exclusive shops in four cities. Apparently she'd gone straight from Chattanooga to Nashville, then on to Memphis before heading for Birmingham. The most recent expenditures on her account came in from West Palm Beach, Florida.

Ms. Perkins was registered at the Palm Beach Classico Hotel, but from a preliminary inquiry, he'd been unable to find out if she was alone. His guess would be that her latest lover was with her. These rich, spoiled heiresses were all alike. Worthless. And from everything he'd learned about Audrey, she was the worst of her kind. Of course, it wasn't his place to judge her, only to find her and bring her home to Daddy. If he boarded the Dundee jet by four, he could be in Palm Beach before dinner, make contact with Audrey and have her home in Chattanooga by bedtime. He should have this assignment wrapped up in less than twenty-four hours.

Using his cell phone, Dom dialed the Bedell home.

"Bedell residence," the butler said. Dom recognized the man's voice.

"This is Domingo Shea, from the Dundee agency. I'd like to speak to Mr. Bedell."

Dom glanced at his unpacked suitcase resting on the stand at the foot of his hotel bed. Good thing he hadn't bothered to settle in since he wouldn't be staying even one night.

"Mr. Bedell is unavailable, sir. May I take a message?"

"Look, this concerns his daughter, Audrey."

"Yes, sir, I understand, but Mr. Bedell isn't here. He's out for a ride and—"

"Fine. I'll try him on his cell."

"Mr. Bedell doesn't take his cell phone when he goes horseback riding."

"Okay, tell him that I've tracked his daughter down and will probably have her home tonight."

"I—er…yes, sir, I'll give him the message."

Dom ended the call, then hurriedly contacted Dundee headquarters. Daisy Holbrook, the office manager answered on the second ring.

"Daisy, my darling, I need the Dundee jet and I need it now."

"Well, you're in luck. The jet just happens to be free."

"Could you send it straight to Chattanooga, like five minutes ago?"

"Hold on and I'll set things in motion." Dom waited

no more than three minutes before Daisy came back on the line. "The jet will be in Chattanooga in an hour. Now, fill me in so I can do the paperwork. You know how Mr. McNamara is about dotting all the I's and crossing all the T's."

"So, it's Mr. McNamara today, huh? What's he done to piss you off?"

"I don't know what you're talking about."

Dom chuckled. "Liar."

Daisy huffed. "I have the greatest respect for Sawyer, but sometimes I agree with Lucie that he's an inhuman robot."

"Whew. Come on, honey, tell me what's going on?"

"He suspended Geoff Monday," Daisy said.

"He what?"

"I don't know all the details, but apparently Geoff did something on his last assignment that Sawyer considered inappropriate, so he's suspended him without pay for a month!"

"Hmm." He'd known for quite some time that Daisy had it bad for Geoff Monday, the former SIS agent who'd joined Dundee's a few years ago, leaving behind a lucrative mercenary career. But Monday seemed oblivious to the fact that sweet little Daisy worshiped the ground he walked on. "Don't try to fight Monday's battles for him, even if you do have a major thing for him."

Silence.

"Come on, Daisy, admit it, you—"

"I like and respect Geoff. That's all and—"

"Don't get mixed up with Monday," Dom warned

her. "He's a good guy and all that, but he's not only too old for you, he's a hundred years older than you are in experience. Listen to me, little sister, find yourself a nice young man and forget Monday."

"Did I ask for you advice? No, I did not. Besides, Geoff thinks of me the same way you and all the other guys here at Dundee's do—as a kid sister. So, don't you dare ever say anything to anyone about my having a silly crush on him. I had no idea you knew. I thought Lucie was the only one who knew."

Anyone who'd seen the way Daisy looked at Monday knew. Everybody except Monday himself. "I'm good at picking up on stuff like that."

"Well, keep it to yourself, okay?"

"Okay."

"Now, give me the details of why you need the Dundee jet so I can fill out all the paperwork."

DOM ARRIVED at the Palm Beach Classico Hotel at six-thirty, inquired about Ms. Perkins and was told the lady was out, but he could leave a message. No amount of persuasion—even a hint of hard, cold cash—rendered any other information.

"I'll wait for her," he'd said and taken a seat that gave him a view of the main entrance as well as the bank of elevators.

It was now six-fifty-five and he was still waiting. He would wait one hour, then he'd try his luck at garnering information from other members of the hotel staff. By nature, Dom was an impatient man. He hated wasting time, his own or someone else's; but his years spent as a SEAL had taught him many things, including, to some degree, patience.

At seven-oh-three, a small redhead, weighed down by shopping bags, entered the lobby. Dom removed the photo of Audrey Perkins from his pocket, took a good look at it, and then scanned the young woman walking past him. Similar coloring, similar height and build, but different facial features. Apparently, Bedell's elder daughter had undergone some minor plastic surgery since this picture was taken.

"Do you need some help, Ms. Perkins?" one of the bellhops asked as he scurried toward her.

"No, thanks, I can manage," she replied, her voice soft, ultra feminine and Southern sweet.

Dom studied her intently, then glared at the photo. In person she was even prettier. Thanks to plastic surgery?And she most definitely had a new hairdo. In the studio photograph Edward Bedell had given Dom, Audrey wore her straight, shoulder-length, red hair in a smooth pageboy. Today a mane of thick, unruly, dark strawberry blonde curls fanned out and down almost to her shoulder blades.

When she brushed off the bellhop and went straight to the nearest elevator, Dom jumped to his feet and rushed after her, catching up just as the elevator door started to close.

"Wait up," he called as he dove toward her. He managed to stop just short of knocking her down, his body colliding with the bags she held in front of her.

"Sorry." He stepped back, looked into a pair of startled, moss-green eyes and smiled involuntarily.

Without hesitation, she smiled back at him, then glanced away, as if she'd just realized her smile could mistakenly be construed as flirting with a stranger. Odd, Dom thought, that a woman with Audrey Perkins's reputation would care.

"Need some help with those packages?"

"No, thank you."

That voice should be illegal. It was the kind that gave a guy ideas. Hot, sweaty, body-heat ideas.

"Have you been in Palm Beach long?" he asked.

"Two days," she replied, then lifted her gaze and connected with his.

This time neither of them looked away, and she smiled at him again. Tentatively. Almost shyly. He couldn't seem to take his eyes off her and it wasn't simply because she was a damn good looking woman. There was something about her, an air of vulnerability, a hint of wariness.

She was lovely. No doubt about that fact. Creamy smooth skin, with only a hint of freckles across her small nose and over her high, sculpted cheekbones. Full red lips that made a man want to kiss her or made him think about all the wicked things that gorgeous mouth could do to him. But it was her eyes that drew Dom to her and held him enthralled.

As a connoisseur of women, he found the opposite sex utterly fascinating. He'd been a ladies' man since puberty and had endured years of kidding from his brother Rafe.

"All the girls have the hots for you, little brother, because you're so damn pretty. Heck, you're prettier than our sisters and almost as pretty as Mama." Rafe had inherited their father's rough, rugged looks, even Dad's Irish blue eyes and ruddy complexion; whereas, except for the Shea height and broad shoulders, Dom's basic appearance was a replica of their beautiful Mexican mother.

Dom had known his share of lovely, fascinating women, but he couldn't recall ever being as instantly attracted to a lady as he was to Audrey Perkins.

Hell, man, you're a damn fool. The lady is not only married, she's a rich, spoiled brat. And a slut to boot.

"Are you all right?" she asked.

Dom suddenly realized that she'd been talking to him and he hadn't responded, that he'd been too busy drooling over this small, elegant piece of fluff.

"Yeah, fine. My mind just wandered. Sorry. Business matters."

"Are you here in Palm Beach on business?" she asked.

Dom nodded.

Without warning, the elevator doors opened and someone entered behind Dom and it was only then that he realized neither he nor Ms. Perkins had punched in a floor number. They'd been talking while the elevator rested at the lobby level.

"You two getting out?" the bald, middle-aged man asked.

Audrey giggled. "No. I—I'm going to the sixth floor."

"What about you, buddy?" the guy asked after he

punched in the fourth floor for himself and the sixth floor for Audrey.

"Seventh, thanks." Since he wasn't registered at this hotel, Dom said the first thing that came to mind.

The three of them remained silent as the elevator lifted; then after the man got off on the fourth floor and the elevator door closed, Dom and Audrey burst into laughter.

"We were just standing here in the elevator and hadn't even punched in our floor numbers," she said. "He must have thought we were crazy."

"Probably." Dom reached out and grasped two of her four large shopping bags. "Those look way too heavy for you. Let me carry them to your room. I swear you can trust me to be a gentleman."

Her smile vanished instantly. "Thank you. They were getting a little heavy. But as far as trusting you… I don't know you and I learned the hard way not to trust anyone."

"You're too young and beautiful—" he surveyed her from head to toe "—and rich to be so cynical."

"Haven't you heard? Money can't buy happiness."

"And are you unhappy, Miss—?"

The elevator stopped at the sixth floor.

"Ms. Perkins," she told him as the door opened. "Audrey Perkins. And right this minute, I'm quite happy."

Using his body as a wedge, Dom held the elevator door open until she exited; then, with shopping bags in hand, he followed her down the corridor.

Glancing back over her shoulder, she paused for a moment and asked, "Are you going to tell me who you are?"

He grinned. "Sure thing. I'm Domingo Shea."

Audrey nodded, then continued down the hall until she reached the double doors that opened into a suite. "Here we are." She rummaged in the pocket of her tailored beige slacks and retrieved a plastic entry key. After shoving the handle on one bag farther up her right wrist, she slid the key through the lock, opened the door and entered the suite. When Dom followed, she dumped her bags on the floor, and then turned and blocked his entrance.

He paused, offered her his most persuasive smile and inquired, "Not going to let me come in?"

She shook her head and held out her hands. "Thanks for your help. I can take those now."

"You're a mighty suspicious lady, aren't you?"

She took the shopping bags from Dom, but didn't close the door in his face, which he'd halfway expected. "Look, Mr. Shea, if you must know, I find you terribly attractive, but I'm not in the market for a one-night stand and I'm not—"

"How about dinner? No strings attached. No expectations."

She eyed him speculatively, a hint of curiosity in those remarkable green eyes. "Just dinner?"

"I can come back at eight and escort you or we can meet at the restaurant, whichever you feel more comfortable doing. I assume they have a nice restaurant here in the hotel."

"The Flamingo Room."

"So, is it a date?"

She hesitated.

He leaned forward, bracing his hands on the door-frame on either side of her and looked right at her. "Why not share a meal and get better acquainted?"

"Just dinner," she told him.

"Just dinner."

"You make the reservations and I'll meet you downstairs at eight."

He grinned broadly, then turned around and whistled to himself as he headed toward the elevator.

Maybe he should have simply told Ms. Perkins that he was a PI sent by her father and husband to bring her home. But if she put up a fuss and refused to return to Chattanooga, all he could do was call her father and tell him where she was. By the time the old man could get to Palm Beach, his darling daughter could well be on her way to Timbuktu. And he could hardly pick her up, kicking and screaming, then carry her down the hall, into the elevator and through the hotel lobby. She was, after all, over eighteen and had a legal right to go wherever she wanted to go, with or without her daddy's approval.

No, the best thing to do was wine and dine her first, then maybe take her on a moonlit stroll along the beach before presenting her with two alternatives. One: she went with him willingly to the airport and flew back to Chattanooga on the Dundee jet. Two: She telephoned her father and assured him she was well and happy and did not want to return home.

DOM HAD EXPECTED to be kept waiting at least half an hour, so when Audrey showed up promptly at eight, he was pleasantly surprised. Once again, the very sight of her stirred something sexual and predatory within him, something he wanted to deny, but couldn't. She was so completely feminine that on a primeval level she appealed to all that was masculine in him.

If every man she met reacted to her the way he did, he could see how easily Audrey could lure men into her snare. He had to remind himself that she was not what she appeared to be. Behind all that beauty lay the ugliness of self-centeredness and betrayal.

When the maître d' approached them, Dom took her arm and draped it over his.

"You look lovely."

That statement was no lie. She did look lovely. The bronze silk dress she wore made her fair skin radiant and her reddish blond hair shimmer with copper highlights.

Audrey didn't reply. Instead she offered him a fragile smile that implied she was pleased with his compliment.

Once seated across the small, linen-covered table in a secluded corner of the dimly lit restaurant, Audrey lifted her gaze and looked directly at him. "Do you make a habit of picking up women in elevators?"

"Actually, you're the first."

"Am I?"

"You find that difficult to believe?"

She shrugged.

Why was she so leery of him? She had no idea he was a PI hired to track her down. He suspected that her distrust extended to all men, perhaps to people in general. Had she spent a lifetime trying to figure out who liked her for herself and who liked her because she was a wealthy heiress?

Don't go making her into a victim, Dom warned himself. Audrey Bedell Perkins was a user, a taker, a woman who'd been unfaithful to her husband most of their six-year marriage.

After they ordered dinner and sat together sipping the merlot, Dom broke the silence with a risky question. "Your name seems familiar," he said. "Your accent is decidedly Southern, but not deep South."

She visibly tensed. "I'm from Tennessee."

"Tennessee, huh? I live in Atlanta. Could I have seen your picture in the newspaper or read something about you in the society columns?"

She took a deep breath, forced a smile and replied. "I'm Audrey Bedell Perkins. It's possible you've heard of my father."

"You're Edward Bedell's daughter, aren't you? Of course, you are. I wouldn't have recognized you from the newspaper photographs I've seen. You're far prettier in person."

Her cheeks flushed a delicate pink. "Thank you."

"If I remember correctly, you're married, aren't you?"

Nodding shyly, she set her wineglass down on the table and folded her hands in her lap. "Yes, I—I'm married."

"And your husband isn't here in Palm Beach with you?"

"No, he isn't."

"Are you traveling alone?"

"Why so many questions, Mr. Shea? You aren't a reporter, are you?"

Dom laughed. "Good God, no. I'm a businessman. And as for all the questions, let's just say that I find you fascinating."

"Do you find me fascinating or do you find the fact that I'm a wealthy heiress fascinating?"

"I suppose you want me to tell you the truth."

"Yes."

"Then the answer is both. If you didn't have a dime to your name, I'd find you very interesting, but the fact that you're Edward Bedell's daughter simply makes you all the more intriguing."

"I appreciate your honesty. It's a rare quality these days."

The waiter set their salads in front of them. Dom lifted his fork, then asked, "Will you answer a question for me and answer honestly?"

She scrutinized his face, as if hoping she could figure out just what he was getting at. "I'll try."

"Are you in the habit of accepting dinner invitations from every man who finds you fascinating?"

She studied him for a moment longer, then replied, "You're referring to the fact that I'm a married woman, aren't you? Would you be shocked if I admitted that I don't feel very married, that you make me wish I wasn't married."

The knot in Dom's stomach tightened. Shit! She was good. Damn good. She was playing him like a fiddle. How many times had she used that line on a guy? If he didn't know her for what she was, he'd take her straight from dinner this evening to bed. And he'd keep her there all night and maybe all day tomorrow.

He reached across the table and grasped her hand. "I usually steer clear of married women, but in your case, I could make an exception. Of course, I wouldn't want your husband or perhaps a jealous boyfriend to—"

"My husband is in Chattanooga," she said. "We—we're sort of separated. And there is no jealous boyfriend."

So, Audrey hadn't run off with Bobby Jack Cash or if she had, she'd dumped him somewhere along the way. Her being alone should make things easier. After dinner, he'd suggest a stroll along the beach and then he'd tell her who he was and ask her to return to Chattanooga with him tonight. If she refused, the best he could do was either persuade her to call her father to set his mind at ease or call the old man himself.

Of course, there was a third option. He could simply throw her over his shoulder, shove her into his car and take her to the airport. Maybe an evening drive might be a better idea than a walk along the beach. He could wait until she realized he'd driven her to the airport before confessing he was a hired gun. If she refused to go with him, he could carry her aboard the Dundee jet and strap her into a seat before she realized what had hit her.

But technically that would be kidnapping. Then again, it would be her word against his.

"You're awfully quiet," she said. "Is something wrong?"

He squeezed her hand. "I was just thinking about how I'd like this evening to end."

She jerked her hand away. "No expectations. You promised."

He held up both hands in an I surrender gesture. "A guy can dream, can't he?"

"All I agreed to was dinner."

"What about a ride around town after dinner? I've heard there are some hot clubs—"

"I'm not into hot clubs."

"Then how about a walk on the beach?"

She sighed. "Maybe."

Her reply was good enough for him. She wasn't the only expert at playing games. He had sweet talked his way into more than one woman's silk panties over the years.

Yeah, but he wasn't trying to get into Audrey Bedell Perkins's panties. His assignment was to track her down and take her home. Home to her worried father.

Home to her husband.

But if the lady didn't want to go home…

CHAPTER THREE

DOM EXCUSED HIMSELF BEFORE dessert arrived and headed for the men's room. Instead of going inside, he found a dimly lit corner and, using his cell phone, dialed the Bedell residence. He needed to speak to the old man himself and find out how to proceed with this investigation.

Surprisingly enough, Edward Bedell answered the call. "Have you found my daughter?"

"Yes, sir, I have."

Silence.

"She seems quite well and happy," Dom said. *Beautiful, desirable, intriguing.*

"Are you sure it's Audrey?"

"Yes, sir. Reasonably sure. She claims to be Audrey Perkins, is registered at the hotel under that name and is using your daughter's credit cards."

"And you've compared her to the photograph I gave you of my daughter?"

"Yes, sir, I have."

"And?"

"Mr. Bedell, do you have any reason to believe that this young woman isn't your daughter?"

"No, no, of course not. It's just that since she disappeared the way she did, I've had all kinds of horrible thoughts about her being kidnapped, murdered. I suppose for just a few seconds there, I let my imagination run wild."

"Yes, sir, I understand."

"Where is she?"

"She's staying at the Classico Hotel in West Palm Beach, Florida."

"Is she with that man?"

"Bobby Jack Cash? No, sir. Ms. Perkins appears to be traveling alone."

"Thank God."

"Mr. Bedell, how do you want me to handle this situation? Do you want me to bring your daughter back to Chattanooga? If so, since she's an adult, that will require her—"

"No, there's no need to bring her home. Apparently she had her reasons for leaving. My guess is her bad marriage. She and Gray haven't had a real marriage in years."

"Yes, sir."

"I'm grateful that you found her so quickly. She's always been a strong-willed person, even as a child. She'll do whatever she wants to do and to hell with…" Bedell paused. "Please tell her that if she needs anything, wants anything…" His voice trailed off, ending on a deep sigh.

"Would you like for me to ask Ms. Perkins to call you?"

"Yes, certainly. But it doesn't have to be tonight. Just whenever she's ready to talk."

"All right." *Was that it? Goal accomplished. Assignment completed.* "Once I deliver your message to your daughter, am I to consider this job finished?"

"Yes, yes. And it was a job well done, Mr. Shea. Thank you. You can return to Atlanta tonight if you wish."

"Yes, sir."

Dom closed his cell phone and clipped it to his belt. This had to have been the quickest, easiest job he'd ever done for Dundee's. In less than twelve hours, he'd found the missing heiress and set her family's minds at ease. So, why was it that he felt something wasn't quite right, that there was more to this situation than met the eye?

What difference does it make? he asked himself. He'd done the job he'd been hired to do. The client was satisfied. Dundee's would get a hefty check and Sawyer McNamara would be pleased that Edward Bedell was pleased.

On his way back to the table where Audrey Perkins waited, Dom considered his own options. If he was a smart man, he'd eat dessert and escort Ms. Perkins to her suite, say goodnight and goodbye. On the other hand, now that he wasn't on the job, he was free to pursue his personal interest in the lady. And God help him, he was interested. But he would be a fool to become involved with a married woman, a woman known for her extra marital affairs.

Would a one-night-stand be considered becoming involved?

When Dom sat down across from Audrey, she smiled. "I've been dying to dive into this cheesecake, but I waited for you so we can savor every bite together."

They had ordered one slice of cheesecake to share. Audrey had bemoaned the fact that if she ate the entire slice herself, she'd put on a couple of pounds overnight.

Dom picked up his fork, sliced into the rich, luscious dessert, and instead of taking the delectable morsel to his mouth, he reached across and aimed it at Audrey's mouth. Her eyes widened, then she opened her mouth. When Dom inserted the bite, she nipped it off his fork, rolled it around over her tongue and sighed.

"Sheer heaven," she said.

"Are all your appetites that easily appeased?" he asked.

Her big green eyes widened even more, her expression one of amused surprise.

"Are you propositioning me, Mr. Shea?"

"Could be."

She laughed, the sound mellow and soft, and somewhat tentative, as if she didn't laugh all that often.

"What about our agreement?" She glanced down at the cheesecake. "Let's eat dessert and take that stroll on the beach, then see what happens."

Smiling, Dom sliced off another bite and once again fed her. He watched the way her mouth opened, the soft fullness of her lips, the curve of her small, pink tongue.

He was getting hard just watching her eat.

Ten minutes later, dessert plate wiped clean and the check paid, Dom escorted Audrey through the restaurant, into the hotel lobby and toward the front entrance. Once outside, they headed straight for the adjacent beach. The Classico Hotel faced the Atlantic Ocean. Lights from the nearby buildings illuminated the path to the beach. Overhead a three-quarter moon and count-less stars brightened the black sky.

Dom eased his arm around her waist as they neared the long stretch of sand.

"Want to take off your heels?" he asked.

She nodded, then clamped her left hand on his shoulder as she used her right hand to remove first one high heel and then the other. Dom took the sleek little bronze leather sandals from her and slipped the straps onto his index finger.

"Are you chilly?" he asked.

She shook her head.

"If you are, I can take off my jacket and—"

"You play the gentleman quite well," she told him.

"It's not an act. I actually can be a gentleman when the occasion—or the woman—calls for it."

"A charming gentleman." Audrey turned and took several steps away from him.

He followed her, draped his arm around her shoulders and fell into step alongside her. They walked together in silence for quite some time, occasionally glancing at each other and smiling. Dom couldn't remember the last time he'd wanted a woman so much.

"MR. SHEA HAS FOUND Audrey," Edward Bedell said to those congregated in his study.

"When?" Cara asked.

"Where is she?" Patrice Bedell glared at her husband.

"Is she with him?" Tears misted Grayson Perkins's eyes.

"Not a one of you asked if she's all right." Edward

clenched his teeth. Damn the whole bunch of them. They didn't love Audrey, didn't care if she was dead or alive. No one loved Audrey the way he did, no one understood her the way he did. Emotion welled up inside him, threatening his composure. He took several deep breaths.

"Of course she's all right," Patrice said. "I knew she'd just run off somewhere with Bobby Jack."

"She's not with that vile man," Edward said. "Mr. Shea says that she is quite alone, that she seems well and…happy."

"Why shouldn't she be happy? She's spending your money and living the high life." When Patrice's gaze connected with Edward's, she shrank away from him, as if she feared he might hit her again.

"Where is she?" Cara repeated her original question.

"West Palm Beach." Edward rose from his leather chair behind the massive desk. "I asked Mr. Shea to tell her to call me, to let me hear her voice."

"How did he find her so quickly?" Grayson asked.

"The Dundee agency was able to track her through her credit card use," Edward said.

"What hotel? I want to fly down there immediately and bring her home." Grayson confronted his father-in-law, a determined expression on his handsome face.

"No, Gray, don't run after her," Cara pleaded. "Not again. Not this time."

"Cara's right." Edward clutched Grayson's shoulder tightly. "None of us are going to chase her down this time. We've all jumped through hoops for that girl. It's high time we step back and let her do whatever she wants to do."

Cara couldn't believe her ears, couldn't believe that her father was actually going to allow Audrey the freedom to live her own life. If only Gray would do the same, if only he would let Audrey go. How could he love a woman who had treated him so badly, a woman who had wanted a divorce for years?

"But Audrey needs—" Grayson said.

"Listen to Daddy." Cara interrupted him mid-sentence as she held out her hands to him in a beseeching manner. "Don't go to Palm Beach. Don't chase after her. It's time for you to accept the fact that Audrey doesn't want to be your wife."

But I do, Cara thought. *Stop loving my sister. She's never been worthy of you. Just once, look my way and see what's right before you—a woman who worships the ground you walk on.*

"I LIKE THIS," Audrey said, the evening breeze gently caressing her face and tousling her hair.

"You like what?" Dom asked as he stopped walking, turned her in his arms and gazed down into her eyes.

Tilting her chin, she looked up at him. "Everything. The beach, the starry sky, the ocean waves, the feel of the sand under my feet." She stood on tiptoe and wound her arms around his neck. "Strolling along the beach, just the two of us, not talking, just…being."

He pulled her closer. "You know what, Audrey Perkins, you're an enigma to me. I can't figure you out."

She sighed heavily. "I'm not all that complicated."

He chuckled. "The hell you're not. Honey, you've got to be the most complicated woman I've ever met."

"How can you say that when you just met me? We don't really know anything about each other, do we?"

"I know that your father is one of the richest men in America, that you're a married woman, that for some reason you're here in Palm Beach all alone."

She eased her hands from around his neck, then turned away from him. "Since I find you very attractive and I'd really like for you to kiss me, that has to mean you're absolutely no good, that if I give in to temptation, you'll just wind up using me, and—"

Dom grabbed her upper arms and whirled her around to face him. "I'm not the kind of man who uses women." He released his tenacious hold on her, reached out and tenderly stroked her cheek. "I'm one of the good guys. I would never hurt you."

"I'd like to believe that, but I'm afraid my track record speaks for itself." She clasped his hand. "I seem to attract the rotten apples. The users, the takers, the…" She sucked in air, released his hand and blew out an exasperated breath.

They stared at each other, moonlight, sandy beach and scenic ocean view fading into a blurred background so that all Dom saw was Audrey, and all she saw was Dom.

"I'm going to tell you the truth," Dom said. "I want you. I'd like to take you upstairs to your suite, strip you naked and make love to you all night."

Her gaze locked with his. Her breathing grew heavy, her breasts rising and falling rapidly. Her lips parted on an indrawn breath.

"If I let that happen, how do I know—"

He laid his index finger over her lips, momentarily silencing her.

"I didn't say it had to happen. I just said it's what I'd like to happen." He lifted his finger from her lips and trailed it over her chin and down her throat, stopping just short of inserting his finger inside the low-cut neckline of her dress. "We're both experienced adults. We've both had one-night-stands before this. Sex without commitment. No promises. No binding ties."

"Just sex." She spoke so softly that he barely heard her.

"It's your call, Audrey."

She went rigid, then broke eye contact.

"What's wrong?" he asked.

"Nothing. I—I… Why don't we just walk for a while longer, then go back to the hotel and get drinks in the bar, maybe talk and dance and…"

"Whatever you want."

"You really mean that, don't you?"

He took her hand in his and squeezed tenderly. "I came to Palm Beach on an assignment that I've completed. I'll be flying back to Atlanta tomorrow, but tonight I'm all yours. If you want to walk and talk and dance, then that's what we'll do."

"Tell me something."

"What?"

"Are you married?"

He shook his head. "No."

"Ever been married?"

"No."

"Ever been in love?"

"Yeah, a couple of times. Or at least I thought I was."

"What happened?" she asked.

"The first time, I was seventeen and she preferred my older brother." Dom hadn't thought about Lori Kaye in years, didn't even know what had happened to her after she married and moved off to San Antonio. "The second time I was older, smarter. We were actually engaged for six months before we realized it just wouldn't work. We wanted different things from life."

"I've been in love twice," she told him.

"Your husband and—"

"Uh-uh." Once again, her entire body stiffened, as if any reminder of who she was, of the fact she had a husband, disturbed her in a way Dom didn't understand. "Both times I made a huge mistake and paid dearly for it. I don't intend to ever fall in love again. No one is ever going to use me or hurt me."

Was it his imagination or had he actually heard genuine pain in her voice?

He tugged on her hand. "Come on. Let's walk, then we'll get a drink and afterward go dancing. If not here, then we'll find some other place."

When she clung to his hand, he got the oddest feeling that at least for the time being she trusted him. Trusted him not to hurt her, not to use her.

HE DIDN'T KNOW THE MAN, had never seen him before, but it didn't matter as long as he paid him in cash. He wasn't particular about who hired him or what they hired him to do, as long as the price was right. Hell, he'd knock off his own grandmother for enough money.

"The job needs to be done tonight."

"Why so fast? I might need time to plan—"

"My client is willing to pay twenty-five thousand if the job is done before daylight tomorrow and if the murder looks like either rape or robbery was involved. Take your pick."

"I don't mix business with pleasure. I'll make it look like a robbery."

"The death should be quick and painless. Is that understood?"

"Yeah, sure. I can slit her throat or shoot her in the head. Does your client have a preference?"

The tall, slender man shook his head. "It doesn't matter."

"I'll need half up front and the other half when the job is done."

"I have the entire amount, in cash, in this briefcase," the man told him. "And I also have a gun in my pocket." He slipped his hand into his pocket and clutched the weapon, showing the imprint of the pistol through the material of his jacket.

"Give me the particulars. Who you want killed, where I can locate them, any problems I might encounter."

"Her name is Audrey Bedell Perkins. She's staying

at the Palm Beach Classico Hotel, in suite number sixten. She's a petite redhead. Early thirties."

"Somebody hates this bitch enough to want her dead, but they don't want her to suffer. Got it." He held out his hand for the money.

The guy hesitated, then set the briefcase on the edge of the bed, flipped it open and dumped the cash. "If the job isn't done by daybreak—"

"It'll be done." He eyed all those beautiful greenbacks. "If the lady's alone, it'll be a piece of cake."

THE BAND PLAYED a soft, jazzy number, giving the dancers a break from the fast, frenetic beat of the last tune. Dom pulled Audrey into his arms, leading her into the slow, intimate dance. They had shared drinks at the Classico Hotel's Mermaid Bar before deciding to take her rented convertible and find a place where the music didn't stop at midnight. The Beachcomber stayed open until dawn, giving customers live music, a dance floor and a bartender who made a mean margarita.

"Having fun?" Dom whispered in her ear.

"Mmm…" Resting her head on his chest, she cuddled closer.

He nuzzled the side of her face, then kissed her ear. She shuddered. "Are you about ready to head back to the hotel or do you want to stay and close the place down?"

"Let's finish this dance before we go," she said.

"Whatever you want, honey."

"Whatever I want," she repeated in a sleepy, little girl voice.

He held her, loving the feel of her, the scent of her. She was small and slender yet nicely rounded. The girl's got meat on her bones, his father would say. The more time Dom spent with Audrey, the harder he found it to believe most of the things he'd read about her in the Dundee report he'd been given. Yes, she was guarded, didn't seem to trust easily and apparently loved to party, but he hadn't seen any evidence of her being a first class bitch. He suspected that beneath that I-can-take-care-of-myself exterior strength lay an inner core of kindness and vulnerability. If his gut instincts were correct, somewhere along the way, someone had hurt this woman, hurt her badly.

When the dance ended, Dom escorted her off the dance floor and out of the club. Once outside he held out his hand.

"Keys, please."

She giggled. "Don't you trust me to drive?"

"Not after two glasses of wine and two strong margaritas."

She rummaged around in her small handbag, yanked out the car keys and handed them to him. "You're right. All you had was a sip of one of my margaritas and a glass of wine about—" she lifted her arm and stared at her wristwatch. "Four hours ago. My gosh, it's nearly three-thirty."

"So it is." He draped his arm around her shoulders and steered her into the parking lot.

When he opened the convertible door for her, she paused, lifted her arm and whirled the bracelet-type watch around on her wrist. "Do you know how much this watch cost?"

"I have no idea." He helped her into the passenger seat, then kissed her on the tip of her nose.

She giggled again. "It cost two thousand dollars. It's real gold, you know."

Dom grinned. She was slightly loopy, after two glasses of wine and two margaritas. If he didn't know better, he'd think the lady wasn't used to drinking.

"What's two grand to you, honey? Your father's a billionaire, isn't he?" Dom slid behind the wheel.

She reached out, grabbed his arm and glared at him. "Is that why you like me? Because—"

Acting purely on instinct, Dom cupped her face with his hands and kissed her. No preliminaries, no sweet nothings. He'd been wanting to kiss her all night. She responded instantly, returning the kiss, opening her mouth, inviting him in. He took full advantage, probing, seeking, passionately loving her mouth. When they were both breathless, he ended the kiss, but didn't lift his head. Instead, he slid his hands down either side of her neck and onto her shoulders, then spread hot, nipping kisses across her cheek and down the side of her neck.

"Dom…"

"Hmm…"

She pushed him away and they stared at each other.

"Could you stay on in Palm Beach another day?" she asked.

"Possibly. If I had a good reason to stay."

The corners of her mouth lifted in a fragile smile.

"I'm not going to ask you in when you take me to my suite, but I'd very much like for us to have lunch tomorrow and then dinner tomorrow night."

"I'd like that, too."

When he started to kiss her again, she shoved against his chest. "It's late. I think we should go back to the Classico now."

Dom covered his heart with his crossed hands and sighed dramatically. "Lady, you really know how to hurt a guy, don't you?"

She laughed. "And you, Dom Shea, know how to tempt a woman beyond reason."

"Oh, honey, if only that were true."

"Believe me, it is."

Dom removed his jacket, lifted her just enough to slip the jacket around her shoulders, then kissed her cheek. "It's pretty chilly out here."

She hugged the coat around her. "Thanks. You really are a nice man, aren't you."

Dom reached across the console and buckled her into her seat belt, then latched his before starting the engine. The cool morning air acted as a slap-in-the-face, making Dom fully alert as he drove back to the hotel. He wondered what Sawyer would say if he stayed on in Palm Beach another twenty-four hours. Would his boss buy the excuse of typing up loose ends on the assignment? If not, he could send the Dundee jet back to Atlanta and simply take a personal leave day.

He knew better than to become involved with a

married woman, even on a temporary basis. But there was something about this particular woman that had grabbed him from the moment he saw her and whatever it was, it wouldn't let him go.

THEY STOOD OUTSIDE Audrey's suite, wrapped in each other's arms. He lifted his head after their third goodbye kiss.

"I don't want to go," he told her.

"You promised," she reminded him.

He groaned. "How about I come back for breakfast?"

"It's nearly four o'clock. Breakfast is only a few hours away."

"I know."

She giggled, then pushed him away. He grabbed the key out of her hand and inserted it in the lock. When the door opened, she took a step inside the foyer, but didn't get any farther before he put his arms around her from behind and pulled her against his chest, pressing his erection against her lower back.

"How about an early lunch? Around eleven," she said.

"How about lunch up here in your suite?"

"If you'll go away now, like a good boy, I'll think about it."

He shoved her mane of long hair to one side and kissed her neck. She squealed. He released her, then turned around and walked away. When he was almost in front of the nearby elevators, she called to him.

"Dom?"

He spun around and smiled. "Yeah?"

"Thanks for the best evening I've had in…in a long time."

"You're quite welcome."

"See you at eleven."

"I'll be johnny-on-the-spot."

After they waved goodbye, she went inside her suite. He punched the elevator down button and waited. Then he realized he still had her key and she still had his jacket. The jacket was no big deal. He could get it tomorrow. But what if she got curious and took a look in the pockets? When he'd wrapped the jacket around her after they left the Beachcomber, he'd forgotten that he'd put the photo of her that Edward Bedell had given him inside the inner pocket. How would he ever be able to explain to her why he had a picture of her?

Dom walked down the hall to her door, but just as he started to knock, he heard an odd noise. Something inside the suite had fallen. He pressed his ear to the door and listened. Another thud, then the sound of scuffling. And finally a muffled cry.

His adrenaline pumping, he slid the plastic key down the lock and opened the door.

"Audrey?" he called to her. "Are you all right?"

Deadly silence.

Then suddenly a loud, terrified scream.

CHAPTER FOUR

DOM'S TRAINING as a SEAL told him how to handle the situation, despite being emotionally involved. And damn it all, he was emotionally involved with Audrey Perkins whether he wanted to be or not.

The suite lay in darkness, which meant the curtains had been closed to prevent outside light from entering the area. Someone had entered the suite, prepared it for an attack and waited for Audrey's return. He could be dealing with a kidnapper, a rapist or a thief, although one of the first two was more likely, unless he had simply walked into the middle of a robbery attempt.

Dom had no way of knowing if he was dealing with one assailant or more. His Glock 30 was in his room in the safe. After making contact with Audrey and finding out she was alone, he had erroneously assumed he wouldn't need his gun. Besides, if he'd carried his weapon on their date, how could he have explained it to her? But Dom seldom if ever went anywhere without being armed, especially not when he was working. Keeping his back to the wall, he eased down, lifted his pants leg and removed the Beretta 950 Jetfire pistol from the holster strapped to his calf. Many of the Dundee agents used the small, 10 ounce, 4.7 inch handgun as a backup weapon.

Not knowing his enemy, Dom took extra precautions. He had to work under the assumption that the person or persons involved posed a threat to Audrey, that they wouldn't hesitate to kill her, especially if this was a kidnapping gone wrong.

When he made his way from the entrance foyer and into the parlor/dining room of the luxurious suite, his Beretta in hand, he heard a loud, agonized grunt, then saw a flash of movement.

Something or someone came barreling toward him, followed by a bulking dark shadow.

Audrey ran straight into him, her breathing labored. "He has a knife," she whispered. "He's trying to kill me."

Before Dom had time to respond, the big, brutal man came at him, but just as Dom aimed the Beretta, the guy rushed past him and Audrey and ran straight for the open door.

"Was he alone?" Dom asked, halfway into the foyer.

"Yes, as far as I know," she replied.

"You stay here," he told her, then headed out the door.

"Don't go. Don't leave me alone," she called after him.

Dom hesitated for a split second, but when he saw the man disappear inside the elevator, he turned around to face Audrey.

"I'll call hotel security," Dom said, then flipped on a light switch and walked over to the phone in the parlor.

"They should be able to catch him when he exits the elevator, if he stays on the elevator."

"Don't call security. Please." Audrey grabbed his wrist. "Don't call anyone."

"Why not?"

"I'm not hurt. I don't think anything is missing. And even so, I really don't want the publicity. If you notify the hotel, they'll call in the police, then the newspapers will get wind of it and Audrey Bedell Perkins will be front page news tomorrow. The press will hound me."

Dom intensely disliked the idea of letting a criminal get off scot-free. It went against everything he believed in, everything he'd fought for as a SEAL, everything he stood for as a Dundee agent.

"Please, Dom."

He replaced the phone on its base. "What's really going on? I thought you said he was trying to kill you. Why would you want a man like that to go free?"

"Maybe I overreacted." Her voice quivered slightly. "I'm not sure. He took me by surprise. He grabbed me from behind. He had a knife. He held it to my throat."

"How did you get away from him?"

"Basic survival techniques. I bit his hand that he held over my mouth, then I elbowed him in the groin. Luckily, I hit the right spot."

Dom looked at her in a whole new light. The pampered heiress had defended herself. She'd fought off an attacker like a spunky streetwise woman would have done. "Where did you learn to fight dirty?"

She exhaled deeply. "Look, there are things I can't

tell you. Not yet. Not until I talk to…my father. I need to go back to Chattanooga."

Dom eyed her quizzically. "I can take you home right now. I have a plane at my disposal." He lifted his leg, eased up the cuff of his pants and put the Beretta in the calf holster.

She stared at him, obviously puzzled by his comment.

"Look, I think we should come clean with each other," he said. "I'll go first, then you."

"What?" She stared at him, obviously puzzled by his suggestion. "I don't understand."

"My name is Domingo Shea and I did come to Palm Beach on business. I work for the Dundee Private Security and Investigation Agency, based in Atlanta. Edward Bedell hired me to locate his missing daughter. I came to Palm Beach to find you."

"Oh."

He couldn't bear the look of disappointment on her face. "But what happened between us had nothing to do with—"

"You had an ulterior motive for being so nice to me."

Dom grabbed her by the shoulders and shook her gently. "I came here on an assignment and expected to find a cold, calculating, spoiled bitch, but you don't come across as any of those things. I was nice to you because I like you. I like you a little more than I should, but once I spoke to your father and told him you were okay, he said fine, just have her call me. Assignment over."

"And that's all I was to you, an assignment."

"No, damn it." He eased his hands from her shoulders, down her arms and then released her. "That's what I'm trying to explain. I became emotionally involved and I shouldn't have. Right now, a potential murderer is getting away because instead of calling hotel security the way I should have, I'm sitting here with you. But once you explain exactly what's going on with you, why somebody tried to kill you and you don't want me to go after them, I'm calling the police."

"No!"

"Why the hell not?"

"Please, believe me when I tell you that if you'll just take me back to Chattanooga, straight to my father—"

"Why are you so anxious to go home to dear old dad when you've been running away for nearly two weeks now? You know who your attacker was or, at the very least, why he was waiting here for you, don't you?"

She shook her head. "No, I swear I don't know who he was or why—" she gulped "—he was waiting here to kill me."

"Which is it—he was trying to kill you or he wasn't?"

"I don't know. You're confusing me. I think he was here to either kidnap or kill me. But it doesn't make any sense. No one was supposed to know where I was. Not yet. Not until…"

"What's really going on here? What are you not telling me?"

"Please, Dom, take me back to Chattanooga as soon as possible. Take me to the Bedell estate. I have to talk to my father."

FOUR HOURS LATER, the Dundee jet landed in Chatta-nooga. Dom had called ahead so that a rental car would be waiting for them. In Palm Beach the temperature had been in the low eighties, but here in southeastern Ten-nessee, this morning's high was seventy. Autumn was in full swing in early October, leaves were already be-ginning to turn from green to golds and reds, and a definite chill was in the air.

On the trip to Chattanooga, Dom had tried to persuade Audrey to confide in him, but she'd refused, telling him that she had to talk to her father before she could say anything else. He suspected that she knew a lot more about her attacker than she was admitting—if not his identity, then the reason he'd been waiting for her in her hotel suite.

Before leaving Palm Beach, Audrey had packed four suitcases, each filled to the brim. But neither he nor she had showered or changed clothes. Dom had retrieved his jacket and put it on; she'd thrown a beige cashmere sweater over her shoulders before they called the bellman.

During the plane ride, Audrey had dozed off to sleep. When she'd rested her head on his shoulder, Dom had slipped his arm around her and readjusted her so that she'd be more comfortable. She had looked so sweet and innocent while she slept.

"I want all my suitcases loaded in the car before we leave," Audrey said after they departed from the Dundee jet.

"Sure thing."

"And I want you to call the house and tell my father that we're on our way."

"Okay."

"And I want you to stay with me when I see my father. Promise me that you won't leave me alone."

"I promise."

On the forty minute drive from the airport to the Bedell estate on Lookout Mountain, Audrey had sat quietly with her hands clutched together in her lap. She appeared to be nervous and worried. And afraid? But why should she be afraid of her father? Maybe that wasn't it. Maybe it was her husband she feared. Could it be that Grayson Perkins had abused her? If that were the case, then Dom would—

He'd stay calm, cool and in control until he found out the truth. That's what he'd do. And he'd keep his promise to Audrey. He'd stay at her side. He wouldn't leave her. Not until he knew she was safe. Not until she asked him to go.

"WHAT THE HELL HAPPENED? You were supposed to make sure that she was taken care of."

"The guy I hired made a mistake. He didn't count on her putting up a fight. He said I should have warned him that she knew how to handle herself. And he had no idea some guy would come to her rescue."

"I don't want excuses. Your failure creates a major problem for me."

"I'm sorry. I swear I've never had any trouble with this guy before. He's good at what he does and—"

"Not good enough to get rid of one small redhead."

"Look, I have contacts all over. Just say the word and I'll put somebody in your area on the job in less than twelve hours."

"No, not yet. Let me see how this is going to play out before I decide on another course of action. Mr. Shea is bringing her home this morning. They should arrive at any moment."

"Just let me know what you want and when you want it. No more slip ups, I promise."

JEREMY LOMAN OPENED the door for Dom and Audrey. "Mr. Bedell and the others are waiting in the study."

Dom noticed that Loman didn't speak to Audrey, didn't even glance at her. And she paid little attention to her father's all-around assistant, which made him wonder if there was bad blood between the two of them.

"The others?" Dom asked, then slipped his arm through Audrey's as they followed Loman down the hall.

"Yes, sir. Mrs. Bedell, Miss Cara and Mr. Grayson. They're all very concerned about Miss Audrey."

Dom felt Audrey tense immediately and his gut instincts warned him that something definitely wasn't right.

Within minutes, they entered the study. Wall-to-wall bookshelves, carved marble fireplace, massive wooden desk, and four somber people stood before them. One by one, the family turned to stare at Dom and then at Audrey. Not one smile. Not one welcome home or thank God you're all right.

"Please come on in," Edward Bedell said. "Would

you—" he glanced at Audrey "—either of you care for coffee?"

"No, thanks," Dom said.

Audrey didn't reply.

"When you telephoned, you said you were bringing Audrey home," Edward said. "Where is she? Did she change her mind about coming back to Chattanooga with you?"

A mental red flag popped up inside Dom's mind the second Edward Bedell's question registered. "What do you mean, where is she? She's right here." Dom turned and looked at Audrey.

"Please, Mr. Bedell, I can explain everything," Audrey said. "I know this looks bad, but remember that I came here with Mr. Shea of my own free will and I did it because I think your daughter is in some kind of horrible trouble. Someone tried to kill me early this morning, someone who thought I was Audrey."

Dom heard several voices questioning, complaining, accusing, but all he could think about was that this woman, a woman he had thought was Audrey Bedell, had just confessed that she wasn't the woman he'd been hired to find.

"I don't understand what's going on here." Bedell glowered at Dom. "What on earth made you think this young woman was my daughter?"

Dom looked right at Bedell. "Maybe because she told me she was Audrey Bedell Perkins and because she was using your daughter's credit cards and had registered at the hotel under that name. And the general description I was given of Audrey fits this woman's general description." Dom snapped his head around and glared at the woman who'd had his insides tied in knots since the moment they met. "Who the hell are you if you're not Audrey?"

"Dom, please understand that I—"

"What have you done to my sister?" Cara demanded as she stormed across the room toward the stranger in their midst. "Did you kill her and steal her credit cards?"

Whoever the woman was, she stood her ground. She squared her shoulders, tilted her chin up and balled her hands into tight fists. "My name is Lausanne Raney. I've worked as a receptionist at Bedell, Inc. for the past six months and I haven't killed anyone. Audrey Perkins hired me to impersonate her so that she and her boyfriend could run away together without being followed."

CHAPTER FIVE

THE TRUTH HAD HIT DOM like a sledgehammer, right between the eyes. Why hadn't he seen what was right before him? Why hadn't he realized that this woman wasn't Audrey Bedell Perkins? He had compared her to the photograph he'd been given and had seen only a superficial similarity. *Great investigative work, Shea,* he told himself. *You were so busy thinking with your dick instead of your brain that you screwed up big time.*

"Why would Audrey do such a thing?" Grayson Perkins asked, genuine puzzlement in his expression.

"Get real," Patrice said. "She figured that if she was gone long enough, either you or Edward would sick the bloodhounds on her. I think it was damn smart of her to hire an impersonator to lead y'all off on a wild goose chase."

"I think we should call the police right now," Cara said. "How do we know this woman is telling us the truth?"

"I swear that I'm not lying," Lausanne told them, her pleading gaze moving around the room, pausing for a split second on each person present.

"What you're saying may be true, but I agree with Cara—we should call the police." Grayson looked directly at Edward. "We don't know where Audrey is or what may or may not have happened to her. If this girl is lying—"

"I'm not lying!" There was a hint of panic in Lausanne's voice.

"Shut up! Everyone, stop talking!" Edward's face reddened, his nostrils flared. "All this quibbling isn't getting us anywhere." He turned to Dom. "You're the professional, Mr. Shea. What do you recommend?"

Torn between being angry at Lausanne Raney for making him look like a fool and wanting to believe that she hadn't committed a crime, Dom hesitated briefly before answering. "Call the police. As a matter of fact, I'll do that for you. I can update them on all the pertinent information." He glanced at Lausanne. "As for you, keep quiet until the police arrive. You can tell your story to them and to us at the same time." He wanted to add, *Do you understand? I'm trying to help you without betraying my client.*

Why the hell did he want to help her? What if she was lying? What if she was somehow involved in Audrey Perkins's disappearance? For all he knew, this woman could be a cold-blooded killer. But if she was a criminal, she wasn't a very smart one; otherwise, she wouldn't have been traveling around the southeast passing herself off as Audrey Perkins while she added up huge bills on the woman's credit cards.

"Very well," Edward said. "I think we should all adjourn to the living room and allow you some privacy to telephone the police." He glanced at Lausanne. "We'll leave Ms. Raney—if that's her real name—in your custody."

Loman followed the others out of the room, closing the study door behind him. Once they were alone, Lausanne rushed over to Dom, who held up a restraining hand. She stopped immediately and stared at him, her eyes dry, her expression stern.

"They don't believe me, do they?" She searched Dom's face, then said, "And you don't, either. You actually think I might have done something to Audrey Perkins and stolen her credit cards."

"Did you?"

"No, I did not."

"Why should I believe you?"

"Oh, I don't know—maybe because I'm telling the truth."

"The way you were telling me the truth when you told me that you were Audrey Bedell Perkins?"

"I was playacting. She hired me to impersonate her. I swear—"

"Save it for the police, honey."

She grabbed Dom's arm and gazed into his eyes. "I'm going to get railroaded on this and we both know it. It's happened to me before. I'm just lucky that way. I should have known the deal I made with Ms. Perkins was too good to be true, that somehow, someway, it would come back and bite me in the butt."

"Are you saying you've been arrested before, that you have a criminal record?"

She released her hold on his arm. "I have never committed a crime, but this isn't the first time I've been
blamed for something I didn't do."

Dom nodded. God, how he wanted to believe her. *Idiot!*

"Have a seat." He pointed to a nearby chair, then
walked over to the desk and picked up the telephone
receiver. He reached inside his coat pocket, removed the
card with Lieutenant Bain Desmond's phone number
that Sawyer had given him and punched in the digits.

The detective answered on the third ring. "Yeah,
Desmond here."

"Lieutenant Desmond, this is Domingo Shea. I'm
with the Dundee—"

"Yes, Mr. Shea, Sawyer McNamara told me I might
be hearing from you. So what can I do for you?"

"Did Sawyer fill you in on any of the details?"

"Nope."

"Okay, here it is in a nutshell—Edward Bedell's
daughter, Audrey Perkins, disappeared nearly two
weeks ago. Bedell hired Dundee's to find her. We traced
her whereabouts through her credit card activity. I found
her in Palm Beach, Florida, where somebody made a
botched attempt at either kidnapping or killing her. I
brought her home to her father this morning. But lo and
behold, the woman turned out not to be Audrey Perkins,
but some lookalike who claims her name is Lausanne
Raney. She swears Audrey Perkins hired her to impersonate her so that if dear old dad hired a PI—that would
be me—to find her, he'd find the impersonator instead."

"Whoa…that's quite a story there, Mr. Shea."

"Yeah, tell me about it," Dom replied.

"Does this Raney woman have any proof that Ms. Perkins hired her?"

"Don't know. Haven't asked."

"Okay, so I guess this means you're waiting for me to do all the questioning, right?"

"Right."

"Sawyer gave you my cell phone number. I'm off duty right now, but if you'll give me about an hour to round up my partner, we'll meet you at the Bedell estate."

LAUSANNE HADN'T BEEN this scared in a long time. Not since she had been arrested as an accessory to armed robbery. Not since she'd trusted the wrong man and paid for her mistake with five years of her life. She felt like the biggest fool on earth for believing she'd hit it lucky when Audrey Perkins offered her a deal she couldn't refuse. It would be so simple, Ms. Perkins had explained. All she had to do was travel around from city to city, stay at four-star hotels, move every few days, and go on shopping sprees as often she wanted. And to seal the deal, Ms. Perkins had given her fifty thousand dollars, which Lausanne had promptly deposited in a savings account. That money was earmarked to pay for an investigator to unearth the whereabouts of Lausanne's daughter.

I'm going to find you, sweet darling. I'm going to make sure you're well and happy and want for nothing.

Lausanne had no intention of interfering in her child's life. But she had to know, had to be certain, that her daughter was living the kind of life she deserved.

That fifty thousand could well be the only proof she had that Ms. Perkins had hired her to gallivant around the southeast pretending to be Audrey. Damn! She'd been paid in cash, something that hadn't concerned her at the time. After all, it wasn't as if she'd thought she'd need to prove she hadn't killed Audrey Perkins and stolen the money from her.

"Is your name really Lausanne Raney?" Dom asked.

She snapped her head up and glared at him. "I'm Lausanne Inez Raney, born twenty-eight years ago in Booneville, Mississippi."

"You know that I can run a check on you and find out if you're lying to me."

Her lips twitched in a hint of a smile. A hard, sarcastic smile that told him she wasn't afraid of him and wouldn't succumb to any bullying tactics.

"So check me out," she said. "I'm not lying."

"Want to fill me in on—"

"No, I don't. I'll tell the police what I know, then if either they or you want to know more, y'all will have to dig up the info on your own. Why should I make things easier for you, especially considering the fact that you don't believe me?"

"You sure fooled me, honey." He sat down in a chair directly across from her.

"And that galls you, doesn't it? It wounds your male pride. You really believed I was Audrey Perkins."

"My male pride will survive. This wasn't my first mistake and it won't be my last. The thing I don't understand is why you insisted on being brought back here to Chattanooga, straight to Edward Bedell."

"Somebody tried to kill me—kill Audrey. Impersonating Audrey for money and the perks of first-class travel and expensive shopping sprees is one thing, but I didn't sign on to be a body double in a murder case."

"So why not just split?" Dom asked. "Why come back to Chattanooga to see Audrey's father and be found out?"

"Because he has the right to know that someone wants his daughter dead and that I'm not going to be her stand-in any longer. He's a rich, powerful man. He can do something to save her life…and mine."

Dom studied her curiously, and she knew he wasn't sure he could believe her. "Do you think Audrey hired you because she knew someone wanted to kill her and set you up as a moving target?"

"Yeah, the thought has crossed my mind a time or two since that guy tried to slit my throat this morning."

"You do realize that the police might come up with another theory."

"I did not kill Audrey Perkins. I didn't harm a hair on her head."

"Can you prove it?"

"Can you or the police prove otherwise?"

"No, but if we can't find Audrey, you might want to hire yourself a good lawyer."

Lausanne shrugged. "I guess I should have known that once you found out I wasn't a rich heiress, you wouldn't give a damn about me, that you wouldn't be on my side, wouldn't stand by me." She shrugged. "That's the story of my life."

"The story of your life, huh? So, you've impersonated a rich heiress before?"

She emitted a mirthless chuckle. "No, this was a first for me. What I meant was that this isn't the first time a guy who whispered sweet nothings in my ear wound up disappointing me. The only difference is I don't think you're really an uncaring, unreliable son of a bitch like the others."

Dom stared at her, but said nothing.

Then again, maybe he was just like the others, only wrapped in a prettier package. Just because Dom professed to be one of the good guys didn't make it true.

So, here she was one her own once again. All alone and in trouble up to her eyeballs. She couldn't count on Dom Shea to help her. The only person she could rely on was herself.

SERGEANT MIKE SWAIN stood five-nine, was built like a fireplug and chewed gum while he talked. His carrot-red hair was cut military short and his large brown eyes were hidden behind a pair of thick glasses. His superior, Lieutenant Bain Desmond, was older, close to forty where Swain wasn't a day over thirty. Tall and lean, with an easy smile that proclaimed him a good old boy, Desmond entered the Bedell living room as if he owned it. The guy wasn't cocky, just self-confident. He surveyed the group of people one by one, then turned his baby blues on Lausanne.

"Start at the beginning, Ms. Raney, and tell us exactly

how and why Dom Shea found you in Palm Beach impersonating Audrey Bedell."

Lausanne swallowed hard. This wasn't the first time she'd been interrogated by the police nor was it the first time she'd been presumed guilty.

"I've been working as a receptionists at Bedell, Inc. for the past six months. Ten—no, eleven days ago, I received a telephone call from Audrey Perkins, asking me to come to her home. She said she'd seen me when she'd visited the main office and thought I'd be perfect for a special job she needed done."

"And so you went to see her?" Desmond asked. "At her home?"

"Yes, I went to her home. After all, she was Audrey Bedell Perkins, the boss's daughter."

"Was there anyone else there when you arrived, a maid…a secretary…anyone who can verify that you met with Ms. Perkins?"

"No, there wasn't anyone else there. She'd made certain that we met alone, in private."

"I see." Desmond nodded. "Go on."

"When I arrived at Ms. Perkins's home, she asked me if I'd like to earn fifty thousand dollars and—"

"Did Ms. Perkins pay you that amount?" Desmond asked.

"Yes, she did."

"Cashier's check, personal check—"

"Cash," Lausanne replied and heard the collective ah-ha sigh reverberating around the room. "I deposited the money in a savings account. Regions Bank."

"And what service were you to provide to earn the fifty-thousand?" Lt. Desmond watched her carefully.

"Ms. Perkins offered me the money, plus an extravagant vacation, new clothes, and use of her credit cards. And all I had to do was travel from one city to another, moving every three or four days, registering under the name of Audrey Bedell Perkins and pretending to be her for a few weeks. She said that the reason she'd thought of me for the job was because she remembered seeing me at the office one day and had noticed that we were about the same height, same size, same coloring and even close to the same age. When she offered me a chance to earn fifty-thousand dollars, she also promised me that my job at Bedell Inc. would be waiting for me when I returned to Chattanooga, that she'd make certain of it."

When murmurs rose from others in the room, Sergeant Swain requested quiet; then Desmond continued with his questioning.

"Did Ms. Perkins tell you why she wanted you to impersonate her?"

"Yes, she did. She told me that she intended to run away with her boyfriend and she didn't want her husband or her father to find them, that all they needed was a good head start on any search her family might instigate."

"And you didn't have any qualms about—"

"Yes, I had my doubts, but when she handed me a bag filled with cash, I pushed aside all my doubts. Fifty-thousand is a great incentive for most of us who don't have that kind of money."

Desmond nodded, as if agreeing. "Do you have any idea where the real Audrey Perkins is right now?"

"No, sir. I have no idea."

"And do you have any proof—other than fifty-thousand dollars in your bank account—to back up what you've just told me?"

"No," she admitted. "The only person who can verify that what I've told you is the truth is Audrey Perkins."

"And Ms. Perkins just happens to be missing."

"Yes, sir. And considering the predicament I'm in, I want her found as much, if not more, than anyone else in this room."

Dom had watched and listened, studying Lausanne's body language, her voice, every aspect of her responses. He wanted to believe her; some part of him did believe her. But was that part his head or his heart? Or a region a little farther south?

"I don't believe anything this woman has told you." Cara Bedell's declaration broke the momentary silence. "She's lying. She knows where Audrey is."

"I agree," Grayson said. "Audrey would never concoct such an elaborate scheme just so she could run away with one of her lovers. She's gone off with other men before this and never found it necessary to—"

"But she's never been in love with any of the others," Patrice pointed out. "Bobby Jack Cash was different."

"Yes, he was different," Edward said. "He was a low-life scum. And he was dangerous. Why Audrey would give a man like that the time of day is beyond me. She was far superior to him in every way."

No one else noticed the stricken look on Lausanne's face at the mention of the name Bobby Jack Cash, but Dom had been staring right at her. He got a sick, sinking feeling in the pit of his belly. He'd bet his last dime that Lausanne knew the man, that there was a connection between them. And here he'd been on the verge of believing all her lies, of being taken in by her sweet, innocent appearance. An ugly scenario formed in his mind, one that put Lausanne Raney and Bobby Jack Cash together in a wicked scheme that ended in murder.

"Ms. Raney, do you know Bobby Jack Cash?" Dom asked.

CHAPTER SIX

LAUSANNE HAD TWO CHOICES—lie or tell the truth. But considering the trouble she was in and the fact that the truth was bound to come out, she chose complete honesty.

Mentally preparing herself for Dom's condemnation and suspicion, she looked directly at him when she responded to his question.

"Yes, I know Bobby Jack Cash."

A loud rumble of angry, accusatory voices bombarded her, but once again Sergeant Swain quieted the Bedell family with a stern warning.

Lausanne hated the expression on Dom's face, knowing that any chance she'd had to persuade him of her innocence had now been lost. Damn it, what was wrong with her? Why did she always pick the wrong guy, the guy who'd disappoint her, get her in trouble and break her heart?

"Ms. Raney?" Bain Desmond spoke her name.

She turned to him. "Yes, sir?"

"How do you know Mr. Cash?"

"I met him when I first went to work at Bedell, Inc. He was employed there as a guard."

"So, you were simply fellow employees and that's the extent of your relationship with the man?" Dom asked.

Keeping her gaze on the police lieutenant and avoiding direct eye contact with Dom, she replied. "No, not exactly. We went out on a couple of dates, but that was months ago and—"

"You were Mr. Cash's girlfriend?" Lt. Bain asked.

"No." Lausanne shook her head. "It was only two dates. That's all."

"Were you lovers?" Dom asked.

Cackling laughter drew everyone's attention away from Lausanne and to Patrice Bedell. Realizing her outburst had removed the spotlight from Lausanne and focused on her, she quieted. Then chuckling softly, she glanced around at the others.

"What's the matter?" Patrice asked. "Don't the rest of you find this as amusing as I do? Bobby Jack was bonking this little nothing receptionist while he was having an affair with Audrey, who fell madly in love with him. My bet is that Audrey found out and—"

"I did not have sex with Bobby Jack," Lausanne swore. "We were not lovers."

"I think she and Bobby Jack murdered Audrey," Patrice said.

"I didn't murder Audrey. And I haven't dated Bobby Jack in months." Lausanne wanted to scream, to rant and rave. But most of all, she wanted to kick her own rear end for getting embroiled in such a complicated mess. First of all, she never should have dated Bobby Jack

Cash; but the guy had been so persistent, so charming and persuasive. And she'd been lonely. But it had taken her only two dates to realize the guy was bad news, just like all the other men in her life, starting with her own father.

Hindsight was twenty-twenty, of course. If only she'd said "thank you, but no thank you" to Audrey Bedell's proposition, she wouldn't be in trouble. Again. No one would be accusing her of murder.

"I want you to arrest this woman for murder!" Patrice got right up in Lausanne's face. "You might as well admit what you did. You and Bobby Jack Cash. You killed her and we all know it."

"For once I agree with Patrice," Cara said. "Make her tell you what they did with poor Audrey."

"No!" Edward Bedell stepped forward, a haggard expression on his wrinkled face. "We have no proof that this girl did anything other than what she said she did—impersonate Audrey. There's a good chance that Audrey is in the Caribbean or in Europe, either alone or with Bobby Jack Cash. Until we find Audrey, we can't be certain of anything."

Lausanne stared at Mr. Bedell, surprised by his attitude, but thankful that he was at least giving her the benefit of the doubt.

Lieutenant Desmond nodded. "Mr. Bedell is right. We have no hard evidence against Ms. Raney, no proof she's done anything illegal. And no witnesses to any crime."

"Are you saying you can't arrest this woman?" Grayson asked.

"Yes, sir, that's exactly what I'm saying." Desmond walked over to Lausanne. "Just because I can't arrest you doesn't mean I believe your story. Until Ms. Perkins is found and can corroborate what you've told us, you will remain a person of interest to the Chattanooga PD. Do you understand?"

"Yes, I understand." Lausanne understood all too well. Once the police ran a check on her and discovered that she had served five years in the TPFW, she would become their number one suspect if anything had happened to Audrey Perkins. And she had a really bad feeling in her gut that if Audrey wasn't already dead, she was in grave danger.

"I'd appreciate it if you'd cooperate by allowing me to ask you a few questions in private," Desmond said. "Of course, you have every right to call a lawyer—"

"I don't need a lawyer, do I?"

"No, ma'am," Lt. Desmond replied. "Not at this time."

"I'm willing to cooperate…up to a point."

"Then why don't we step outside in the hall for a couple of minutes."

All eyes were on the two of them as Desmond and she exited the room. She caught a glimpse of Dom in her peripheral vision and wondered if his strained expression was concern or condemnation.

Once Lt. Desmond closed the door behind them, he led her a good eight feet down the hall, then paused and confronted her.

"When Dom Shea called me in on this case, he gave me your name and I ran a preliminary check on you and found out that—"

Lausanne finished the sentence. "I served five years in the Tennessee Prison for Women in Nashville."

"The reason I didn't mention this in front of the others is because I didn't figure that bit of information was anyone's business. At least not at this point in my investigation."

Lausanne met the detective's gaze head-on, trying to figure out if he was on the level or if he was playing her. "Thanks. I guess."

"If you had anything to do with Audrey Perkins's disappearance, now would be a good time to tell me. Cooperate and I'll do what I can to help you."

"I've had all the help I want from men and that includes policemen. But I'll tell you again, I have no idea where Audrey Perkins is. And keep in mind one thing—you don't know that anything has happened to her. Not yet."

"What do you mean not yet?"

"Didn't Mr. Shea tell you that somebody attacked me in my hotel room in Palm Beach?" She glared at Lt. Desmond. "Somebody who thought I was Audrey tried to slit my throat."

"Yeah, Shea told me. But for all I know, whoever tried to kill you was after you, not Ms. Perkins."

"Get real, will you. Why would anybody want to kill me? But I'll bet you could find quite a few people who might want Audrey dead." Lausanne glanced over her shoulder and nodded toward the closed living room door down the hall. "Starting with some people in that room."

"What happened to you in Palm Beach could have been an attempted robbery."

"I don't think so. This guy could have stolen everything in my suite and been gone before I returned," Lausanne said. "No, I'm pretty sure he was waiting for me. He intended to kill me."

Lt. Desmond studied Lausanne for a couple of seconds, then grunted. "Look, I don't need to tell you not to leave town, do I?"

"The only place I'm going is to my apartment in East Brainerd," she told him. "Then first thing tomorrow, I'll be job hunting." She could live for quite a while on the fifty grand she'd stashed away in the bank, but she didn't want to waste it on living expenses. So, that meant finding another job ASAP.

"I'll have Sergeant Swain take you home."

"I can call a cab." But before she left, she intended to get her suitcases out of Dom's car. Audrey Perkins had told her that whatever she bought during her all-expenses-paid vacation, she could keep. She wasn't about to hand over thousands of dollars in clothes and jewelry and... She'd bought several things that she thought any ten-year-old girl might like. Things she hoped to somehow give her daughter as gifts. But first, she had to find her child.

"Just wait around for a few minutes, okay?" Lt. Desmond told her.

She shrugged.

"After I talk to Mr. Bedell, I'll probably have a few more questions for you."

"If you've got more questions, I want a lawyer."

Desmond's lips curved upward in a tentative smile.

"For the sake of argument, let's say I believe you about Ms. Perkins hiring you and about someone trying to kill you, thinking you were she."

"What are we doing, playing pretend?"

He chuckled. "From what Dom Shea tells me, you're quite good at that game."

Lausanne huffed. "He's just pissed because I fooled him." *Yeah, and he fooled me, too. I thought he actually liked me and all the while he was just chasing down a runaway heiress.*

Desmond took her by the arm and led her farther down the hall. Then he opened the door to the study and gave her a nudge over the threshold. "Wait in here. And don't even think about leaving without my permission."

"I REGRET THAT THINGS turned out this way," Dom Shea said. "I'm sorry that the woman I found in Palm Beach turned out to be an imposter."

"It's not your fault," Edward Bedell said. "Apparently my daughter is determined not to be found. She went to great lengths and some expense to put us off track."

Cara glowered at her father. "You can't mean to tell me that you believe that woman's lies. Something terrible has happened to Audrey and we all know it."

Edward groaned. "Now, Cara—"

"No, she's right," Grayson said. "There's something all wrong about this. If Audrey wanted to run off with Bobby Jack Cash, she'd have simply run off with him." Grayson shot Patrice a withering glance. "Even if she was madly in love with the man, she would hardly have given up everything for him. We all know that Audrey could never survive without Edward's money supporting her."

"Perhaps they're right," Patrice agreed. "Maybe Audrey just wanted to put a good scare into you, make you think she'd left for good, then when she got in touch with you, you'd be so relieved that you'd forgive her and accept Bobby Jack as your new son-in-law."

"Never!" Edward all but growled the word.

Grayson turned to his father-in-law. "I think we should have Mr. Shea continue his search for Audrey. Now that his first lead unearthed an imposter—"

"I'm not sure what to do, where to go from here," Edward said. "I'd like to know that Audrey is well and happy, but if she doesn't want to be found…"

"What if she's in trouble?" Cara said. "What if Bobby Jack Cash did leave with her? What if he's keeping her from contacting us?"

"Mr. Shea," Grayson said. "What do you recommend?"

Yeah, put him on the spot, ask him to make a decision that shouldn't be his. Apparently everyone in the Bedell family had slightly different opinions of the situation, including their suspicions about Lausanne Raney. Was the woman telling the truth or was she lying? He didn't have the answer to that question any more than the rest of them did.

Glancing from Grayson to Edward, Dom said, "Mr. Bedell hired Dundee's, so the call is his. If he wants us to continue the search for Ms. Perkins, we will. If not, then my involvement in this case is over."

"Daddy, please, do something." Cara grasped her father's arm.

Tensing at her touch, Edward eased his arm from his daughter's and took a step away from her. She clenched her jaw and sucked in a deep breath, apparently making an effort not to cry.

"I'd like you to stay on the case," Edward said. "Stay on in Chattanooga and do what you can to find out where my daughter went when she left town. And also, keep an eye on Ms. Raney. We can't rule out the possibility that she is lying, that she knows a great deal more than she's telling us."

"Yes, sir."

Before Dom could say anything else, before he could discuss the details of exactly what Edward Bedell meant by keeping an eye on Lausanne Raney, Lt. Desmond entered the living room.

Apparently having overhead the last bit of conversation between Dom and Edward, Desmond said, "I think you're wise to keep track of Ms. Raney. Although we intend to make sure she doesn't leave town, having someone watch her movements for the next few days will help us a great deal."

"Then you think she's somehow involved in Audrey's disappearance?" Edward asked.

"Possibly. But there's no way to be sure. I'd say there's a fifty-fifty chance she's telling the truth," Desmond said.

"Which means there's a fifty-fifty chance she's lying," Dom said.

Desmond grimaced. "Yeah."

"Where is she?"

"Waiting for me to release her so she can go home. I offered for Sergeant Swain to drive her, but she said she'd call a cab."

"I'll take her." The words were out of Dom's mouth before he realized he'd even thought them.

Desmond cocked an eyebrow.

"Good idea, Mr. Shea," Grayson said. "Don't let that woman out of your sight."

"I'll want a daily report," Edward told Dom. "On the search for Audrey and on Ms. Raney. If necessary, bring in another agent to help you. Money is no object."

"Yes, sir. I'll contact you daily with updates. And if I think it necessary, I'll ask for assistance." Dom glanced at Desmond. "May I take Ms. Raney home now?"

"Yeah, sure. And one more thing—whatever Dundee's finds out about Ms. Perkins and Ms. Raney, keep the Chattanooga PD informed."

"I have your cell number," Dom said.

Desmond nodded.

LAUSANNE WAITED in the study. Tapping her foot nervously while she sat, she folded and unfolded her hands, rubbing the perspiration into her palms. Her gaze scanned the elegant room, which was like something out of a magazine or off one of those TV shows about the rich and famous. Wonder what it cost to decorate a room like this? More than fifty thousand, she'd bet.

As her gaze traveled around the room, she paused on the marble fireplace and looked upward to the gold-framed oil painting of a woman. Slender and petite, with her golden red hair styled in a sleek page-boy cut the woman was pretty but not classically beautiful. Wonder who she is? Audrey Perkins's mother perhaps. While working at Bedell, Inc., she'd heard rumors that Edward Bedell's first wife had been the love of his life.

When the study door opened, Lausanne jumped up, intending to face Lt. Desmond and demand he allow her to go home. But instead she came face to face with Dom Shea.

"What do you want?" She scowled at him.

"I'm taking you home."

"No, you're not."

"Lieutenant Desmond is releasing you and he instructed me to take you home."

She eyed him speculatively.

"Ready?" he asked.

"Why did he tell you to take me home?"

"To make sure you get there safe and sound."

"And if I don't want an escort?"

"It's either me or Sergeant Swain," Dom told her.

"Some choice."

Dom reached out and grasped her arm. "Let's go, honey. Make it easy on both of us and cooperate."

Lausanne glanced at his hand tightly gripping her arm. "Are you still working for Mr. Bedell?"

"Yes, I am."

"So, who wants you to keep tabs on me, Mr. Bedell or Lieutenant Desmond?"

"Both of them," Dom replied

"I take it that they don't buy my story about Audrey hiring me to impersonate her?"

"They'd be fools to trust you. I trusted you and look where it got me." Dom forcefully turned her around to face the fireplace. "Take a good look at the lady you were impersonating. There's only a vague resemblance and yet it didn't enter my head that you might not be who you said you were. It even crossed my mind that you might have had a little cosmetic surgery."

A tight knot formed in the pit of Lausanne's stomach as she stared at the portrait. That was Audrey Bedell Perkins? It couldn't be. This was not the woman who had hired her, not the redhead who'd given her fifty-thousand dollars in cash and sent her off on a spending-spree holiday.

Oh, my God!

"What's wrong?" Dom asked.

"Nothing's wrong. What makes you think something's wrong?"

"You look like you've seen a ghost."

"I said nothing's wrong. I just want to get out of here and try to forget about what an idiot I am. I should have known that if something seems too good to be true that it probably is."

Why didn't she just tell him that she now knew the woman who hired her to impersonate Audrey Bedell Perkins was not Audrey herself? Because he might not believe her. And if he didn't, then what? Better to err on the side of self-preservation and keep quiet for now.

With the realization that Audrey hadn't hired her, the situation had suddenly gone from complicated to alarmingly convoluted.

"Is there something about that portrait that bothers you?" Dom asked.

She shook her head. "Not really. I was just thinking that Audrey Perkins and I really don't look anything alike."

After escorting her out of the study, Dom paused in the open doorway and glanced back at the portrait over the fireplace. Then his gaze met Lausanne's. As he studied her closely, she realized he suspected she was lying to him. Again.

CHAPTER SEVEN

LAUSANNE HADN'T SAID MUCH on the drive from Lookout Mountain to East Brainerd. A couple of times, Dom had tried to start a conversation, but her one-word replies had let him know she wasn't interested in talking. Fine with him. There didn't seem to be anything either of them could say to change the situation. Neither of them had turned out to be who the other had thought they were. Each had lied to the other, either by omission or misrepresentation. And neither trusted the other. But on some basic, sexual level, they were still painfully aware of each other, which made things worse. Much worse.

Dom had to admit that this was a first for him. He wasn't the type of guy easily fooled or manipulated. In all his relationships, he'd held the upper hand, been the one sought after, the one who'd always been able to pick and choose the best of the best. His taste in women was fairly eclectic, but as a general rule, he preferred lovely, sophisticated, well-bred ladies. Of course, in his youth, he'd sampled a few bad girls, variety being the spice of life and all. But he knew trouble when he saw it and had learned to avoid becoming embroiled in messy personal situations.

Lausanne Raney was trouble with a capital *T*. Whatever the hell was going on with her, whatever brouhaha she'd created in her life, wasn't his problem. A smart guy would steer clear, cut his losses and run. Even though keeping close tabs on her was part of his job assignment, that didn't mean he had to become personally involved.

"Take the next right," Lausanne said. "Two blocks over. Glennview apartments."

Dom nodded, then took the next right at the red light.

"How long have you lived here?" he asked.

"Six months. Ever since I moved to Chattanooga. I needed a place that was cheap, already furnished and close to the bus line, since I don't own a car."

Dom caught a glimpse of her profile in his peripheral vision. Stoic. Proud. Her gaze focused straight ahead and not on him. "Where'd you live before that?"

"Nashville."

Dom maneuvered his rental car into the parking lot of the apartment complex.

"Why did you leave Nashville?" he asked.

"I needed a change of scenery."

Dom pulled his car to a stop in the nearest available parking slot, then turned off the motor and reached for the door handle.

"There's no need for you to get out," she told him. "Just put my suitcases on the sidewalk and I'll get them up to my apartment on my own."

"When I take a lady home, I always see her to her door." He opened the car door and stepped outside, then rounded the hood and opened the passenger door.

"Somebody taught you good manners."

He held out his hand to her. When she took it, he helped her to her feet. For a split second, they stood there, their bodies almost touching. She looked up at him as he glanced down at her. He was a good nine inches taller, despite the fact she was wearing two-inch heels. Staring into her moss green eyes, the expression on her china-doll face deceptively sweet and innocent, Dom had the overwhelming urge to kiss her.

Don't do it, he warned himself. *She's trying to reel you in, trying to sucker you. Remember, she's a master manipulator, capable of making lies sound like the truth.* For all he knew, this woman was a cold-blooded killer. At the very least, she was hiding something from him and from the police.

Dom grasped her upper arm and turned her around so that they were no longer facing each other. "Come on. Let's go."

"I need my luggage," she told him.

"So you're keeping all the loot you acquired using Audrey Perkins's credit cards, huh?"

"Damn right I am. It was part of the deal."

Dom popped the truck lid and removed the Louis Vuitton luggage, one piece at a time. If what was in these bags was as expensive as the cases themselves, then the lady had spared no expense when she went shopping.

Lausanne grabbed the two smaller pieces of Louis

Vuitton. "I'm in the building to the left," she told him. "Apartment 2-B."

He picked up the other two suitcases, then followed her across the sidewalk and up the flight of exterior stairs that led to the second level of the building. She stopped in front of a bright blue door, the paint cracked and peeling.

"This is it." She set the bags on the floor, then rummaged in her purse, retrieved her house key and inserted it in the lock. After opening the door, she turned around and gasped when she bumped into Dom, who had moved toward her instead of away from her. "Thanks for bringing me home."

"Are you sending me packing?"

Narrowing her gaze, she stared at him questioningly. "What is it that you really want?"

"I'd like a cup of coffee," he told her. "How about inviting me in and fixing us a pot?"

"Why would I invite you into my apartment?"

"So we can talk in private."

"What if I don't want to talk?"

"Then I'll do the talking."

"My story isn't going to change, you know." She bent down and picked up the two pieces of luggage. "I told you and the police the truth. I don't have any idea where Audrey Perkins is."

Dom gave her a gentle nudge into her apartment. When she didn't resist, he walked inside behind her and, using one of the larger suitcases, shoved the door closed. They stood a few feet into her living room, gazes locked, muscles tense. If he could look at this woman and not want to drag her off to the nearest bed, his job would be a lot easier. But there was something about her, something that appealed to him in some oddly primitive way. She was small and delicate, with a soft, sexy voice and a face like an angel. A false aura of innocent sweetness surrounded her.

Dom dumped the luggage on the floor behind him. "Were you lying when you said that you and Bobby Jack Cash weren't lovers?" He wanted to kick his own butt for asking her a question that made him sound like a jealous fool.

She cocked her head to one side and gave him a hard, condemning look. "I had my fill of bad boys long before I met Bobby Jack. My mistake was dating him, but I thought he was a nice man. I was wrong. We had two dates and neither ended in our doing the horizontal."

Lausanne put the two suitcases she'd been holding on the floor next to the ones Dom had deposited behind him.

"Did you know he was having an affair with Audrey Perkins?"

"No, I didn't know. Like I told you, after our second date, I didn't see Bobby Jack again, except occasionally at work."

"Hmm…" Dom broke eye contact and moved past Lausanne. Glancing at the outdated, floral sofa, he nodded in that direction. "Mind if I sit down?"

"Sit if you want," she said. "Stay all afternoon, but you're not going to learn anything you don't already know. I was hired to impersonate Audrey Perkins. I have no idea where she is. I didn't kill her. I'm not involved with Bobby Jack Cash."

"Let's say I don't believe you."

She glowered at Dom.

"Let's say I believe that you and Bobby Jack were lovers who plotted together to swindle Audrey Perkins out of a great deal of money." Dom watched Lausanne for a reaction, but all she did was stare at him with those big, sad green eyes, practically no expression on her face.

"It's a free country. You can believe whatever you want." She marched over to the kitchenette, separated from the living room area by a small vinyl-topped bar. After laying her purse on the bar, she removed her cashmere sweater and hung it on the back of the metal bar stool.

"But something went wrong," Dom said. "Maybe he fell for Audrey or maybe he decided that he could get more money from her by cutting you out of the picture and running off with her. So, you killed both of them."

"Interesting scenario." Lausanne opened one of the three wall cupboards over the single sink and compact stove. "Regular or decaf?"

"Huh?"

"It's after one o'clock. Do you prefer regular or decaf coffee?"

"I never drink decaf."

She reached up into the cupboard, removed a bag of ground coffee and proceeded to prepare the coffeemaker.

"Or maybe you're the one who double-crossed him,"

Dom said. "You two bumped off Audrey together, then you took the fifty grand and Audrey's credit cards and left Bobby Jack high and dry."

"Cream and sugar?"

Dom had to give it to her—Lausanne was as cool as a cucumber. He was accusing her of murder and she hadn't blinked an eye. But did that unemotional reaction mean she was guilty or innocent?

"I take my coffee black."

"Black it is," she said.

"I figure the guy who tried to slit your throat at the Classico Hotel was Bobby Jack. You betrayed him and when he finally caught up with you, he—"

Lausanne laughed. Startled, Dom stopped talking mid-sentence and stared at her. Smiling at him, she shook her head, the action tossing her mane of reddish gold curls from side to side. Dom's body tightened. Damn!

Grumbling under his breath, he willed his body under control. "Do you find being accused of murder humorous?"

"I find your fantasy scenarios humorous. I had absolutely no reason to kill Audrey Perkins or Bobby Jack Cash. Besides that, there's no evidence that either of them are dead. For all we know, they're off somewhere together basking under a tropical sun."

"Maybe. But until we find them—or least find Audrey—part of my job is to keep you under surveillance. No one trusts you. Not Lieutenant Desmond, not Edward Bedell, not—"

"Not Domingo Shea."

"I'd like to believe you. But you played me for a fool once and I'm not in the habit of handing out second chances."

Lausanne removed two plain white mugs from the cupboard, then poured hot coffee into each. "That's too bad. I think everybody deserves a second chance. After all, there aren't many people who haven't made a few mistakes and wish they could change the past."

When she picked up the mugs and walked toward him, he rose from the sofa and took one of the mugs from her. "What mistakes have you made?"

She sat down in the dingy, plaid chair across from the sofa and held her mug cradled in both hands. "I trusted the wrong people. The wrong men."

"Was Bobby Jack—?"

"Change that tune, will you? Bobby Jack was a guy I dated twice. I didn't really know him and certainly didn't trust him. Besides, by the time I met him, I'd wised up. I don't really trust anybody and haven't in a long, long time."

"You trusted Audrey Perkins." Dom took a sip of coffee.

"It wasn't a matter of trust. She hired me to do a job and paid me well to do it. Beginning and end of story."

He eyed her skeptically. "No, that's not all." He shook his head. "There's more to it. There's definitely something you're not telling me."

"If you say so." Lausanne sipped on her coffee.

"What if I told you that I want to believe you and that I want to help you?" He was being honest with her. He did want to believe her. And God only knew why, but she brought out all of his macho protective instincts.

She set her mug down on the scarred wooden cocktail table anchored between the chair and the sofa. "I'd say you're lying and it's time for you to leave now."

Dom shrugged. "You don't believe me."

She stood. "Yeah, sure I believe you. Just like you believe me."

Dom placed his mug beside hers on the table, then rose to his feet. "I'm going to give you my card. It has my cell number on it. If you need anything or if you decide you want to talk some more, give me a call."

He slipped a business card from his inside jacket pocket and held it out to her. She stared at the card for a couple of seconds, then grabbed it and tossed it down on the table.

Dom walked to the door. Lausanne followed, keeping several feet between them. He opened the door, then paused and said, "The chemistry we had going on between us in Palm Beach—that was real, wasn't it?"

She looked him right in the eyes. "Was it?"

Dom momentarily hesitated, then entered the exterior corridor that led to the open staircase. Before he had a chance to say anything else, Lausanne closed the door. He heard the distinct click of the lock.

Why the hell did he want to beat on her door, demand she let him back inside, then pull her into his arms and tell her that he believed her, that come what may, he'd take care of her?

Because he wasn't thinking straight. He wanted

Lausanne Raney. Wanted her stripped naked and lying beneath him. Wanted to be inside her, listening to her cry out his name when she came.

God damn fool!

Dom tromped down the corridor, took the steps two at a time and all but ran to his rental car.

LAUSANNE STOOD at the door. Waiting. Listening. Hoping? No, she didn't dare hope that Dom would knock, that she would open the door and there he'd be, arms open, telling her that he believed her, trusted her, would stand by her and help her prove her innocence.

She didn't need Dom Shea. She didn't need anybody. She'd learned the hard way that if you trusted someone enough to lean on them, to believe they'd be loyal and steadfast, you'd only end up disappointed. And in her case, worse. The first time she'd loved a man, she'd been seventeen and wound up pregnant, unmarried and alone. You'd have thought that experience would have taught her a lesson she'd never forget, but did it? No, not desperate-for-love, gullible Lausanne Raney. Less than four years after she gave her baby girl up for adoption, she fell in love again. She trusted again. And for the second time, she paid dearly for her stupidity. But after five years in prison, she finally wised up.

Lausanne trekked across the living room, opened a bottom drawer in the single end table—a seen-better-days maple veneer—and pulled out a dog-earned phonebook.

Flipping through the Yellow Pages, she tried to erase

Dom Shea from her mind. If he'd go away and never come back, she might be able to do that. But the fact was he wasn't leaving Chattanooga. He'd be keeping an eye on her for his boss, Edward Bedell. And the police were bound to question her again, maybe even press some kind of charges against her, if Audrey Perkins didn't show up soon. And even if she did, since she wasn't the woman who'd hired Lausanne, Audrey couldn't back up her story.

Lausanne spread the phonebook apart on the page that listed attorneys. Unless she was badly mistaken, it was only a matter of time before she'd need a good lawyer. The only problem was, she couldn't afford a lawyer, good or bad.

Don't forget that fifty grand you stashed away in a savings account. If you have to, you can use part of that money for legal fees.

Who was she kidding? A good lawyer would take the entire fifty thousand and then some. She could hock the jewelry she'd bought on her trip and the expensive luggage, but she'd keep the clothes because she'd need them when she got a new job. Besides, used clothes sold cheap.

How did a person go about choosing a lawyer? When she'd been arrested as an accomplice to armed robbery nearly six years ago, the court had appointed an attorney to defend her. He'd been young, fresh out of law school and eager to win. He'd lost, but he had gotten her a lesser sentence. She owed him that much anyway.

Lausanne read through the list of criminal attorneys.

Do you see a name that you like? Ever heard of any of these people? Damn! Frustrated, she ripped out a page from the phonebook, folded it in half and stuck it in her slacks pocket.

She eyed the two half-empty mugs on the cocktail table.

Don't you dare moon over that man. He's no good for you. He's not your friend. He's your enemy. Remember that the next time you see him. And if your heart starts fluttering when he looks at you, remind yourself that he believes you're capable of murder.

After picking up the mugs, she took them into the kitchenette, dumped the coffee into the sink and stuck the mugs in the ancient dishwasher. Knowing she didn't have the luxury of wasting time, she yanked the ripped phonebook page from her pocket, stuck it in her purse and then grabbed both her purse and sweater as she headed for the door.

She should choose a lawyer and get in touch with him; and she would—later. But first things first. She'd take the bus to the grocery store to buy the basics she needed and while there, she'd pick up a copy of today's newspaper so she could search the want ads. What she needed even more than a lawyer was a job.

CHAPTER EIGHT

NOW WAS THE TIME to make a move on Gray. Cara had never been more certain of anything in her life. He was lonely and vulnerable, worried sick about Audrey and feeling terribly betrayed. In the past, she had kept her feelings to herself. She'd never interfered in Gray's marriage, never crossed the line between concerned sister-in-law and being madly in love with her sister's husband. But this time, it seemed that Audrey was gone for good and might not be coming back. Ever.

Did she want Audrey dead? Yes and no. If there was any other way to free Gray of his obsession with Audrey, then Cara wouldn't wish her sister dead. But being totally honest with herself, she knew that as long as Audrey was alive, Gray would forgive her and take her back no matter how many times she ran off with another man. Gray would never let Audrey go, would never set either of them free to find happiness with other people.

Pausing in the hallway to check her appearance in a floor-to-ceiling mirror, she moaned. Even at her best, she could never be as attractive as her older sister, never as sleek and slender, never as sexy and enticing. But she possessed qualities that Audrey didn't have. She was loyal and loving and faithful and...

And she loved Gray more than Audrey ever had, more than anyone ever could. He was the sun and moon and stars to her. The beginning and end of her world.

Cara's hand trembled as she reached for the crystal door handle. Before she'd left Gray in the living room with her father twenty minutes ago, she'd made him promise that he'd stay for lunch.

"You need to be with family," she'd told him. "With other people who love Audrey." She hadn't actually lied to him. Their father loved Audrey and in her own way, she did, too. She loved her sister as much as she hated her.

After sucking in and blowing out a deep breath, Cara grasped the handle and eased open the door. Putting a pleasant expression on her face, she waltzed into the room, but came to a dead stop when she saw Gray and Patrice. With her arms draped around Gray's waist, Cara's wicked step-mother kissed him on the cheek.

"What the hell's going on?" Cara demanded.

Gray jumped as if he'd been shot, yanked out of Patrice's embrace and turned to face Cara, his face slightly flushed.

"We didn't hear you come in." Patrice gave Cara a haughty, cat-that-ate-the-canary smirk.

"Patrice was merely comforting me," Gray said innocently.

And Cara believed him. Wanted to believe him. Needed to believe him. But if anyone was going to comfort Gray, she was. Not her tramp step-mommy dearest.

"Shouldn't you check with Cook about lunch?" Cara issued Patrice a condemning glare. "She needs to know that Gray will be here for lunch and for dinner tonight, too."

Looking helpless and confused, like a pitiful child, Gray murmured, "Cara, I shouldn't impose on—"

"Don't be silly," Cara told him. "You're always welcome here. You're family and always will be, no matter what happened to—happens with Audrey."

Squaring her shoulders in order to bring attention to her expensive silicone breasts, Patrice smiled at Gray, but spoke to Cara. "I thought surely you'd told Cook yourself. I know how eager you are to keep Gray here with us for as long as possible."

"I would never overstep my bounds," Cara said. "Daddy informed me when you two married that you were the lady of the house and would take care of all those little wifely duties."

Patrice's smile vanished. "I'll go speak to Cook. I know how much you want to be alone with Gray…to comfort him."

When Patrice exited the living room, Gray slumped down on the sofa, rested his arms against his thighs and dropped his hands between his spread knees. Nervously tapping the tips of his fingers together, he hung his head.

Poor, darling Gray. Such a sweet, delicate disposition. Far too gentle and kind for a woman like Audrey.

Cara sat beside him, but made no attempt to touch him.

"Patrice is a viper," Cara said, keeping her voice level

and calm despite the anger and hatred boiling inside her. "Please be very careful around her."

"She was trying to be kind." Gray's voice cracked. "She knows how much I love Audrey, how desperately I want her to be all right."

Cara lifted her hand and laid it on Gray's back, careful to keep her touch light and sisterly. "What if Audrey doesn't come home? You have to face that possibility. We all do."

Gray lifted his head and glared at Cara, his mouth gapping in a mournful sigh. "You think she's dead, don't you?"

"I think it's possible. That Raney woman is lying. I know she is. Hiring someone to impersonate her isn't something Audrey would do. And if that woman knows Bobby Jack Cash, then it's highly probable that the two of them…" Cara paused for effect, wanting Gray to believe that she was as traumatized as he by the thought that Audrey might be dead. "I can't bear to think about it."

"I did everything I could to make her happy." Gray sighed dejectedly.

Cara patted his back, ever mindful to keep her touch non-sexual. "I know you did. No one could have been a better husband. Audrey just needed something else. She was never satisfied, not even when we were kids. She always wanted what she couldn't have."

Gray glanced at Cara. "To be sisters, you two are so very different."

Cara's hand on his back stilled. If anyone else, other than her father, had said that to her—that she and Audrey were very different—she would have taken the comment as a compliment. But coming from Gray, she wasn't sure.

"We had different mothers," Cara reminded him. "I suppose that's part of the—"

"God, how I wish Audrey could be more like you." Gray covered his face with his open palms.

"What?" Had she heard him correctly or were her ears deceiving her? Was she simply hearing what she longed to hear?

"You—you wish that Audrey was more like me?"

Gray removed his hands from his weary face and cocked his head to one side in order to look up at Cara. "If only I'd fallen in love with you instead of Audrey, my life would be so different."

Overcome with sheer joy, Cara barely contained her emotions. She wanted to hug Gray and kiss him and confess her undying love. But now was neither the time nor the place. He wasn't ready to find out how desperately she loved him, how much she'd always loved him.

Keeping one hand unmoving on Gray's back, Cara reached out with the other and tenderly cupped Gray's chin between her thumb and fingers.

They sat there in the elegant living room of Edward Bedell's ancestral mansion and gazed into each other's eyes for a long, heart-stopping moment; then Gray pulled away from her tentative hold and rose to his feet. He walked across the room, paused by the windows facing the front veranda and heaved a sonorous sigh.

"Please don't misunderstand," Gray said, his back to Cara. "I love Audrey. I've been besotted with her for ages.

But we've made each other so miserable. If only she could have truly loved me. If only I'd been enough for her."

Cara wanted to run to him, to comfort and console him. *Not yet. Wait*, an inner voice cautioned. *It's too soon. Once we know for sure that Audrey is gone and will never return, then Gray will be mine. All mine.*

DOM PULLED INTO the parking lot of a fast-food restaurant in East Brainerd. He'd called Bain Desmond right after leaving Lausanne's dismal little apartment. He couldn't shake the negative vibes he'd gotten from the place. After seeing her in West Palm Beach, dressed to the nines and living in the lap of luxury, it came as a surprise to see how she really lived when she wasn't impersonating an heiress. But what he couldn't decide was whether her being that poor meant she was more or less likely to have killed Audrey Perkins.

After going inside the restaurant and placing his lunch order, Dom checked his watch. Two-thirty. Desmond had agreed to meet him right about now. It looked like the detective was running late. Dom picked up his order, prepared his cola and got his condiments. After grabbing a straw and a handful of napkins, he carried his tray to a booth near the bank of front windows.

He cleared his tray, sat down and glanced out the windows at the kiddie playground. A young woman stood guard over two preschool-age children and an older woman kept watch over a toddler as the three little ones ripped and romped, laughing and squealing with delight. Dom had a twelve-year-old nephew and a nine-year-old niece back in Texas, his elder sister Pilar's two kids. He hadn't seen them—hadn't seen any of his family—in over five months. But Thanksgiving was just around the corner and he intended to go home for the holiday and then back again for Christmas. He'd already put in for the time off and gotten Sawyer's approval. Family meant everything to Dom. One of these days, he'd have a wife and children of his own.

"Wishing you were that age?" a male voice asked.

Snapped out of his thoughts, Dom looked up to see Lt. Desmond, a cola in one hand and a bag of fries in the other, standing by the booth.

"I didn't see you come in." He gestured to the opposite bench. "Have a seat. And yeah, there's nothing like being a kid, is there?"

Desmond set his cola and fries on the table, then slid into the booth. "Not if you have a happy childhood."

Dom nodded, not wanting to get into a discussion of their personal lives. "I appreciate your meeting me. I just dropped off Lausanne Raney and—"

Dom's cell phone rang. He groaned, then yanked the phone from his belt loop and flipped it open. He noted the caller ID. The Dundee Agency. "Dom Shea here."

"Hi, Dom. I thought I'd better get in touch right away with the info you requested on Lausanne Inez Raney," Daisy Holbrook told him.

Dom glanced at Desmond, who asked, "Do you need some privacy for this call?"

Dom shook his head and motioned for the detective to stay put.

"Shoot," Dom said. "Tell me what you've found out about her."

"It's not good," Daisy said.

Dom's stomach tightened. "Somehow I knew you were going to say that."

"The lady turned twenty-eight in August. Born and raised in Booneville, Mississippi. Ran away from home at sixteen, got pregnant at seventeen, gave the child up for adoption. Not much on her from eighteen to twenty-one. At twenty-one, she was arrested as an accessory to armed robbery."

"Shit!" Dom muttered under his breath.

Desmond gave him an inquisitive stare, which Dom ignored.

"Go on," Dom said.

"She spent the past five years in the Tennessee Prison for Women in Nashville. Got her GED while there and took advantage of the vocational programs the prison offered. She studied office education. She was a model prisoner. Not one black mark against her."

"Anything else?"

"Bedell, Inc. has a policy of hiring rehabilitated ex-cons," Daisy said. "Lausanne didn't lie on her job application about her background. She didn't have to."

"What about Bobby Jack Cash?" Dom asked.

"He's an ex-con, too. Spent a few years behind bars for being the brains behind a swindle that took the life savings of four old women. He's done some petty stuff, too. Written bad checks. And he was acquitted on manslaughter charges. It seems he killed a guy in a bar fight."

"Nice guy. Did Bedell, Inc. think this guy was reha-bilitated when they hired him as a guard?"

Daisy chuckled. "I don't think it mattered. It seems the guy had a recommendation from Mrs. Bedell."

"Patrice Bedell?"

"Right."

"Interesting. See if you can find out why she'd rec-ommend him. Dig deep enough to find out if there was something personal between them."

"Sure thing."

"Later." Dom closed his cell phone and clipped it to his belt.

"I take it that was a report on Lausanne Raney," Desmond said.

Dom nodded. "You knew she had a record, that she'd spent five years in the TPFW."

"Yeah, I knew."

"And you didn't share that info with me because…?"

"I thought it best for your agency to fill you in about Ms. Raney's background," Desmond said. "I got the impression that your interest in the lady went beyond the professional. Was I wrong?"

Dom started to vehemently deny the detective's assumption, but knew the guy was too intuitive to fool. Honesty with a man like Lt. Desmond was the best policy.

"You weren't wrong," Dom admitted.

"Then you have a conflict of interest, don't you?"

Dom huffed. "My only interest is to find out the truth."

"For your client or for yourself?"

"For both of us."

"The truth is what I'm interested in," Desmond said. "Where's Audrey Bedell? Is she all right? If she's not okay, then what happened to her and who's responsible for her disappearance?"

"Any theories?"

"Too many."

"I realize that you're on this case because Sawyer McNamara wanted you to handle things, so I'm assuming you two go way back or something."

Desmond shook his head. "Not really. I think the commander and McNamara go way back and Commander Crowell recommended me when he was informed y'all might need the police on a certain case involving someone living in my precinct."

"I assume you've already filed a missing person's report, per Edward Bedell's request."

"I'm sure you're working with the same info," Desmond said. "Physical description and photo. The identity of the last person who saw Ms. Perkins. Any knowledge of her plans, habits, routines and personal interests. And—"

"And any suggestion of foul play."

"What are your gut instincts telling you? Is Audrey Perkins alive or dead?"

"Dead."

Desmond nodded. "Murdered?"

"Probably."

"Suspect?"

"Suspects," Dom said.

"Hmm… The husband, of course. The spouse always heads the list."

"And then there's the stepmother. Did you know Patrice Bedell recommended Bobby Jack Cash for his job at Bedell, Inc.?"

Desmond grinned. "No, I didn't."

"Dundee's is looking into the possibility that there's a past history between those two."

"Just as there's a past history between Cash and Ms. Raney?"

"She said they had two dates, weren't intimate and—"

"And you really want to believe her, don't you?"

"Like I told you before, all I want is the truth, whatever that truth turns out to be."

Desmond took a swig of cola, then looked right at Dom. "I'm bringing Ms. Raney in first thing tomorrow morning for further questioning." Desmond held up his hand. "And before you ask, the answer is no, you cannot be there when I question her."

"She's going to need a lawyer, right?"

"Yeah, she's going to need a lawyer."

CHAPTER NINE

AFTER CONTACTING eight law firms and being politely refused by each, Lausanne came to the conclusion that somehow the Bedell family had put the word out that they didn't want any reputable firm to represent a woman suspected of possibly murdering Audrey Perkins. Call her paranoid, but she couldn't figure out any other reason. She had cash to pay up-front to retain a decent lawyer, so why had she gotten one rejection after another? That is, until she'd gone for broke and called the most prestigious criminal attorney in the city.

"Yes, Mr. Oliver is in," the receptionist had said. "I'll put you through to him."

"Ms. Raney, what can I do for you?" Berton Oliver had asked.

After she recovered from the initial surprise of him taking her call, Lausanne explained her situation. Then she received an even bigger shock when he told her he would represent her, if it became necessary.

Well, it had become necessary. At precisely eight-thirty this morning, she had received a call from Sergeant Swain requesting that she come to the police station for questioning. So, here she was in the interrogation room with her lawyer beside her and Lt. Desmond sitting across the table from them. His partner stood quietly to the side, a condescending scowl on his face.

The moment she phoned Mr. Oliver's office this morning, she'd been assured that her message would be relayed to him ASAP. Frantic, knowing that with the way her luck ran, things were bound to end badly, she'd paced the floor, waiting and praying. Fifteen minutes later, Mr. Oliver had phoned to tell her that he was on his way to her apartment to pick her up, that he would escort her to the police station.

Berton Oliver looked very much as she had expected. A man in his early fifties, dressed in a tailor-made suit and sporting a Rolex on his wrist. He was short, no more than five-eight, apparently in superb physical condition and was rather good looking for a man his age. He had a mane of salt and pepper hair and the bluest eyes Lausanne had ever seen.

They had been at police headquarters for the past two hours and she had answered questions the entire time, many of the questions simply repeated more than once or worded in a slightly different manner. She suspected they were hoping shc'd slip up, get confused, change her story. But the police were working under the premise that she was lying. She wasn't. No matter how many times they asked her how she'd wound up in Palm Beach with Audrey's credit cards, her reply never changed because she was telling the truth.

Lt. Desmond remained calm and in total control

despite the fact that by now he was undoubtedly frustrated at being unable to shake her. There had been a time in the past when she'd have fallen apart under this kind of pressure. But she wasn't that same green kid who'd wanted so badly to believe that sooner or later life would give her a break. She had learned every lesson the hard way. She'd taken her lumps, paid her dues and wasn't about to show any weaknesses. Especially not now.

She had let her guard down with Dom Shea and just look how that had turned out. If she hadn't been enjoying her disguise as Audrey Perkins so damn much, hadn't gotten such a kick out of pretending to be a carefree heiress, she would have protected herself from becoming emotionally involved with a stranger.

"Lieutenant Desmond, I can't see that this line of questioning is getting us anywhere," Berton Oliver said in his authoritarian voice. "Ms. Raney has answered every question you've asked her. She's been honest with you about everything. But she cannot tell you what she doesn't know. No matter how many times you ask her or in how many different ways, her reply to your question about Ms. Perkins's whereabouts will remain the same. She does not know where Audrey Perkins is or what, if anything, has happened to her."

Wearing a pensive, sympathetic expression on his face, Lt. Desmond leaned forward and focused directly on Lausanne. "If Bobby Jack Cash coerced you into helping him—"

"My client has repeatedly denied any involvement with Mr. Cash other than two casual dates that occurred months ago," Mr. Oliver said.

Lt. Desmond scooted back his chair, took a long, hard look at Lausanne and grunted. "Don't leave town, Ms. Raney. And if you can think of anything you've forgotten, anything that might help us find Audrey Perkins, please contact me immediately."

Before she could reply, Mr. Oliver said, "I can assure you that she will." He rose from his chair, clasped her arm and helped her to her feet. "Gentlemen." He nodded to each detective in turn, then escorted Lausanne out of the interrogation room.

"He thinks I'm guilty," Lausanne said. "They all think I'm behind Audrey Perkins's disappearance."

"Don't say anything else until we're outside and in my car," Mr. Oliver told her.

She hushed immediately.

Should I tell him the one little bit of information that only I know? Lausanne wondered. But *I'm not the only person who knows that Audrey Perkins was not the woman who hired me to impersonate her. That other woman, whoever she is, also knows the truth.*

No one would believe her if she told them the truth. Going by experience, she figured that the police would find a way to use the information against her. After all, she'd been so adamant, to Dom and to the Bedell family, that Audrey had hired her to impersonate her, to lead any PI her father or husband might hire on a wild goose chase. If she changed her story now, told them that the woman wasn't Audrey Perkins but someone else, wouldn't that make her look like a liar?

She was already in enough trouble as it was. The police thought she was involved in Audrey's disappearance. No one believed her.

Once seated in her lawyer's Mercedes, she turned to face him. "Thank you, Mr. Oliver. I can't tell you how much I appreciate your taking my case. I can admit to you that I'm scared. If I didn't have you in my corner, I'd be even more frightened than I am."

He patted her hand in a friendly, supportive manner. "You can count on me, my dear. The police have no case against you. As a matter of fact, at this point all they're working on is a missing persons case."

"May I ask you something, something that I've been wondering about?"

"Of course, ask me." He patted her hand again, released his hold and sat back in the cushy leather seat.

"Why did you agree to be my lawyer?"

He smiled. "You really don't know, do you?"

She shook her head. "What do you mean—"

"I believe you're acquainted with Domingo Shea."

Lausanne tensed. "Yes, I am. What does he have to do with your agreeing to be my lawyer?"

"Mr. Shea contacted me on your behalf," Mr. Oliver said. "He wanted to make sure you had the best legal representation possible if you needed it. And as it turned out, you did need me."

"Why would he…? Why would you…?" Lausanne tried to collect her thoughts, tried to make sense of what she'd been told, but it didn't make any sense. First of all why would Dom help her? He thought she was a murderer, didn't he? And secondly, how had Dom persuaded such a prestigious lawyer to take her on as a client?

"As for why he contacted me on your behalf and agreed to pay your legal fees, I don't know. That you'd have to ask him." Mr. Oliver smiled, a devilish twinkle in his eye. "As for why I agreed to take you on as a client...well, let's just say that I owe the Dundee Agency, and Mr. Shea in particular, a favor and leave it at that."

Lausanne felt as if her world had tilted on its axis. "That's all you're going to tell me?"

He nodded. "All you need to know is that whatever happens, I'll take good care of you legally. And Mr. Shea is picking up the tab."

"I have my own money. I can pay you."

"You have fifty-thousand dollars given to you by Audrey Perkins," Mr. Oliver told her. "I don't want you to touch that money. Keep it where it is—in your savings account. At this point, it's the only sort of proof, flimsy as it is, that Ms. Perkins hired you to impersonate her."

"I can't take money from Dom. There has to be another way to—"

"Why don't you speak to Mr. Shea before you make any rash decisions?"

He was right. She needed to talk to Dom, to find out just what he thought he was doing, why he was paying for her lawyer.

MR. OLIVER DROPPED Lausanne off at her apartment complex in East Brainerd, once again urging her to be sensible about her situation.

"I'm only a phone call away, if you need me," he told her. "Day or night."

With her mind jumbled, all kinds of crazy thoughts duking it out for attention, Lausanne climbed the exterior stairs leading to her apartment. So mentally engrossed in the what-ifs dominating her life right now, she didn't notice the man standing outside her front door, not until he spoke to her.

"How'd it go?" Dom Shea asked.

Lausanne gasped. "Damn it, you scared me. What are you doing here? No, don't answer that. I don't care." She marched right up to him, glared furiously and demanded, "What did you think you were doing hiring me a lawyer?"

The corners of Dom's mouth lifted with amusement. "I thought I was helping you."

"I don't want your help." *Yes, you do,* an inner voice reminded her. More than anything, she wanted Dom to believe her, to believe in her. From the moment they boarded the Dundee jet to return to Chattanooga, she'd started hoping that once he learned the truth about her, he would stand by her.

"If you wind up being charged with a crime—any crime—you'll need the best defense money can buy, not some court-appointed lawyer."

Lausanne stared at him in disbelief. "Explain something to me, will you? You think I killed Audrey Perkins and yet you hired a lawyer for me. Why?"

"I don't think you killed Audrey Perkins," he told her.

"You don't?" Hope welled up inside her. "You believe me, believe that I've told you the truth?"

Shuffling his feet, Dom glanced down at the floor, avoiding eye contact with her. "I want to believe you."

Anger replaced hope. Anger and disappointment. Lausanne whirled around and put her back to him; then she unzipped her shoulder bag and delved inside to find her key. "Go away and leave me the hell alone. If it becomes necessary, I'll take my chances with a court-appointed attorney."

"The way you did the last time you were charged with a crime?"

Lausanne tensed, then snapped her head around and shot him a go-to-hell look.

"Didn't take you long to find out about that, did it? I suppose Lt. Desmond told you."

"Nope. You forget, honey, I work for the Dundee Agency. We can find out facts just as quick, sometimes quicker, than our law enforcement counterparts."

"Okay, so you know I served five years in the TPFW. So what?"

"You have a criminal record. If you're arrested for another crime—"

"I didn't have anything to do with Audrey Perkins's disappearance. End of discussion." She turned away from him, inserted the key in the lock and opened the door.

"Lausanne?"

"Go away and leave me alone," she repeated. "And I don't want your lawyer!"

She went inside her apartment, but before she could close the door, Dom stuck his foot over the threshold. She pressed the door against his foot. He didn't budge.

"I know a lot more about you than the fact you spent five years in prison," he said.

"Good for you. Now go away."

"Let's talk." He shoved against the door.

She put all her strength into closing the door, determined to keep him out. "I don't...want...to...talk." Shoving as hard as she could, strained and out of breath, she cried out, "Damn you, Dom Shea."

Realizing she couldn't win a battle of brute strength, she stopped fighting him and choked down tears she absolutely refused to release. She walked away from the partially open door, raced through the living room, into her bedroom and straight through to the bathroom. After slamming the bathroom door and leaning back against it, her breathing labored, she sucked in huge gulps of air.

Don't trust him. Don't lean on him. Don't expect anything from him. Whatever he says, whatever he does, reject him. No matter what he promises, don't fall for his lies. He's just another good looking, sweet talking man. He may be older and more sophisticated than Brad or Clay, but he wants exactly what they wanted. He wanted to fuck her. Plain and simple.

And what did she want? God help her but she wanted what she'd wanted when she was seventeen and gave her virginity to Brad White, what she'd wanted when she was twenty-one and became involved with Clay Terry. She wanted to be loved.

Not going to happen. Love and happily ever after were not in the cards for her. She had to face facts. If she thought for one single minute that Dom Shea was the answer to her prayers, she was an utter fool and deserved whatever happened to her.

"Lausanne?"

Please, please, please go away.

"Honey?"

Leave me alone. Haven't I been hurt enough for one lifetime? Can't you understand what you're doing to me?

He rapped repeatedly on the bathroom door.

"I'm not leaving until we talk," he told her.

Sooner or later, she'd have to leave the bathroom, so she might as well get this over with right now.

Lausanne checked her appearance in the mirror. Lordy, she looked pale. Really pale. Even though she was naturally fair—strawberry blonde fair—and had never had a tan in her life, today she looked almost ghostly, despite the rich russet bronze lipstick and matching blush. A hint of dark circles beneath her eyes reminded her that she hadn't slept more than a couple of hours last night.

You look fine, she told herself. She wore one of the new outfits she had charged on Audrey Perkins's credit card. The straight brown skirt in a soft, moleskin fabric coordinated perfectly with the gold silk blouse and the brown and tan hound's-tooth check jacket.

What difference did it make how she looked? She wasn't walking out of here to meet her lunch date. She was going to meet her fears head-on. She was going to stand her ground with Dom Shea.

Lausanne opened the bathroom door, squared her shoulders, tilted her chin and prepared to do battle. When she emerged, Dom stepped backward.

"Are you all right?" he asked.

She gazed at him incredulously, wondering if it was possible that he actually did care. Stop right there. One look into his gorgeous black eyes and she was already wishing for the impossible.

"I'm okay," she replied and marched straight into the living room.

Dom followed her; and when she spun around to face him, they stood there and stared at each other for a full minute before he asked, "Were the police pretty rough on you? I figure Desmond for a good guy, but he has to do his job."

Clenching her teeth tightly, emotions raw and tears near the surface, Lausanne reminded herself that crying was useless, that allowing her emotions to rule her always turned out to be a disastrous choice.

She swallowed hard. "Lieutenant Desmond hammered away at me for two hours, asking me the same questions over and over again. About Audrey Perkins, about Bobby Jack Cash and about why I didn't just come clean and tell him the truth."

"It's his job to get to the truth. And it was Mr. Oliver's job to—"

"Oh, you got your money's worth there. Mr. Oliver did his job."

"I plan to keep him on retainer. Just in case."

"Do whatever you like." Lausanne walked away from Dom.

He caught up with her just as she entered the kitchenette, pausing on the opposite side of the vinyl-topped bar. "I know that you ran away from home at sixteen and I know about the baby you gave up for adoption when you were seventeen."

"So?"

"So, I realize you haven't had it easy, that there are probably reasons why you—"

"Why I killed Audrey Perkins!"

"No, that's not what I was going to say. I was going to say that there are probably reasons why you've got such a big chip on your shoulder."

She emitted a chuckling huff.

"Look, honey, I want to believe you. I want to help you. But you're not making it easy for me."

"Why? What difference does it make to you?"

"Damn if I can explain it," he told her. "Let's just say that you got under my skin and leave it at that."

Sweet talker. Charmer. He knew what to say and just how to say it. If she hadn't been burned so badly before, hadn't found out just what sneaky, lying bastards men could be, she just might fall for his line of bull. The old, naive Lausanne would have. The smart, cynical Lausanne wouldn't.

"You're still working for the Bedell family, aren't you? Your loyalty belongs to them. They've bought and paid for you. How will they feel if they find out you hired a lawyer for me?"

"Yeah, I'm still working for the Bedells. And my loyalty is to the truth, to locating Audrey Bedell. Finding her is what her family wants and it's what you want, too, isn't it? There's no conflict of interests, as long as you're not lying to me."

"What will it take for you to believe me? I could take a lie detector test or sign an oath in blood or maybe I could just screw you. That is what you want, isn't it? You've got this pesky little itch for me that won't go away until I scratch it."

Dom shook his head sadly. "Who hurt you so badly that you think all a guy could possibly want from you is sex?"

Her heartbeat pulsed loudly in her ears. She hated the way he was looking at her, with such tender concern, such genuine sympathy.

"Don't you dare feel sorry for me!" She rounded the corner of the bar separating them and came at him, her hands knotted into rigid little fists.

"Why shouldn't I feel sorry for you? You've had a really shitty life, gotten a lot of tough breaks. Why does it bother you so much that I care, that I wish I could make things better for you?"

She stopped dead still less than a foot from him,

lowered her fists and snarled at him. "Who asked you to care? Who needs you?"

"You do, Lausanne. You need me."

Don't you dare let him see any weakness. If you do, he'll take advantage of you.

Her throat was tight and dry, her eyes blinking to hold back unwanted tears. "Let's get something straight—I don't need you. I don't need anybody. I take care of myself."

"What are you so afraid of?" he asked, a tone of pity in his voice.

I'm afraid I'll fall for you, that I'll believe all your sweet lies and that you'll hurt me. You'll get what you want and then you'll leave me and I'll be all alone again. Alone and in trouble.

"Who said I was afraid?"

"Aren't you?" He took a tentative step toward her.

She drew in a deep breath. "If I agree to keep Mr. Oliver as my lawyer, will you go away and leave me alone?"

He smiled. "You're afraid of me, aren't you? Afraid that if you let me get too close—"

She shoved against his chest. "Get out of here. Go!"

Dom grabbed her hands and held them over his heart. Every nerve in her body came to full alert. He yanked her forward so that she fell into him, her breasts to his lower chest, her head at his shoulder. Realizing what he intended to do and helpless to stop him because she wanted it as much as he did, Lausanne lifted her face and looked up at Dom.

He lowered his head and took her mouth in a gentle

yet all-consuming kiss. She shivered. A tingling sensation ignited in her feminine center and spread through her body. He deepened the kiss as he pressed her closer, one hand on the small of her back and the other cupping her hip.

Every feminine instinct within her yearned for him, wanted to be with him, to give herself to him and find physical release.

Just when she was on the verge of crumbling, of giving in to her basic needs, Dom lifted his head and stared into her eyes.

"I want you," he said. "And you want me." When she opened her mouth to respond, he tapped his right index finger over her lips. "Shh..."

"But Dom," she mumbled.

He lifted his finger from her lips. "I want us to have sex. I'm only human. But I need to prove to you that I want to help you because you deserve a break, because I think there's a good chance you've been telling me the truth. I need to become your friend before I become your lover."

Lausanne stared at him as he released his firm hold on her. What sort of game was he playing? Or was he being honest with her? Did he really want to be her friend?

"I need a friend," she said.

Dom grinned. "How about giving me a chance to prove myself to you, to prove that I can be a good friend?"

"I guess maybe I can do that—give you a chance." She gazed at him hopefully. "And you can do something for me, if you want us to be friends."

"What's that?"

"Try just a little harder to believe I've told you the truth."

And I have told you the truth, just not the complete truth.

CHAPTER TEN

DOM SMILED AT LAUSANNE when she set a plate of scrambled eggs, bacon and hash browns in front of him. "Looks good," he said.

"I don't cook it, I just deliver it," she told him, a hint of a smile on her lips.

For the past five days, she'd been working at the Chicken Coop, a fast-food restaurant that specialized in chicken, fixed any way you wanted it, and eggs, which made the place a favorite of people who wanted an inexpensive breakfast. And for the past five days, Dom had been eating at least one meal a day here. They weren't dating, weren't seeing each other at all unless you counted the fact he made sure she was his waitress when he ate here. He'd called her a few times but had found out she wasn't much of a conversationalist, that she mostly responded when he talked.

She hadn't given him any real encouragement, so he kept asking himself why he couldn't stay away from her. Sexual attraction was definitely a part of it, but there was more. And it was that "more" that bothered Dom. On an instinctive level, he sensed that Lausanne needed him and not just because she was still "a person of interest" in Audrey Perkins's disappearance. All these years, after countless women coming and going in Dom's life, he realized that Lausanne Raney was different. She was the first who brought out both his protective and his possessive instincts.

"Need more coffee?" she asked.

He glanced down at his almost empty mug. "Yeah, I sure do."

When she walked away, heading for the row of coffeemakers behind the counter, he watched her, appreciating the view. Her movements had a naturally feminine sway to them, her hips and legs working together in a seductive manner that proclaimed her all woman. Glancing around at the other customers, Dom noted that he wasn't the only man who'd been watching Lausanne. Even in her uniform of brown slacks and a yellow and brown striped shirt, she didn't look like the other waitresses. She was the type of woman who stood out in a crowd. Part of her uniqueness was that mane of curly, reddish-blonde hair, even when it was secured in a ponytail the way it was today. And part was her build, small-boned, slender yet nicely rounded. And then there was her face—the face that haunted his dreams.

"Pretty little thing, ain't she, son?" A white-haired guy in a plaid shirt and overalls, who sat in the booth across from Dom, grinned good-naturedly at him. The guy had to be at least seventy, if he was a day.

"Yes, sir, she certainly is."

"If I was thirty years younger and not married, I'd ask

her out," the old man said. "So, what's keeping you from asking her?"

He couldn't begin to explain to a stranger how complicated the situation was.

"You'd better make your move, son, before somebody else does. A pretty little peach like that won't stay on the tree very long before being picked." The man chuckled softly. "My Ernestine was a looker in her day. Had a swarm of boys buzzing around her, but I just cut me a path through all that buzzing and stole her away from the rest of 'em. We've been happily married for fifty-two years."

As if on cue, a plump, gray-haired woman, in dark slacks and a hip-length beige sweater, walked down the aisle separating the booths and scooted in on the opposite side of the old man. She was round-faced and rosy cheeked; and Dom could see the beauty in her wrinkled face.

"Sorry it took me so long in the ladies' room, sugar pie," the lady said in a voice as soft and sweet as any twenty-year-old's. "But there were four ahead of me."

Her husband reached across the table and gave her hand a loving squeeze, then cocked his head to one side and winked at Dom.

If Dom's mother had lived, that's the way his parents would be now—an older couple still in love, still enjoying each other's company. And that's what Dom wanted when he settled down and married.

Lausanne came over to his table, the glass coffeepot in her hand. "This is fresh."

Dom held up his mug for her to fill it, which she did. Just as she turned to leave, he called to her. "Lausanne?"

"Yes? Is there something else you want?"

"What time do you get off work today?" he asked.

"I get off at five, why?"

"How about I pick you up, we grab a bite to eat and I take you home?"

After studying him for a full minute, she said, "Okay." Then she leaned down and spoke quietly, for his ears only. "But I'll get us something from here. I'd rather not go out. If we go somewhere for dinner, it'll seem more like a date. If I grab us a bite here and we eat at my apartment, then it'll just be two friends sharing a meal."

"If that's what you want."

"It is."

When she sashayed away, the old man caught Dom's eye. He gave Dom a thumbs-up sign. Dom simply nodded.

If only his relationship with Lausanne was as simple as a guy asking a girl for a date. Yeah, if only… With a girl like Lausanne there wasn't much chance for a future. She was nothing like his mother. Nothing like this lady sitting across from him, with her husband of fifty-two years. Lausanne was a wild card. A man couldn't be sure what he'd get with her. Heaven or hell? Maybe a little bit of both.

Dom's cell phone vibrated against his side. He snapped it off his belt. Immediately recognizing the number, he flipped open the phone and said, "Shea here."

"Dom, it's Bain Desmond."

"Yeah, what's up?"

"I'm on my way to Edward Bedell's office with some unpleasant news. I thought you might want to be there since you're the PI on Mr. Bedell's payroll."

Unpleasant news? Had the police discovered Audrey Perkins? Was the lady dead?

"Want to fill me in?" Dom asked.

"Some fishermen dragged a body out of the Tennessee River a couple of days ago. The guy had several bullet holes in him, so we knew we had a homicide case on our hands."

"And this is news Mr. Bedell needs to know because—?"

"The body's been identified."

"By whom?"

"I played a hunch," Desmond said. "I had a check run on Bobby Jack Cash. Things like dental work, blood type, fingerprints and—"

"Bobby Jack Cash was murdered?" Dom inhaled sharply.

"Yep. Shot five times. Whoever killed him wanted to make sure he was dead."

"It would take someone fairly strong to dump a man's body in the river," Dom said. "A small woman probably couldn't manage it."

"Nobody's accusing Ms. Raney. Not yet."

"She's not physically strong enough to have—"

"He could have been shot near the river, then just rolled into the water."

Dom didn't like that line of thinking. But damn it, Desmond was right.

"Has there been a preliminary autopsy?" Dom asked.

"Yes. And I'll be filling Mr. Bedell in on the particulars."

"So, if I want to know those particulars, I'd better get myself down to Bedell, Inc. in a hurry, right?"

"Right," Desmond said. "See you there."

Dom cursed under his breath.

"Something wrong?" Lausanne asked as she laid his bill on the table. She eyed the cell phone he still held in his hand. "Bad news?"

"Just business." There was no point in ruining her day, no need for her to start worrying. Not yet. Once he had all the facts, he'd tell her. Tonight. He clipped the phone to his belt, then pulled out his wallet and left her a generous tip before reaching for his bill. "I'll pick you up at five."

"Have a good day," she called after him as he headed toward the cashier.

"Yeah, you, too, honey."

BEDELL, INC. HEADQUARTERS was located in downtown Chattanooga, where it had been for over a century, housed in an older building now renovated and expanded by tearing down the adjacent buildings and constructing new ones. Dom drove his rental car into the underground parking deck. Lt. Desmond was there waiting for him.

"I thought we'd go up together," Desmond said. "I'm

not sure how Mr. Bedell is going to take this news. If Audrey Perkins ran away with Cash and now he's dead, then the odds are, if she didn't kill him, she's dead, too."

No point beating around the bush. "Is Lausanne Raney your number one suspect?" Dom asked.

"She heads the list, along with a couple of others. It was obvious that Edward Bedell and Grayson Perkins hated Bobby Jack."

"I suppose the question is did either Bedell or Perkins hate Bobby Jack enough to kill him."

"Perkins knew his wife was in love with Cash," Desmond said. "In my book, that makes him head the list of suspects."

"Right. And Bedell hated Cash because he didn't think Cash was good enough for his daughter."

"That would be one motive for Mr. Bedell to kill Cash."

One motive for murder? And the other would be? Apparently the Chattanooga PD had investigated the tip that Dom had shared with Desmond at the fast-food restaurant. "You know more than you're letting on, don't you?" Dom asked.

"Know what?" Desmond played it cool.

"The dirt on Cash and Mrs. Bedell."

"If you're talking about the fact that Patrice Bedell and Bobby Jack were once involved, then yes, we have confirmation."

"Look, no big surprise there," Dom said.

"Then how come you didn't share your suspicions with your client?"

"We figured that unless it had some bearing on

Audrey Perkins's disappearance, which we didn't know if it did or not, then why tell the guy his wife and Cash were old lovers? That would be like pouring salt into an open wound."

Desmond indicated that they should head for the elevators. Dom fell into step alongside him.

"I'm afraid Cash's body being discovered changes things. It adds more elements into the mix." When they reached the elevators, Desmond punched the up button.

"More suspects?"

Desmond nodded. "That's what you wanted, wasn't it? You don't want to believe that Lausanne Raney is responsible for Audrey Perkins's disappearance. Now, she's not our only suspect."

"It's highly improbable that Lausanne killed Bobby Jack," Dom said.

"Hmm… She could have lured him to the river, killed him and managed to get his body into the water. Or she could have had an accomplice."

"An accomplice? Who?" He hated the very idea. If there was any possibility that Lausanne was playing him for a fool, he needed to know now.

"It's just a theory," Desmond told him. "So far, our investigation into Lausanne Raney doesn't indicate that she had a relationship with anyone. No friends. No boyfriend. She dated Cash months ago and a couple of other guys, but none of them more than two or three times. Does that match Dundee's investigation of her?"

"Pretty much."

"Look, the bottom line here is that I can't afford to rule out anybody."

"My money's on the husband," Dom said.

"Which husband?"

"Audrey's husband, Grayson Perkins."

The light over the elevator indicated it was preparing to stop at their level. A distinct ding sounded when the door opened. Dom stepped back, allowing Desmond to enter first; and by the time he got on, the detective had already hit the button for the top floor.

EDWARD BEDELL'S OFFICE screamed money. Sleek and modern, with lots of glass and metal and artwork that looked like hen-scratch to Dom, which meant the paintings had probably cost an arm and a leg. The only color in the gray, black and white room was the vibrant hues in the paintings.

Edward wasn't alone. His son-in-law, Grayson Perkins, stood alongside him. Both men wore somber, serious expressions. Edward came forward and extended his hand, greeting them with a cordial if restrained welcome.

"When you telephoned, you assured me that you had not found my daughter, so what is this urgent matter?" Edward asked.

"A body was dragged out of the Tennessee River—"

Grayson gasped. "Not Audrey!"

"No, sir, not Mrs. Perkins," Desmond said.

Grayson sighed with relief. "Thank God."

"Who was it?" Edward's intimidating stare demanded an immediate answer.

"Bobby Jack Cash." Desmond watched the men for a reaction as closely as Dom did.

Edward maintained his composure, not batting an eye, but Dom noted a vein in his neck bulged slightly.

"Mr. Bedell, I have to ask you a question," Desmond said.

Edward Bedell looked Desmond in the eye.

"Were you aware that your wife and Bobby Jack Cash were once involved?" Desmond asked.

Edward snarled. "Yes, I've known about my wife's affair with that man since it happened. That was one of the reasons I couldn't bear the thought of my daughter becoming another of his victims. Cash was the type who sought out rich women and used them. I saved my wife from him, but…" Edward shook his head. "My poor little girl. If she found out for herself what kind of man he was and that he was in cahoots with that Raney woman, then God only knows where she is or what happened to her."

"Have you arrested Lausanne Raney?" Grayson inquired, a slight quiver in his voice.

"No, we haven't made an arrest in the case," Desmond said. "We don't have any hard evidence against anyone. Only suspicions."

Edward turned to Dom. "This makes it even more imperative that you find Audrey. God, when I think what might…" He gulped several times and turned away from the others.

"Lieutenant, you believe that Audrey is dead, don't you?" Grayson laid his trembling hand on his father-in-law's back. When Edward's shoulders slumped, a misty-eyed Grayson patted the elder man's back in a comforting manner.

"The honest truth is that we don't know," Desmond admitted.

"Dundee's will increase our efforts to locate Ms. Perkins," Dom said.

"As will the Chattanooga PD," Desmond added.

Edward lifted his shoulders and slowly turned around, his eyes glazed with tears. "I want that Raney woman questioned until she breaks and admits the truth. She knows what happened to Audrey. If she killed her—" Tears trickled down his weathered cheeks.

Grayson Perkins approached Desmond. "We want to be kept informed, every step of the way with this investigation."

"Yes, sir, we'll do that." Knowing he'd been dismissed, Desmond said, "It's my duty to ask both of you not to leave town. It's merely a matter of procedure. Bobby Jack Cash had an affair with both of your wives and it's not beyond the realm of possibility that—"

"Neither of us is going anywhere." Edward Bedell glowered at Desmond. "You have my word on that, Lieutenant."

Desmond nodded, then glanced at Dom before exiting. The minute Desmond left, Edward zeroed in on Dom.

"Find my daughter! Alive or… Just find her. Bring in as many Dundee agents as you need to get the job done. And work with the police, if possible. But if not, then find a way to go around them."

"May I speak frankly?" Dom asked.

"Yes, of course," Edward replied.

"We've been searching for Ms. Perkins for the past five days and there is no evidence that she was seen by anyone after she hired Lausanne Raney to impersonate her."

"Assuming we can believe Ms. Raney," Grayson said.

"If Ms. Raney is lying, then you, Mr. Perkins, were actually the last person to see your wife alive." Dom narrowed his gaze.

"Are you accusing me of—"

"No sir, I'm not accusing anyone of anything, just stating a fact."

"I believe the Raney woman was working with Bobby Jack Cash and something went wrong between them," Edward said. "I don't care if she killed him. Good riddance to bad rubbish, if you ask me. But if that woman has harmed my Audrey, I want her punished."

Dom wanted to believe one-hundred percent in Lausanne's complete innocence. If only he had some sort of proof that he could show Edward and Grayson, that he could take straight to the police. But the truth was that he had no proof, that as much as he wanted to believe she wasn't guilty of any crime, he still had good reason to doubt her.

"I'll get in touch with Mr. McNamara right away and update him on the situation," Dom said. *And unless I can be totally objective about this case, I'll have no choice but to ask Sawyer to take me off this assignment.*

LAUSANNE FRESHENED UP in the Chicken Coop's bathroom. After breaking the rubber band that held her ponytail in place, she shook her hair free and then brushed it vigorously. All her life she'd been blessed or cursed, depending on how her thick, curly hair behaved on any given day. All she had to do to keep it healthy and shiny was wash it, condition it and brush it.

She applied fresh blush and lipstick, both items purchased on her recent shopping sprees, both high dollar cosmetics, the kind she'd never been able to afford.

It wasn't that she'd been born dirt poor and grown up in poverty. Just the opposite. Her maternal grandfather had been a doctor, her mother a teacher and her father, a lawyer, had been elected mayor of Booneville when Lausanne was twelve. Life had been good. Too good. In the span of one year between her twelfth and thirteenth birthdays, her entire world turned upside down and had never righted itself since then.

Fastening only the top button of her tan cashmere sweater, Lausanne hurried out of the bathroom, through the restaurant and, as she passed by, grabbed two sacks off the counter. Nervous and much too excited, she reminded herself that this wasn't a date. *Take a deep breath, count to ten, do whatever you have to do to gain control of yourself.* Okay, so Dom hadn't cut and run. Not yet. And maybe he was beginning to believe in her just a little. But that didn't mean she could trust him— with her heart or with her life. As far as she knew, he was still working for Edward Bedell. She shouldn't forget that if it came to choosing between her and his job, he'd certainly pick his job.

Maybe it wasn't fair to judge Dom by all the other men in life, all the men who'd let her down and broken her heart, but that was the only type she'd had any experience with, except for her grandfather Marshall. If she could find a man like that… But loving, loyal, old fashioned Southern gentlemen were most definitely a dying breed.

When she saw Dom's car turn into the parking lot, her heartbeat did a silly rat-a-tat-tat. She had it bad for this guy and that wasn't good. Her brain told her to keep this man at arm's length. But her heart… Damn her foolish heart.

Dom pulled up to the curb, parked the car, got out, and opened the door for her. She smiled at him.

"You look mighty pretty," he told her.

She couldn't allow herself to be pleased by his flattery. After all, it might not be sincere. "Thank you."

After she settled inside the car, he buckled her seat belt and kissed her cheek. "Did you have a good day?"

She stared at him, her cynical mind suspecting he had an ulterior motive for asking her. "It was long and hard, but not a bad day. How about you?"

"Yeah, my day was long and difficult. And informative."

He closed the door, rounded the hood and got in on the driver's side. When he pulled out of the parking lot and into traffic, Lausanne hazarded a glance in his direction. His gaze focused on the road ahead.

"I guess it's against the rules for you to tell me about the case, huh, even if the case you're working on concerns me?" She tightened her grip on the two white sacks sitting in her lap.

"There's been a development in the case," Dom said. "Something you need to know."

Her stomach flip-flopped nervously. "What development?" *Please, God, don't let Audrey Perkins be dead.*

"Bobby Jack Cash's body was pulled out of the Tennessee River a few days ago. Lieutenant Desmond told us today that they have a positive ID."

Lausanne felt sick to her stomach. "How did he die?"

"He was shot."

"Then he was murdered?"

"It would appear so."

"A guy like Bobby Jack must have had a lot of enemies, so there has to be any number of suspects."

Dom turned on the street leading to her apartment complex. "Yeah, there are several possible suspects."

"Including me?"

"Honey—"

"I've never owned a gun, never used a gun. Dom, I swear that I've never touched a gun. Not ever."

He parked his car in a slot close to her apartment, shut off the motor and turned to face her. "I'd like to believe you. But you had a boyfriend who used a 9mm to rob a convenience store. Are you saying you never handled the gun?"

"No, I never handled Clay's gun. I didn't even know he had a gun. Not until…"

"Until what?"

"Until he came running out of that store with the gun

in his hand and a bagful of money and told me to get us out of there as fast as I could."

"And you did what he told you to do, didn't you?"

Gritting her teeth, determined not to get all emotional and beg him to believe her, Lausanne dumped the twin sacks she'd been holding onto the floorboard and flung open the car door.

Dom grabbed for her, but she managed to get out of the car before he reached her. Once outside, she ran toward the stairs, but Dom caught up with her on the second step and whirled her around. Then he grasped her shoulders and shook her gently.

She struggled, but he held her firmly.

"Please, just let me go, will you?"

"I wish I could."

She looked up into his eyes and saw the same hunger, the same raw need she felt. Was he as powerless against his own desires as she was? "You hate feeling this way, don't you? You don't trust me, you know I'm all wrong for you, but you want me anyway."

"Is that how you feel about me?" He tightened his grip on her shoulders, biting into the softness of her cashmere sweater.

"Yeah, it's exactly how I feel." She squirmed. He held fast. "But if I've learned one lesson in my life, it's to protect myself, even if I have to protect me from me."

"Do you have any idea how much I want to trust you?"

Why couldn't he? Why couldn't he just go on blind faith? But then again, why should he? She sure as hell couldn't.

"I didn't kill Bobby Jack Cash," Lausanne said, her gaze locked with Dom's.

Dom heaved a deep sigh, then released her.

"You actually think I might have killed him and maybe Audrey Perkins, too, don't you?"

He shook his head. "My gut tells me that you didn't. But that stupid, logical part of my brain won't let go of that one last doubt."

She stood on tiptoe and kissed his cheek. "I understand. My heart tells me that you're one of the good guys, but past experience won't let me risk being hurt all over again. So, let's end this thing before it starts. No matter how much we want things to be different, they aren't."

"Yeah, I'm afraid you're right."

"Take care of yourself, Domingo Shea."

"You, too, honey. And if you ever need me…"

She turned and ran up the steps as fast she could, swallowing her unshed tears. When she reached her doorstep, she paused and looked back to see Dom getting in his car.

"Goodbye," she whispered.

CHAPTER ELEVEN

IF NOT FOR THE TIPS she earned at the Chicken Coop and the extra she earned walking dogs for three residents in her apartment building, Lausanne wouldn't be able to make ends meet. And it helped that her boss, Effie Pounders, was such a sweet woman, who gave Lausanne a free meal every day.

"I've had my share of tough breaks in the past, kid," Effie had told her. "I know what it's like to get the short end of the stick time and again."

Today, Lausanne had worked the evening shift and had gotten home a little after ten-thirty. Luckily, a couple of the other waitresses drove right by her apartment building to and from the restaurant, so she'd been able to catch a ride since starting work. After dumping her purse on the bar and using the bathroom, Lausanne headed out the door in a hurry. The Bakers across the hall were expecting their first child in a month and Molly Baker was on bed rest for the duration. Johnny Baker worked twelve-hour shifts, from seven to seven, so he'd had to find someone to walk their black-and-white English spaniel at night. Lausanne had volunteered to do it for nothing, but the Bakers had insisted on paying her. It wasn't much, but every little bit helped.

Lausanne knocked on the Bakers's door, then called out, "Molly, it's me, Lausanne. I'm coming in to get Freckles."

The minute she used the key the Bakers had given her and opened the door, the energetic spaniel came bounding toward her. She dropped to her haunches and opened her arms to surround the dog.

"Hey, boy, are you ready for your walk?"

"He's been waiting," Molly said from her resting place on the sofa.

Lausanne closed the door behind her, then walked into the living room with Freckles at her heels. "How are you feeling tonight?"

"So-so," Molly replied. "I feel like a beached whale. And Johnny won't let me lift a finger to do anything."

"That's because he loves you and that baby." Lausanne wondered what it would feel like to have a man love her that way. Watching Johnny look at Molly was almost embarrassing because it was so intimate. The look of love. But not for me, Lausanne reminded herself.

"I know, but I get so bored just lying around." Molly pouted.

"Enjoy it while you can." Lausanne retrieved Freckles's leash from the wall hook in the kitchenette. "When that baby gets here, you'll be so busy you won't have a minute to yourself."

"I know, and I can't wait to hold this big boy—" she patted her huge belly "—in my arms."

Lausanne hooked the leash to Freckles's collar. "I can only imagine. You're so lucky, Molly. You know that, don't you?" She marched the dog to the door.

"Yes, I know, but sometimes I just need reminding."

Lausanne opened the door. "We'll be back in a few minutes."

"Don't forget to lock the door behind you."

"I won't forget."

With the door locked and Freckles chomping at the bit, Lausanne headed down the exterior stairs leading to the sidewalk. If the sky wasn't so clear and a three-quarter moon wasn't lighting the path, Lausanne would have brought along a flashlight, but it was such a perfectly beautiful evening that she didn't need one. Besides, the pole lights in the parking lot illuminated a large area of the sidewalks and the small grassy areas around the apartment complex.

While Freckles sniffed his way along, stopping periodically to hike his leg, Lausanne thought about things she shouldn't be thinking about. She hadn't seen or spoken to Dom Shea in three days, not that she had expected him to phone or to show up unexpectedly on her doorstep. But she had thought maybe he'd drop by the Chicken Coop for breakfast or lunch. He hadn't. They were both better off not becoming involved, but damn-it-all, she missed the guy.

Yeah, well, get over it, she told herself. *If Dom doesn't believe you, can't take you at your word, then you don't need him in your life.*

She didn't need anybody. She was just fine alone. She

could take care of herself, couldn't she? That's what she'd been doing since she ran away from home twelve years ago, when living with her stepmother had become unbearable.

Renee Latimer Raney had been the stepmother from hell. From day one. And things went from bad to worse with each passing week, month, year, until finally Lausanne couldn't endure one more day living under the same roof with that despicable woman. If only her father had interceded, if only once he'd taken her side in a battle of the on-going war with his new wife. It never happened. Her father, who had once adored her, became a stranger to her, a man she neither liked nor respected. But even now, a part of her still loved her father, still needed— No, she didn't need him. She didn't need anybody. Besides, it didn't matter. Her father had died two years ago, while she was still in prison.

"Are you going to poop or not?" Lausanne asked Freckles. "We can't stay out here all night, you know."

As if understanding her, the dog dragged her onto a grassy knoll that was shrouded in darkness since it was situated between a wooded area and the apartment complex. Dried leaves crunched under her feet and beneath the spaniel's paws. A cool breeze rustled through the nearby trees and shrubbery, reminding Lausanne that she'd soon need a winter coat. Luckily, she had bought one while she'd still had Audrey Perkins's credit cards. When she'd offered Dom the cards, after their return to Chattanooga, he'd told her to toss them, that they were worthless. Edward Bedell had reported the cards stolen and closed out the accounts.

While Freckles circled his chosen spot, Lausanne caught a glimpse, in her peripheral vision, of movement to her left. A stray dog or cat? Or—

Before her next complete thought, a dark, looming shadow appeared behind her. Gawking over her shoulder, she saw a man approaching her. A stranger. Reacting purely on gut instinct, Lausanne grabbed Freckles, who fortunately had done his job, and ran like hell. Even if the man meant her no harm, she wasn't about to wait around to find out. It was nearly eleven at night, she was alone and he was a stranger.

Hearing nothing over the roar of her own heartbeat, Lausanne wondered if the man was following her, so she hazarded a glance over her shoulder. God, he was only a few feet behind her and gaining ground fast. During that one quick glimpse, all she'd noted was that he was tall, had a dark mustache and was wearing a jacket and a baseball cap.

Not watching where she was going, Lausanne tripped over a raised section of cracked sidewalk and went tumbling to her knees. Afraid she might fall on Freckles, she released her hold on him as she hit the broken concrete.

A big hand grasped her shoulder. Lausanne screamed. With his hackles raised, Freckles barked repeatedly, loud enough to wake the dead. Struggling to free herself from the man's tight grip, Lausanne dropped onto her stomach and rolled, surprising her attacker and enabling her to pull away from him.

"What's going on out there?" a male voice called from the parking lot.

"Help!" Lausanne cried as she managed to get to her feet. "Please, help me!"

The man who had followed her looked right at her, a menacing frown on his shadowed face, then he glanced in the direction of the parking lot.

"I'll see you later," he told her, his tone threatening. "To finish the job." Then he ran in the opposite direction.

Breathing hard, her body shaking, Lausanne stood there quivering from head to toe. Pete Harris came running across the parking lot, heading straight toward her.

Freckles trotted over to Lausanne and nuzzled his wet nose against her pants leg.

"Are you all right, Lausanne?" Pete asked as he came up to her. "I heard you screaming and the Bakers's dog barking and then I saw that man with you. Did you know him?"

"No, I—I didn't know him." Lausanne's voice quivered.

"Did he hurt you?"

"No, just scared me to death."

Pete reached down for Freckles's leash, then nodded to the apartment complex. "Come on and I'll walk you back upstairs before I head on out to work. I'm on the twelve-to-eight shift this week. I was just leaving for work when I heard you hollering."

"Thank goodness you did. I don't know what he might have done to me."

I'll see you later. To finish the job. The man's words echoed inside her head.

When she, Pete and Freckles neared the exterior stairs, she realized they were not alone. At least half a dozen of the complex's residents had come out of their apartments and were staring at them.

"What's wrong?"

"What happened?"

"Was that you screaming?"

"Is anybody hurt?"

Everybody started talking at once.

Pete stopped and faced the small crowd. "Some guy she didn't know grabbed Lausanne. But he's gone. I scared him off."

"I called the police when I heard you scream." Mrs. Potter, who lived in the building next to hers was a sweet old lady, but a bit of a busybody. "I expect they'll be here soon."

The police? Damn! But then again, maybe it was a good thing that someone had called the law. After all, she'd been attacked tonight, at least had been on the verge of being attacked and might have been killed if not for Pete Harris. Lausanne could have passed the incident off as a potential robbery or rape, but the man's threat kept repeating itself over and over in her mind. *I'll see you later. To finish the job.*

He had meant to kill her. And it was personal.

She had expected to hear from Lt. Desmond after they'd dragged Bobby Jack Cash's body from the river, had figured she'd be their number one suspect, but that had been days ago and she hadn't heard anything from the Chattanooga PD. Well, she'd hear from them tonight. And they'd hear from her. Call her crazy, but she knew in her gut that the attack on her tonight had something to do with Audrey and Bobby Jack.

THE PATROLMEN WHO ANSWERED Mrs. Potter's call took down all the info Lausanne could give them and cautioned her to be careful about walking her dog so late at night. With no more to go on than a general description—white male, tall, dark hair, dark mustache, nondescript clothing and an inability to ID his face—there was little chance the police would ever apprehend the guy. Molly had invited Lausanne to spend the night with her, but she'd declined, wanting nothing more than to hide away in her apartment.

Sitting on her sofa, alone and still shaken from her experience, Lausanne jumped sky-high when she heard someone knocking on her door. Get real—no self-respecting attacker would announce himself.

Pattering to the door in her aching sock feet, she called, "Who is it?" She peeked through the viewfinder.

"Ms. Raney, it's Lieutenant Desmond."

Oh, great, just what she needed. "What do you want? Why are you here?"

"I understand you were attacked tonight. I'd like for you to tell me about it."

"Why?" Something wasn't quite right about this. "How did you find out—"

"Open the door and talk to me."

Reluctantly, Lausanne unlocked the door and opened it just a fraction. Peering through the narrow gap, she glared at the detective. "Are you still keeping tabs on me?"

"Only in a round about way. If anything comes into headquarters concerning you, I'm notified immediately."

"Oh, I see."

"You're all right?" he asked. "You weren't harmed, were you?"

Lausanne eased the door open halfway. "Do you really care?"

"I care the same as I'd care if any law-abiding citizen was harmed by an attacker." Desmond eyed her skeptically. "And you were attacked, right?"

"Yes, I was…well, I would have been if Pete Harris hadn't scared the guy off."

"You didn't know the man who grabbed you?"

She shook her head.

"Did he say anything to you?"

"Why do you ask?"

"Then he did say something. What was it?"

"He said that he'd see me later…to finish the job."

"Hmm… Do you have any idea what he meant?" Desmond asked.

"I have an idea," she told him.

"And that would be?"

"I'm not sure exactly why, but I think it has something to do with Audrey Perkins's disappearance and Bobby Jack's murder."

"And it might not," Desmond said.

"You don't believe me. Why am I not surprised?"

"I believe someone approached you tonight and frightened you and that another Glennview Apartments resident scared the guy off. And I believe it's possible this guy intended to rob you or rape you, but as for a connection to Audrey Perkins or—"

"You asked me if I had any idea why this man tried to attack me and I told you what I thought."

"It's quite possible that you fabricated this attack and the theory that it was somehow connected to Ms. Perkins and Mr. Cash in order to throw suspicion off yourself and onto some unknown person. Maybe you knew this guy. Maybe he's an old boyfriend. Maybe—"

"Maybe you're nuts," Lausanne said. "That's a load of malarkey and you know it."

"I agree with her." The voice—Dom's voice—came from somewhere behind Lt. Desmond.

Lausanne's heart skipped a beat. "Dom?"

The detective stepped aside and turned to face Domingo Shea. "You certainly got here in a hurry. You must have broken every speed limit between here and your hotel."

Dom frowned at Desmond as he passed him and went straight to Lausanne. He shoved open the door, then grabbed her by the shoulders and searched her face. "Are you all right?"

"Yes, I'm okay."

"When I heard what happened, I—"

"How did you find out?" she asked.

"I called him," Lt. Desmond said.

Dom glowered at the detective. "Look, I appreciate

your contacting me. I owe you one. But harassing Lausanne is no way to conduct an investigation."

"I'm not conducting an investigation. I'm merely having a nice, friendly talk with Ms. Raney."

When Dom slid his arm around her waist, her stomach did a silly flip-flop; then when he said, "She doesn't have anything else to say to you without her lawyer present," Lausanne wanted to hug him.

"I knew I should have waited before I called you," Desmond said, a hint of humor in his voice. "How do you think it'll go over with Edward Bedell when he finds out that you're Ms. Raney's champion?"

"Is Mr. Bedell your next phone call?" Dom asked.

"Nope. Not tonight."

"Look, if it's any of your business, I'm not taking sides here," Dom said. "Not exactly. I'm on the side of the truth. And that's what Mr. Bedell wants, isn't it?"

"Yeah, but he could still see this—" Desmond eyed Dom's arm around Lausanne's waist "—as a conflict of interest."

"If and when I feel that things have reached that point, I'll take myself off this assignment."

Desmond grunted, then looked directly at Lausanne. "I'm leaving you in good hands, Ms. Raney." He turned to go, then glanced back at her. "Remember not to leave town."

Dom maneuvered her around and nudged her into her apartment, then closed and locked the door. "Tell me what happened. And don't leave anything out."

Clinging to his arm, she asked, "Will you believe

me or will you doubt me the way Lieutenant Desmond does?"

"Tell me the truth—the complete truth—and I'll believe you, honey."

DOM SAT WITH LAUSANNE on her sofa and listened as she talked, telling him every detail of what had happened to her tonight while she was walking the Bakers's dog. If she was lying about anything, then she was an Academy Award-winning actress. He saw real fear in her eyes, sensed genuine anxiety when she told him what the man had said to her.

"He'll come after me again," Lausanne told Dom. "I know he will. He said he'd be back to finish the job. He's been hired to kill me."

"Why would someone hire him to kill you?" Dom asked. "In Palm Beach, you thought the man who tried to kill you was after Audrey Perkins, but now that you're no longer impersonating her, then why—'"

"You don't believe me." She jumped up off the sofa. "You promised that you'd believe me if I told you the truth. But you lied to me. You lied, damn you, you lied."

She stomped toward the door. Dom shot up off the sofa and ran after her, catching her seconds before her hand connected with the doorknob.

After swinging her around, he held both of her wrists tightly. "God, woman, you're the most aggravating female I've ever come across. You go on the defensive before there's any reason to and you don't give a guy half a chance before you cut him off at the knees."

Glaring uncertainly at him, she tugged on her wrists, but he held fast. "We've had this discussion before and we agreed that since we can't trust each other, we need to go our separate ways."

"I believe you about the man trying to attack you tonight," Dom said. "And unlike Lieutenant Desmond, I'm not dismissing your theory that the man who came after you is somehow connected to Audrey Perkins's disappearance."

Dom wanted to believe every word out of Lausanne's mouth. For days now, he'd been waging an internal war with his own emotions. When Desmond had called to tell him about Lausanne being attacked, he'd been half out of his mind with worry until he'd seen for himself that she was all right. On the ninety-to-nothing mad dash from his hotel to her apartment, he'd gone over everything from the moment he first saw her in Palm Beach until they had said their goodbyes in her apartment doorway three nights ago. He had come to several conclusions, but no decisions. He wanted to trust Lausanne, but what were the odds that a woman with her background was on the level? Then on the other hand, what if she really was innocent of any wrong doing in the ongoing case and he didn't do all he could to help her? He'd feel like a heel. And he'd lose the one chance he had not only to help her, but to screw her.

He wanted her. Wanted her in the worst way. Every day they'd been apart, he'd had to force himself to stay away from her.

She looked up at him with those hungry green eyes

and all he could think about was making love to her. Slow and sweet. Hot and nasty. Over and over again.

"Are you saying you believe me?" she asked.

"Yeah, honey, I believe you."

"And you think it's possible that I'm right about someone trying to kill me and it somehow having a connection to Audrey Perkins?"

Did he really believe she might be right? Maybe. Maybe not. *Damn it, man, tell the lady what she wants to hear, what she needs to hear. You can work through any lingering doubts later.*

He released her wrists, lifted his hands and cupped her face between his open palms. "Yeah, I think it's possible."

"Oh, Dom." She swallowed hard. "Thank you for believing me."

The gratitude and the hope he noted in her expression really got to him, making him wonder how many times she had been hurt and disappointed, how many times she'd had her heart broken.

He eased his hands down her neck and across her shoulders, resting them there while she gazed up at him, a tentative smile on her lips.

"You can't possibly know how much it means to me that you're taking a leap of faith like this and at least giving me the benefit of the doubt. It's more than…"

She ended the thought midsentence, making him wonder what she'd been about to say.

"Lausanne, do you have any idea why someone connected to Audrey and Bobby Jack might want to kill you?"

"I'm not sure, but...well, there's something I know, something I haven't told anyone."

Dom's stomach muscles tightened. "Will you tell me?"

When she nodded, he squeezed her shoulders.

"The morning we flew in from Palm Beach and went to the Bedell mansion, I saw a portrait in Mr. Bedell's study, a portrait of Audrey."

"Yeah, so?"

"So, it was then that I realized the woman who hired me to impersonate Audrey Perkins wasn't Audrey herself, just someone else impersonating her."

CHAPTER TWELVE

"I'M BEGINNING TO THINK I need to hire a new cleanup guy. It's obvious that you're no longer capable of handling the job."

Okay, so he'd had things go wrong twice now, had sent less-than-competent goons out on assignments. He'd made the mistake of hiring locals—one in Palm Beach and the other in Chattanooga—to terminate Lausanne Raney. But he'd thought that he could save a few bucks that way and keep the profit for himself. Big error in judgment on his part.

"Look, I've never let you down before and I swear if you give me another chance, I'll make sure—"

"You've made that promise before and failed to deliver."

"Just say the word and I'll have somebody in Chattanooga tomorrow who will guarantee to get the job done."

"No. Not tomorrow. After two attempts on her life, she'll be very careful. Wait. I'll tell you when. But go ahead and line up someone. And this time, he'd better be the best my money can buy. Do you understand?"

"Yes, I understand."

The dial tone hummed in his ears. He understood, all right. This Raney woman knew something she shouldn't know or had done something she shouldn't have done. The only way to keep her quiet or to punish her was kill the bitch.

Okay, so he'd lose money on this deal, but it paid to keep a repeat customer happy. If he screwed up just one more time...

He knew just the man for the job. Corbin didn't come cheap, but he was the best. He had a ninety-nine percent success rate. That one failure was now in a permanent vegetative state, which in the grand scheme of things was as good as dead.

DOM STARED AT LAUSANNE in disbelief, as if he thought perhaps he'd misunderstood her, so Lausanne repeated her confession. "Did you hear me? I said that Audrey Perkins was not the woman who hired me to impersonate her."

"I heard you, honey. It's just that you've been so adamant about Audrey having hired you that I'm having a difficult time understanding this."

"What's to understand? Someone else was impersonating Audrey when she hired me to—"

"Yeah, yeah, I get that part," he told her. "What I don't understand is why you didn't know right away that the woman wasn't Audrey Perkins. After all, you'd been working at Bedell, Inc. for months. You must have seen Audrey when she came to the office to visit her husband or her father."

Just when she'd thought he believed her, that she could trust him, he proved her wrong. "Do you think I'm lying about this?" Furious and disappointed, she broke eye contact.

"Look at me, Lausanne."

She stubbornly refused to meet his gaze.

"Damn it, woman, look at me."

She glared at him. Their gazes locked, a battle of wills ensuing.

"I don't think you're lying," he said. "I just don't understand why you didn't recognize the woman who hired you as a phony."

"I'd never seen Audrey Perkins. During the six months I worked at Bedell, Inc. she never came to the office while I was there. I swear to you that the first time I met her, or thought I met her, was the day I was summoned to her house."

Dom nodded. "Okay. So tell me about that meeting. Tell me about the woman."

"I've told you before. She hired me to impersonate her, to impersonate Audrey Perkins. And she paid me—"

"You met her at her home, at Audrey Bedell's downtown penthouse apartment. And no one else was there, not even the maid. Didn't that seem odd to you?"

Lausanne shook her head. "No, not really. What are you getting at?"

"Whoever this woman was, she was able to arrange to meet you alone, to dismiss any servants, to make sure Grayson Perkins wasn't there and she had access to the house."

"You're right. That means she was somebody close to the family, someone who had a key to the house and knew when no one would be there."

"Patrice Bedell," Dom suggested. "Or Cara Bedell."

"The stepmother? Yes, I can see that." Lausanne's own stepmother would have gladly killed her if she'd thought she could get away with it. "But I've met her and it wasn't Mrs. Bedell."

"Okay, what about Cara, the sister who's in love with Audrey's husband."

"You picked up on that, too, huh? But no, it wasn't Cara, either."

"Let's not rule out the husband," Dom said. "Grayson Perkins could have hired someone to impersonate his wife."

Lausanne groaned. "You think Audrey Perkins is dead, don't you?"

"I figure it's a good possibility. Whoever killed Bobby Jack probably killed Audrey. Unless…"

Lausanne's nerves rioted. "Unless I'm lying? Unless I killed Bobby Jack? Unless—"

"Unless Audrey killed Bobby Jack," Dom said.

"Oh. I hadn't thought of that. And I'm sorry I jumped to the wrong conclusion, that you'd automatically think I was the one who'd killed Bobby Jack."

He held out his hand to her. She stared at that simple truce offer, his outstretched hand, and hesitated accepting.

"This trust business works both ways, honey," he told her. "If you want me to trust you, to believe in you, then you're going to have to reciprocate. You're going to have to trust me."

"Hmph." Lausanne stared at Dom's hand. "I guess I've been so concerned about your not trusting me that I didn't think about the fact that I'm having just as difficult a time trusting you."

"I'm not asking for unconditional trust," he said. "But we have to start somewhere. I'm not making any promises and you don't have to, either." He wiggled the fingers on his outstretched hand. "Let's make a bargain that we'll work at building the trust between us."

"I can do that." She put her hand in his.

He led her over to the sofa. When they sat down, each turned to face the other. Not touching, they sat there, their gazes connected.

"I don't think you killed Audrey Perkins or Bobby Jack Cash," he said.

She breathed a deep sigh of relief. "I didn't. I don't have it in me to kill. If I did, believe me, I'd have killed my stepmother, years ago, when I was sixteen."

He reached over, lifted a strand of her hair and curled it around her ear, then glided his fingertips across her jaw before removing his hand. "Is she the reason you ran away from home?"

"Just how thorough is that check you ran on me?" Lausanne couldn't look away. He held her spellbound with the tender concern she saw in his black eyes.

"Just a preliminary check. Basic facts." He paused, then said, "Dundee's is running an extensive check on you. Edward Bedell requested it and he's our client."

Bubble bursting. "For a few minutes there, I'd forgotten that fact, that you're working for Mr. Bedell."

"If the time comes when your best interests conflict with my doing the job I was hired to do, I'll ask my boss to send in another agent."

Huh? Had she heard that right? "Are you saying what I think you're saying?"

"I'm saying that if I have to choose between protecting you and doing my job, I'll take myself off the Bedell case."

"Oh, Dom." She barreled into him, threw her arms around him and kissed him.

After she'd dotted his face with grateful kisses, she pulled back and smiled at him. "Please, don't be lying to me."

"I'll make you one promise here and now. I promise that from here on out, I'll never lie to you."

She nodded. "And I promise you the same. I'll never lie to you ever again."

He took both of her hands in his. "You have to go to the police and tell them that the woman who hired you was not Audrey Perkins."

"What good will that do? They won't believe me."

"They might. But your best bet is to be honest with them from now on. It's up to them whether or not they believe you."

"I wish I had some idea who the woman was." Lausanne tried to remember exactly what the woman had looked like, what she'd been wearing, how she'd spoken.

"She had red hair and I believe her eyes were blue,

but they could have been gray. They definitely weren't brown. And she was taller than I am, maybe five-six, but she was slender and rather pretty."

"And she was young?" Dom asked. "About your age?"

"Yes, probably between twenty-five and thirty-five. Definitely no older."

"What about her voice? Her mannerisms?"

"A typical East Tennessee accent. As for her mannerisms— Wait, there was something, now that I think about it."

"What?"

"She seemed nervous."

"How?"

"Fidgety, like she wasn't comfortable in her own house or her own skin for that matter. I just chalked it up to her being anxious about running off with her lover."

"She was concerned that you might figure out she wasn't really Audrey Perkins."

"That was probably it." Lausanne asked aloud the question that had been nagging at her ever since she realized the woman who'd hired her wasn't Audrey. "Why would someone other than Audrey hire me to impersonate her?"

"Good question."

"Got any ideas?"

"At least a dozen," he replied. "But I could be dead wrong about all of them. The best way to find out the answer to your question is to find the woman who hired you."

"How do we do that?"

"First thing in the morning, we'll talk to Bain Desmond. If he believes us, we'll go from there."

If he believes us. *Us.* That one word repeated itself in Lausanne's mind and in her heart. Dom hadn't said if he believes *you;* he'd said if he believes *us.*

"And if he doesn't believe us?"

"Then we'll do our own investigation."

"We will?"

"Yes, we will, starting with other Bedell, Inc. employees. If Grayson Perkins or the stepmother or the sister got somebody to pose as Audrey so she could hire you, then it's possible that they used another employee...someone they already knew."

"How are you going to conduct a private investigation for me while you're working for Mr. Bedell?" Lausanne asked.

"I'll be doing the investigation for Mr. Bedell," Dom told her. "Once he learns that his daughter didn't hire you, but someone else posing as her, he'll want to know that woman's identity, won't he?"

"Oh, Dom, you're right."

"Her father wants to find out what happened to Audrey and so do you. You both want the same thing— the truth."

"I should have told you about this as soon as I realized Audrey wasn't the person who hired me, but I didn't know what to do, who to trust, so I kept it to myself."

"You do realize that whoever attacked you in Palm Beach and again tonight might have tried to kill you so that you couldn't identify the woman who hired you."

Nausea. A sick, sinking feeling in the pit of her belly. She was such an idiot. Why had she ever thought she could make some easy money, have a little fun and not pay the piper? She'd paid dearly for every mistake she'd ever made. Paid with the loss of her baby, paid with five years of her life. Now, she might pay the ultimate price.

Dom pulled her into his arms. She went willingly, with no resistance, needing him more than she'd ever needed anyone. He held her close, his mouth soft against her temple as she rested her head on his shoulder.

"I know you're scared," he said. "I'm scared for you, honey. You've gotten yourself into a real mess."

"It isn't the first time. I seem to be really good at screwing up and getting myself into trouble. I thought that was all over, that finally I'd learned how to stay out of trouble." She buried her face in his shoulder and clung to him. "I'm the worst kind of bad news. You should run from me while you can."

Yeah, why should Dom stick around, when no one else ever had? No matter what he said or did, she had to remember one thing—she couldn't count on him for the long haul. She couldn't count on anyone except herself.

Needing another person was a sign of weakness. Oh, God, how she wished she could be weak, that she could be needy, that she could forget the harsh lessons she'd learned through sheer misery.

Dom pressed his lips against her temple and kissed her, a featherlight touch, his breath warm against her skin. "I'm not going anywhere. I couldn't even if I wanted to." He slipped his hand under her chin and cradled it between his thumb and forefinger; then tilted her face so that they could look into each other's eyes. "I'm a sucker for damsels in distress."

She mustn't cry. Crying showed weakness. The first few weeks in the TPFW, she'd cried herself to sleep every night, but she'd soon learned that crybabies got pushed around and taken advantage of by the hardasses. It hadn't taken her long to toughen up, to at least fake being a hardass herself.

"I stopped believing in white knights coming to the rescue a long time ago," she told him.

He ran his thumb across her bottom lip. She sucked in a surprised breath.

"Maybe you stopped believing too soon. Maybe your white knight just hadn't shown up…until now."

Her heart fluttered foolishly. *Don't listen to him. Don't fall for his line, albeit a great line. Dom Shea wants what every other man in your life has wanted—to get in your pants. As soon as he's had you, as soon as he's used you for his own needs, he'll walk away and never look back.*

At least this time, she knew what he wanted, knew how things would end. She had no expectations beyond a day by day relationship built on physical attraction. If he'd just stick around long enough to help her out of this jam, that would be enough. She'd use him. He'd use her. They'd both get something out of it. No harm. No foul.

And it wasn't as if she'd have to pretend she wanted him. Her body ached with wanting him.

It had been a long time since she'd been intimate

with a man. Over five years. Not since Clay. Not since she'd been barely twenty-one. And even back then she hadn't been all that experienced. What she'd been was a sadly used and abused kid who so desperately wanted to be loved.

Lausanne wrapped her arms around Dom's neck, then she looked at him, hoping her gaze conveyed her feelings. She'd never seduced a man in her life and wasn't quite sure how to go about it, actually wasn't even sure it was what she wanted. But she figured it was what he wanted, maybe even what he expected from a woman like her.

With half closed eyelids, she scooted closer, pressing herself against him until her mouth brushed his. "Domingo Shea, I'm going to kiss you and kiss you and—"

Dom didn't wait for her to finish speaking or for her to make the next move. Before she realized what was happening, he took her mouth in a hungry, devouring move that left her dizzy and weak. Without thinking, only feeling, she responded eagerly. Opening her mouth, she kissed him back, giving as good as she got.

Every cell in her body came alive. Vividly, bouncing-off-the-walls alive. Without being consciously aware of what she was doing, Lausanne inched the fingers of her right hand up the back of his neck. Her fingertips embedded themselves in his short, thick hair. Using her left hand, she gripped his shoulder tightly.

His big hands held her, caressing her tenderly, but not intimately; and all the while Dom and she kept on kissing and kissing…until almost breathless, they broke apart. They looked at each other, the longing between them palpable, so real and honest that neither of them could deny it.

With his hands around her waist and hers twined behind his neck, they sat there in silence for endless moments.

Dom finally spoke. "Wow, lady, you sure know how to curl a guy's toes."

The tightness in her chest eased and she was able to breathe normally again; then she smiled. "You're some kisser yourself, Mr. Shea."

"Thanks, I've never had any complaints."

How many other women had he kissed? Dozens? Hundreds? "I guess practice makes perfect, huh?"

"In my case, maybe. But I'll bet not in yours."

She blinked, slightly taken off guard by his comment. "Why do you say that? I thought you liked the way I kissed you? Did I do something wrong, something that made you think I don't have a lot of experience?"

Acting so quickly that she had no time to protest or even react, Dom lifted her onto his lap, then wrapped his arms around her so that she couldn't escape.

"I loved the way you kissed me," he told her. "You did everything absolutely right...for a beginner."

"A beginner!"

When she tried to escape, he refused to release her. "It was a compliment, honey. You're a natural. You did curl my toes. Just think what you'd do to me if you had more experience."

"You know that I'm not a virgin," she said defensively. "I haven't been since I was seventeen. And I've had more than one lover."

"Hmm… They must have been a couple of duds."

"What makes you think there have been only two?"

"Intuition."

"Oh."

"Am I right?" he asked.

She shrugged. His intuition was a little too accurate to suit her.

"Number one was the guy who knocked you up when you were seventeen," Dom said. "And number two was the guy who got you sent to prison for being his accomplice in a convenience store robbery."

"Okay, let's say that you're right. So, if you get to know about the men in my past, do I get to know about the women in yours?"

"I've never been married, never been engaged, have no children and have been in love only once. She preferred my big brother, but in the end, she married somebody else. I've made love to maybe a dozen different women and I've had just sex with possibly a dozen more."

He'd been with at least twenty-four different women. That didn't surprise her. What surprised her was that there hadn't been more.

"For me, it was making love," she told him. "For both of them, it was just sex. I've never had a man make love to me."

He leaned his forehead against hers, took a deep breath and whispered huskily, "Then I'll be your first."

Her eyes widened with anticipation and wonder. "You're going to make love to me?"

He lifted his head, then cupped her face between his open palms. "Yeah, honey, I'm going to make love to you."

Gulping, she stared at him questioningly. "Tonight?"

He chuckled. "No. Tonight isn't the right time. You're not ready. We're both still working on our trust issues."

"Oh. No, not tonight. Not yet." She didn't want him to leave her, but she couldn't bring herself to ask him to stay.

"No lovemaking tonight, but I'd like to stay, spend the night, if you'll let me," he said, as if reading her mind.

"You don't have to." *But please stay. Don't leave me alone.*

"I want to stay," he said. "I'll sleep on the sofa. I'm not going to leave you alone, not after what happened tonight."

My protector. My white knight. Oh God, Lausanne, don't do this to yourself. Don't kid yourself. Whatever's going on between you and Dom won't last. It's a temporary thing. No promises. No commitments on either side.

"Okay, you can stay." She pulled away from him and stood.

"Thanks."

She offered him a shaky smile. "I'll get you a pillow and a blanket." She headed toward the bedroom.

"Lausanne?"

She glanced over her shoulder as she paused in the open doorway. "Yeah?"

"You wanted me to stay, didn't you?"

"Sure…if you want to."

He grinned. She hurried into the bedroom, got an extra blanket from the closet and the second pillow from her bed, then took the items back into the living room.

Dom had removed his jacket and hung it on the back of a bar stool. When she approached him, he turned and took the blanket and pillow from her, then tossed them on the sofa.

"You'd better turn in and try to get some sleep," Dom said. "I'm going to call Bain Desmond and ask him to come over here first thing in the morning. Knowing that the woman who hired you wasn't Audrey Perkins should take some of the suspicion off you."

"That's assuming he believes me."

"I think he might. Desmond's smart. He'll know the truth when he hears it."

CHAPTER THIRTEEN

LAUSANNE WOKE to the smell of coffee, and for a couple of groggy seconds wondered where that delicious aroma was coming from. Then she remembered that Dom had spent the night. On her sofa. He must have prepared the coffee. Yawning as she threw back the covers and stretched, Lausanne smiled. She had slept soundly, but only because she'd known she was safe, that Dom was nearby. Crawling out of bed, she reminded herself not to get used to having Dom around. Once the Audrey Perkins case was solved, he'd go back to Atlanta, back to his real life, and she'd be alone again.

After using the bathroom, washing her hands and face and brushing her hair, she put on a matching robe over her beige silk pajamas, both purchased while she'd been impersonating Audrey. When she entered the living room, she noted that Dom had folded his blanket and laid the pillow on top of it. Both rested on the sofa arm. She scanned the living room and the open kitchenette and found both empty. Where was Dom? Had he set the coffeemaker and then left?

Just as a wave of disappointment washed over Lausanne, the front door opened and Dom, with two paper sacks in one hand, came breezing in, whistling. After removing her key from the lock, he kicked the door closed behind him. When he turned around, he saw her.

"Morning, beautiful."

Her stomach flip-flopped. Because he'd called her beautiful? Or because she was so glad to see him? "Good morning."

"Sleep well?" He walked through the living room and set the two sacks down on the bar.

"Yes, quite well, thank you."

"Hungry?"

"I guess so."

"You'd better be," he told her, a humorous twinkle in his eye. "I made a quick run to the bakery." He lifted one sack. "We have cinnamon rolls." He set that sack down and lifted the other. "And French toast sticks."

"You've been very busy this morning, haven't you?" She took a good look at him. He was clean-shaven and neat despite his slacks and shirt being slightly wrinkled from him having slept in them. "You've showered, shaved, made coffee and gone out for breakfast, while I slept late."

He removed his jacket, hung it on the back of a bar stool and grinned at her. "Never let it be said that Camila Shea's baby boy doesn't know how to treat a lady."

Lausanne's heart stopped for a millisecond. He'd referred to her as a lady. Did he mean it or had he used the word lightly?

Lausanne approached him, feeling strangely timid. Having a man spend the night in her apartment was unusual enough, but having him cater to her this way seemed really odd. She was unaccustomed to a man treating her with such respect and with such care. "I take it that your mother taught you good manners."

"Yes, ma'am, that she did." He opened one sack and then the other. "What's your preference this morning? Or would you prefer some of each?"

"Just coffee right now. I usually can't eat anything when I first get up." She moved past him hurriedly and went straight to the coffeemaker.

"That's good to know," he said. "I'll file that info away for future reference."

Dom came up behind her, his chest almost touching her back. Her breath caught in her throat. He reached around and above her, opened the cupboard and removed two white mugs. His arms brushed against hers, sending a tingling sensation through her entire body.

Why did she react so strongly to his mere touch? What was it about him that ignited such passion in her?

"You pour the coffee, honey," he said, easing backward. "Remember, I take mine black." He moved over enough to open the second cupboard and remove two plates. "I want a couple of cinnamon rolls now, but I'll just leave your plate on the bar until you're hungry."

With slightly unsteady hands, she lifted the coffeepot.

"I called Bain Desmond on my way to the bakery," Dom told her.

"And?" She poured two mugs to the brim with the hot coffee.

"He'll be here around eight-thirty."

"What time is it now?" She glanced at the electric clock, circled with a black plastic case, that hung on the kitchenette wall. "Oh, it's not quite eight. I thought it was later."

"You have plenty of time for coffee and a bite to eat before changing out of your pajamas."

She handed Dom one of the mugs, then glanced down at her silky attire. "So, you don't think I should entertain the detective in my sleepwear, huh?"

Dom set his mug on the bar alongside his empty plate, then took hers and placed it next to his. Commanding her attention with his dark stare, he slipped his right index finger between the lapels of her silk robe and spread the lapels apart. She sucked in a startled breath. With their gazes locked, he glided his finger inside her pajama top. Leisurely. Seductively. The tip of his finger stopped between her breasts.

"I don't want any other man seeing you like this."

Her heartbeat accelerated, the quick rhythm pounding in her ears. "You don't?"

Grinning sheepishly, he slid his finger up and out of her pajama top, then retrieved his mug from the bar. "Better drink your coffee and eat something before Lieutenant Desmond gets here."

Coming out of the romantic haze Dom's words and touch had created, Lausanne followed his lead, picked up her cup and sipped the strong, hot brew.

"You make good coffee," she said, surprised that her voice sounded so calm because, inside, she was a quivering mass of emotions.

"When you get to know me better, honey, you'll discover that I'm very good at a lot of things."

"And very modest."

He chuckled. "Yeah, there's that, too." After taking a couple more sips of coffee, he removed a cinnamon roll from the sack and bit into it.

"It must be nice to have so much self-confidence." Damn, why had she let her thoughts pop out of her mouth that way?

"It's hard to believe you have a self-esteem problem. Most beautiful women—"

"Haven't lived my life."

He stared at her and she knew he was trying to analyze her comment. "Sometime you'll have to tell me about it…about all of it. I'd be very interested in learning what made you you."

"I thought Dundee's was conducting a thorough check on me for Mr. Bedell. That should tell you everything you want to know." She grunted. "Hell, no need to wait for the report, I can give you the pitiful tale of Lausanne Raney's life in a nutshell."

"I didn't mean to hit a nerve." Dom narrowed his gaze, focusing on her flushed cheeks. "I'm personally interested in you and therefore in your past. My interest has nothing to do with the case I'm working on."

"Doesn't it?"

"Are we back to not trusting each other?" Dom asked.

She grumbled under her breath. "I'm trying."

"Yeah, me, too."

"So, do you want the nutshell version of my life or not?"

"Only if you want to give it."

"I was born to two loving parents and had a wonderful childhood. Then my mother died and the world as I knew it ceased to exist. My father shut himself off from everyone, including me. Then a little over a year later, he remarried. Renee was a cruel, jealous woman. She made my life so miserable that I ran away when I was sixteen." She sighed deeply as the memories washed over her. "Somehow, I managed to survive without turning to drugs or prostitution. I met a guy not much older than I was, we hooked up, he fed me a line of bull, I slept with him, got pregnant. Yada-yada-yada. I gave my baby girl up for adoption, steered clear of good-looking, sweet-talking guys and drifted from place to place.

"Then right before I turned twenty-one, I met another good-looking, sweet-talking guy. This one talked love and forever after. I believed all his lies and wound up being arrested as his accomplice when he robbed a convenience store."

"I'd say it's past time you got a break," Dom told her. "And if you think I'm just another good-looking, sweet-talking man, you're wrong. The last thing I ever want to do is hurt you."

"We're back to that little matter of trust again."

"You can't rush it. Trust takes time to build, especially when a relationship starts out the way ours did."

"Yeah, with lies and lies and more lies."

"No more lies between us. Agreed?"

She nodded. "Agreed."

BAIN DESMOND LOOKED a little too handsome to suit Dom and a little too friendly with Lausanne. What was the detective up to by being so nice?

Desmond sat on the sofa with Lausanne, sipping on the coffee she'd poured for him, and the two were chatting about the weather, about how at this time of year, it can feel like summer one day and winter the next.

"I know you don't have time for idle chit-chat." Sitting across from Desmond, Dom glared at the detective. "So, maybe we should get down to business."

"Whenever Ms. Raney is ready," Desmond said.

Dom gritted his teeth.

"I'm not sure where to start," Lausanne admitted. "So I'll just start with the morning Dom brought me back from Palm Beach." She looked to Dom for approval.

When he nodded, she continued. Desmond watched her closely. Dom was beginning to wonder if the detective's interest in Lausanne, like his, was as much personal as professional.

"Perhaps I should say first that I truly believed the woman who hired me to impersonate Audrey Perkins was Audrey Perkins," Lausanne said.

With an inquisitive look in his eyes, Desmond lifted one eyebrow. "And she wasn't?"

"No, she wasn't, but I thought she was. I didn't realize

the truth until I saw a portrait of Audrey in her father's study. That's when I knew that she—Audrey—hadn't hired me, that the person who did was someone else."

Desmond didn't respond immediately, just sat there staring at Lausanne.

"You can see how this changes things," Dom said.

"Hmm…" Desmond nodded.

"Find the woman who hired Lausanne and you'll find out what happened to Audrey Perkins." Dom studied the detective's face for a clue as to what he might be thinking. The guy's face was blank.

"*If* Ms. Raney is telling us the truth." Desmond looked directly at Lausanne. "Are you being completely honest with me, telling me everything?"

Dom barely stopped himself from answering for her. He wanted to bellow out the reply. *Yes, damn it, yes, she's telling you the truth.*

"I've told you the truth about everything," Lausanne reiterated.

"Why should I believe you?" Desmond asked. "What proof can you give me? What evidence do you have?"

Seemingly stumped by the detective's questions, she sat there thinking, her green eyes reflecting her deep concentration. Dom held his breath. Desmond waited for a reply.

Finally, Lausanne said, "I can identify the woman who hired me and I don't think someone wants me to do that. I've been attacked twice." She hesitated, then added, "And I have fifty thousand dollars in my bank account. If I wasn't paid that amount to impersonate Audrey Perkins, then where did I get hold of so much cash?"

"You or Bobby Jack Cash could have stolen the money from Audrey Perkins," Desmond said. "And as for your being attacked twice—there's no reason to believe either incident was connected to Ms. Perkins's disappearance."

"Are you being obstinate on purpose or are you just plain stupid?" Dom barked the question, anger in every word. "Why would Lausanne deposit stolen money in a bank account under her own name? And being attacked twice in less than two weeks is no coincidence. Any fool could see that. And didn't you hear her say she can ID the woman who hired her? Whoever this woman is, she's your lead to finding out what happened to Audrey Perkins."

"So, you're saying that you believe everything Ms. Raney has told you?" Desmond asked point-blank.

"Yes, I believe her," Dom said without giving his response a thought.

He *did* believe her. With his heart, with his gut and with every ounce of testosterone in his body.

"Okay, let's say I believe you, Ms. Raney," Desmond said. "I'll need a description of this woman and—"

"She was between twenty-five and thirty-five. Tall, slender, pretty and had red hair. But her hair could have been dyed or it could have been a wig." Lausanne spoke rapidly. "Her accent sounded pretty much like everybody else's who lives in this area and there was nothing distinctive about it. She seemed a bit nervous, but I chalked that up to her being eager to run off with her lover."

"If you saw her again, are you sure you'd recognize her?"

"Yes, I'm sure."

"Do you think you could ID her from a photograph?"

"Yes, I believe I could. Why? Do you have any idea who this woman might be?" Lausanne asked.

"Not really," Desmond said. "But a good place to start looking would be with the people closest to Ms. Perkins."

"We know it wasn't her sister or her stepmother." Dom gave Lausanne an encouraging glance and noted her immediate response. Momentary relaxation. Temporary relief. And gratitude. "You should look beyond Audrey's friends. You need to check out the employee data for Bedell, Inc."

"Bedell, Inc. employs thousands of people world-wide," Desmond said.

"Just check out the females under thirty-five who are employed here in Chattanooga," Dom suggested.

When Desmond stood, Dom did, too, and then Lausanne.

"Keep this revelation to yourselves for now," Desmond told them as he headed for the door. "As soon as I come up with something, I'll let you know."

"Thank you, Lieutenant," Lausanne said as she stood between Dom and Desmond. She offered the detective her hand.

Desmond took her hand, shook it and held it a little too long to suit Dom.

"You be careful coming and going, especially at night," Desmond told her. "I'd be glad to keep check on you—"

"That won't be necessary," Dom said. "I'm staying here with her."

Desmond's mouth lifted in a why-am-I-not-surprised smile. "So does this mean you're working for Ms. Raney now instead of Edward Bedell."

Dom clenched his teeth tightly.

Lausanne glanced back and forth between Dom and Desmond, then when neither man spoke again, she stepped in to defuse the tension.

"May I see you to the door, Lieutenant?"

"Thank you, Ms. Raney."

When she closed the door and turned to Dom, he huffed loudly. "He's got the hots for you."

Lausanne rolled her eyes. "He does not." Then she smiled broadly. "But I love it that you're jealous."

"Me jealous? No way."

She came up to him, wrapped her arms around his waist and stood on tiptoe to look him square in the eyes. "You're going to get in trouble, you know that, don't you? You can't be my protector and continue working for Mr. Bedell."

"Then I'll just have to contact my boss and tell him to assign another agent to the case."

"You mustn't do that." She released him and stepped back.

"Why not?"

"I won't let you jeopardize your job for me."

"Your life is a lot more important than my job," Dom told her. "Besides, I doubt I'll lose my job just because I resign from this case."

"If Mr. Bedell finds out why you resigned, he won't like it. He may demand that your boss fire you. I've heard Mr. Bedell can be a very unforgiving man."

Dom took her hands in his. "No matter what happens, I'm not going to let you go through this alone. Until we unearth the truth and know that you're safe, dynamite couldn't blast me away from you."

CHAPTER FOURTEEN

AT 1:20 THAT AFTERNOON, Lieutenant Desmond arrived at Bedell, Inc., along with his partner, Sergeant Mike Swain. When they asked to speak directly to Mr. Bedell, they were informed the big boss had gone home early, but that Mr. Perkins was still here and taking all of Mr. Bedell's afternoon appointments. As soon as they were announced, the secretary escorted them down the hall and directly into Grayson Perkins's huge, swanky office. Having grown up dirt poor on his uncle's farm in Dayton, Bain possessed an innate distrust of the rich, especially the filthy rich. Even though Mr. Perkins wasn't wealthy in his own right, his wife stood to one day inherit at least half of an estate estimated in the billions. That is, if Ms. Perkins was still alive. And Bain definitely had his doubts about that. He'd be interested in taking a look at Audrey Perkins's will. He'd bet his pension that her husband was the major beneficiary.

"Please be seated." The secretary indicated two plush leather chairs. "Would you care for coffee or tea?"

"No, thanks," Bain replied.

Mike shook his head.

An Important Message
from the Editors

Dear Reader,

*Because you've chosen to read one of our fine novels, we'd like to say "thank you!" And, as a **special** way to thank you, we're offering you a choice of <u>two more</u> of the books you love so well **plus** an exciting Mystery Gift to send you — absolutely <u>FREE</u>!*

Please enjoy them with our compliments...

Pam Powers

Lift here

Peel off seal and place inside...

What's Your Reading Pleasure...
~~ROMANCE?~~ *OR* SUSPENSE?

Do you prefer spine-tingling page turners OR heart-stirring stories about love and relationships? Tell us which books you enjoy – and you'll get 2 FREE "ROMANCE" BOOKS or 2 FREE "SUSPENSE" BOOKS with no obligation to purchase anything.

Choose **"ROMANCE"** and get **2 FREE BOOKS** that will fuel your imagination with intensely moving stories about life, love and relationships.

FREE!

Choose **"SUSPENSE"** and you'll get **2 FREE BOOKS** that will thrill you with a spine-tingling blend of suspense and mystery.

FREE!

Whichever category you select, your 2 free books have a combined cover price of $11.98 or more in the U.S. and $13.98 or more in Canada.

And remember... just for accepting the Editor's Free Gift Offer, we'll send you 2 books and a gift, ABSOLUTELY FREE!

YOURS FREE! We'll send you a fabulous surprise gift absolutely FREE, just for trying "Romance" or "Suspense"!

® and ™ are trademarks owned and used by the trademark owner and/or its licensee.

Order online at www.FreeBooksandGift.com

The Editor's "Thank You" Free Gifts Include:

- *2 Romance OR 2 Suspense books!*
- *An exciting mystery gift!*

Yes! I have placed my
Editor's "Thank You" seal in the
space provided at right. Please
send me 2 free books, which
I have selected, and a fabulous
mystery gift. I understand I am
under no obligation to purchase
any books, as explained on the
back of this card.

**PLACE
FREE GIFT
SEAL
HERE**

	ROMANCE
	193 MDL EE4Y 393 MDL EE5N

	SUSPENSE
	192 MDL EE5C 392 MDL EE5Y

FIRST NAME

LAST NAME

ADDRESS

APT.#

CITY

STATE/PROV.

ZIP/POSTAL CODE

Thank You!

The Reader Service — Here's How It Works:

If offer card is missing write to: The Reader Service, 3010 Walden Ave., P.O. Box 1867, Buffalo, NY 14240-1867

POSTAGE WILL BE PAID BY ADDRESSEE

BUSINESS REPLY MAIL
FIRST-CLASS MAIL   PERMIT NO. 717-003   BUFFALO, NY

THE READER SERVICE
3010 WALDEN AVE
PO BOX 1341
BUFFALO NY 14240-8571

NO POSTAGE
NECESSARY
IF MAILED
IN THE
UNITED STATES

"Mr. Perkins will be right with you." The secretary exited discreetly.

"Think he'll give us what we want without a search warrant?" Mike asked.

"Possibly."

"You're going to ask first, huh? Then if he doesn't agree, you'll—"

A side door to the inner sanctum opened and an elegantly attired Grayson Perkins breezed into the room. "Gentlemen, what may I do for you?"

"We need to ask you a few questions," Bain said. "And we also need to see the Bedell, Inc. personnel files."

"Ask me whatever you need to ask." Grayson propped his slim hips against his massive desk and crossed his arms over his chest, the movement revealing his shirt cuffs and the sparkling diamond links.

"Who, other than her sister and stepmother, are the women closest to your wife? Her friends, employees, that sort of thing." Bain studied Grayson, wondering just what went on inside the guy and if there was anything else to him other than his *GQ* body and cover-model face.

"Audrey doesn't really have any female friends," Grayson replied. "Numerous acquaintances, but no friends. She and Cara live very different lives, but they care about each other. And they both despise Patrice." Grayson mused for several seconds then said, "We have several female employees. There's the cook and the housekeeper, but neither live in and aren't there every day."

"Either of those women thirty-five or younger?" Mike Swain asked.

"No, Vivian and Cathy are in their late forties."
Grayson frowned. "I'm puzzled by why you're interested in the women in Audrey's life. What does this have
to do with her disappearance?"

"I'm just covering all the bases," Bain said. "Can you
think of anyone else, any young woman more connected
to your wife, someone who possibly had a key to your
penthouse?"

"Well, there's Audrey's personal assistant, Megan
Reynolds."

"Is she under thirty-five?" Bain asked.

"Yes, I think so. My guess is that she's around
thirty. Why?"

Disregarding the question, Bain continued. "What
about female employees under thirty-five here at Bedell,
Inc.'s main headquarters? How many—"

"You expect me to answer all your questions, but you
won't answer even one for me?" Grayson uncrossed
his arms and pushed himself away from the desk.

"I'm going to need photo IDs of all female employees under the age of thirty-five," Bain said. "And that
includes all personnel employed in your home and Mr.
Bedell's home."

Obviously frustrated by having his demands ignored,
Grayson glowered at Bain. Their gazes met for half a
second before Grayson looked away and said, "I don't
believe that will be a problem. Everything is computer-
ized. I'll call our personnel department and tell them
what you need."

"What about the people who work in your home and in—"

"They're all paid through the Bedell, Inc. payroll department, so their records are on file here at company headquarters."

"We appreciate your being so cooperative, Mr. Perkins." Bain stood and held out his hand.

Grayson Perkins had a firm, confident handshake. "My secretary will show you to the personnel office. I'll inform them to cooperate with you in every way."

A few minutes later, when the secretary left them outside the double doors leading into the personnel office suite, Mike paused and said, "So, what do you think about Mr. Perkins? He just up and agreed to give us whatever we wanted. Guess that makes him look less guilty, right?"

"Not necessarily."

"Huh?"

"Mr. Perkins has no idea why we want the personnel files on these women. He's unaware of the fact that we want photos to show Ms. Raney to see if she can identify the woman she says hired her."

"Man, you don't trust anybody, do you? You still consider Perkins a suspect in Bobby Jack Cash's murder and his wife's disappearance and you think the Raney woman is lying about—"

"I think Lausanne Raney is probably telling us the truth, but I learned a long time ago not to take anybody's word for anything, especially not if that person is suspected of committing a crime."

Bain opened the door and walked into the office. An

attractive young woman rose from her desk and met him. "Lieutenant Desmond?"

"Yes."

"Mr. Perkins has told us to cooperate with you fully. Just tell me what you need and I'll do my best to provide it as quickly as possible."

DOM MET BAIN DESMOND and Mike Swain outside the Chicken Coop at seven-fifteen that evening. They took a back booth, ordered coffee and asked Lausanne to take her next break as soon as she could.

"It'll be another fifteen minutes at least," she told Dom. "Does Lieutenant Desmond have some new information?"

"He has photos of all Bedell, Inc. female employees under the age of thirty-five," Dom said. "He wants you to take a look at them."

Lausanne nodded, then scurried off to deliver chicken salad and iced tea to a customer.

Dom glanced at the laptop Mike Swain laid on the table in front of him.

"The employee photos are on a disc," Desmond said.

"How many photos?" Dom asked.

"Out of seventy-six female employees, forty-two are under the age of thirty-five," Swain said.

"You realize that with that many photos to look at, it'll be easy for Lausanne to become confused," Dom said. "She might not be able to ID the woman, especially considering the fact that the woman probably wore a wig and—"

"Making excuses for her just in case?" Desmond asked.

"Just stating a simple fact."

"Well, the facts are these—I have a murder case on my hands as well as a missing person's case. And until both cases are solved, Ms. Raney will remain a person of interest to the Chattanooga PD."

"You don't really think she's capable of murder," Dom said.

"Just because she's a beautiful woman that any man would find desirable doesn't mean she's not capable of murder." Desmond looked pointedly at Dom. "Believe me, I'd like to see her proven completely innocent, but I haven't lost my objectivity."

The way you have. Those four words hung silently between them.

"What if Audrey Perkins killed Bobby Jack and she's on the run?" Dom tossed out a plausible scenario. "Knowing Cash's body was bound to be found eventually, she arranged to have an impersonator lead police or private PI's off her trail."

"Why hire two impersonators?" Desmond asked.

"There could be numerous explanations."

"Name one."

Lausanne showed up that very minute, as if on cue, saving Dom from having to produce a reply when he had none. "Effie told me to go ahead and take my break since we're not busy now that the car club customers just left."

Dom scooted over to allow her to sit by him.

"So, where are the photographs you want me to look at?" Lausanne asked.

"They're here." Sergeant Swain patted the top of the closed laptop.

Lausanne glanced quizzically at the computer.

Swain flipped the laptop open and turned it around so that the screen faced Lausanne. "I have the disc loaded. All you have to do is hit Next when you're ready to move from one photograph to the next."

"Take your time," Lt. Desmond told her.

She nodded.

"Do you need for me to show you how to do it?" Sergeant Swain asked.

"No, thanks, I know how to use a computer."

Dom couldn't help noticing the way both Desmond and Swain watched Lausanne with more than professional interest. Apparently both men found her attractive. But that was no big surprise. They weren't blind. What red-blooded male wouldn't get a hard-on just looking at her?

Lausanne clicked through photograph after photograph, pausing several times, looking closely, then moving on to the next picture. After she'd gone through the first twenty or so, she stopped and checked her watch. The classy little Rolex had probably been purchased with Audrey Perkins's credit card. For some crazy reason that bothered Dom. He hated like hell that Lausanne had passed herself off as another woman, spent that woman's money so easily and had kept all the bounty from her numerous shopping sprees.

"I've got five more minutes until my break is over," Lausanne told them.

"Keep looking," Desmond said. "You're more than halfway through the file."

Lausanne nodded and began again.

"I'll check with your boss and see if you can have a little extra time." Dom nudged her. She slid out of the booth, to allow him room to get out.

Before sliding back into the booth, she said, "Don't say anything to Effie that might get me fired. I need this job."

Dom nodded, then went looking for Effie Pounders, the fast-food restaurant's manager. When he explained to the lady that Lausanne was helping the police with a missing person's case, Mrs. Pounders was more than accommodating.

When Dom slid back into the booth beside Lausanne, she looked up from her search. "Mrs. Pounders said to take all the time you need."

Lausanne immediately returned to the task at hand.

"How many does that make?" Dom asked.

"I'm on number thirty-one," she replied, then clicked Next to move on to number thirty-two.

She studied that photograph longer than any of the others, but didn't say anything. Dom inched closer and looked at the laptop screen. The photo, like all the others, was not studio quality, just a snapshot probably taken by a personnel staffer solely for the employees's files. The woman was sort of pretty, with small features, big blue eyes and short dark hair. Dom didn't see any resemblance between this woman and either Audrey Perkins or Lausanne.

"Does she look familiar?" Dom asked.

"Have you found her?" Desmond tapped the edge of the screen.

"Give me another minute, will you? I'm trying to picture her with red hair."

Seconds seemed like minutes and minutes like hours as Lausanne studied the photo. Finally, she turned to Dom and said, "This is the woman who hired me to impersonate Audrey Perkins. Only her hair was longer and it was red."

Dom grasped the edge of the laptop and pivoted the screen so that Desmond and Swain could see the woman's face. "Who is she?" he asked.

Swain turned the laptop around and pulled it over to him, then hit one of the keys and typed in something. "Her name is Megan Reynolds."

"Does that name mean anything to you, Ms. Raney?" Desmond asked.

She shook her head. "No. Nothing."

"Ms. Reynolds is Audrey Perkins's personal assistant," Swain said. "She's worked for Ms. Perkins for five years and was hired personally by Ms. Perkins herself."

Desmond tapped one of the computer keys, then catty-cornered the laptop around so that they all could see the screen. He pointed to the photo that popped up. "You're sure, no doubt in your mind, that this is the woman who posed as Audrey Perkins and paid you to impersonate her?"

"I'm sure," Lausanne said. "No doubts whatsoever."

"Then our next step is to question Ms. Reynolds and

see what she has to say for herself." Desmond closed the laptop and handed it over to Swain.

"What if she denies everything?" Lausanne asked.

"Then, Ms. Raney, we have a problem," Desmond told her.

CHAPTER FIFTEEN

WHEN LAUSANNE'S SHIFT at the Chicken Coop ended at ten that night, Dom was outside in his car waiting for her. He had spent the past few hours on the phone, first with Lieutenant Desmond, then with his client and finally with his boss. At least with those three, there wasn't any conflict of interest, not the way it could turn out to be with Lausanne. He'd been up-front with Sawyer about the situation.

"I have a personal interest in Lausanne Raney," Dom had admitted. "I'm fairly certain she's telling the truth about her involvement with Audrey Perkins and if it comes down to choosing sides..."

"Do you want me to relieve you of duty?" Sawyer had asked. "Deke Bronson's new assignment got delayed until next month, so he's free right now. I could send him in to replace you."

"Let's hold off on that for the time being. Okay?"

"All right, as long as you can assure me that Edward Bedell will have no reason to complain about Dundee's services."

"Right. I understand."

Lausanne said goodbye to the other waitresses as they headed for their vehicles. When she saw Dom, she waved at him and smiled. He liked seeing her smile. His guess was that she hadn't done much smiling in her life, at least not since her mother died when she was twelve. If it were up to him, she'd have something to smile about every day.

Lausanne opened the car door and slid inside, then faced Dom. "Any word from Lieutenant Desmond about Megan Reynolds?"

"Yeah. It seems Ms. Reynolds is on a two-week vacation. By some odd coincidence she left Chattanooga the day after you did."

"Then she should be back by now, right?"

"Wrong. It seems she called and asked for more time off and since she had two more weeks vacation time accumulated, the extra time was approved."

"Where is she? Have the police been able to contact her? They have to talk to her and find out why she pretended to be Audrey Perkins, why she hired me to—"

Dom tapped her lips to quiet her. "Slow down, honey. One question at a time."

"Where is she?"

"As far as we know she was in Mexico and then moved on, but we're not sure where. From cell phone records that the police obtained, it seems when she called Bedell, Inc. to ask for an extension on her vacation, she was in Rio de Janeiro."

"Has Lieutenant Desmond contacted her? Has he spoken to her?"

"He's tried, but she's not answering her cell phone."

"Damn, I knew something like this would happen, that I'd still come off looking guilty."

Dom reached over and buckled her seat belt. He lifted his hand and caressed her cheek. "We'll find her. I promise."

Her gaze met his. "*We* as in the police or Dundee's?"

"Both. Dundee's always works with local authorities whenever possible."

"What did Mr. Bedell say about my identifying Ms. Reynolds as the woman who hired me?"

"He seemed surprised and very concerned," Dom said. "He can't figure out why Audrey would have gotten her assistant to pose as her and then hire you to gallivant around the southeast impersonating her."

"Does he believe I'm telling the truth?"

"I'm not sure. I think he's confused, just like the police are. This is a puzzle no one seems to be able to figure out." Dom hooked himself into his seat belt, then started the engine and checked his rearview mirror.

"You have to find Megan Reynolds," Lausanne said.

Dom backed out of the parking slot and drove onto the main road. "Dundee's is busy right now investigating Ms. Reynolds and trying to track her down. My boss has already authorized me to fly out of the country when she's found, if it's necessary. Regardless of how the police handle this investigation, I plan to speak to Ms. Reynolds personally."

"Is that what Mr. Bedell wants you to do?"

"He wants me to do whatever is necessary to find his daughter."

"Dead or alive?"

"Yeah, dead or alive."

Silence. What else was there to say? They both knew that if Audrey Perkins came up dead, Lausanne would head the list of suspects.

USING A PHONY NAME and address, Megan Reynolds had purchased a new cell phone and paid for her minutes up front. When she'd phoned Bedell, Inc. and requested an extension on her vacation, she hadn't given a thought to the fact the call could be traced. She'd gotten her ass chewed out about that earlier today and ordered to toss that phone in the trash and hop the next jet out of Rio de Janeiro. And that's just what she intended to do. She certainly didn't want to answer any questions about Audrey Perkins, those posed by the police or by the private PI that the Bedell family had hired.

If she was going to have to live outside the U.S. from now on, perhaps even assume a new identity, she was going to need more money. And if she didn't get what she asked for, then she'd just blow the whistle and expose all the lies.

Megan punched in the private number and waited as it connected. She hadn't installed phone numbers or information of any kind in the new cell phone, just in case she had to dispose of it, too.

"Hello."

"It's Megan."

"Did you do as I instructed?"

"I did. I have a new cell phone. Want the number?"

"Yes."

She recited the number, then said, "I'm at the airport. I bought a ticket to Buenos Aires."

"Good. Stay there until I contact you."

"Look, I didn't agree to stay away from the U.S. indefinitely. If you want me to keep under the radar, I'm going to need more money."

"You were paid handsomely for your services."

"Not handsomely enough."

"How much more do you want?"

"Double what you paid me."

Silence.

"It's your choice," Megan said. "Either cough up more money or I come back to Chattanooga and tell the police everything I know."

"I can't wire you the money or overnight you a check. Either could be traced."

"Hey, I don't care. That's your problem. You figure out a way to get me what I'm asking for in forty-eight hours or I'll hop a plane home and go straight to the police and spill the beans."

"I'll see what I can do."

"And one other thing—I'm going to write myself up a little insurance policy, just in case you're thinking about bumping me off."

"That won't be necessary."

Megan laughed. "You forget, I know just how dangerous you can be."

"What are you planning?"

"I thought I'd write Lausanne Raney a letter, describing in detail why I hired her to impersonate Audrey Perkins and tell her who was behind the master plan. I figure I can find me a lawyer in Buenos Aires who'll mail the letter if anything happens to me."

"You'll get your money. Once that's done, I don't ever want to hear from you again. Is that understood?"

"If I get what I want, I'll give you what you want. My silence."

She flipped her cell phone closed, left the secluded corner near the wall of windows facing the runway and glanced around at the other passengers waiting for the flight to Buenos Aires. From here on out, she'd have to play it smart or her life wouldn't be worth a damn.

DOM TOOK LAUSANNE'S KEY from her and opened the door to her apartment. She was dead on her feet from a long and exhausting shift. This wasn't the first time she'd worked as a waitress, but after getting the fabulous job as a receptionist at Bedell, Inc., she had hoped she'd never have to be a waitress ever again. So much for hopes and dreams.

Dom flipped on the overhead light switch, bathing the room with a hundred watt glow. After closing and locking the door, he said, "Why don't you take a nice hot bath and relax."

She sighed. "That sounds like a good idea, but I'm not sure I have enough energy to—"

Dom swooped her off the floor and up into his arms. Startled, Lausanne yelped, then flung her arm around his neck and held on while he carried her through her bedroom and into the small, outdated bathroom. He closed the commode lid and set her down very gently, then knelt in front of her. After removing her sweater, he undid the buttons on her blouse.

She grasped his hand. "What are you doing?"

"Helping you undress." He grinned.

"I think I can manage to undress myself."

"Suit yourself." He winked at her, then got up and went over to the tub. "You get undressed and I'll draw your bath water."

What? He was going to draw her bath water? Surely she was dreaming. This couldn't be real.

He turned on both faucets and the water flowed into the tub. He glanced back at her and asked, "Do you have any bubble bath?"

She shook her head.

He surveyed her from head to toe. "You aren't undressing."

"And I'm not going to until you leave the bathroom."

"Modest, are we?"

"Yes, we are."

He chuckled. "Where do you keep the extra towels? You'll need one for your hair."

"In the bedroom, top drawer in the dresser."

"Get undressed, I'll hand you the towels and I promise not to peek."

After he left the bathroom, partially closing the door, Lausanne removed her blouse and slacks and folded them neatly. She tried to get two wears out of her uniform and usually could if she didn't drop any food on herself during her shift.

"Here you go," Dom said.

She glanced at the doorway and saw his big hand extended around the door, an extra towel dangling from his fingers. Reaching out, she grabbed the towel, then shoved on the door. He moved out of the way, but not before he caught a quick glimpse of her in her underwear. He let out a long, loud whistle.

Lausanne's cheeks flushed and heat suffused her body. She slammed the door in his face. "You promised not to peek."

"I tried not to, but I just couldn't help myself. After all, I'm just a man and you, honey, are one gorgeous woman."

Smiling to herself, Lausanne tossed a washcloth into the tub and laid the towels on the back of the commode.

Dom thought she was gorgeous. She supposed she'd always been pretty, even as a little girl. Her mother had always told her she was, but had reminded her that "pretty is as pretty does." She'd gone through a plump stage that began at ten and she'd finally outgrown it around age fourteen, but not before her stepmother had done everything in her power to ruin Lausanne's self-confidence. Renee had been horribly jealous of Lausanne and the memory of Lausanne's mother. She had despised her husband's deceased wife and his only child with a hatred that bordered on madness.

Then later on, when Lausanne met Brad, he'd told her she was too skinny, her boobs not big enough and her freckles were ugly. But those unflattering comments had been made after he'd taken her virginity and gotten her pregnant.

Suffering from really low self-esteem, years later she'd hooked up with Clay, who'd actually told her she was pretty. *Pretty and dumb,* he'd said. *Just the way I like my women.* He hadn't been too far wrong about the dumb part, but in retrospect, Lausanne realized she hadn't been so much dumb as naive.

When the tub filled halfway to the rim, she turned off the faucets, striped off her underwear and stepped into the warm water. Sliding down so that her head rested on the back of the tub, she submerged herself in the liquid blanket and sighed. It wouldn't take much for her to fall asleep in here. Usually she just jumped in the shower every morning to save time, so a tub bath seemed like a real luxury.

Oh, how easily a person could become accustomed to luxury. For the ten days she had impersonated Audrey Perkins, Lausanne had wallowed in the kind of luxury most people only dream of; but that dream had ended all too soon for her and apparently would cost her dearly. Try not to think about it, at least for tonight. What's done is done.

Lausanne allowed herself several minutes to savor the warmth, the comfort, the sweet solitude. Then she removed the bar of soap from the holder, lathered the wash cloth and washed her face. Next she shampooed and conditioned her hair with the expensive products she'd purchased at a trendy little spa in Palm Beach. Now, she wished she'd bought other items, bubble bath, scented powder and body wash. But each hotel where she'd stayed had provided gift baskets filled with all that stuff because she'd rented only deluxe suites when she'd traveled as Audrey Perkins.

If only she'd had sense enough to have turned down that woman's offer to impersonate her boss's elder daughter. She'd told herself at the time that the deal was too good to be true, that there had to be a catch. But she'd allowed that fifty thousand dollars—in cash—to blind her to the obvious. There are no free rides in this life. There's always a price to be paid. How many times did she have to learn that bitter lesson before it took?

For one night, couldn't she just forget the past and all her stupid mistakes? Couldn't she pretend it was possible to wipe the slate clean and start all over again? If only she could go back and change things. But where would she start? Even if she could go back, she didn't have the power to prevent her mother from dying or stop her father from marrying a crazy woman.

Brad and Clay were two huge mistakes that she wouldn't make again. Not even if it meant never being pregnant, never giving birth? Out there somewhere was a ten-year-old little girl, loved and adored, the center of her parents' universe. And Lausanne had given that little girl life. Would she, if she could, erase her daughter's very existence?

No. No, she wouldn't.

But you don't know that she's loved and adored, that she is the center of her parents' universe.

That's why the fifty thousand that Audrey had offered her—no, not Audrey, Megan Reynolds—was so important. That money could enable her to search and find her child, to make certain her daughter had the life she deserved. Once Lausanne knew her baby girl was well and happy and secure, she could move forward with her own life.

But she couldn't do anything—neither search for her child nor move on with her life—until the mystery surrounding Audrey Perkins's disappearance was solved.

Lausanne finished bathing quickly, got out, dried off and yanked her silk robe from the hook on the back of the door. After putting on the robe, she towel-dried her hair, then fingered through it to untangle the curls.

Her stomach growled, reminding her that she hadn't eaten since lunch today and then she'd been too preoccupied with other things to eat more than a few bites. All she had in the fridge were a couple of microwave dinners, milk, mayo, mustard and fat-free bologna.

Tightening the robe's silk belt, she braced herself to face a second night alone in her apartment with Dom. How long would she be able to resist temptation? Every time he looked at her, she went weak in the knees. When he smiled at her, butterflies danced in her belly. And when he touched her, she melted.

Her bedroom was semi-dark, only a single bedside lamp emitted a forty-watt glimmer. As she neared the open door leading into the living room, she noticed the lights had been turned off out there. What was going on? What was Dom up to? Why had he turned off all the lights? The minute she emerged from her bedroom, she gasped.

In the center of the dark room, atop the coffee table,

half a dozen fat candles flickered brightly, casting a mellow radiance over the area. Two plates filled with food and two glasses of wine graced either side of the coffee table. A single peach rose in a bud vase between the plates blushed prettily in the candlelight.

Dom Shea stood by the sofa and held out his hand to her. "Dinner is served."

"How…? When…? This is such a surprise."

"A pleasant surprise, I hope," he said.

"How did you manage all this?" she asked.

"I bought the wine, the glasses, the food and the rose before I picked you up from work. Everything was in the back seat."

Tears threatened to choke her. She would not cry. She didn't dare. It had been such a long time since she'd cried that she was afraid if she started, she wouldn't be able to stop.

He wiggled his fingers at her. She smiled and walked toward him. He took her hand and eased her down on the floor atop one of the two pillows he'd taken from her bed. Once she was seated, he maneuvered his big body down onto the floor atop the other pillow, then crossed his legs and got comfortable.

"It's nothing fancy," Dom said. "Just gourmet sandwiches from the deli, along with potato salad and chocolate pecan pie for dessert."

"Do you have any idea how hungry I am?" Realizing her comment could be taken more than one way, she glanced over at him.

He winked at her. "No matter how hungry you are,

you're going to have to eat first. I went to a lot of trouble to put together this romantic meal."

It took her a full second to realize he was teasing her. She laughed. He laughed. Then he lifted his glass.

"A toast," he said.

She picked up her glass.

"Here's to us. To being one step closer in getting to know each other better and learning to completely trust each other."

"Here's to us," Lausanne said. Oh, Dom, is there really an *us?*

"THERE HAS BEEN A CHANGE in plans," the familiar voice over the telephone said.

"I'm listening."

"This is your last chance. If you screw this up—"

"No more screws up. I promise. You want the Raney woman dead, she's as good as dead right now." He was blowing hot air and he knew it. He'd tried to make contact with the guy known only as Corbin, but it wasn't all that easy getting in touch with one of the top assassins in the country.

"There's a more important job that needs to be done first."

For the past fifteen years, he'd been in the business of procuring services of every kind for those rich enough to pay the price for whatever they wanted. He had worked for this particular person on various other occasions and had never disappointed the client. However, he was relatively new to providing hired assassins because, at heart, he wasn't a ruthless man, just a greedy one.

"You name it, you got it," he said. "For the right price, of course."

"Do you have any contacts in South America? In Argentina to be specific?"

"Uh…yeah, sure." He didn't, but for enough money, he'd find somebody either there or willing to go there."

"I'll overnight you the particulars. The person I want eliminated, her name, description and location. The cost is unimportant. Whatever it takes."

"This is another woman, someone besides Ms. Raney?"

"That's correct. Megan Reynolds. I want her taken care of first. Then once she's eliminated, I'll want Lausanne Raney taken out immediately afterward, so put two men on the job."

"Right. Two men on the job. Can do."

"If my wishes aren't followed to the letter this time, your services will no longer be required in the future. Not for anything. Do I make myself clear?"

"Perfectly clear." He had to arrange for two women to die, otherwise the gravy train he'd been riding for years, thanks to the business this special client sent his way, was going to derail.

CHAPTER SIXTEEN

LAUSANNE SIGHED SLEEPILY. She'd had a warm bath, a nice supper and lots of special attention from a wonderful man. So now the questions was: would Dom expect payment for having gone out of his way to take such good care of her? Still sitting on the floor, she leaned her back against the sofa and closed her eyes.

"I guess I'm disappointing you by practically falling asleep after dessert." Lausanne glanced at him and smiled, an unspoken question foremost on her mind.

Dom returned her smile. "You're tired, honey. You should go to bed."

Here it comes, she thought. *Let's hop in the sack. It's payback time.*

Before she could form a reply, he stood, came around the end of the coffee table and swooped her up into his arms.

"This is becoming a habit with you," she said.

With her firmly in his arms, he reached down and picked up her pillow. "Are you complaining?"

She didn't reply.

He carried her into the bedroom and set her at the foot

of the bed, then pulled down the spread, blanket and sheet and laid her pillow at the head. While she watched him, waiting for him to make his move, he maneuvered her around on the bed, then pulled the covers over her. When she didn't lie down, he gently pressed her shoulders until she eased back and rested her head against the pillow. Looking up at him, she waited for him to climb into the bed with her. But he didn't. Instead he leaned down and kissed her forehead.

"Sleep tight, honey."

He turned around and headed for the door.

"Dom?"

"Huh?" He glanced back at her.

"Thank you."

"You're welcome."

He closed the door, leaving the bedroom in semidarkness. Lausanne reached over and turned off the bedside lamp, then curled up into a fetal ball and closed her eyes.

Domingo Shea puzzled her. She'd never known a man like him. She knew he wanted her, yet he wasn't pushing her to have sex, wasn't rushing her to do something she wasn't ready to do. Was he too good to be true or what? Usually the answer to that question was yes, but she was beginning to think Dom really was a good guy and if she gave herself to him, he wouldn't turn out to be just another terrible mistake.

Yawning, Lausanne snuggled into the warmth of her bed. Her feet and legs ached from her having been up and running at the restaurant for so many hours.

Her mind drifted off into that half-awake/half-asleep

state. Dom filled her thoughts, banishing everything else. Sweet thoughts. No worries, no past, no future. Just Dom.

She was naked. Her body tingled with sexual need. Her nipples peaked, her feminine core throbbed.

"I want you. Oh, Dom, please make love to me."

He hovered over her, big, naked and aroused. She circled his hard sex and stroked him, loving the feel of him in her hand and the growling sound he made deep in his throat. Without saying a word, he put his knee between her legs and parted her thighs, then lifted her hips. As her femininity clenched and unclenched in preparation, gushing with moisture, he lowered his head and suckled at first one breast and then the other. She keened softly, wild with need.

"Now, Dom. Please, now."

He thrust into her with one hard, deep lunge. She cried out with pleasure. He rode her hard, in a frenzy of need, and within minutes they came together, unraveling with fulfillment.

Perspiring and breathless, Lausanne clung to Dom, loving him, needing him, wanting to hold on to him forever.

But as suddenly as he had appeared, he disappeared. He was no longer in her arms. He was gone. Evaporated like a morning mist.

"Dom," she screamed. "Dom, where are you?"

Lausanne woke with a start, her heart hammering like mad.

Oh, God, it was a dream. Just a dream. But it had seemed so real.

Her body had come apart when she'd climaxed. She could still feel the aftershocks of her orgasm tingling through her.

The bedroom door flew open. Wearing only his black briefs, Dom Shea stood in the shadows. "Honey, are you all right? I heard you crying my name, calling for me."

She crawled out of bed, and unsteady on her feet, rushed toward him. He met her halfway and when she threw herself into his arms, he encompassed her in a protective embrace.

"I had a bad dream," she said, then corrected herself. "No, it wasn't a bad dream. It was a wonderful dream. It just ended all wrong."

Holding her close, he stroked her back and nuzzled her cheek. "Everything's okay. You're safe. I'm here."

Yes, her heart cried. *I am safe, safe in your arms. As long as I have you, nothing can hurt me.*

"Want to tell me about the dream?" he asked.

Lord, no, she couldn't tell him that she'd had an erotic dream about him and had actually climaxed. What would he think of her? *Damn it, Lausanne, it's not as if he thinks you're pure as the driven snow.*

She shook her head. "No, it's not important."

"Are you sure? Sometimes it helps to talk about a frightening dream and dispel its power."

She clung to him, appreciating the comfort she found in his strong arms, loving the feel of his muscular chest beneath her fingertips. Suddenly she realized that Dom was practically naked and so was she. She still wore only her loosely belted silk robe, which was now gaping from mid-thigh to calf-length hem, separated just enough to reveal the inner curve of her breasts. If Dom was wearing only his briefs, that meant he had already stripped off and bedded down for another night on her sofa.

"What time is it?" She lifted her head from his chest.

"I'm not sure." He glanced at the digital lighted clock on her bedside table. "It's two-fifteen."

"Oh. I thought I'd just fallen asleep. I had no idea I'd been sleeping for nearly two hours." She looked directly at him. "I'm sorry I woke you."

He caressed her shoulders, then wrapped his hands around her upper arms. "Can I get you something? A glass of water? Some decaf cola?"

Keeping her gaze connected with his, she shook her head.

"Want me to sing you a lullaby or tell you a bedtime story?"

She laughed. "You're so sweet, Dom. So absolutely, wonderfully sweet." She laid her hand flat in the middle of his chest, her palm partially resting over his heart. "Are you for real or did I just dream you up?"

His eyes darkened from deep brown to inky black as he stared at her, his heartbeat quickening and his pulse racing. When she became aware of the tension in his hard body, she felt an irresistible urge to tell him everything.

"Your dream, it was about me, wasn't it? About us?" he asked, his voice whisper soft.

"Yes." That single word came out on a hushed sigh.

He yanked her to him, then lowered his head. With

his lips almost touching hers, he whispered, "Were we making love?"

Her bones melted. Her blood ran hot.

"Do you want to make that dream come true?" he asked.

"Yes," she whispered and accepted that whatever happened, it had been her choice. Whatever the outcome, she couldn't blame Dom.

CARA WAS GLAD that Grayson had decided to stay here at the family home on Lookout Mountain, at least until Audrey had been found. She had hoped that their living under the same roof would give her the opportunity to see more of him, but so far, that hadn't been the case. She saw him at breakfast and at dinner, but he spent his days at Bedell, Inc. headquarters and his evenings alone in Audrey's old room upstairs.

She so desperately wanted to reach out to him, to comfort him, to make him forget Audrey.

As Cara passed by her father's study on her way to the kitchen for a cup of herbal tea, he caught a glimpse of her and called out her name.

"Cara?"

She paused outside the door and glanced at him. "Yes, Daddy?"

"Come in here and talk to me," Edward said.

She moved to just inside the study, but didn't approach him where he sat in his favorite old leather chair in front of the fireplace. "Yes, sir, what do you want to talk to me about?"

"About Audrey." His gaze connected with Cara's and she noticed that he'd been crying. Again. Odd, to see him cry. In her entire life, she'd seldom seen him shed a tear. But then again, he'd never been afraid that his precious Audrey might be as dead as her lover was.

"What about Audrey?"

"Come in and sit with me."

"It's late, Daddy, nearly two-thirty, and I was just on my way to the kitchen for some herbal tea."

"Damn it, girl, sit down. Can't you spare your father a few minutes of your time?"

"Yes, sir. Of course."

When she walked over to her father, intending to take the chair opposite him, he reached up, grabbed her hand and pulled her down so that they were face to face. Instantly, she smelled liquor on his breath and realized he was probably soused.

"You look like me, you know. Shame. Your mother wasn't a bad looking girl. And Audrey's mother was—"

Cara jerked away from him. He stared up at her through bloodshot eyes.

"Poor Cara, the ugly duckling," Edward said. "You've always been jealous of her, haven't you?"

"Why are we discussing this now?"

"Why not now?"

"Because my being jealous of Audrey is old news. Because my sister is missing and possibly dead. Because you're drunk and—"

"I don't want her to be dead. I can't bear the thought

of…" Tears streamed down his cheeks. "You don't hate her enough to wish her dead, do you?"

Cara gasped silently. Her eyes widened in shock and disgust. "You old son of a bitch! You think I had something to do with her disappearance, don't you? Do you honestly think I could kill my own sister?"

"You hated Audrey."

"I hate you, too, but I haven't killed you, have I?"

Cara turned and hurried toward the door.

"Cara, wait!"

She paused, her heart racing, tears threatening to choke her.

"I'm sorry. I know I haven't been a very good father to you. I wish I could go back and change things. If I could, I would."

She sucked in a deep breath. Did he truly mean what he'd said or was it the liquor talking? Maybe the liquor and a great deal of self-pity. Had he suddenly realized that if Audrey was dead, Cara was the only child he had left?

"I wish things had been different," she told him, her back to him.

"Is it too late for us?"

"Probably. I—I don't know."

She rushed out of his study and back down the hall, forgetting about the herbal tea she'd wanted. With tears partially clouding her vision, she raced up the stairs.

As she walked by Audrey's old room, she didn't notice the door stood wide open or realize that Gray had seen her. Not until he called her name.

"Cara, are you all right?"

She stopped immediately, swallowed several times and swatted the trickle of tears from beneath her eyes. Forcing a half-smile to her lips, she turned and faced him.

"Hello, Gray. What are you doing still awake at this hour? It's after two o'clock."

"You're awake." He surveyed her sleeping attire, purple knit pajamas covered with a lavender robe made from a fuzzy chenille fabric. "What are you doing roaming around in you PJ's?"

"I couldn't sleep," she admitted. "I have so many things on my mind. I thought some herbal tea might help me rest."

He visually scanned her hands for a mug or a cup and noted she held neither. "Did you change your mind about the tea?"

"I got sidetracked."

When he lifted an inquisitive eyebrow, she said, "Daddy's in his den and he's quite drunk. He was seeking solace from the daughter he's never loved or wanted."

"Oh, Cara, my dear girl." Grayson walked out into the hall. "Edward loves you, in his own way." Grayson took Cara's hand.

"Daddy loves Audrey and no one else, just as you do." Cara gazed into Grayson's eyes, hoping beyond hope that she would see something more than pity.

"Unlike Edward, I hate Audrey as much as I love her." Grayson hung his head, as if he was ashamed of having spoken such a terrible truth.

She squeezed his hand. "It's all right. Really. I feel the same way. You can't help loving Audrey. She's incredible in so many ways. But she's selfish and self-centered and can say the most hurtful things and do such god awful things to the people who love her."

"Come with me." Grayson tugged on Cara's hand.

She followed him into her sister's rooms, the bedroom and sitting room of a young woman who had not lived in this house in years, not since she and Gray moved out when they purchased a penthouse loft in downtown Chattanooga. That had been six years ago.

Cara glanced around the sitting room, all white and gold, with delicate peach and cream accents. Even after she married, Audrey had kept her room totally feminine, as if Gray didn't matter in the least.

"It's a lovely room, isn't it?" Gray gazed tenderly at the watercolor portrait of Audrey at age sixteen that hung over the white marble mantle.

"She's not coming back." When Cara saw the stricken look on Gray's face, she wished she could retract what she'd just said.

"You think she's dead, don't you?"

Cara nodded, then rushed to Gray and grasped his upper arms. "Whether she's dead or not, she won't come back to you. Not this time. You have to face the fact that your marriage is over."

"I've known my marriage was over for a long time." Gray laughed morosely. "I simply have a difficult time letting go."

"You deserve to be loved and cherished," she told him. "I—I want that for you."

"Do you, sweet Cara?"

She released him, but didn't move, simply stood there looking at him. *Can't you see that I love you, that I worship the ground you walk on, that I'd do anything for you?*

"Yes," she told him. "I can't bear to think of you being so miserable."

He smiled. "Audrey once told me, several years ago, that you were in love with me. I told her she was wrong, that you were just a dear, sweet girl who was quite fond of her brother-in-law."

Cara felt as if she'd been sucker punched. Swaying slightly, she reached out into thin air, searching for something to grab hold of to steady herself.

Gray slipped his arm around her. She gasped when he touched her.

"Was I wrong?" Gray asked. "Was Audrey right?"

Cara looked him square in the eyes. "I love you. I've loved you for as long as I can remember. Long before you married Audrey."

She wasn't sure what she'd expected him to say or do, but laugh in her face was not the reaction she'd wanted. Feeling as if he'd slapped her, she glowered at him.

"Oh, sweet Cara, don't be angry with me. You have no idea how wonderful it feels to laugh."

"It's not wonderful for me. I hurts to have you laugh in my face when I just confessed that I love you."

He caressed her cheek. She shuddered.

"I'm not laughing at you. I'm laughing because it's so obvious that I'm the biggest fool on earth. I never looked past Audrey to see someone far more worthy of my love, someone who actually could have loved me in return."

"Gray?"

He brushed his lips over hers. Cara lost her breath.

"You should go to bed now," he told her. "If you stay, we might do something we would both regret in the morning."

No, her heart cried. *I wouldn't regret anything we did. Let me stay. Let me show you how much I love you.*

"Don't send me away," she pleaded.

"It's too soon. I'm not going to take advantage of the way you feel about me. I'm a wreck of a man. I'm emotionally spent after years with Audrey. You're the one who deserves far better."

"I want you, Gray. Only you."

"Please, dearest Cara, go now. We both need time to think about this, to see if there is any way we can be together in the future."

Cara's heart swelled with hope. He hadn't said he loved her, but she could wait. She could wait forever if it meant Gray would finally be hers.

"I'll see you in the morning," she told him.

He lifted her hand to his lips, kissed it and told her, "Until then."

Quivering inside, Cara left Audrey's sitting room and walked down the hall to her own bedroom, not once looking back, but she knew that Gray stood in the doorway and watched her.

He's mine now. You're gone, Audrey, and you can't come back and hurt him.

BAIN DESMOND HATED being awakened from a sound sleep, but it happened all too often due to the fact he was a police detective. As he pulled his '59 red and white Corvette up behind the two Black and Whites parked behind the county coroner's vehicle, he glanced at the time showing on the dash clock. Two-thirty. This was a hell of a way to start a new day.

When he emerged from his car, he saw Mike Swain's truck parked on the other side of the road. His partner had been the one who'd called him.

"The river just spit out another body," Mike had told him. "Seems this one's a woman. Her body washed ashore near the Walnut Street Bridge. Jeff Webster gave me a call. Said he figured we might be interested…just in case."

If this woman turned out to be Audrey Perkins, Bain would be very interested; and he could cross one theory off his list—that Audrey had killed Bobby Jack Cash. If she was dead, her husband would become the number one suspect, especially considering the fact his wife had left him for her lover. Second on Bain's list would be Lausanne Raney. It was possible she had killed both Audrey and Bobby Jack. But in all honesty, he didn't think she'd murdered anybody. Of course he was going on gut instincts, that and the fact he didn't want Lausanne to be guilty. Huffing, Bain wondered if his instincts might be off center the way Domingo Shea's were. And for the same reason. They both found Ms. Raney very attractive.

Making his way toward Bain, Mike threw up his

hand. "Over here. If you want to take a look at her before they haul her off, you'd better hurry."

Bain spoke to the uniformed officers, Jeff Webster and Riley Davidson, the first ones to arrive after being called to the scene. It seemed a homeless man who had been looking for a place to huddle for the night, had stumbled over the bloated body. When Bain approached the county medical examiner, Dr. Jimmy Stevens, zipped up the body bag and motioned for his assistants to take the bag to the van.

"Mind if I take a look?" Bain asked.

"Suit yourself, but there's no need. Your partner told me what y'all wanted to know."

"So?"

"So, until we get a positive ID and I perform an autopsy, I can't tell you for certain who she is or how she died. But I'd say there's a good possibility that our lady of the river is the Perkins woman. She's Caucasian, about five-four, redheaded and there's a diamond the size of Rhode Island on her ring finger."

"Thanks, Jimmy. I'll want a preliminary report as soon as possible."

"You'll get it."

When Jimmy followed his assistants toward the van, Bain followed him.

"I'll get in touch with Grayson Perkins and ask him to come by first thing in the morning and see if he can ID the body."

"He's the husband, right?"

Bain nodded. "Any educated guesses on how she died?"

"The lady has a bullet hole almost directly over her heart, so I'd say the odds are that was the cause of death," Jimmy told him. "I'll know more after the autopsy."

"There was only one bullet hole?"

"One was all it would take, if it was a direct hit to the heart."

"If our victim is Audrey Perkins, then whoever killed her shot her once as opposed to shooting Bobby Jack Cash repeatedly. Of course that's assuming the same person murdered both of them. If so, it tells me the killer probably had a reason to hate Cash a great deal more than Audrey."

"The husband would have hated Cash more, right?"

"Possibly. But we're counting chicks before they hatch," Bain said. "No use wasting time on theories until we've got more facts and a positive ID."

But Bain knew, the way a seasoned detective knew a lot of things, that the redheaded lady of the river was Audrey Perkins. Shot once. In the heart.

CHAPTER SEVENTEEN

DOM TOUCHED LAUSANNE with gentle reverence, as if she were made of spun glass. His tenderness was her undoing. He was such a big, vitally alive man, so masculine in every way. She had expected him to be ruthless and demanding, but he was the exact opposite. He undid the tie-belt loosely holding her silk robe together, then slowly spread the robe apart to reveal what lay beneath, Lausanne's hot, damp body.

Gazing at her, he drew in a deep breath, then smiled. "You're perfect."

Perfect? He thought she was perfect? No other man had ever looked at her body without finding fault. Her breasts weren't big enough, her hips were too wide, her legs too short, the smattering of freckles on her shoulders and chest were ugly.

He eased the robe from her shoulders, over her arms and off. It dropped to her feet and formed a shimmering circle. Her nipples peaked. Pulsing need throbbed between her thighs. Standing before Dom, naked and aroused, Lausanne suddenly felt uncertain. She lifted her gaze to meet his and gasped when she saw the raw need in his eyes.

As if sensing her nervousness, Dom yanked his briefs down and off, then kicked them aside. "Better?" he asked.

She simply stared at him.

"We're on equal footing now. Both of us naked and totally exposed."

"Yes, thank you."

Chuckling softly under his breath, Dom stood there and allowed her to survey him from head to toe. She began her inspection with his handsome face, but quickly traveled south, over his broad shoulders and wide, bronze chest. Every inch of him was muscular and fit, his skin like subtle leather, but scars marred the perfection. One gashed across his left side, a long, thick scar she assumed had been created by a knife. Another one on his chest was more round in shape, probably caused by a bullet. Was his line of work that dangerous or were those marks military battle scars?

Her gaze continued its downward path, then paused at the tip of his impressive erection, just shy of reaching his navel.

Lausanne swallowed hard. He was big and hard and ready.

"Touch me, if you want to," he told her.

Her body clenched and unclenched, sending a sensual message to her brain.

Without replying to his comment, she reached out and ran her fingertips over his chest, pausing to circle each tiny nipple. He sucked in a deep breath. She moved on, across his belly, and then she slid her hands over his slim hips before reaching behind him to cup his firm buttocks.

His sex twitched against her belly.

She shivered, her hunger intensifying with each passing moment.

"May I touch you?" His voice was a husky groan.

"Yes…please."

The moment he placed both of his hands on either side of her lower back and pressed her intimately against him, she knew she was lost. She'd never wanted a man the way she wanted Dom, had never experienced such raw passion.

He lowered his head until his lips touched hers. "I'll protect you."

Her mind already fuzzy with desire, she didn't immediately comprehend what he'd meant; and when he kissed her, all coherent thought left her mind. She arched her arms up and slipped them around his neck, pushing her tingling breasts against his hard chest. Their kiss deepened, transforming from sweetness to utter abandon when he probed inside her mouth, his movements mimicking the ultimate joining.

When she didn't think she'd be able to stand another minute, when her legs went limp and her knees buckled, Dom ended the kiss. With her eyes closed and her pulse racing, she swayed unsteadily. He wrapped his arm around her and led her to her bed.

After easing her down on the edge of the bed, he ran his hands over her arms from shoulders to wrists. "I'll be right back, honey. I need to get a condom out of my duffle bag."

"Oh." She nodded.

Even that brief separation was too long. She needed him so badly, wanted him inside her now, loving her and allowing her to love him in return.

Lovemaking isn't love, Lausanne reminded herself. *No matter what Dom says, this will be sex.*

He returned to the bedroom quickly, but she noted that he hadn't put on the condom. When he came to her, he paused, dropped a couple of foil wrappers on the bedside table and then went down on his knees in front of her.

What was he doing?

He bowed his head, lifted her left foot and kissed each toe, then went to the other foot. "You have such cute little feet, honey."

Lausanne sighed.

He circled her ankles, then eased his hands up her calves. Before parting her knees, he kissed the top of each thigh. "Your skin is like silk. I love touching you."

Lausanne breathed deeply.

He skimmed his open palms up her outer thighs, all the while kissing a path from her knees, up her inner thighs to the apex of her body. When his warm breath fanned the curls covering her feminine mound, she gripped the edge of the bed with both hands.

"Dom?"

"Just relax and enjoy."

He parted her thighs enough to insert himself between them, then kissed her mound. Lausanne quivered. He nuzzled her, then slipped his tongue between her damp feminine folds.

Lausanne whimpered.

He pressed his tongue against her core and then flicked repeatedly.

Lausanne moaned with pleasure.

Dom moved his hands upward, over her hips and waist, then around to cover both breasts; and all the while his talented tongue stroked harder and harder, faster and faster.

Lausanne gripped Dom's head, her fingers playing with his short hair, her body tightening, tensing, preparing for release.

When he rubbed her nipples with his thumbs, she cried out with a pleasure/pain that shot through her entire body. While his mouth worked relentlessly to bring her to fulfillment, his fingers tormented her tight, aching nipples.

The world inside and out of her exploded like sky-rockets. She shook and shivered, her release so intense that she felt as if she were shattering into pieces.

"Oh, Dom…Dom…" She huffed his name repeatedly.

While her climax radiated through her, Dom lifted his head and reached up, entangling his fingers in her hair. He pulled her head down to his and kissed her, her musky scent strong on his lips. Then he pushed her backward onto the bed before reaching for one of the foil packs.

While the orgasmic aftershocks rippled through her body, she watched, fascinated by everything about him, while he slipped the condom over his penis.

When he came down over her, she opened her arms to hold him and her legs to accept him into her body.

"You have no idea how much I want you," he said.

"Yes, I do," she told him. "If you want me half as much as I want you."

He entered her with one quick, deep lunge, filling her completely, stretching her to accommodate his size. She clutched his shoulders. He cupped her buttocks and lifted her up as he eased in and out of her, the rhythm slow and steady.

"This is so good," she said.

He increased the tempo of his thrusts, then slowed again.

Groaning against her mouth, he kissed her, then maneuvered them so that his mouth came down over one breast. He toyed with her breasts, alternating back and forth between licking and sucking.

She felt the tension building and couldn't believe she could be this aroused again so quickly, but if anything, this time she was spiraling out of control even faster.

She bucked up against him, meeting each thrust with equal intensity. When he buried his face against her neck, she whimpered, "I'm going to come again. Oh, Dom…"

"That's it, honey. Come for me. Let me feel you falling to pieces a second time."

He hammered into her relentlessly until she cried out when another orgasm hit, spiraling her completely out of control, beyond anything she'd ever experienced.

She clung to him, savoring each millisecond of earth-shattering pleasure.

And then when Dom came, she felt it in every fiber

of her body. He groaned and shook, then collapsed on top of her.

They lay there, their bodies sticky with perspiration, their breathing labored. Totally spent and feeling as if she'd died and gone to heaven, Lausanne kissed Dom's naked shoulder.

"Wow!"

He chuckled. "Yeah, honey. Wow!"

He lifted himself up and off her, then rolled them over so that she lay in his arms, cuddled and cosseted, safe and secure.

"We're good together," he said, as he caressed her flat belly.

"Almost too good. It was unbelievable."

"There's no such thing as too good, but I'm curious to find out if it'll be as good the next time."

"The next time?"

"Not right away." He nuzzled her neck. "But give me an hour or two and—"

"And if it is as good the next time?" Would he stay with her, love her, never hurt or disappoint her? No, of course he couldn't make such a promise. Sex, no matter how great, was still just sex. Love was a horse of a different color. He might consider what they did lovemaking, but that didn't mean he loved her or that he ever would.

"If the next time is as good, I'm not going to be able to keep my hands off you," he said. "You'll have to get a whip and chair to stop me from attacking you every chance I get."

"And what if I don't want to stop you?"

"Then I'd say we're going to be spending an awful lot of time in this bed."

He hugged her close and kissed her. For a few brief, blissful moments, Lausanne forgot to worry about the future.

BAIN DESMOND ESCORTED Grayson Perkins and his sister-in-law, Cara Bedell, to the morgue. He had telephoned Mr. Perkins an hour ago and explained the situation, then had volunteered to pick him up, but Perkins had said he'd drive himself. However, as it turned out, he had told his sister-in-law about Desmond's call and she had insisted on not only accompanying him to the medical examiner's, but on driving.

"I should warn you, Mr. Perkins, that this body appears to have been in the river for quite some time and it's bloated and some decomposition has begun," Bain said, recalling that several weeks after death, the hair, skin and nails become loose and the skin begins to burst open, revealing muscle and fat. And a body that had been in the water almost always showed signs of being fish food. Literally. "There will be an autopsy and Dr. Stevens will use forensic odontology and DNA testing to determine the victim's identity—"

"The victim?" Cara asked.

"Yes, ma'am. The lady from the river is considered a murder victim," Bain replied.

With a stricken look on his face, Grayson asked, "If she can be identified by other means, then why must Cara and I—"

"You don't have to ID the body," Bain said. "You might not be able to, but it would help us if you could."

Perkins turned white as a sheet. If Bain didn't consider Perkins the chief suspect if the body turned out to be Audrey, he would actually feel sorry for the man.

"I'll do it," Cara said. "There's no reason for Gray to go through such a horrible ordeal."

Sighing heavily, his shoulders slumping with relief, Grayson grabbed his sister-in-law's hand. "Thank you, Cara. I—I don't think I could have… If it is Audrey, I couldn't bear to see her that way."

Cara squeezed Grayson's hand. "I know. I know. It'll be all right. I'll do it."

Bain watched the interplay between those two and wondered about their relationship. It was obvious Cara cared deeply for her brother-in-law, that she felt protective where he was concerned. And one other thing was quite evident—Cara Bedell had balls; Grayson Perkins didn't.

"Before I take you back and introduce you to Dr. Stevens, there's something I'd like to show you," Bain said. "The victim was wearing a diamond ring. If you could ID it as belonging to your sister—"

"Audrey wore a large diamond on her ring finger," Cara said. "No wedding band. No other rings."

Bain motioned to Jimmy Stevens's assistant. "Could we see the ring that was removed from the victim?"

The young woman nodded, went into another room and came back with a small envelope. She opened the envelope, then put on a pair of protective gloves before dumping the envelope's contents into the palm of her hand.

Cara and Grayson looked at the diamond ring. Grayson gasped and clutched his throat. Cara clenched her teeth.

"Well?" Bain asked.

"It's Audrey's ring," Cara said. "Or one just like it."

"You're certain?" Bain looked from Cara to Grayson.

"There's an inscription inside the band," Grayson said. "The words 'forever and always' will be there, if it's Audrey's ring."

Jimmy's assistant picked up the ring, took it to her work station and slipped the band under a magnifying glass. After giving the ring a thorough inspection, she lifted her head and looked directly at Bain.

"The inscription is there."

"Oh, God, no!" Grayson crumpled, doubling at the waist as he wept. "My precious Audrey."

Not being an emotional person, Bain had some difficulty watching another man fall apart in front of him. He cleared his throat. Cara cast him a withering glare, then wrapped her arms around Grayson and led him over to a nearby chair.

"Hush, hush." She stroked the guy's back, petting and consoling him as if he were a child. "We knew this was possible, that Audrey might be dead. It's a terrible thing, but we will deal with it."

Grayson lifted his head and stared at Cara through his tears. "Go see her." He clutched Cara's hand. "It's possible someone stole Audrey's ring. Maybe that Raney woman... She could have sold it and someone else bought it and..." He wept again, almost uncontrollably.

Lowering her voice to a mere whisper, Cara comforted him, soothing him in a maternal fashion. When he calmed enough so that he was merely sobbing softly, Cara stood up straight and turned to Bain. "I'm ready."

"Are you sure, Ms. Bedell?"

She nodded.

DOM WRAPPED HIS ARMS around Lausanne as they stood together in the shower, the warm spray pelting them as he kissed her shoulder. She sighed dreamily, turned in his arms and kissed him. They had made love for the third time, here in the shower, only minutes ago and yet they couldn't break apart, couldn't end this delicious closeness. She had never felt so exuberantly alive.

"What shift are you working today?" He cupped her damp buttocks.

"I'm working a short shift today. I go in at eleven and I get off at three. Just four hours to cover the lunch crowd." She draped her arms around his neck, stood on tiptoe and kissed him.

"I wish we could stay here all day, not go out, not see another living soul."

"I have day after tomorrow off." She kissed him again.

"Let's stock up on supplies and lock ourselves away."

"I like that idea." Smiling up at him, she asked, "What supplies will we need?"

"Oh, a couple of bottles of wine, maybe some cheese

and eggs and bread, a couple of romantic CDs and a big box of condoms."

She giggled. "Planning a lovemaking marathon, Mr. Shea?"

He slipped his hand between her thighs and petted her intimately. "Yes, ma'am, that's exactly what I'm planning. Are you interested?"

"Very."

When he leaned down to kiss her, he stopped midway.

"What's wrong?" she asked.

"I think that's my phone."

"Let it ring."

"I'm expecting a call from Dundee headquarters," he told her. "Daisy was supposed to get back to me this morning with a report on Megan Reynolds."

Dom shoved back the shower curtain halfway and stepped out onto the floor mat, then turned to Lausanne. "I'll be right back."

"No, I'll get out. You go answer your phone."

After he wrapped a towel around his waist and disappeared into the bedroom, she turned off the faucets and got out of the shower. She wrapped a towel around her head, then using a second towel, dried her body. Her breasts were tender, so she took special care when drying them. Dom had been gentle, but he had given her breasts thorough attention each time they'd made love. Her nipples turned pebble hard just at the thought of his mouth on her body.

As she moved the towel between her legs, she realized she was slightly sore from their vigorous lovemaking. When the terrycloth touched her nub, she quivered with renewed arousal.

Lausanne walked into the bedroom and found it empty, so she retrieved her silk robe from the floor and put it on, then went into the living room. Dom was in the kitchenette preparing the coffeemaker while he held his cell phone sandwiched between his ear and his shoulder.

"Yeah, thanks, Daisy," Dom said. "If you can get me an exact location, like the name of a hotel, that would be great." He glanced at Lausanne, smiled and blew her a kiss.

She smiled tenderly at him.

"Be sure to tell Sawyer that I need to speak to him as soon as possible and go ahead and line up Deke Bronson." He flipped on the coffeemaker. "Talk to you later." He closed his cell phone and laid it on the bar.

"Was it an important call, the one you'd been expecting?" Lausanne asked.

He nodded. "The information Dundee's dug up about Megan Reynolds is very interesting and it's something the Chattanooga PD will find out about soon, if they don't already know."

"Did Dundee's locate Ms. Reynolds?"

Dom came over to Lausanne and stood directly in front of her. "Yeah. She's in Buenos Aires and I'm going to fly down there and talk to her."

"When?"

"Today. Dundee's should be able to arrange things so I can leave by late this evening or early tonight."

"I want to go with you."

"Honey, you can't do that. First of all, it could be dangerous. And secondly, you've been ordered not to leave town."

Lausanne nodded, reluctantly agreeing. "You're right, but…"

He tilted her chin with his forefinger, encouraging her to look right at him, which she did. "Dundee's was able to check on Ms. Reynolds's finances. Up until recently, she lived rather modestly, had a small savings account and pretty much lived paycheck to paycheck. Then the very day she hired you to impersonate Audrey Perkins, Megan deposited a million dollars in a money market account."

Lausanne let out a loud whistle. "Where did she get— Oh, my God, somebody paid her to hire me? Is that what you think? If that's the case, then I was badly gypped. I only got fifty grand."

Dom grinned. "I'm glad to see that you haven't lost your sense of humor."

"I realize that this is no laughing matter, but you don't know how relieved I am. If she was paid a million bucks, then she either killed somebody or she's covering up a huge secret, right?"

"Right," Dom said. "My guess is that Megan Reynolds knows what happened to Audrey and probably knows who killed Bobby Jack."

"Then we have to talk to her, somehow make her tell the truth and get me off the hook." Lausanne clutched Dom's arms.

"Not we," he reminded her. "Me. I'm going to Buenos Aires alone."

She nodded. "Of course." That's what he thought. This was her life on the line. She'd been set up. But by God, she wasn't going to take the fall for someone else. When Dom flew off to South America, she intended to either be on the plane with him or on the very next one out of Chattanooga.

Another woman might stay put and wait for Dom, the trained professional, to handle the situation. But not Lausanne. Even though she trusted Dom, past experience had taught her not to put her fate entirely in someone else's hands. She wanted to be there when Dom found Megan Reynolds. She needed to confront the woman who had set her up and learn the truth first hand.

CHAPTER EIGHTEEN

LIEUTENANT BAIN DESMOND swirled around in his swivel desk chair and chewed on the side of a pencil while he thought things over, trying to put all the information into the proper perspective. He figured official identification of the lady of the river was a mere formality. The corpse had been wearing Audrey Perkins's ten-carat diamond ring, the flashy engagement ring that Desmond would bet his last dime her old man had paid for and not her husband. And when Cara Bedell had taken a look at the body, she'd tensed like a dog raising its hackles and preparing to fight.

"I can't be sure, but she looks like Audrey," Cara had said as she studied the woman's barely recognizable face. "Is there a tiny serpent tattoo on the inside of her left wrist?"

Jimmy Stevens had looked at Bain and said, "There is a small tattoo of a snake on the underside of her left wrist."

Tears had welled up in Cara's eyes. "Then that—" she gazed at the corpse "—is my sister."

Over the years, Bain had learned to steel his nerves and not become emotionally involved with the victims or their families. A police detective, like a doctor or a nurse, faced tragedy on a regular basis. If you didn't harden your heart to some degree, you'd be worthless to yourself and those you were sworn to help.

"Jimmy should know something from the dental records by the end of the day," Mike Swain said, bringing Bain back to the present moment. "But there's not much doubt our lady of the river is Audrey Perkins, is there?"

Bain removed the pencil from his mouth. "Hmm...no, not much doubt at all."

"So, what's your take on this? Who killed her and did the same person kill Bobby Jack Cash?"

Bain tapped the pencil on his desk. "In a jealous rage, Grayson Perkins killed his wife and her lover, then dumped their bodies into the river. He then paid his wife's personal assistant to help him cover up the crime by having her hire Lausanne Raney to impersonate Audrey, thus making everyone assume she was still alive."

"Hey, we now know that the Reynolds woman was paid a million bucks, which makes me wonder if she witnessed the murder. That's a hefty sum of money to pay out otherwise."

"Despite the fact that Megan Reynolds deposited a million in a money market account in a Nashville bank, we can't get a name of the person who transferred the money because it was wired from a Swiss account. If we knew for sure who paid her, we'd have our killer."

"I thought you said Grayson Perkins killed—"

"That's one theory," Bain said. "There are others."

"Like Lausanne Raney killed them both."

Bain tossed the pencil atop the stack of files in the corner of his desk. "Lausanne Raney was in cahoots with Bobby Jack, but something went wrong and she killed him and Audrey, then stole Audrey's identity and fifty grand in cash, then left Tennessee."

"If that's what happened, then she's pretty stupid," Mike said. "She left a trail a blind man could have followed."

"Yeah, I know, that's why I tend to believe her story. That and the fact Megan Reynolds is somehow involved and if Lausanne Raney killed Audrey and Bobby Jack, how does Megan fit in?"

"Then we're back to the husband."

"Or possibly the half-sister or even the stepmother. There was no love lost between the stepmother and Audrey," Bain reminded him. "Maybe she was jealous because of Audrey's affair with Bobby Jack or maybe she wanted to eliminate one of the heirs to her husband's fortune and Bobby Jack just got in the way."

"One less heir would mean a great deal more money. I hear the old man is worth billions, so it's possible wife number four might have bumped off the elder daughter. But do you really think the sister could have killed Audrey?"

"Remember what Audrey's friends and acquaintances have told us," Bain said. "Cara Bedell is in love with her brother-in-law and hated the way her sister treated him."

"So, the sister killed her to get her out of the way. But why kill Bobby Jack? And if she did kill him, why shoot him more than once?"

Bain shrugged. "Maybe he tried to stop Cara and she shot him. Or maybe Cara didn't know he was anywhere around and when she realized he'd seen her kill Audrey, she had to kill him, and shot him several times to make sure he was dead."

"It makes sense."

"All my theories make sense," Bain said. "The problem is, which one is correct, if any of them are?"

CARA AND GRAYSON didn't go back to the Bedell mansion on Lookout Mountain, nor did Gray go to work. Instead, they went to Gray's penthouse apartment, the one he'd shared with Audrey for the past six years. Neither of them could bear facing her father, not yet. She had no idea how he would react when he learned that Audrey was dead. Would he fly into a rage? Would he fall apart completely? Perhaps both. The two things she knew for sure was that Edward Bedell would never be the same again and that he would move heaven and earth to see that Audrey's killer was punished.

"Would you like something to drink?" Gray asked. "I know it's not quite noon, but I—I—" his voice cracked. "I think I need a little brandy."

"Why don't you sit down and let me get it for you? I know where the liquor cabinet is."

"You're too good to me."

Grayson appeared weary and defeated as he sat down in the white leather chair facing the floor to ceiling row of windows that overlooked downtown. He leaned his head against the back of the chair and closed his eyes. Poor darling. He'd sobbed intermediately on the drive all the way from the medical examiner's office on Amnicola Highway to his downtown penthouse.

Audrey had loved this huge open apartment the moment she saw it and insisted that their father buy it for Gray and her. She'd hired an interior designer from New York to come to Chattanooga and decorate the five spacious rooms and three baths. Then once she had everything just the way she'd wanted it, Audrey had thrown herself a lavish housewarming party, inviting the who's who of local society. Although Audrey wasn't well liked, no one dared refuse her invitation out of fear they might offend Edward Bedell.

Cara busied herself fixing Gray's drink. Despite needing the soothing influence of liquor, she decided against joining him. After all, she couldn't properly look after Gray if she didn't keep a clear head.

"Here you go." She handed him the brandy snifter. "Just relax and try to rest, if you can. I know you didn't get much sleep last night."

Gray took the snifter with one hand and reached out for her with the other. Grasping her wrist, he looked up at her. "You won't leave me, will you? I can't bear being alone. Not now." Tears filled his eyes.

She eased her wrist from his grip. "I'm not going anywhere. Not until you're feeling better." She walked over and sat down on the hot pink and white striped sofa. "But eventually, I'll have to talk to Daddy. I can't put off telling him for more than a few hours."

"Edward won't be able to handle this. He loved Audrey as much as I did."

Cara shook her head. "No, he loved her more than you did. He loved her more than life itself."

Gray took a sip of brandy, then sighed. "Who do you think killed her?"

"I don't know. Maybe she and Bobby Jack shot each other." That would have been justice, but the odds of that were slim to none. "Or maybe that Raney woman killed them both."

"There will be so much to do." Gray sipped on the brandy. "Once the police release Audrey's body…" He closed his eyes and shook his head sadly. "We'll have to arrange for a funeral. I want no expense spared. A white casket, don't you think? Lined with pink satin. Hot pink satin. We should special order something unique. Audrey hated being like everyone else. She always wanted to be different. Orchids and roses for the blanket. And we should have a violinist play her favorite songs."

"Yes, of course."

Gray lifted his half empty glass in the air. "Would you be a dear and top this off?"

Cara hurried to do his bidding, all the while wishing he would stop talking, stop rambling on and on about Audrey's funeral. He had become far too calm and seemed engrossed in the details of how best to handle the funeral arrangements.

"White limousines, don't you think?" He glanced at Cara. "We may have to order them from Nashville, if we can't find enough locally."

She handed him the refilled brandy snifter. "There will be plenty of time to make arrangements. It could be a week or more before the police department releases Audrey's body."

He downed a large gulp of brandy, then coughed several times before asking, "How did she look?"

"What?"

"How did Audrey look when you saw her? I imagined her as beautiful in death as in life. Was she? Was she still beautiful?"

Dear God, had he lost his mind? Yes, he had. He was insane with grief. She couldn't tell him the truth, that the corpse she'd seen at the medical examiner's had born little resemblance to Audrey, little resemblance to any living human.

"She didn't look like herself," Cara finally managed to say. "But you have to remember that the Audrey we knew—and loved—is gone. She left that body weeks ago."

Gray chugged down more brandy. "You won't desert me, will you, Cara? You won't let Edward toss me out like yesterday's trash."

"You're talking nonsense. Daddy is very fond of you. He handpicked you to be Audrey's husband, didn't he?"

"And I made a lousy husband. I disappointed her. I made her terribly unhappy. So unhappy that she had to go to other men to find satisfaction." Gray finished off the brandy, then held out the snifter to her. "Just a little more, please."

"Are you sure? Haven't you had enough?"

"Just a little more...to deaden the pain."

Reluctantly, she did as he requested.

"Why don't you lie down for a while," Cara said. "I'll turn down the covers for you."

"Not in her bedroom," he said, his speech slightly slurred. "I use the guest room. We haven't shared a bedroom in years."

"Oh, Gray, what did she do to you?"

He snapped his head up and glared at Cara. "It was me...all my fault. I was a lousy lover. She told me so. She laughed at me."

Cara knelt in front of him and put her arms around him. "Audrey could be cruel, but I had no idea that she could be that evil."

"Pretty boy with a pretty little dick. That's what she'd say. You've got a tiny little dick and you don't know what to do with it." Tears poured down Gray's cheeks.

Cara held him tighter and tighter, wanting more than anything to ease his pain, to erase her sister's unforgivable taunting. "She didn't deserve you. You were always too good for her."

He lifted his left hand and patted the back of Cara's head. "I should have fallen in love with you. Everything would have been so different."

The snifter slipped from his right hand and hit the white carpet, spreading a dark stain over the luxurious pile.

"Oh, Lord, look what I've done," Gray gasped. "Audrey will be so angry. She can't abide stains on this carpet."

Gray shoved Cara aside, almost toppling her to the floor. She managed to right herself and stand, then turned to find Gray on his hands and knees, rubbing his palm over the stain, spreading it, making it bigger and bigger.

"But Audrey's not here to scold me, is she?" He looked up at Cara. "She's dead. Dead…dead…"

"Yes, my poor darling, she's dead. She can't ever hurt you again."

LAUSANNE HAD BROUGHT HOME grilled chicken sandwiches and potato salad from the Chicken Coop for their supper. When they finished, Dom cleared the bar where they'd eaten, then poured them each a cup of coffee and removed a couple of doughnuts from the fresh six-pack he'd purchased at the grocery store before picking Lausanne up from work a little after three.

He laid her dessert on a clean napkin in front of her. "Cream filled. Those are your favorite, right?"

She smiled at him. "I mentioned that fact only once and you actually remembered."

"I remember everything you tell me, honey. Everything about what you like and dislike, what you want and—"

"You're buttering me up for a reason," she said. "And I think I know why."

He shrugged.

"You're still planning on leaving for Buenos Aires tonight, aren't you? And you're not going to let me tag along." Lausanne glared at him.

"Sawyer is flying Deke Bronson into Chattanooga on the Dundee tonight. He'll take over the Bedell case and work with the Chattanooga PD on behalf of the Bedell family in the continuing search for Audrey. I'll take the jet to South America, find Megan Reynolds and bring her back to the U.S. if it all possible. If not, I'll get the necessary information from her. And while I'm gone, Deke will keep an eye on you." Dom winked at her. "Just not too close an eye."

Lausanne frowned. "I wish there was a way I could go with you."

"I know, but we've already gone over the reasons why that's not possible." Dom grasped her shoulders. "Besides, I shouldn't be gone more than a few days, if I don't have a problem locating Ms. Reynolds. In the meantime, you stay put, behave yourself and don't give Deke any trouble."

When she didn't respond, just gazed at him with those hypnotic green eyes, he shook her gently. "Promise me."

"I promise that I'll behave myself."

Dom eyed her skeptically, his gut telling him that she had given in far too easily. But before he could question her sincerity, a loud, repetitive knocking on the door announced they had a visitor.

"You stay put." Dom tapped her playfully on the nose.

"Are we expecting somebody?"

"Not that I know of."

Dom crossed the room, peered through the viewfinder and groaned. "It's Lieutenant Desmond."

Lausanne slid off the bar stool as Dom opened the door.

"Evening folks," Desmond said. "May I come in?"

"Depends," Dom said.

"Let him in." Lausanne came up behind Dom.

Desmond stepped over the threshold and Dom closed the door behind him.

"Please come in and sit down, Lieutenant," Lausanne said.

"Thank you, ma'am."

As soon as Desmond took the single chair in the room, Lausanne sat on the sofa across from him. Dom stood behind her, one hand resting protectively on her shoulder.

"Why are you here?" Dom asked.

"To give you the news in person," Desmond replied. "It'll be front-page headlines in tomorrow's *Chattanooga Times Free Press* and I thought you deserved to hear about it from me instead of reading about it in the newspaper."

Lausanne held her breath.

Dom narrowed his gaze. "Tell us."

"Audrey Perkins's body washed ashore near the Walnut Street Bridge," Desmond said. "She was identified by her sister earlier today and dental records verify that the woman is Audrey Perkins. Ballistics reports say the bullet came from the same gun that killed Bobby Jack Cash."

Lausanne went chalk white. Dom tightened his grip on her shoulder.

"She's dead?" Lausanne's voice quivered. "Audrey Perkins is dead."

"I now have a double homicide on my hands," Desmond said. "And unfortunately, Ms. Raney, you remain a person of interest to the Chattanooga police department."

CHAPTER NINETEEN

DEKE BRONSON WORE a tan overcoat, unbuttoned and hanging loosely on his large, muscular frame. He entered Lausanne's apartment with the deadly quiet of a warrior sneaking up on his enemy, a feat she found quite remarkable considering the man's size. He was taller than Dom by a couple of inches and outweighed him by at least twenty pounds. His face was lean, his cheekbones high, his jaw square, and there was a hint of a cleft in his chin, but the day's growth of beard stubble concealed the depth of the indentation. Although dark-haired, with leather-tan skin, this man possessed none of Dom's remarkably handsome Hispanic features. He was neither good looking nor ugly, but he was over-poweringly masculine in a rough and rugged way.

"Come on in," Dom said. "I want you to meet Lausanne. I'll need you to keep an eye on her while I'm gone."

Deke glanced past Dom to where Lausanne stood in the kitchenette, a dish towel in her hand. "Ma'am." He nodded.

Lausanne offered him a hesitant smile.

"Daisy contacted me on the flight from Atlanta," Deke said. "I understand the assignment has changed, that Audrey Perkins has been found."

"Yeah, Mrs. Perkins's body washed ashore this morning, near a downtown pedestrian bridge," Dom replied. "You'll need to report to the Bedell family in the morning and tie up any loose ends. But even if they dismiss Dundee's now that Audrey has been found, I want you to remain in Chattanooga until I return from Buenos Aires."

Deke glanced at Lausanne again, this time allowing his gaze to linger on her for a long moment before focusing on Dom. "I'd planned to check into a hotel tonight, but if you prefer, I can stay here with Ms. Raney."

"That won't be necessary." Lausanne tossed the dish towel onto the kitchen counter and rounded the bar. "I mean there's no need for you stay tonight. I won't leave my apartment until I go to work in the morning. I promise. I'm not doing any dog walking now, so—"

"Pick her up for work in the morning at five-forty-five. She has to be there by six," Dom said. "Then pick her up tomorrow afternoon and bunk here every night while I'm gone."

Deke simply nodded.

Lausanne sensed that the two agents wanted to converse without an audience, so she took the hint and excused herself. "I have a few things to wash out by hand. I'll just go take care of that now." She looked right at Deke. "Nice to meet you, Mr. Bronson. Thank you for agreeing to keep watch over me for Dom."

"Yes, ma'am. My pleasure."

Lausanne hurried into her bedroom and closed the door. Pausing for several seconds, she listened, hoping she could hear Dom and Deke talking, but all she heard were the creaks and whines of an old apartment building. Scurrying about, she gathered up several pairs of silk panties and two lace bras, then headed for the bathroom. After drawing water in the sink and adding liquid soap, she dumped the garments into the suds and then dried her hands. She tiptoed into the bedroom, removed the phone book from the bedside table and picked up the portable phone. Knowing that she had to work quickly, before Dom finished his conversation with Deke Bronson and came looking for her, she crept back into the bathroom and shut the door.

After closing the commode lid, she sat down, placed the phone on the edge of the sink and laid the phone book in her lap. Flipping through the yellow pages, she searched and found what she was looking for rather quickly.

Dom had made it perfectly clear that he would not allow her to fly to Buenos Aires with him, but she had no intention of letting that stop her from going. Why couldn't Dom understand her need to talk to Megan Reynolds face to face, to find out directly from this woman why she'd hired Lausanne and either intentionally or inadvertently set her up for a possible murder rap.

Dom couldn't understand why she needed to be part of this, why she couldn't simply allow him to handle things. Hell, even she didn't fully understand why she felt this desperate need to personally confront Megan

Reynolds. Maybe it was simply a matter of not fully trusting anyone else. Once she was released from prison, she had promised herself that never again would she put her future in anyone else's hands, that she would take full responsibility for her life.

The operator put her through to the booking agent, who gave her the information she needed. Thinking fast, Lausanne booked her flight from Atlanta to Buenos Aires. Once Dom left, which was bound to be soon, she would call a cab and go by her bank where she'd use her ATM card to remove all the money she had in her checking account. Although she had one credit card in her own name and had used it to book her flight, she knew she might need some cash to convert to pesos when she got to Argentina.

Delta had a 10:25 p.m. flight leaving Atlanta tonight, but there were no direct flights in the evenings from Chattanooga to Atlanta. She'd need to rent a car, make the two hour plus drive and be at the Atlanta airport in time to make the flight to Sao Paulo, Brazil, the only stopover.

Lausanne opened the closet, stood on tiptoe and grabbed the edge of her carry-on bag. When it toppled from the shelf, it barely missed hitting her face, but slammed against her upper chest instead. Reeling backward, she struggled to steady herself as she latched on to the Louis Vuitton case. She'd travel light, several changes of underwear and socks, a couple of lightweight tops and a pair of pajamas. Before packing, she removed her passport from the satin pouch inside the case. Strange how things happen, she thought. She'd never had a passport, never dreamed she'd ever need one. But when she went to work at Bedell, Inc., she learned that one of the requirements for employment was having an up-to-date passport.

She put her passport in her purse, then packed quickly. Only moments after she slid the carry-on under her bed, Dom opened the door.

Acting as innocent as possible, Lausanne smiled warmly at him. "Is Mr. Bronson gone?"

"He just left."

"And you're going to leave now, aren't you?"

"Yeah."

"Let me go with you," she said, knowing he'd refuse her request yet again. But she also knew that if she didn't ask one more time, he'd wonder why.

"Honey, we've gone over this—"

"I know. I know. It's just I hate to be left out of the loop. After all, this is my life, my problem. I should be allowed to question Megan Reynolds myself."

Dom came toward her. She slid her foot across the carpet and kicked the edge of the Louis Vuitton case out of sight, hiding it completely beneath the bed.

He took her hands in his, pulled her to him and kissed her. With his face lowered to hers, his breath warm against her lips, he sighed. "I'll call you when I get there in the morning."

She nodded meekly, knowing she would be in flight when he called, winging her way to Argentina, only a few hours behind him.

"Deke filled me in on what to expect when I get there," Dom told her. "Dundee's has arranged for a man named Tito Gomez to do some digging for us. Dundee's has used him on several previous assignments. He has an excellent reputation for unearthing secrets."

"Do you think he can find out where Megan Reynolds is staying in Buenos Aires?" Lausanne asked.

"If she can be found, he'll find her. Apparently she's using an alias and that's the reason we've been unable to locate her using routine methods. Deke said that Señor Gomez has promised to locate Ms. Reynolds by noon tomorrow."

"He's very sure of himself, isn't he?"

Dom brought her hands to his lips, kissed them both, then gazed into her eyes. "Be a good girl while I'm gone and don't give Deke too much trouble."

"I promise I won't give Mr. Bronson any trouble." She wouldn't be a problem for Deke Bronson because she wouldn't be in Chattanooga.

When Dom wrapped his arms around her, they exchanged a passionate kiss that left Lausanne weak. He released her slowly, apparently as reluctant as she to let go.

"I'll be back as soon as I get some answers from Ms. Reynolds." Dom caressed Lausanne's cheek.

"Be careful, okay?"

He grinned. "I will. And you stay safe, honey."

"I'll try."

She walked with Dom into the living room, then when he lifted his duffle bag and headed for the door, she stood back and watched him. He paused in the doorway.

"Lock up as soon as I'm gone," he told her. "And don't open the door for anyone except Deke."

She nodded.

"Lausanne…"

"You'd better go."

"Yeah, I…uh… Just take care of yourself while I'm gone."

As soon as he shut the door, she locked it before rushing into her bedroom to find the phone book. After arranging for a rental car to pick her up, she dragged out a pair of jeans, a cotton knit sweater and a medium weight jacket. After dressing, she slipped on a pair of high dollar athletic shoes. Her attire was fashionable enough for travel. She'd easily fit into the crowd at the airports. Atlanta. Sao Paulo. Buenos Aires.

THE DUNDEE JET LANDED at the Ezeiza International Airport at 10:46 the following day. With the three-hour time difference, it was a little after seven back in Chattanooga. That meant Lausanne had been at work for over an hour and was probably right in the middle of serving the breakfast crowd at the Chicken Coop. Maybe he should wait until nine, when she'd be due a break, to contact her. But he had promised her he'd call as soon as he landed.

"Señor Shea," a small, well-dressed man in his late forties approached Dom on the tarmac, making Dom wonder if he was an airport employee.

"I'm Dom Shea."

The man greeted him warmly, with a wide smile and an extended hand. "*Hola.* I am Tito Gomez. I have arranged for you to go through customs *rapidamente,* without delay. And I have arranged for *remise,* car service. Come with me, *por favor.*"

Following Señor Gomez, Dom entered the terminal through a special entrance reserved for those traveling on private airplanes. Just as Gomez had told him, Dom passed through customs rapidly, his single carry-on not even checked.

"Tiene algo para declarar?" the custom's agent asked.

"No, no." Gomez shook his head.

"No tengo nada para declarar," Dom said.

"You speak Spanish *muy bien,*" Gomez said.

"My grandparents were from Mexico," Dom replied.

"Ah, *sí, sí.*" Gomez picked up Dom's black vinyl bag. "It is best we speak English. Many here understand the language, but all understand Spanish. Yes?"

Dom nodded. Yes, he understood. For their private conversations, fewer people would understand what they were saying if they spoke in English.

Gomez led Dom from the terminal to the waiting car, a black, late-model Japanese make, with leather seats and a sunroof. The driver took Dom's duffle bag, then opened the back door for his clients before depositing the bag in the trunk.

Once seated, Gomez turned to Dom. "We are thirty-five kilometers southwest of the city. We will talk now while we ride. I will explain what I know."

Dom checked his wristwatch. He needed to phone Lausanne soon and give her an update. She was probably concerned that he hadn't called her.

While Gomez talked, Dom removed his cell phone from the belt clip and groaned when he realized he had not turned his phone back on after the Dundee jet landed.

"There is a Señorita Mary Ray staying at the Alvear Palace Hotel," Gomez said. "I have seen the lady with my own eyes—" he tapped the edge of his temple next to his right eye "—and I look at the picture faxed to me and I look at this Mary Ray. If she is not Megan Reynolds, they are twins."

The minute Dom turned on his cell phone, he noticed he had four messages. Had Lausanne been trying to contact him? Uneasiness knotted his stomach muscles.

"Then you're saying you found Megan Reynolds, that we know where she is?" Dom asked.

"*Sí.*"

"I want to go straight to the hotel and see her immediately. I don't want her to have any advance warning. It needs to be a surprise visit. Do you understand?"

"*Sí,* yes, yes. But we must wait."

"Why?"

"We do not have her room number." When Dom glared at Gomez, the man shook his finger back and forth. "No, no problem. We will get the room number. Soon.

"I know a bellman who does not come to work until *mas tarde,* later in the day."

Dom nodded. "I need to make a phone call."

"*Sí.*"

When Dom checked his first message, the voice he heard was not the soft sweet voice of the woman he'd left safely behind in Chattanooga.

"Damn it, Shea, we have a problem. Call me as soon as you get this message," Deke Bronson had said.

"Is something wrong, Señor Shea?" Gomez looked at Dom, an expression of concern in his black eyes.

"I'm not sure," Dom replied, then listened to the second recorded message.

"Yeah, it's Bronson here. Your lady friend has flown the coop. She wasn't at her apartment when I arrived to take her to work this morning. I checked at the restaurant. No one had seen her or knows where she is."

Dom cursed under his breath.

"There is a problem?" Gomez asked.

"Yeah, but it's nothing you can fix."

Gomez stared at him, puzzlement on his face.

"This is my problem," Dom said. "I will have to take care of it."

Gomez nodded.

Dom listened to the third message.

"Lausanne booked a flight out of Atlanta last night. Her plane should land in Sao Paulo, Brazil at ten forty-five," Deke said. "If there are no delays, she'll be at Ezezia around two this afternoon."

"God damn it!" Dom clutched the small cellular phone until he heard a distinct crack, then realized what he was doing and loosened his hold.

Gomez simply stared at Dom, saying nothing.

Dom listened to the fourth and final message.

"Hi, Dom, it's Daisy. The Bedell assignment is officially closed. Mr. Bedell no longer requires Dundee's services. If you don't need Deke in Chattanooga..."

Dom deleted the message, then turned to Gomez. "Have the driver turn around. We're going back to the airport."

"*Qué?*"

"I need to go back to the airport and wait on a flight arriving from Sao Paulo at two o'clock," Dom explained, then dialed the preprogrammed Dundee headquarters number on his cell phone.

"Dundee Private Security and Investigation Agency," Daisy said.

"It's Dom."

"Are you in Buenos Aires?"

"I was on my way from the airport to downtown, along with Señor Gomez. We're turning around and heading back."

"You got my message."

"Bring Deke in," Dom said. "There's no reason for him to stay in Chattanooga."

"I know you're probably very upset with Ms. Raney—"

"You think!"

"I'm sorry, Dom. I know you're worried about her. But it's not as if she'll be all alone in a foreign country. She'll be with you."

"I may not be checking in for a while. Let Sawyer know that I'll be on my own time not only down here in Argentina, but when I return to the U.S., too. I'm taking a leave of absence. I'll book a commercial flight home."

"The Dundee jet is staying there in Buenos Aires for now," Daisy said. "I won't bring it back to Atlanta until it's needed. It's yours as long as it's free. And I'll contact you before I recall the plane."

"Thanks."

"Good luck down there."

Dom clipped his cell phone on the belt loop and turned to Señor Gomez. "This is only a minor delay. I have to pick up a friend at the airport, then we'll all go to the Alvear Palace Hotel together."

But not before he'd given Lausanne a piece of his mind.

LAUSANNE BOARDED the Aerolineas Argentinas afternoon flight for Aeropuerto Internacional Ministro Pistarini de Ezeiza. After finding her seat by the window and placing her carry-on in the overhead, she situated herself comfortably and fastened her safety belt. By now, Deke Bronson would have reported her absence to Dom and no doubt he was fighting mad. He'd know she had disregarded his orders about staying put in Chattanooga and would figure she was heading for Buenos Aires. And so she was. In less than three hours, the Boeing 737 would land and there wasn't a doubt in her mind that Dom would be there waiting for her. Yes, he would be upset, even angry with her. But she'd deal with him. She had to make him see that her taking a separate flight to South America was all his fault. If he'd simply agreed to take her along on the Dundee jet with him, then... It sounded perfectly logical to her, but what if Dom didn't see it that way?

She had promised him she would behave herself, but she hadn't promised not to follow him to Argentina.

Later, after the plane was in the air and the seat belt light went off, Lausanne leaned her head against the cushioned rest and closed her eyes. Had Dom's contact in Buenos Aires found Megan Reynolds? Would Dom have already had time to question the woman? She had no idea how much quicker Dom had made the long overnight trip from Chattanooga to Argentina than she had, but flying on a private jet had to have cut his air time by several hours. And her hour long layover in Brazil had added extra time to her journey.

It was possible that when she arrived in Buenos Aires, Dom would have all the answers, that when he met her at the airport, he might actually have Ms. Reynolds with him. If that were the case, they could all board the Dundee jet and fly home, back to Chattanooga, where Ms. Reynolds would tell the police who had paid her off and why.

If only it could be that simple. But in Lausanne's experience, nothing was ever that cut and dried. Even if Ms. Reynolds was still in Buenos Aires, it might take days or even weeks to find her, if then. And there was always the possibility that she would slip through their fingers and disappear off the face of the earth.

MEGAN KNEW she couldn't stay on in Buenos Aires indefinitely. But she had to wait until arrangements had been made for her to receive her final payment. Once she had another million deposited to her account, she would move on, perhaps to Hawaii, then to Australia.

Of course, she needed to put her funds in an international bank, either the Caymans or Switzerland. For the first few years, she'd need to keep moving from place to place, then eventually she'd settle somewhere, maybe the south of France. She'd heard it was beautiful there.

But she'd really hate leaving Buenos Aires, especially leaving this luxurious room here at the Alvear Palace Hotel. Although the exterior of the hotel was under renovation, the available interior rooms were elegant. Her room was decorated in Louis XVI style and featured personal butler service, which she absolutely adored. Having someone at her beck and call, using Hermès de Paris and being pampered in the luxurious spa gave Megan a preview of what her life was going to be like from now on.

She'd lived from paycheck to paycheck for years, before, during and after her marriage that had ended three years ago. Trey Colby had been a big mistake, one she had rectified by acquiring a divorce. Her employer, Audrey Perkins, had applauded her for having the guts to get rid of her deadbeat husband.

"I'd divorce Gray tomorrow, if I could," Audrey had said.

"Why can't you?" Megan had asked.

Audrey had laughed. "Because Daddy handpicked Gray for me and he wouldn't like it if I divorced the man he thinks is such a perfect son-in-law."

There had been times when she'd felt sorry for Audrey. But not often. Audrey hadn't made it easy for anyone to like her. She'd been a royal, first-class bitch.

A light rapping on the door snapped Megan out of her thoughts about her former boss. That would be Andres with the late lunch she'd ordered: *parrillada,* a salad and fried potatoes.

Megan opened the door to find a tall, slender man behind a serving cart. But the man was not her usual butler, Andres.

"Who are you?" she asked.

"Mi nombre es Julio," he replied.

"Your name is Julio?"

"Sí, Señorita Ray."

"Where is Andres?"

The man looked at her, puzzlement in his dark eyes. "You don't speak English do you? Well, never mind. Bring the cart on in and place my lunch on the table." Using hand movements, she indicated what she wanted him to do.

He pushed the cart inside, closed the door behind him and studied her hand signals. Once he had set the meal on the table, he pulled out her chair and smiled.

"Thank you," she said as she took her seat. *"Muchas gracias."*

He handed her the bill, which she signed and returned to him, then she reached for her *mate,* a traditional Argentinian drink similar in taste to tea.

Sensing that Julio was still standing directly behind her, Megan lowered her hand. Was he new at this job? Didn't he know his tip was included in the price of lunch? She'd have to make him understand somehow. But before she managed to turn around and dismiss him, he slipped a cord around her neck and tightened it quickly, making it impossible for her to speak. She clutched at the cord with clawing motions as she gasped for air.

CHAPTER TWENTY

WHEELING HER CARRY-ON behind her, Lausanne disembarked, went through customs and searched the crowded airport for Dom. She knew he'd be waiting for her, probably angry and upset that she'd disobeyed his orders. Not being able to speak Spanish, the snippets of overheard conversation all around her were nothing more than background noise. As she moved deeper into the hustle and bustle of the Ezeiza Airport and couldn't locate Dom, she started worrying. Just a little. What if he wasn't here? What if he wasn't going to meet her? Then she'd be alone in a foreign country. The prospect was daunting for a woman who'd never traveled outside the U.S., who actually hadn't traveled farther west than Texas or farther north than Kentucky.

He's here, she told herself. He wouldn't leave her to fend for herself. Dom cared about her. He'd never desert her. Would he?

She'd been wrong about guys in the past. What made her think she really knew Dom Shea?

A big hand came from behind and clamped down on

Lausanne's shoulder while another hand removed hers from the handle of her carry-on and took the case from her. Startled by the unexpected action, she gasped as she glared over her shoulder.

"Welcome to Buenos Aires, Ms. Raney," Dom said.

Breathing a deep sigh of relief, she turned to face him. Ready to throw her arms around him, she hesitated, noting the stern expression on his face.

"Hi," she said meekly.

He eyed her carry-on. "Is this all your luggage?"

"That's it."

He grasped her arm. "Let's go. I have a car waiting."

She hurried to keep in step with his fast, agitated pace. "Dom?"

He kept walking, acting as if he didn't hear her.

"Please, talk to me. Let me explain."

Silence.

He was really angry with her. No doubt about it.

"I had to come and talk to Megan Reynolds myself. Please, try to understand."

When he continued with the silent treatment, Lausanne halted, giving him two choices: either walk away and leave her or stop. He stopped.

"Let's not do this here," Dom told her. "Mr. Gomez, Dundee's contact in Buenos Aires, has found Ms. Reynolds. She's at the Alvear Palace Hotel, registered under the name Mary Ray. My guess is that she won't be in Argentina much longer, so we need to confront her as soon a possible."

Lausanne nodded. "Okay." She looked at Dom,

hoping he could see the plea for understanding and for-giveness in her eyes.

"Why couldn't you have just stayed in Chattanooga?"

She tried to smile but the effort failed miserably. "I'm sorry I couldn't do as you asked. I'm sorry I'm not the type of person who can sit back and let someone else fight her battles, take all the risks, do all the dirty work." When Dom didn't reply, simply stared at her, she rushed on. "Megan Reynolds is the person who put me in the dangerous position I'm in right now. I think I have a right to confront her, to demand some answers."

Dom groaned. "Now you listen to me and hear me good—when we confront Ms. Reynolds, you keep quiet and let me do all the talking." Lausanne opened her mouth to protest but Dom cut her off. "Trust me, honey. I know what I'm doing. I've had experience at this sort of thing. You haven't."

She hated admitting that he was right, but he was. What if she started shooting questions at Megan Reynolds and the woman clammed up and refused to talk? But did she trust Dom to handle things the right way, if there was a right way?

Think about it, Lausanne, she told herself. Dom showed up here at the airport just as she'd known he would. He hadn't let her down, hadn't deserted her. But could she trust him completely? After all, this was her life, her future, they were talking about, and in the past when she'd put her faith in a man, she'd wound up regretting it. *But Dom isn't Brad and he's not Clay. He's a far better man than either of them and you damn well know it.*

"All right," she said, taking a giant leap of faith. "I'll trust you to handle things with Megan Reynolds."

"Enough so that you'd wait for me in the hotel lobby? I'll leave Mr. Gomez with you and—"

"I'll keep quiet while you question her, but I'm going with you."

Dom huffed. "I was afraid you'd say that." He grasped her arm and herded her outside to the parking area where a dark sedan waited for them.

A small, debonair man, chatting casually with the driver, stood outside the late model car. When he saw them approaching, he turned, smiled and came forward to greet them.

"Tito Gomez, at your service, Señorita Raney." He bowed his head in a gentlemanly fashion. "Welcome to Buenos Aires."

"Thank you, Mr. Gomez. Or should I say *gracias*. I'm afraid I don't speak Spanish."

"It is not a problem, señorita," Gomez said. "I speak good English, no?"

"No, I mean yes." Lausanne laughed.

Dom growled. Her laughter died when her gaze met his.

The driver took her carry-on from Dom and deposited it in the trunk, then opened the back door. Dom nudged her into action. She slid into the back seat. Dom spoke to Señor Gomez in Spanish for a couple of seconds, then Gomez got in the front seat. Dom slipped into the back seat with Lausanne and the driver closed the door.

Once they were on their way, Lausanne tugged on Dom's jacket sleeve and whispered, "What were you and Mr. Gomez talking about? Was it something you didn't want me to hear?"

"I'm not keeping secrets from you," Dom said. "Gomez reverted to speaking in his native language since he knows I speak fluent Spanish. He was simply telling me that his source at the Alvear Palace phoned him while I was in the airport waiting for you. It seems we now know Ms. Reynolds's room number."

"Then we haven't missed her. She's still there, at the hotel." A rush of anxious anticipation swept through Lausanne. "She has to tell us who put her up to hiring me to impersonate Audrey. If we can find out who it was, then we'll have the name of the real killer."

"Maybe. Maybe not."

"What—?"

"Don't count on anything," Dom told her. "Whoever hired Ms. Reynolds paid her a million dollars. That kind of money can give a person amnesia. Just because we've tracked her down doesn't mean she's going to open up and tell us anything."

"What if she doesn't talk? What will we do then?"

"We'll tell her that someone has attacked you twice because of your involvement in Audrey's disappearance. If she realizes she could be next, that whoever paid her a million dollars has possibly already killed two people, she might be willing to tell us what we want to know."

"Do you think she was duped the way I was or did she know the person who hired her had killed Audrey and probably Bobby Jack, too?"

"You were paid fifty thousand. She was paid a million. Do the math, honey, and you'll have your answer."

SEÑOR GOMEZ ESCORTED THEM into the Alvear Palace Hotel through a back entrance and up to the fifth floor on the service elevator. Gomez's contact had met them before they boarded the elevator and told them he'd been unable to obtain a key to Mary Ray's room, but that the lady had eaten lunch in and had not left the hotel all day.

The hotel, although in the midst of extensive renovations, still exuded elegance and class, the way only a historic building such as this could. Dom had traveled the world, had been exposed to the best and the worst society had to offer. Nothing surprised him, little impressed him, not even this magnificent old hotel.

They got off the service elevator on the fifth floor and, following the numbered signs, Dom led them down the long, plush corridor.

"There's her room," Lausanne whispered as they rounded the corner leading into another hallway.

Dom paused. "I want you to stay here, out of sight, with Mr. Gomez. And keep quiet."

Lausanne frowned. He knew she was eager to confront Megan Reynolds, but since they had no idea what they might be walking into, he wanted to protect her as much as possible. What he really wanted was her back home in Chattanooga, but she was here now and he had to deal with reality.

"Remember, you're going to trust me," Dom said.

She nodded.

Dom headed down the hall. When he reached Ms. Reynolds's door, he glanced back at Lausanne and gave her a thumbs-up signal. She returned the gesture. He then locked gazes with Gomez, who squinted his eyes and nodded in a barely discernible manner. Knowing that Dundee's man in Buenos Aires understood that Dom was entrusting his woman to him, Dom knocked on Ms. Reynolds's door.

No response.

He knocked again.

Nothing.

He knocked louder, harder, and longer.

Silence.

Dom clutched the door handle, turned it and, to his surprise, the door swung slightly ajar. Would a woman deliberately leave her hotel door unlocked? Perhaps, if she was expecting someone. A friend? A lover?

A sinking feeling hit Dom in the belly, one of those something's-not-right-here reactions that warned a person they were heading straight into trouble.

He eased the door open enough to allow him entrance, then stepped over the threshold. Scanning the room, he noted the bed was unmade, clothing lay haphazardly over the bed, the chairs and the floor. Lamps lay overturned on the tables, one broken on the floor, and items were scattered over the thick, luxurious carpet. Someone had ransacked the place!

As his gaze moved across the large room, he saw a pair of feet sticking out from beneath an overturned armchair. More than half certain that those bare feet with red toenails belonged to Megan Reynolds, Dom made his way across the room. He stood over the tumbled chair and looked down at the woman lying trapped beneath it. Her eyes were open, and had begun to flatten. A shocked expression was etched on her features and her face and neck were dark red.

Dom eased down on his haunches to better examine the body. That's when he saw the corded rope hanging loosely around her neck. He quickly checked for a pulse. None. But her body was warm, which meant she hadn't been dead for very long. When he examined her neck, he found a straight line bruise.

Megan Reynolds had been strangled. Rigor mortis had not set in, which was another indication that she hadn't been dead for very long. Maybe an hour or two, possibly less.

Dom's mind registered several things all at once. Megan Reynolds, the woman they had hoped could lead them to a killer and clear Lausanne of suspicion, was dead. A wheeled cart clanked down the hallway and stopped abruptly, then a woman screamed. That terrified scream and the thunder of running feet flying down the corridor warned Dom he was not alone. When he stood and turned around, he saw a maid standing in the doorway, a horrified look on her face.

"Telefonee a la policia inmediatamente!" Dom called out to the maid.

She turned and ran screaming down the hall, leaving her cart in the doorway. By the time Dom reached the door, Lausanne was there, shoving the cart aside and

staring at him, her eyes filled with questions. Tito
Gomez came up behind her and glanced into the room.

"What happened?" Lausanne asked as she glanced
past Dom. "Oh my God!" When she tried to enter the
room, Dom grabbed her shoulders and shoved her back
into the hall.

"Is she Señorita Reynolds?" Gomez asked.

"Yeah, that's Megan Reynolds," Dom replied.

"Is she—" Lausanne gulped "—dead?"

"Yeah, honey, she's dead. And my guess is that it
happened within the past hour or so."

"Señor, we should leave now," Gomez said. "The
police will arrive soon and you do not want to be questioned."

Dom nodded, then grabbed Lausanne's arm and led her
hurriedly down the corridor, Gomez following quickly
behind them. A couple of people in the other rooms opened
their doors and peered outside, but no one said anything
or made an attempt to stop them from leaving.

Once inside the service elevator, Gomez said, "You
take Señorita Raney to the car and go to the airport. I
will remain here and contact you with an update."

"Yeah, thanks," Dom said.

"Why are we running?" Lausanne asked. "We didn't
do anything wrong."

"We know that, but it could take days, maybe weeks
to prove that to the local authorities," Dom told her.
"We're Americans. Foreigners. You have a police record
and I...well, I have a military record that the local police
might find suspect."

When she gave him a puzzled look, he grimaced. "I was a navy SEAL. I know countless ways to eliminate an enemy."

Her mouth formed a shocked oval.

When the elevator hit the bottom level, Dom all but dragged Lausanne off, not bothering for any last words with Gomez. Dundee's had contacts worldwide, men and women who knew their jobs, performed them well and were paid handsomely. Dom had no doubts that Tito Gomez would handle this situation in a professional manner.

"Come on, honey, we need to get out of here," Dom said.

When they reached their waiting car, the driver started to open the back door. Dom motioned to him and instructed him, in Spanish, to get them to the airport as fast as possible; then Dom shoved Lausanne into the back seat and slid in beside her.

"Dom?"

"Huh?"

"Megan was killed because she knows who murdered Audrey and Bobby Jack, right?"

"Yeah, that would be my guess."

"Then the attacks on me—they were meant for me, not Audrey."

"Yeah."

"I'd hoped… I guess I knew, but I didn't want to believe it."

She looked like a lost puppy, alone and uncertain. God, how he wanted to take care of her, to make sure nothing bad ever happened to her again. He pulled her into his arms and held her. "You're safe, honey. I'm not going to let anyone hurt you. I promise."

AN HOUR LATER, the Dundee jet took off from the private airstrip at Ezeiza. Dom didn't draw a free breath until they were out over the Atlantic, heading up the coast, past Uruguay. Lausanne rested in his arms, huddled against him like an exhausted child seeking warmth and comfort.

When her stomach growled, Dom asked, "Are you hungry?"

"I suppose I am," she said. "But I don't know if I can eat anything."

"I'll fix us something." He untangled her from his embrace and stood. "The jet has a fine galley and the refrigerator and cupboards are always kept fully stocked. Do you have a preference?"

She shook her head, a sad, weary half-smile on her face.

"Why don't you stretch out on the sofa and rest while I whip us up a bite."

She obeyed him instantly, easing out her small, slender body on the long, wide lounge sofa. He watched her for a couple of minutes, unable to keep his eyes off her, wishing he could erase those worry lines from her brow and take away all the fear inside her. She tried so hard to project a tough, don't-give-a-damn image, but he knew better. Just below the surface of that protective shield she'd built around herself lay a kind, loving woman. A vulnerable woman.

When her eyelids closed, Dom smiled. Poor baby.

He entered the galley, all stainless steel shiny and spotlessly clean. He hadn't eaten anything since he'd prepared himself coffee and toast aboard the jet before landing in Buenos Aires this morning. He had assumed that after talking to Megan Reynolds, he'd eat an early dinner at one of the local restaurants. The last time he'd been in Argentina—on Dundee business last year— he'd enjoyed *empandas,* which was a dough filled with ground meat, olives, boiled eggs and spices. But what he'd like to have right now was a delicious flan, served with *dulce de leche,* a luscious sweet caramel.

Damn, he must be hungrier than he'd thought.

He checked the refrigerator and found the ingredients for salad, along with a stack of deli lunch meats and various cheeses. Soup and sandwiches might hit the spot. He opened an overhead cupboard and smiled when he saw a variety of canned soups. He grabbed the can marked "vegetable."

Halfway through preparing their meal, Dom halted his hand stirring the warming soup when he heard his cell phone ring. He laid the spoon on the counter and snatched his phone from the belt hook.

He was relieved when Tito greeted him on the other end of the line. "It's good to hear from you."

"*Sí, sí.*" Gomez spoke rapidly to Dom in Spanish. "You are safely out of the country, yes?"

"Yes, we're over the Atlantic now," Dom replied in Spanish.

"The police are searching Buenos Aires for a man

fitting your general description. But it is assumed the man is from South America. The maid told the police that he spoke fluent Spanish, but his accent was not Argentinian."

"You got away without any problems, right?"

"But of course. However, while you and Ms. Rancy were on your way to the airport and the police were being called, I returned to Ms. Reynolds's room."

"You what?"

"I did not stay long and I was very discreet. But I thought perhaps I might discover something of interest if I simply looked over the room before the police arrived."

"And did you find anything interesting?"

"The lady had expensive tastes," Gomez replied. "And she had either contacted a local attorney or was considering contacting one."

"How do you know this?"

"I found a business card lying on the desk, alongside a letter that I assume Ms. Reynolds was writing."

"What did the letter say?"

"The letter had not been written. Only the salutation. It read, *Dear Lausanne*."

"She was writing a letter to Lausanne. No last name?"

"No last name."

"What about an envelope?" Dom asked.

"One lay beside the letter, but it had not been addressed."

"So there's no way the police can find out who Lausanne is."

"They will assume Señorita Reynolds was writing to a friend," Gomez said.

"What about the business card—who's the lawyer?"

"Alejandro Lopez."

"Ever hear of him?"

"Not until I saw his card in Ms. Reynolds's room, but I have already met with the gentleman. As a matter of fact, I have just now left his office."

"You work fast, Gomez."

He chuckled. "Ms. Reynolds had spoken to Lopez over the phone and had an appointment this afternoon, one she did not keep, of course."

"Did he know why she needed a lawyer?"

"He told me—after I had paid him handsomely for the information—that Ms. Reynolds wanted him to hold a letter for her. She was to bring it to him today."

"Did he—?"

"That is all he knew," Gomez said.

"And you believe him?"

"Yes, I don't think he would lie to me. You see, Señor Lopez and I have an understanding."

Dom knew exactly what Gomez meant. "Thanks. If you find out anything else, call me."

"Sí, señor."

After replacing his cell phone, Dom finished preparing two sandwiches, two bowls of soup and snapped open the lids on two cans of lemon iced tea. Placing their meal on a large serving tray, Dom carried it out of the galley and into the lounge. After placing it on a table in front of the sofa, he sat down in a chair across from the sofa and called Lausanne's name softly.

Her eyelids fluttered.

"Supper's ready," he told her.

Sighing deeply, she opened her eyes, smiled at him and stretched before sitting up. "I fell asleep, didn't I?"

"You needed it, honey."

"Mmm...something sure does smell good." She eyed the tray on the low table between them.

"Just soup and sandwiches."

"You're so good to me," she told him. "I'm not sure I deserve such special treatment, not after the way I totally disregarded your orders and flew off to Buenos Aires on my own. Most men would be furious with me."

"I'm not most men."

"No, you're not. And I'm beginning to realize just how different you really are from the men I've known in the past."

He removed a linen napkin from the tray, snapped it open and laid it across her lap. "And you, Lausanne Raney, are not like any woman I've ever known."

"Is that a good thing or a bad thing?"

"I haven't decided," he said, only half joking.

CHAPTER TWENTY-ONE

LAUSANNE ATE the last bite of her sandwich, then wiped her mouth and hands on the linen napkin. "I didn't realize I was so hungry. That was delicious."

"I aim to please." Dom guzzled the final drops of tea from the can, then set it on the tray.

"You do please," she said. "You please me very much."

"Flattery will get you anything you want." Dom winked at her as he stood and reached down for the tray.

"You prepared the meal." She hopped to her feet. "The least I can do is clean up."

He lifted the heavy tray. "Why don't we do it together?"

"All right."

Together was such a beautiful word. A word that meant not being alone. A word that conveyed a closeness with another person that Lausanne had never truly known, at least not as an adult.

Dom drew water into the sink, then looked in the lower cupboard for detergent, found it and added it to the flowing water. "While you were asleep, Señor Gomez called." He dumped their dirty bowls into the foam.

Lausanne's stomach fluttered with apprehension. "What did he have to say?"

Dom explained that Gomez had found a letter Megan Reynolds had begun writing, starting with the words *Dear Lausanne.* "He also found a business card for a local attorney, Alejandro Lopez, and Gomez has already spoken to Señor Lopez." Dom went on to give her details about Gomez's "talk" with the lawyer.

"I don't understand," Lausanne said. "Why would Megan Reynolds have been writing to me?"

"Apparently there was something she wanted you to know." Using a clean sponge, Dom washed one bowl and handed it to Lausanne.

"Then why did she plan to give the letter to the lawyer instead of mailing it directly to me?" Lausanne dried and put away the first bowl, then the second one.

"Insurance." Dom handed her the clean spoons.

Lausanne stared quizzically at Dom as she dried the spoons. "I don't get it."

"She probably knew that whoever paid her off was a dangerous person, a person capable of murder, and she wanted some insurance to protect herself."

"Oh, I see. If this person knew she'd written a letter to me, to be forwarded only if she died, then they would be less likely to kill her." But it hadn't worked out that way, had it? Someone had strangled Megan Reynolds before she could write the letter. "Where do these go?" Lausanne held up the dried spoons.

Dom took them from her, opened a bottom drawer and laid them in the silverware tray. "Apparently Megan never got a chance to finish the letter."

"Why didn't the killer take the letter or destroy it?" Lausanne asked. "Why leave it for the police to find?"

Dom shrugged. "Maybe he figured that since the page was blank except for your first name, the letter was of no significance. Or maybe he had to leave quickly for some reason, before he got a chance to take the letter."

"But he must have seen it, right? After all, he was sent to kill her before she could write it."

"Which means she had threatened whoever had paid her off, otherwise they wouldn't have known." After drying his hands, Dom turned Lausanne to face him, gripped her shoulders and looked right at her. "You realize that you're the only loose end the killer needs to tie up, don't you?"

She shivered as the truth of Dom's statement sank in—whoever had paid an assassin to kill Megan Reynolds had probably already hired someone to try to kill her. Again. Third time charm?

"Aren't I special." A shiver of pure fear rippled through her. "The police suspect me of murdering two people and the real murderer is after me, too."

Dom cupped her face with his hands. "No one is going to hurt you. Not the police. Not some hired killer. The only way anyone will ever get to you is through me."

Tears pooled in her eyes. "Oh, Dom…" She sniffled, trying her damnedest not to cry. "You're too good to be true, you know. I just don't have this kind of good luck, especially not with men."

"I'm the lucky one." He leaned down and brushed his lips over hers.

Lausanne cried, holding nothing back, permitting herself the freedom to truly feel.

Dom hugged her to him, whispering softly in her ear. She melted into his strength, giving herself over to her emotions, a luxury she had not allowed herself in years. She had been alone for such a long time, with no one who truly cared about her. But now, with Dom, she felt safe.

After she'd cried her last tear, she lifted her head from his chest, wiped her damp eyes and looked up at him. "Thank you."

"For what?"

"For being you."

Dom grinned, then reached down and took her hand in his. "Come on, honey. We've got a long flight home. Why don't we go cuddle on the sofa and swap life stories?"

"You don't want to hear mine. It's a sob story practically from beginning to end."

He led her back into the lounge and over to the sofa, then sat and pulled her onto his lap. She curled up against him, loving the feel of him, knowing that for now, for these next few hours, no harm could come to either of them. On the Dundee jet, high in the sky, soaring over the Atlantic Ocean, she and Dom were in their own little world.

"You go first," she told him. "Domingo Shea was born in Texas. How many years ago?"

"Thirty-seven."

"Ooh, you're an old man. Nine years older than I am."

"Does that make me too old for you?"

She rubbed her hand over his chest, the feel of his cotton shirt smooth under her palm. "No, I think that makes you just right for me."

Dom chuckled. "I don't think I've ever been just right for someone."

"Well, you're just right for me," she told him. "What about me? Am I too young for you? Too wild for you? Not good enough for you?"

He grasped the back of her neck and forced her head up so that she had to face him. "I don't ever want to hear you put yourself down like that, not ever again. Not even jokingly. Understand?"

Her heart caught in her throat. She nodded.

"You're just right for me, too," he told her. "No one else has ever been so right."

"Damn it, Dom, you're going to make me cry again."

He tickled her in the ribs, which made her giggle and squirm, then he wrapped her in his embrace and said, "Promise not to cry again and I'll regale you with tales of the life and times of Domingo Ronan Shea."

Twisting around just enough to gaze up at him, she asked, "Ronan?"

"Ronan. 'Tis a fine old Irish name, me girl. Ronan Shea was my great-grandfather, born and bred in County Tyrone."

"Someday when you have a son, that's what you should name him—Ronan Shea."

Dom pressed his cheek against her temple. His warm breath fanned over her ear and wafted through her hair. She closed her eyes and sighed.

"If I have two sons, I might name the second one Ronan," Dom said. "But if and when I have a son, I'd like to name him after my brother Raphael and call him Rafe."

"That's a wonderful name, too."

Dom remained quiet for several minutes.

"Tell me about Rafe," she said.

Dom kissed her forehead. "Rafe was my big brother and a lot like our old man. Big, rugged, rough. As Irish as the day is long. He and our father were as close as any son and father could be and so much alike in looks and personalities." Dom grunted. "Me, I was Mama's son. Too pretty to be a boy. That's what the old man told me. I had inherited Mama's Mexican features, except I got Dad's height and build."

"Were you jealous of the relationship between Rafe and your father?"

"Yeah, I guess I was, in a way, but it didn't keep me from loving them both. I idolized Rafe. And hell, we both thought the old man hung the moon."

"What happened to Rafe?"

"How do you know—"

"I heard it in your voice." She laid her arms over his where he held her around the waist. "Rafe's dead, isn't he?"

"Yeah. He was killed in the Gulf War, that first damn war with Iraq. He was making the army his career, so as soon as I finished college, I joined the navy. He was a Ranger. I was a SEAL. We were always competing."

"I didn't have any siblings, but I hear healthy competition is normal between brothers or between sisters."

"When Rafe was killed…" Dom swallowed hard.

"Nothing has ever been the same since then."

"Yeah, you're right, but how did you know?"

"Because when my mother died, my life changed and nothing has ever been the same since."

"I've spent the past fifteen years living the life I thought Rafe would have wanted to live. The guy was a hell-raiser, a womanizer and the apple of the old man's eye. I tried my best to step into Rafe's shoes, but… Hell, I'm not Rafe. I'm Domingo, but I've lived in Rafe's shadow for so long, I'm not sure who I am anymore."

"I understand." Lausanne nestled closer to Dom, wishing she could lose herself in him. "My mother's precious twelve-year-old Lausanne was a sweet, naive little girl adored by both her parents. She lived an idyllic life, with a beautiful room filled with toys and dolls and pretty clothes. Then one day her mother died and her father became a cold stranger who married a crazy woman. And that wicked stepmother made Lausanne's life a living hell."

"And you ran away from home to escape this crazy woman."

"Out of the frying pan and into the fire. If I'd stayed in Booneville and endured Renee's abuse, I'd never have met Brad White, the good-for-nothing. Of course, it's not nice to speak ill of the dead, but Brad was worthless."

"Brad White was your child's father?" Dom asked.

Huffing out a cleansing breath, Lausanne replied, "He got me pregnant, but I never thought of him as my baby's father. He wasn't around long enough to be anything other than a sperm donor."

"You must have loved him, in the beginning."

"I thought I did, but let's face it, I was seventeen, alone, scared and needed somebody. Anybody would have done. It just happened to be Brad."

"How could a man leave a woman who was carrying his child?"

"Brad wasn't a man. He was a nineteen-year-old boy who loved beer and motorcycles and girls. I was just one of his girlfriends. The last thing he wanted was to get tied down with a wife and baby."

"How did you manage, being a kid all alone and pregnant?" Dom hugged her comfortingly.

"I didn't manage, not very well. When I was seven months pregnant, I swallowed my pride and went to Brad's house to ask him to help me, to help us, the baby and me. I was desperate. That's when I found out he was dead. His sister told me he'd been killed in a motorcycle wreck less than a month earlier. His mother had died when he was little and he had a stepmother, just like I did, but she was a nice woman. Brad's father was dead, too, so it was just the sister and the stepmom."

"There was no one to help you."

"That's why I gave her away, you know. My baby girl. I wanted her to have a good life, the kind of life I'd had before my mother died."

That incurable, gut-wrenching pain she always felt when she thought about her daughter clutched Lausanne's heart. For a few seconds, she couldn't breathe.

Dom turned her in his arms so that he could see her face. "Lausanne..."

"I wanted to keep her. You don't know how much I wanted to be a mother to her, but..." She choked back the tears. "That's why I agreed to impersonate Audrey Perkins. That's why I took the fifty thousand dollars."

Dom curved his index finger and thumb around her chin and jaw. "You lost me, honey. What did the money have to do with your baby?"

"I gave her away to strangers. I've always wondered if the people who adopted her cherished her as the precious gift she was, if she has the life she deserved. A good life. I promised myself that when I got out of prison, I'd turn my own life around and I'd save up enough money to do whatever it took to find my little girl."

Releasing his grip on her chin, Dom narrowed his gaze, giving her a hard stare. "You want to find your child and take her away—"

"No!" Lausanne covered his mouth with her fingertips. "I would never try to take her away from two loving parents and a happy life. I just want—no, I need—to know for sure that she's all right, that she does have the wonderful life I wanted for her."

He captured her hand in his and kissed her fingertips. "Lausanne...ah, honey."

Dom kissed her lips. Tenderly.

That tormenting ache in her heart eased the slightest bit, as if sharing the pain with someone who truly cared how much she had suffered lessened the severity.

"I thought taking the money and impersonating

Audrey would be a slam dunk, that I'd not only get the money I needed to search for my daughter, but I'd get to enjoy the kind of spending spree vacation most women only dream about." Lausanne grunted in self-disgust. "I should have know I'd only wind up in an unholy mess. No matter what I do, how hard I try, I just keep screwing up. And this time, instead of somebody else dragging me down, I'm the one doing the dragging. I'm dragging you down into my personal hell."

When she lifted herself, intending to get off his lap, Dom wrapped his arm around her waist, pulled her down and turned her around so that she sat sideways, her side to his chest. She wiggled, trying to free herself from his hold, but he enfolded her in both of his big, strong arms and pressed his cheek against hers.

"Haven't you figured it out yet?" he asked. "There is nowhere I'd rather be than with you. In heaven or hell or someplace in between."

Lausanne's heart stopped. She knew it did. She couldn't breathe, couldn't think, couldn't react in any way. Then suddenly her heartbeat drummed inside her head. She gasped for breath, sucking in deep gulps of air.

"You're crazy, Dom Shea. You know that, don't you?"

She jerked away from him and this time he let her go. When she made it to her feet, she turned and glared at him. He looked up at her, love and passion in his eyes.

"You just don't get it, do you?" she said. "I don't deserve a wonderful man like you. I'm not good enough for you. You're one of the good guys. I'm one of the bad girls who just keeps fucking up her life and I don't think that will ever change. My advice to you is run like hell."

"You don't mean that."

"Yes, I do. If you stay with me, keep on trying to help me, you'll wind up regretting it."

Wanting to run away and hide, she turned her back on him; then she realized that there was no place to run. They were aboard the Dundee jet. If she wanted to escape, she'd have to find a parachute and jump.

Dom came up behind her, but he didn't touch her. She held her breath, a part of her wanting him to hold her again, to tell her that he loved her and they had a future together. And the other part of her, the realistic woman who knew there was no such thing as happily ever after, didn't want him near her. If he touched her, she'd be lost. She wanted him so much that she'd be powerless to resist.

And you love him, a wicked inner voice taunted. *You've gone and fallen head over heels in love with Dom Shea.*

"If you want some time alone, there's a bedroom in back," Dom said. "There's a CD player and a case filled with books and a private bath. You can hole up in there until we reach Chattanooga, if that's what you want."

"Thank you. I'd like a little time by myself."

"Want me to call you for supper? I thought I'd whip us up a bite in four or five hours."

"Yes, thank you." She glanced over her shoulder. "I'll be glad to help you prepare dinner."

"Okay." He offered her a wavering smile.

Lausanne forced herself not to run from him. Instead,

she walked slowly toward the bedroom door and with every step, she wished he'd ask her to come back to him.

"MEGAN REYNOLDS has been eliminated," he said.

A deep sigh. "And the letter? What did you find out about the letter?"

"I was told that he saw a letter lying on her desk at the hotel and—"

"Did he get the letter and destroy it?"

"No, there was no reason to remove the letter. All that was written on the stationery was the greeting *Dear Lausanne*."

Another heavy sigh. "Good."

He wished the man in Buenos Aires he'd hired to kill Megan Reynolds had found a completed letter, one naming his client as a killer. If there had been a letter, something incriminating, he could have used it to blackmail his client, if he ever needed that type of self-defense weapon. "Then you're satisfied with the outcome?"

"Very satisfied."

"Will you require anything else?" Would the Raney woman need to die, now that Megan Reynolds was dead and there was no letter naming his client as a murderer?

"Yes, I want Lausanne Raney eliminated. And the sooner the better. If by some chance Megan wrote another letter… I can't afford to take the chance."

"If that's what you want, then—"

"It's not what I want, but it's necessary. Do you think I wanted to have Megan killed? I didn't. And Audrey…" Silence.

"I'll make contact with my sources in the morning and arrange for a specialist to go to Chattanooga and handle the hit." He needed Corbin for this job. Only Corbin.

"No more screw ups. No more near misses. Understand?"

"It could take several days to make the arrangements. And if you want one of the best, it'll cost you a mint." The best didn't come cheap.

"Damn the cost. Just get it done this time."

FIVE AND A HALF HOURS later, Dom knocked on the bedroom door. Lausanne didn't respond. He eased open the door and peered inside the room. A dim bedside lamp glimmered softly. She lay atop the covers on the bed, curled into a fetal ball, and appeared to be sound asleep. He had prepared the meal himself, taking a prepackaged dish of Eggplant Parmesan from the small freezer and heating it in the microwave. He'd set the small dining table, placed salads and bread sticks and wineglasses on the sleek surface and lit a couple of fat candles that he'd put in the middle of the table.

As he entered the bedroom, he called to her in a whisper. "Lausanne…"

She whimpered, as if halfway hearing him, but unable to fully awaken.

"I have dinner ready," he told her

Moaning softly, she uncurled and flipped over on her back. "Dom?"

"Yeah, honey, it's me."

Her eyelids fluttered. "I must have fallen asleep." She opened her eyes. "How long have I—"

"About five hours."

"I must have slept really hard," she said. "I feel slightly hung-over."

Dom ventured several feet into the room. "You needed to rest."

"I needed to escape."

"From me?"

She pushed herself up into a sitting position. "Yeah, that's what I thought. But as it turned out, I needed to escape from myself. From who I am. From who I don't want to be. But you know what—you can't escape from yourself."

"Honey, don't do this."

"God damn it, Dom, stop being so nice to me. I don't deserve it."

Dom stomped across the room. "I've had all of this I can take. I'm going to tell you one last time, I don't want to hear you putting yourself down, ever again." He paused by the side of the bed. "I won't stand for it."

Lausanne gazed up at him, her beautiful green eyes wide with wonder. "You won't?"

He sat down on the edge of the bed and confronted her. "No, I won't. Okay, so you've made a few mistakes. Who hasn't?"

"A few mistakes?" She laughed sarcastically. "I got pregnant at seventeen and had to give my baby away, then at twenty-one, I wound up being arrested as an accomplice to an armed robbery and serving five years in the pen. Those aren't your typical mistakes. Those were whoppers. And just when I thought I'd turned my life around, I went and did something totally stupid—I agreed to impersonate a rich society woman who wound up dead, along with her boyfriend, and now I'm one of the chief murder suspects."

Dom grinned. "Okay, so your mistakes are whoppers. But that doesn't mean you're less worthy of happiness than anyone else. The way I look at it, maybe it means you deserve a little more."

Tears misted her eyes. "I don't deserve—"

Dom placed his index finger over her lips to silence her. "No more talk like that. Not now. Not ever."

Teardrops glistened on her thick, dark eyelashes. "I'm no good for you. I'll just mess up your life and—"

Dom grabbed her and kissed her. It tore him up inside to see her like this, to hear her self-condemnation, to know how desperately she needed to be cherished and how afraid she was to trust herself and him.

The moment he took her mouth, she responded, all resistance erased as if it had never existed. They were a combustible combination, explosive when bonded together. He wanted her, wanted to bury himself deep inside her, to possess her body and soul. But he wanted more for both of them. He wanted to show her that she was worthy of all good things in life. He wanted to protect her from hurt, to wrap his arms around her and keep her safe.

Minutes later, they broke apart, both of them breathless and unbearably aroused. He felt her hunger as strongly as he did his own, as if they were a part of each other.

Without either of them speaking, they gazed into each other's eyes and reached out, ripping at each other's clothes in a frenzy of need. When his shirt hit the floor, atop her sweater, they paused and took deep breaths. If he didn't slow things down, he'd be inside her and finished within three minutes flat. He wouldn't take her this way, to appease his own desire. She deserved better and he intended to prove that to her.

"Dom?" His name was a pleading whisper on her lips.

"We've got hours," he told her. "There's no need to rush."

"But I want you."

He grinned. "And you're going to want me even more when I get through loving you."

After kissing the tip of her nose, he rose from the bed, walked across the room and put several CDs in the five-disk player. Classical piano music filled the room, the first recording Grieg's *Notturno*. Dom went into the bathroom, turned on the lights, then closed the door almost all the way, leaving only a narrow crack of light. When he returned to the bed where Lausanne sat waiting and watching, he flipped off the bedside lamp, casting the bedroom into semidarkness.

He reached out, clasped his hands around her waist and pulled her out of the bed and onto her feet. She gasped when he kissed her neck. He removed his hands from her waist, then kept his hands to either side of his body, forcing himself not to touch her. He kissed a path down her neck, across each collar bone and to the other side of her neck. She shivered. His sex hardened.

With the utmost gentleness, he turned her so that he faced her back, then lifted her long, wild hair with one hand as he brought his lips down on the base of her neck.

She whimpered when he kissed her there. Loving the reaction, Dom licked a moist trail from her neck to the top edge of her bra, then skipped over the bra and continued down the hollow of her back to the waistband of her jeans.

Her skin was like warm satin.

He reached out and undid the hook on her bra, then very slowly eased the straps down her arms. She stood there, tense with anticipation, while he removed her bra. And then he caressed her shoulders.

Moaning, she swayed toward him until her naked back encountered his bare chest. He slipped his arms around her as she leaned against him; then cupping his hands, he covered her breasts. A perfect fit.

He lowered his head and whispered in her ear. "I'm the luckiest man in the world."

"Huh?" Her voice quivered.

"I said I'm the luckiest man in the world...because I'm your lover." He rubbed his thumbs across her peaked nipples.

"Oh..."

"You're beautiful and smart and perfect for me in every way," he told her. "Allowing me the privilege of making love to you is a gift you're giving me, one I'll always cherish."

He lowered his hands to unzip her jeans. While he shimmied her jeans down her hips and over her legs, she helped him, and even removed her panties herself. With her back still to him, he inserted his right hand between her thighs. While his thumb brushed over her mound, his fingers found her core and strummed across the tip in a slow, tantalizing rhythm.

As he nipped at her neck and shoulders, sweet little love bites, he used one hand to alternate between her breasts. The fingers of his other hand worked inside her feminine lips to excite and pleasure her. Within a couple of minutes, he felt her body tighten and knew she was on the verge. He murmured how much he wanted her, using graphic words, as he increased the speed of his strokes.

Lausanne cried out when she climaxed, moisture gushing to coat his fingers. While she shivered and shook, he stripped out of his slacks and briefs.

Damn it, he didn't have a condom.

The barely rational part of his brain remembered that there was a box in the bathroom. The Dundee jet was equipped with all the comforts of home, including contraception, just in case a client might need it. Why hadn't he thought of that sooner and gotten the condoms when he'd turned on the bathroom lights?

When he lifted her and placed her on the bed, she held open her arms. He lowered his head and kissed her belly. "I need to protect you."

She sighed dreamily and waited while he made a mad dash to the bathroom. When he returned, fully prepared to make love to her, he found her on her knees in the center of the bed.

God in heaven, she was beautiful. Like a curvaceous

little porcelain doll, every curve, every feature sheer perfection. The triangle of fluff between her thighs was as brilliantly golden red as the long, thick mass of straw-berry blonde curls cascading over her shoulders. Her breasts were firm and high, her waist long and slender, her hips rounded and her butt a tight inverted heart.

"You're the most beautiful thing I've ever seen."

"Then you haven't taken a good look at yourself," she told him. "Because you're the most beautiful thing I've ever seen."

He chuckled softly as he approached the bed. The moment his knees hit the edge of the mattress, she threw herself at him and flung her arms around his neck. They toppled into the bed, their legs and arms tangled together as they kissed and touched and rolled around on top of the covers. Managing to straddle him, she pinned him to the bed.

"You're in charge, honey." Dom spread his arms out on either side of his chest. "I'm all yours."

She rose up over him, circled his penis with her tight fist and brought him up between her thighs until his tip touched her feminine folds. Then she took him inside her, sliding over him, taking him fully. Once buried to the hilt within her, he longed to thrust upward, but waited for her to make the next move. If she made him wait much longer, he'd die. He was so close to losing it that he wasn't sure he could hold off until she came again. But he sure as hell was going to try.

Leaning over him, her breasts like tempting melons, she gazed down at him and smiled. Dom lifted his head and suckled one breast and then the other. Groaning with pleasure, she rubbed against him, putting pressure exactly where she needed it. Unable to restrain himself, Dom clutched her hips and pulled out of her, then thrust up and deep. She tossed her head back and keened while their bodies moved together, the pace growing more frantic by the minute.

Dom knew he was going to climax any second now and there was no way to slow the process. He wished he could make it last longer. Maybe next time.

"It's good, honey," he said. "So good."

She tightened around him like a squeezing fist and within seconds she came. Jerking. Shivering. "Uh! Uh! Uh!" She huffed and moaned, unraveling completely.

When Dom climaxed, his ears rang and he felt as if the top of his head was going to explode. Every nerve in his body experienced the orgasm.

She melted into him, her body spreading over his like butter on a hot biscuit. He stroked her buttocks. She nuzzled his neck.

"I don't know about you, honey," Dom said. "But that was the best damn sex I've ever had, so I guess what they say is true about sex being better when you have deep feelings for the other person."

She sighed contentedly and kissed his chest. "We are good together, aren't we? I mean really good."

He caressed her hip. "We're better than good. We're perfect."

"Perfect," she whispered, then closed her eyes and sighed dreamily.

A few minutes later, Dom realized she was asleep. He eased her off of him and onto the bed, then maneuvered the sheet and blanket down and back up to cover her. After getting out of bed, he retrieved his cell phone from his pants and headed to the bathroom. He laid the phone on the back of the commode, then removed his condom, tossed it into the trash and washed himself. After he'd cleaned up and relieved himself, he closed the commode lid, sat down and picked up his phone. He brought up Sawyer McNamara's private number.

His boss answered on the fourth ring. "Shea, this had better be important. I'm in the middle of a lovely evening with a charming lady."

"I want Dundee's to find someone for me," Dom said.

"This can't wait?"

"No. She's already waited long enough."

"Who are you talking about?" Sawyer asked.

"Lausanne Raney gave a baby girl up for adoption over ten years ago. I want Dundee's to find that child. I want to know who adopted her, where they live, what the child's name is and if she's with a good, loving family."

"Are you footing the bill for this?"

"Yeah, send all the bills to me. And see what you can do to expedite the search. I have a woman who can't go on with the rest of her life until she knows that her daughter is safe and happy."

"You've got a woman who can't go on with her life until she's no longer under suspicion for double homicide," Sawyer said. "And you should know that when the Dundee jet sets down in Chattanooga, Lieutenant Desmond will be there to meet you."

"Damn! He knows Lausanne left the country."

"Yes, he knows. And he's none too happy about it."

"She's innocent," Dom said. "She didn't kill anybody."

"Even so, she did leave Chattanooga after the police told her not to. Hell, she left the country."

"She was with me every minute from the time she arrived in Buenos Aires. Maybe I can make Desmond understand that she wasn't fleeing the country. After all, she's coming back of her own free will."

CHAPTER TWENTY-TWO

THE DUNDEE JET LANDED in Chattanooga early the following morning. As Sawyer had warned Dom, Lieutenant Bain Desmond was there to meet them, a uniformed female officer with him.

"Lausanne Raney," Lieutenant Desmond said, "you're under arrest."

"Everything will be all right," Dom told Lausanne. "Trust me."

"I do trust you, but—"

He took her hands in his and squeezed reassuringly. "Just go with the policewoman and cooperate. Go through the process of being booked, but you won't spend one minute behind bars, I promise."

"I don't understand."

"You're going to have to go with the policewoman—" He glanced at the tall, athletic black woman waiting patiently for Lausanne. "I don't have time to explain everything now." He hugged her, then whispered in her ear. "You're safe. I'm taking care of you."

Closing her eyes momentarily, she clung to Dom, not understanding what was going on. But knowing she

could trust him, she released him and turned to the policewoman. "I'm ready to go now."

The young black officer, whose name badge identified her as B. Fuqua, read Lausanne her rights, then
handcuffed her and helped her into the back seat of the
patrol car. When the door closed, she felt a sudden sense
of panic, as if she'd been shut off from the world, away
from Dom and the security he represented.

Willing her jangling nerves under control, Lausanne
sat quietly in the back seat as the patrol car sped along
the highway. She was being charged with disregarding
a direct order from the Chattanooga police. According
to Lt. Desmond, she had fled the country. Well, she
supposed things could be worse—he could be charging
her with murder.

She recited the same sentence over and over inside
her mind, believing it with her whole heart. *Dom will
take care of me.*

No one had taken care of her since her mother died.
She'd been forced to fend for herself, to fight her battles
alone, to trust no one. But every human being needs
somebody in their life that they could count on to be
there for them, to go into battle at their side, someone
with whom they could celebrate the triumphs and be
comforted by in times of tragedy.

Was she a fool to believe that Dom was that person
for her?

"Are you all right, Ms. Raney?" Officer Fuqua asked.

Lausanne nodded. "Yes, I'm okay." As okay as a

person under arrest, handcuffed and in the back of a police cruiser on her way to jail could be.

Leaning her head back and closing her eyes, Lausanne said a silent prayer. *Please, God, help me get out of this mess I've gotten myself into. I know I've made promises before and you know I've tried to keep those promises, but somehow I just keep screwing up.*

And if you're listening, how about doing a couple of other things for me. It sure would be nice if my faith in Dom Shea hasn't been misplaced. You know how difficult it is for me to trust anybody. But I do trust Dom. And I love him. Heaven help me, I love him something awful.

And I guess I really don't need to ask this since it's a prayer that never leaves my heart, but... Keep on watching over my baby girl. Make sure she's with people who love her and are taking good care of her.

DOM WAITED in the interrogation room, along with Bain Desmond and Mike Swain. He just hoped that when they explained the situation to Lausanne, she wouldn't take a swing at him. If she did, he'd understand. After all, they were playing a game she knew nothing about, not yet. And although he'd been the one who had called Desmond from the Dundee jet before they arrived in Chattanooga, it had been Desmond who'd come up with the plot to use Lausanne to trap a killer. Dom hadn't agreed to using his woman as bait, but knew Lausanne well enough to realize that she would insist on making her own decisions. If she was willing to go along with Desmond's plan, then Dom intended to be involved every step of the way. No way in hell was he going to let anything happen to her. Not now. Not ever.

When Lausanne marched into the room, her head held high, her shoulders back and a defiant look in her beautiful green eyes, Dom felt like laughing out loud. No meek little lamb being led to the slaughter. Not his girl. Damn, he was proud of her. She glanced at him. He gave her a thumbs-up. The corners of her mouth lifted ever so slightly; then she glared at the two detectives.

"Please, come in and take a seat, Ms. Raney." Lt. Desmond pulled out a chair for her.

Lausanne sat, folded her hands in her lap and darted her gaze around the room.

Dom walked over behind her chair and placed his hands on her shoulders. At first, she tensed, then when he gave her a gentle squeeze, she relaxed.

He lowered his head and whispered in her ear. "I'm right here, honey, and I'm not going anywhere. I'm with you all the way, whatever you decide to do."

Before she had a chance to question his comments, Lt. Desmond sat down across from her on the opposite side of the table. "I apologize for having you arrested, handcuffed and—"

"Hold on just one minute." She pivoted halfway around in her chair and looked up at Dom. "Whatever's going on here, you're in on it, right?"

"Lausanne...honey—"

"I've been arrested before, you know," she said. "And I know that the way I've been treated tonight isn't the norm. Everybody is too concerned with how I feel and if I'm all right. So, how about cutting to the chase and just tell me what's going on."

With his gaze locked to hers, Dom replied, "While you were asleep on the plane coming back from Argentina, I spoke to my boss, Sawyer McNamara. He told me Lieutenant Desmond was meeting us at the airport to arrest you for fleeing the country."

"I didn't flee the country." Lausanne paused for a couple of seconds, then said, "Well, I guess that, technically, I did flee the country. But I had every intention of coming back." She faced Desmond. "I did come back to Chattanooga of my own accord."

"Yes, ma'am, you did," Desmond agreed.

Dom gave her shoulders another squeeze. "After I got off the phone with Sawyer, I called Lieutenant Desmond."

"You what?" Lausanne whirled around and came halfway up out of her chair.

Dom eased her back down, pressing her into place with his hands on her shoulders. "I told him everything that happened in Buenos Aires, everything about Megan Reynolds, including the letter she had started writing to you and about her hiring an attorney."

"Mr. Shea convinced me that you had nothing to do with Bobby Jack Cash's and Audrey Perkins's murders, that you were set up, Ms. Raney," Desmond said.

"He did?" She looked wide-eyed at Dom, then turned around to face Desmond. "Then why am I here? Why was I arrested?"

"Because we want the real killer to feel safe, to think he or she got away with two murders," Desmond told her. "Although we can't arrest you for the murders, we can imply that we're on the verge of doing just that."

"You've lost me completely," Lausanne said. "I'm not following your line of reasoning here."

"Ruling you out as a suspect, along with the now deceased Ms. Reynolds, leaves us with three people with reason to want Audrey Perkins dead and one person we know for sure who wanted Bobby Jack out of the way. And all three are wealthy enough to afford a hired assassin to kill Ms. Reynolds. And to kill you." Desmond waited to see if Lausanne would question or comment on what he'd said. She didn't. "Grayson Perkins had motive to kill both his wife and her lover. It's also possible that Patrice Bedell wanted to see both victims dead. And Cara Bedell hated her sister."

"How is pretending that I'm the primary suspect, who is on the verge of being arrested for the murders, going to smoke out the real killer?"

Silence. Deafening silence.

Dom almost shouted, *Don't agree to Desmond's plan. Don't put your life on the line.* But he had to let her do whatever she wanted to do. Besides, they all knew that her life was already in danger and probably would be until the killer was apprehended.

Lausanne glanced from Lieutenant Desmond to his partner, Sergeant Swain, then to Dom. "I'm not going to like the answer, am I?"

"Lieutenant Desmond has come up with a plan to capture the real killer," Dom said.

"What sort of plan?" she asked.

"I'm going to speak to the Bedell family later today and tell them about Megan Reynolds being killed and explain that we arrested you for leaving the country." Desmond's gaze met Dom's and the two exchanged a knowing look. "I want the killer to draw a free breath. I'm going to imply that we suspect you might have killed Megan Reynolds for whatever reason, but there's nothing we can do about it. However, we're close to charging you with the murders of Audrey and Bobby Jack."

Lausanne couldn't believe her ears.

"Dom explained about Megan Reynolds's letter and about her hiring a lawyer in Buenos Aires," Desmond said. "If she was murdered to prevent her from writing that letter, then whoever was behind her murder and the murders of Audrey and Bobby Jack knew she would name him or her as the killer."

"And?" Lausanne asked.

"And tomorrow morning, we want you to make three telephone calls," Desmond told her. "To Grayson Perkins, Patrice Bedell and Cara Bedell. We want you to tell each of them that you have received a letter that was overnighted from Argentina. Tell each that you think he or she will be very interested in the information the letter contains. Then before they can reply, hang up. And don't answer your phone. Not until we tell you to."

Lausanne sat there quietly for several minutes. Dom tightened his hold on her. She lifted her right hand and patted his left hand clamped to her shoulder.

"You want to use me as bait." She glanced away from Desmond and up at Dom. "Do you think I should do it?"

"Do I want you to put yourself in the line of fire— no. I want to take you as far away from all of this as I possibly can. But this is your decision and I'll stand by you, whatever you decide."

Lausanne took a deep breath. "I'll do it."

Dom's muscles froze and his gut tightened. He'd been pretty sure she would agree to Desmond's plan, but hearing her say it out loud made it all too real.

"Thank you, Ms. Raney," Desmond said. "For now, we'll follow through on your arrest. We've already arranged bail for you and you'll be able to leave with Mr. Shea shortly. Stay with him from now until in the morning." Desmond glanced at Dom. "Y'all have a reserved room at the Chattanoogan Hotel, under the name Sawyer McNamara. I don't want Ms. Raney going to her apartment and I figure if anyone is looking for her, an expensive place like the Chattanoogan will be one of the last places they'd look."

"The fewer people who know where you are, the safer you'll be," Sergeant Swain said to Lausanne. "Once we get everything set up, we'll come to the hotel in the morning and monitor your phone calls to the suspects, then wait and see if one of them takes the bait."

"If one of them does, they may want to come to you," Desmond said. "But my guess is that he or she will want you to meet them. If that happens, we'll send you out to hook up with them at their chosen rendezvous point. Naturally, you'll be wired. And you'll be under constant surveillance."

She looked at Dom. "Will you be with me?"

"He'll be with us," Desmond replied. "You'll have to go in alone. And I won't lie to you—there is an element of risk involved."

"You know what, Lieutenant? I'm damned if I do and damned if I don't."

"Yeah, it seems you are, Ms. Raney."

JEREMY LOMAN MET Bain at the door and escorted him into the living room at the Bedell mansion. "Mr. Bedell is expecting you."

Glancing around at all the opulence surrounding him in this big, old mansion, Bain wondered why in the world anybody would need a twenty-five room house and an eight-car garage. Because need and want wasn't the same thing. Rich people wanted everything and more. They wanted the best their money could buy.

Loman opened the double pocket doors and announced, "Lieutenant Desmond is here."

Scanning the room quickly, he noticed Patrice Bedell sitting in a chair by the massive fireplace, perched there like a queen on her throne. She was an attractive woman, but a little too phony for Bain's tastes. Grayson Perkins sat on the sofa. Cara Bedell stood behind him, her hand resting on the sofa back, almost touching Perkins's shoulder.

What did she see in a guy like Perkins? Yes, he was handsome—too handsome—in a rather effeminate way. During the course of the investigation into the two homicides, Bain had learned a great deal about Grayson Perkins. The man possessed some business savvy, but was lost in the corporate world without his father-in-law to guide him, step-by-step. The guy spent a fortune on his clothes, got a weekly haircut and manicure and even indulged in frequent massages and body wraps. He drove an expensive sports car and the jewelry he wore— watch and rings—cost more than Bain's yearly salary. From what they'd learned about Audrey Perkins's husband, Bain's assessment of the guy could be summed up in two words: weak and useless.

Edward Bedell approached Bain, his big hand outstretched. They shook hands, then Edward said, "When you telephoned, you said you had news for us about Audrey's murder."

Bain nodded, then casually glanced around the room. He needed to make a quick study of each face after he gave them the news about Megan Reynolds and even more so when he suggested that the police might be on the verge of making an arrest in the double homicide case.

His gaze lingered on Cara Bedell. She wasn't the beauty her sister had been, but he sensed a strength in her that impressed him. The investigation into her life had surprised him. While Audrey had spent her time as a social butterfly and an adulterous wife flitting from one man to another, Cara Bedell actually worked. At twenty-four, she was a vice president in her father's company; and word at Bedell, Inc. headquarters was that when the old man retired she would be first in line to take over as CEO.

"Please, Lieutenant, if you have news for us, then don't hesitate to tell us," Cara said. "No matter how unpleasant your news might be, it can't be any worse than our learning about what happened to Audrey."

"Straight to the point, Ms. Bedell," Bain said. "All right. We received word that Megan Reynolds has been located in Buenos Aires."

A hushed silence fell over the room.

"Well, you can tell her that she's fired," Edward said.

"I'm afraid that won't be possible," Bain told them.

"Why not?" Cara asked, her gaze connecting with Bain's.

Some weird sort of current passed between Cara and him and for half a second, he couldn't think straight. Mentally shaking himself free of whatever had happened, he cleared his throat and looked directly at Edward Bedell.

"Ms. Reynolds is dead."

Patrice's mouth gaped. Cara's eyes widened.

"Dead," Edward whispered the word. "What happened to her?"

"According to the Buenos Aires police officer I spoke to earlier today, Ms. Reynolds was strangled in her hotel room."

"Who would want to kill Megan?" Cara asked.

Bain realized that he didn't want Cara Bedell to be a murderess, that his gut instincts told him she was no more a killer than Lausanne Raney. But being attracted to both women might have his normally keen instincts slightly off center.

You're attracted to Cara Bedell? Hell, are you out of your mind? She's not your type. She's not even pretty.

And she's an Amazon. An Amazon with freckles and an attitude. Man, did the lady have an attitude.

Before Desmond could reply to Cara, Edward asked the question Bain had hoped one of the suspects would ask. "Do the Buenos Aires police have any idea who killed Megan?"

"Well…yes and no." *Okay, here's your chance to test your acting talent, Desmond told himself.* "It seems they have a description of an American woman who was seen leaving Ms. Reynolds's hotel room shortly before her body was found."

"An American woman?" Patrice entered the conversation. "How did they—"

Bain cut her off mid-sentence. "I arrested Lausanne Raney this morning on her return from Buenos Aires."

"Oh, my God!" Patrice gasped as if suddenly putting two and two together. "The Raney woman killed Megan just as she killed poor Audrey and Bobby Jack."

"Now, Mrs. Bedell, don't put words in my mouth," Bain said.

"But it makes sense, doesn't it, Lieutenant Desmond," Grayson Perkins said. "If this Raney woman left town and went to Buenos Aires, she and Megan were somehow connected, perhaps Megan was involved in murdering Audrey and—and that man. That would give Ms. Raney a reason to kill Megan."

"It's possible," Bain agreed, but thought how totally illogical the theory really was. But then again, it didn't matter what conclusions Grayson Perkins or any of the others drew, as long as the real killer believed he or she was in the clear. At least until the morning, when Lausanne would drop her little bombshell.

"Do the Argentinian authorities have any evidence against Ms. Raney?" Edward asked.

"No, not really," Bain replied. "But we are gradually building a case against her." Bain grimaced. "I've said too much, but...well, since y'all are Audrey Perkins's family, I suppose you have the right to know that I personally think it's only a matter of time before we make an arrest in our double homicide case."

For some reason, Bain found himself looking at Cara. She removed her hand from the back of the sofa and met Bain's stare head-on. Her cheeks flushed slightly and she clenched her jaw as if she was agitated.

"Then you have evidence against Ms. Raney that you aren't at liberty to discuss at this time?" Cara asked.

"Not exactly, but we expect to procure that evidence very soon."

"If she killed my darling Audrey, I want her prosecuted to the fullest extent of the law." Grayson clutched his chest in an overly dramatic manner, making Bain wonder just who he was performing for—Edward Bedell or perhaps Cara. Had the son of a bitch decided he needed a new meal ticket?

Bain glanced from Grayson to Cara, who glowered at him. How was it possible for a smart, sophisticated woman like Cara Bedell to be so fooled by a scoundrel like Perkins? He was a weak, lily-livered sycophant. Couldn't she see past his pretty-boy facade?

According to those who had known her all her life,

Cara had been carrying a torch for her brother-in-law since she was a kid. Even if she was now all grown up, smart, savvy and a tough-as-nails businesswoman, maybe emotionally she was still a teenager who had a crush on her big sister's fellow.

"When you arrest Ms. Raney, we would like to be notified," Edward said.

Bain turned to the elder man and saw the suffering in his eyes. A father's pain. He'd never thought he would be capable of feeling sorry for a rich old bastard like Bedell, but right this minute, he did. Rich or poor, powerful or insignificant, all parents experienced the same torture when they lost a child.

"Yes, sir," Bain said. "Once an arrest is made, you will be the first to know."

"Jeremy, please see Lieutenant Desmond to the door." Edward shook hands with Bain again. "Thank you."

"I'll see the lieutenant out." Cara marched across the room and preempted the butler's orders by shooing Jeremy Loman aside and indicating with a sweep of her hand to Bain that they should exit the living room.

Halfway down the hall, Cara paused. "When you arrest Ms. Raney, I'd appreciate it if you contacted me personally and allowed me tell my father and Gray. They're both quite fragile right now. Gray is on the verge of a nervous breakdown and Daddy...well, Daddy isn't handling things as well as he appears to be. He's drinking quite a bit and...no one knows this, but he has a heart condition. Hell, he's not aware that I know, but his doctor felt someone in the family should be told and—"

"And you're the responsible one, right? You're the strong, in-charge caretaker for the rest of this bunch."

"You don't like us very much, do you, Lieutenant Desmond?"

He shrugged, but didn't reply.

"Are you trying to be diplomatic by not responding?" she asked.

"Yeah, something like that."

They resumed their walk toward the foyer. Once there, Bain turned and faced her. "It's none of my business, but… Never mind."

When he opened the front door, she reached out and grasped his arm. "No, please, tell me what's none of your business."

When he glanced down at her hand clutching his forearm, she released him immediately.

"Just in case no one has ever pointed it out to you before," Desmond told her, "you're way too much woman for Grayson Perkins. A woman like you deserves a hell of a lot better."

While she stood there staring at him in shock, Bain left the Bedell mansion. And with every step he took toward his vintage Corvette, he mentally kicked his own butt. Why would Cara Bedell give a damn what he thought?

CHAPTER TWENTY-THREE

THE CHATTANOOGAN, occupying a corner at 12th and Broad Streets in the heart of downtown Chattanooga's Southside, was a luxury hotel. Lausanne seriously doubted that the CPD was picking up the tab for her overnight stay. If she had to hazard a guess, she'd bet Dom would be paying the bill. After they checked in at three that afternoon, under the guise of Mr. and Mrs. Sawyer McNamara, the bellman carried their bags and led them to the elevator.

When they reached their fifth floor room, which had a waterfront view, Dom tipped the bellman and requested he fill their ice bucket. After he left to do Dom's bidding, Lausanne stared at the king-size bed, then looked at Dom.

"You don't like it?" he asked, all innocence.

"I like it just fine," she told him. "Since we're Mr. and Mrs. McNamara, there's nothing wrong with our sharing a bed, is there?"

Dom grinned. "If you're uncomfortable with—"

She rushed to him, wrapped her arms around him and said, "Stop talking nonsense. The way you're acting, you'd think we weren't already lovers."

Dom heaved a deep breath. "It's just that I don't want you to think that I think just because we've made love that I expect—"

She kissed him. "I know you're trying to be a gentleman and I appreciate it. You really are too good to be true. But you have to know that I want to be with you—" she rubbed herself against him intimately "—the way we were together on the plane flying home."

Just as Dom lowered his head to kiss her, the bellman returned with their filled ice bucket. "Excuse me, Mr. and Mrs. McNamara."

Dom released Lausanne, took the ice bucket from the bellman, set it on the table, and then walked him out into the hallway. "I'd like a couple of medium steaks, with all the trimmings, a bottle of the Broad Street Grill's best red wine and two crème brûlée desserts, if they're on the menu." Dom handed the bellman more money. "See that it's delivered around six."

"Yes, sir." The bellman grinned from ear to ear when he saw the amount of his second tip.

When Dom came back into the room and shut the door behind him, Lausanne flopped down in the comfy armchair by the window. "The way you're throwing money around, a person would think you're made of it."

"I'm not hurting for money," Dom told her. "I don't have any ex-wives I'm paying alimony to, no child support payments, and I've managed to make some wise investments over the years. I'm not wealthy by Edward Bedell's standards, but I'm comfortable."

"You don't have to spend a lot of money on me, you know. We could have stayed at a much cheaper hotel."

"So you figured out that the CPD isn't paying for this room." He came over to her and sat down on the edge of the bed across from her chair. "I figure it's money well spent. After all, I wanted to impress my best girl."

Lausanne patted his knee. "You impress me just by being you, Dom Shea. Don't you know that you're one in a million?"

Dom grinned sheepishly. "Maybe you'd better talk to my sisters before you definitely decide about that."

"Oh, would your sisters tell a different tale?"

"Would they ever."

"Just how many sisters do you have?"

"Three. One older, two younger. Pilar is married to Hart Lawton and my dad lives with them on their ranch in Texas. They've got two kids, a boy and a girl. My sister Marta lives in New York City. She's a clothing designer and just came out with her own line this past year. She's thirty-four and has no plans to ever get married. Then there's the baby, Bianca. She's in her last year of college at Texas A&M. She was our parents' surprise baby."

"It must have been wonderful growing up in a big family with a brother and three sisters and happily married parents." Lausanne's gaze connected with his. "Your parents were happily married, weren't they?"

"Yes, they were, for thirty-five years, until my mother passed away six years ago."

"Your father hasn't remarried?"

"Nope. He says that once you've had the best, you won't settle for anything else."

Tears moistened Lausanne's eyes.

Dom reached out and took both of her hands into his. "I want what my folks had. A marriage that's rock solid. A woman I love more than anything on earth, who loves me the same way, and a pack of kids keeping us on our toes."

"I—I hope you get what you want. It sounds like a beautiful dream."

"Dreams come true every day, honey."

"For some people, but not for—"

Dom yanked her out of the chair and pulled her over onto his lap. She grabbed him around the neck to keep from toppling over into the floor.

"What's your dream, Lausanne, the dream you think can't come true?"

She sighed heavily, then smiled. "I'm married to a man I adore, who adores me, and we have a couple of kids and…" Her smiled disappeared. "The other part of my dream is very selfish. My baby girl is with me and my wonderful new family." She nuzzled against Dom. "Is it so terribly wrong for me to want a chance to be her mother?"

"No, honey, it's not wrong. Just highly unlikely."

"I know. That's why it's a dream."

CARA TOOK GRAY HOME after dinner. He'd drunk a little too much, and although he had offered to call a taxi, she'd volunteered to drive him. He was quiet on the drive from Lookout Mountain to downtown, but several times he reached over and patted Cara's arm. When she glanced his way, he smiled at her, but her heart didn't leap to her throat or do an erratic rat-a-tat-tat the way it so often had over the years whenever he'd paid her the least bit of attention.

It doesn't mean anything, she told herself. You're tired, you've been under a great deal of stress and you know that it'll be up to you to hold everyone together through Audrey's funeral next week.

At least now that the police were on the verge of arresting Lausanne Raney, Cara could stop worrying about a member of her family being accused of Audrey's and Bobby Jack's murders.

When she pulled her Jaguar into the basement parking area of Gray's apartment building, she turned to him, intending to give him a sisterly goodnight kiss, but Gray grabbed her hand.

"Please, come up with me," he said. "I really can't bear to be alone."

For longer than she could remember, she'd dreamed of Gray turning to her, with that look of need in his beautiful eyes, and asking her to spend the night with him.

"You should have stayed at the house with the family."

"Perhaps you're right. But I didn't want to wear out my welcome."

"I tell you what. I'll come up with you, but I shouldn't stay the night."

"People who know us would understand that you were here with me only as a dear, kind and loving sister-in-law."

"Of course." Those old feelings of inadequacy and unimportance reared their ugly heads. "People would know you could never be interested in me. Not in that way."

"Oh, Cara, that isn't true." He brought her hand to his lips and kissed it. "Audrey's barely gone and it would be improper for me to court her sister so soon after... But in the future, the near future, I hope that you will give me a chance to rectify the mistake I made by marrying Audrey instead of waiting for you."

Her heart did skip a beat then and hope resurfaced. "Just what are you saying, Gray?"

Holding her hand and gazing adoringly into her eyes, he smiled that million watt smile that made most women swoon. It certainly had been making her swoon ever since she'd been a kid. But right now, so close to possibly hearing what she'd longed for Gray to say to her, Cara suddenly felt oddly unsure.

"When a proper amount of time has passed—at least six months—I'd like the privilege of dating you, and in time, perhaps a year from now, we might discuss marriage."

Marriage to Gray. The dream of a lifetime. So, why wasn't she overjoyed? Why didn't she feel the ecstasy she'd so often experienced in her daydreams about being his wife?

You still love him, she reminded herself. Of course she did. She had loved Gray since she'd been twelve years old and she would probably love him until the day she died, but...

But what?

Gray laughed, the sound almost too cheerful, then he said, "You're speechless, aren't you, my darling? Have I made you so happy that you can't talk?"

"I…uh…you've surprised me," she told him. "That's all. I never expected you to…well, to practically propose like this."

His smiled vanished and a sorrowful expression quickly replaced it. "Oh, I know it's much too soon to make plans, and we must keep this our little secret for now, but just think how pleased Edward will be when…say this time next year, perhaps at Thanksgiving or even Christmas…we tell him that I'm going to remain a true member of the Bedell family."

Pop! Cara's balloon burst.

More than anything, she wanted Gray to love her the way he'd loved Audrey. She had fantasized about being his wife, the woman he worshiped and adored. And here he was proposing to her, albeit a year in advance of their being able to announce their engagement. But Gray hadn't mentioned the word *love,* hadn't proclaimed his undying affection for her, hadn't said he couldn't live without her.

Think how pleased Edward will be. I'm going to remain a true member of the Bedell family.

The truth hit her like an unexpected slap across the face, brutally honest and painfully real. Gray didn't love her, had never loved her and never would. Had he ever truly loved Audrey or had it all been for show, for Edward Bedell's sake? Had Gray cared deeply for Audrey as he proclaimed or did he simply love being

Edward's son-in-law more than he could ever love anyone or anything?

"Cara, darling, are you all right?" Gray pressed her hand to his heart.

She managed to resist the instant impulse to jerk her hand away. Instead she stared at him, at his absolutely beautiful face, and for the first time since she was twelve years old, she saw beyond the grand facade. Instinctively, she lifted her other hand and caressed his smooth, flawless cheek. Her heart ached with love for the phantom Gray who had never existed, who had been a figment of her overactive, hormone-driven, adolescent imagination.

"I'm fine, Gray. Really." You poor darling, she thought, realizing just how truly perfect Gray had been for Audrey. Two totally self-centered, egotistical people. Audrey, who had possessed sadistic tendencies, and Gray who had and still did possess masochistic traits, had been a match made in heaven—or perhaps in hell. Did her father realize what a magnificent job he'd done pairing his elder daughter with Grayson Perkins?

"Will you come up with me?" Gray asked. "I really hate being alone."

"I shouldn't," Cara said. "But if you truly don't want to be alone, why don't I go up with you, help you pack a bag and then you come back to the house with me and stay for a while longer, at least until after Audrey's funeral." *Or stay for weeks or months or years. Come home with me and plant your roots so deep at the mansion that Daddy will never kick you out, despite the fact you aren't his son-in-law any longer and never will be again.*

"I suppose that's what I should do," Gray said, as if the thought of living in the Bedell mansion had never crossed his mind. "It would be unbearable staying here in the apartment. There are so many memories of Audrey here." He glanced at Cara, checking her reaction.

She patted his hand. "I understand. You loved my sister. She was your wife."

"You're the most kind and understanding woman I know, dear Cara." He gazed at her longingly, just a hint of sadness in his expression. "One day…"

Yes, one day, dear Gray, when you ask me to marry you, I'll say no.

Cara supposed she should hate Gray, but she didn't. She still loved him. But her eyes were open now and it was such a pity that, until tonight, she hadn't been able to see the man he truly was. Realization dawned in the far reaches of her consciousness. Dear God, Audrey had seen the real Gray, had known how shallow and pathetic he really was. But Cara had looked at him, judged him all these years, through the eyes of a young girl, worshiping her idol from afar.

"Come with me, darling, and help me pack," Gray said, unable to completely disguise the giddiness in his voice.

"Of course, Gray, whatever you want."

But only for now. I've paid too high a price for loving you, so from now on, things will be different. Once Audrey is laid to rest and Lausanne Raney is arrested for her murder, things are going to change drastically. After that, it will be whatever I want and to hell with everyone else.

DOM AND LAUSANNE LAY spoon fashion in the king-size bed in the fifth-floor room of The Chattanoogan Hotel facing the Tennessee River. They had eaten dinner by candlelight, finished off a bottle of excellent wine and made slow, maddeningly passionate love. The thought of making love to her aroused Dom all over again. But he would not wake her. She needed to rest. Tomorrow would be a difficult day for her. A day that could change their lives. A day he dreaded in a way he'd never dreaded another. He couldn't bear thinking about the possibility of something going wrong. If he lost her...

Completely naked, Dom eased out of bed and walked to the windows overlooking the river. He stared out into the nighttime stillness and tried to erase the worst case scenarios that kept playing inside his head.

Nothing will go wrong. She'll be protected at all times. I'll be nearby. If the police don't act quickly enough, I will.

If only they knew who the real killer was. Knowing his or her identity would help them follow through with Desmond's plan and keep Lausanne safe. At least they had been able to narrow down the suspects to three. Better than a dozen, but not as good as singling out one person.

Desmond thought Grayson Perkins had killed his wife and her lover; the odds were that he had. But they couldn't rule out Patrice or Cara, both with motives of their own. And what if the killer sent a hit man after Lausanne, instead of coming himself?

Dom's cell phone rang. Damn! He rushed over, picked up the phone off the nightstand and opened it before it rang the second time. He didn't want anything to disturb Lausanne. Before putting the phone to his ear, he noted the time on the lighted digital face. Ten-fifty. Then he checked the caller ID.

"Yeah, Sawyer, what's up?" Dom asked quietly as he headed to the bathroom.

"I have some information I thought you might want right away," Sawyer said. "It's about the child Lausanne Raney surrendered for adoption."

Dom's heart pounded. "Have you located the child?" He went into the bathroom and closed the door.

"Yes, we've located her."

"Is she—"

"The child's name is May, named by the hospital staff where she was born, since she was born in the month of May," Sawyer said.

"I don't understand. If she was adopted, why—?"

Interrupting again, Sawyer said, "May was never adopted. She's been living in foster care most of her life."

A knot of apprehension stuck in Dom's throat. He cleared his throat and asked, "Why wasn't she adopted?"

"Because there was a problem. Nobody wanted her."

CHAPTER TWENTY-FOUR

LAUSANNE HAD FORCED DOWN a few bites of toast and drunk a cup of coffee this morning, but for a while she'd felt as if she might throw up at any minute. Dom had been her rock, helping her in every possible way he could. And Lieutenant Desmond, Sergeant Swain and the other members of the CPD, who had showed up promptly at nine-thirty, had all been polite and supportive.

"You'll make the calls using this phone. We have it fixed so that the person on the other end will see a specific number and your name on their caller ID. We'll be recording each call."

"We already have people in place to keep track of all three suspects, which won't be that difficult since all three are at the Bedell mansion this morning," Sergeant Swain explained.

"Whenever you're ready, Ms. Raney," Lt. Desmond said. "Do you need to go over what you're going to say one more time?"

She looked directly at Dom when she replied. "No, I'm fine. I know exactly what I'm supposed to say."

From where he stood across the room, Dom gave her

a thumbs-up sign. She inhaled deeply and exhaled, then sat down at the desk where the police officers had connected the special phone she would be using.

"Okay, everybody, clear out," Lt. Desmond said. "Y'all take your places in the adjoining room." He glanced at Dom. "Are you staying?"

Dom narrowed his gaze. "Damn right I am."

Lt. Desmond focused on Lausanne. "Ready?"

"Ready."

When she reached for the phone, she thought it odd that her hand wasn't shaking, not in the least. That's when she realized she was functioning off pure adrenaline, that she'd shoved fear and uncertainty deep inside in order to do what had to be done.

She glanced at the list of numbers, each a cell phone, private numbers that she would have no way of knowing. Would that fact register with the suspects—would they question where she'd obtained their telephone numbers?

"Is something wrong?" Sergeant Swain asked when he noted her hesitation.

"Won't they wonder how I got hold of their private cell phone numbers?"

"Possibly," Lt. Desmond said. "But the guilty person will probably be too concerned with the fact you're in possession of a letter written by Megan Reynolds to even think about how you got his or her private number."

Lausanne nodded.

"Do you need a few more minutes, honey?" Dom asked.

She shook her head, then picked up the phone and dialed the first number. It rang five times before Grayson Perkins answered.

"Hello, Ms. Raney." His voice resonated with uncertainty.

"Good morning, Mr. Perkins. I suppose you wonder why I'm—"

"How dare you contact me," he said, as if suddenly getting over the shock of her phone call. "I thought you were in jail."

"I'm out on bail."

"I'm not speaking to you. I'm hanging up—"

"I wouldn't do that if I were you," Lausanne told him. Silence.

"I thought you might want to know that I received an Express Overnight delivery from Buenos Aires only a few minutes ago."

"Buenos Aires?" Grayson's voice quivered.

"Mmm…hmm. The delivery package contained a very interesting letter that Megan Reynolds's attorney, Senor Alejandro Lopez, was instructed, by Megan, to send to me."

"What does the letter say?"

"I think you know."

"What sort of game are you playing, Ms. Raney?"

"The game is called *I Want To Be a Millionaire,*" Lausanne told him, then ended their conversation.

When she replaced the receiver, she looked at Lt. Desmond. "Did I do all right?"

"You were great."

"What if he calls me right back?" she asked.

"He will get a busy signal no matter how many times he tries," Sergeant Swain said. "After you make the next two calls, we'll wait for a couple of hours before letting any calls come through to you. We want to give the killer a little time to sweat."

Lausanne took a deep breath, then lifted the receiver and dialed the second number.

Patrice Bedell answered on the third ring. "Ms. Raney, why are you calling me? And just how did you get my private cell phone number?"

Lausanne cut her eyes up toward Lt. Desmond, who gave her a hand signal to continue.

"I thought you'd might want to know that I received an Express Overnight delivery from Buenos Aires only a few minutes ago."

"Isn't that where you found Megan Reynolds and killed her?" Patrice said.

Disregarding Patrice's accusation, Lausanne forged ahead. "The delivery package contained a very interesting letter that Megan Reynolds's attorney, Senor Alejandro Lopez, was instructed, by Megan, to send to me."

"Then I suggest you turn the letter over to the police. I can't imagine why you'd think the letter would be of any interest to me."

Did Patrice Bedell's reaction indicate she was innocent? Or was she just a very good actress?

"You really don't want me to give this letter to the police, do you, Mrs. Bedell?"

Lausanne slammed down the receiver, then turned

to Lt. Desmond. "She told me to turn the letter over to the police."

Lt. Desmond grinned, then tapped the earpiece he wore. "I heard what she said. And the lady wasn't finished talking to you. She's calling you back as we speak."

"Oh." Lausanne twined her fingers together, released them and rubbed her hands together. Her pulse accelerated. Her palms dampened.

"Call the last name on the list," Lt. Desmond told her.

After dialing the number, she waited for Cara Bedell to answer, but after the sixth ring, the call went directly to voice mail. Lausanne looked up at Lt. Desmond, silently questioning him. He mouthed the words, *Leave a message.*

"Ms. Bedell, this is Lausanne Raney. I received a package from Buenos Aires this morning from Megan Reynolds's attorney. The package contained a letter from Megan, a letter I'm sure you'll find quite interesting."

Lt. Desmond zipped his index finger across his throat, giving her a "hang-up" signal. Lausanne replaced the receiver, then whooshed out a thank-God-that's-over sigh.

Dom came out of the corner where he'd been watching over her, shoved Lt. Desmond aside and pulled a visibly shaken Lausanne securely against him.

"You did a great job, Ms. Raney," Sergeant Swain said.

Lausanne looked up. "What now?"

"Now we wait and let them stew," Lt. Desmond replied. "Perkins and Mrs. Bedell have tried to call you back."

"Which means?" Lausanne asked.

"Nothing…something…everything," he told her.

She emitted a chuckle, her nerves finally unraveling.

As if instinctively knowing she needed to lean on him, Dom walked her over to the bed and the two of them sat down, side by side. He took her hand in his and she rested her head on his shoulder.

"I'M SORRY, but if you want the best—"

"I want Lausanne Raney eliminated immediately. The woman has a letter in her possession written by Megan Reynolds."

Interesting that there would be a second letter, one perhaps written before the unfinished missive found in Ms. Reynolds's room at the Alvear Palace Hotel.

"My contact has assured me that this gentleman will be available tomorrow and can fly directly to Chattanooga," he explained.

"I thought I made myself clear. I can't wait another day. The woman has a letter, which I assume makes an accusation against the person she believed killed Audrey and Bobby Jack Cash. I cannot allow this letter to fall into the wrong hands."

"I understand, and if you're willing to let me use someone already in the area, then—"

"You've used incompetent locals twice before and they failed miserably to eliminate Ms. Raney. No, I will not pay one red cent for another botched job."

"Then perhaps you can speak to Ms. Raney, make her an offer she can't refuse, buy yourself some time."

"I would prefer not to get my hands dirty, but it seems I have no other choice. I'll take care of Ms. Raney myself."

"But wouldn't that be a mistake? Her death could be traced back to you and—"

The dial tone hummed in his ears. Damn arrogant... He'd just lost a hefty commission because his client was running scared. He had tried to explain the proper course of action, one that involved bribery and patience, but it was apparent that his client had run out of patience.

HER NERVES FRAYED and her patience wearing thin, Lausanne paced the floor in her hotel room. Everyone had cleared out for an hour, leaving Dom and her alone. They hadn't talked much. He had held her in his arms for most of that time, the two of them sitting quietly, and for a few brief moments, she'd felt safe.

A knock sounded on the outer door. "It's Lt. Desmond."

Lausanne eased off Dom's lap and sat down in the chair opposite him, then said, "Yes, come on in."

Lt. Desmond glanced at the telephone on the desk. "We've let our suspects stew for a couple of hours. It's time to allow calls to come through now."

"Any word on their reactions?" Dom asked.

"All three have left the Bedell mansion," Lt Desmond said. "We have someone tailing each of them. Mrs. Bedell has gone to her hairdressers for her weekly appointment. Mr. Perkins went to his penthouse apartment. And Ms. Bedell telephoned police headquarters and asked to speak to me. I sent Sergeant Swain to meet her."

"Why would she want to speak to the police, to you in particular?" Lausanne asked. "Do you think she intends to report my phone call?"

"Maybe. We won't know until Mike talks to her and finds out what she wants."

"In the meantime?" Dom asked.

"We wait to see if anyone took the bait."

Five minutes passed. Lausanne paced. Ten minutes passed. Dom paced with her. Fifteen minutes passed. Lt. Desmond joined them and when his phone rang, the three of them bumped into each other.

Lt. Desmond flipped open his phone and said, "Yeah, Mike, what have you got?"

Dom's gaze met Lausanne's and they waited anxiously for the detective to finish his brief conversation. When he closed his phone, he glanced from Dom to Lausanne.

"Cara Bedell just told Sergeant Swain that Lausanne Raney telephoned her earlier this morning and left a message telling her that she had received a letter, via Senor Lopez, from Megan Reynolds. It seems Ms. Bedell believes Ms. Raney wants to blackmail someone in the Bedell family."

"Well, I'll be damned," Dom said.

"Ms. Bedell told Mike that undoubtedly Ms. Raney didn't kill Audrey or Bobby Jack, but knows who did."

"Well, that certainly narrows down our suspects, doesn't it?" Dom slipped his arm around Lausanne's waist and gave her a comforting hug.

As if on cue, Lausanne's phone rang. Three pairs of eyes zeroed in on the telephone. She looked to Lt. Desmond.

"Let it ring three times, then answer it," he instructed.

She did just that and picked it up after the third ring.
"Hello."

"Ms. Raney?"

"Yes." She didn't recognize the voice, but it was definitely male. It had to be Grayson Perkins.

"I understand you have a letter written by Megan Reynolds, is that correct?"

Whoever she was talking to, it wasn't Audrey's husband, but his voice sounded vaguely familiar. She glanced at Lt. Desmond, knowing he could hear the conversation, and gave him a questioning stare, silently asking him if he recognized the voice. He shrugged and shook his head.

"Yes, that's correct," Lausanne replied.

"I wish to purchase that letter."

Lausanne swallowed hard. "That's good, because I want to sell it."

"What's your price?"

She looked at Lt. Desmond. He mouthed, *A million dollars. Cash.*

"A million dollars," Lausanne said, keeping her gaze focused on Lt. Desmond. "In cash."

"I can't get my hands on that large amount today, but I can make a sizable down payment."

"How sizable?"

"Let's say a hundred thousand. Call it good faith money."

"All right. I'll want the money deposited—"

"No! If you want the money, you'll meet me when and where I say."

Her gaze collided with Lt. Desmond's. He nodded his head.

"All right," Lausanne replied.

"Bring the letter with you."

"Do you think I'm crazy? No million dollars, no letter."

"I need some assurance that you will not hand the letter over to the authorities," he said.

How did she respond to his request? Thinking fast on her feet, Lausanne blurted out, "If you can get your hands on five hundred thousand today, I'll bring the letter with me. It's a real bargain at that price."

"You have a deal, Ms. Raney."

"When and where shall we meet?"

"Bedell, Inc. In the basement parking garage. At nine o'clock this evening. And come alone. Our business is private."

"Tonight at nine."

She hung up the phone, shot out of the chair and faced Lt. Desmond. "That wasn't Grayson Perkins."

The lieutenant shook his head. "No, it wasn't. The call was traced to the Bedell mansion and I'm relatively certain the man you just spoke to is Jeremy Loman, the Bedell butler."

"You're right," Lausanne said. "I thought his voice sounded familiar. But he's not even one of the suspects."

"He is now," Dom told her. "Right, Desmond?"

"Yeah. This is a new, unexpected twist," the detective said. "In our investigation, we didn't come up with any reason why Jeremy Loman would want to kill Audrey or Bobby Jack. He's been a devoted employee for over twenty years and it's the opinion of everyone who knows the man that he'd cut off his right arm before harming anyone in the family."

"If your information is correct, it means Loman didn't kill anyone," Dom said. "He made that phone call to Lausanne on someone else's behalf."

"Grayson Perkins," Lausanne said.

"Possibly," Dom agreed. "Or maybe Cara Bedell went to the police to throw them off track and had Daddy's devoted servant do her dirty work."

"When you meet with Loman tonight, you'll be wired, so we'll be able to hear everything that's said," Lt. Desmond told her. "During the day today, we'll gradually move our people into position in the underground parking deck at Bedell, Inc., and we'll have to do it so that they're not detected. At this point, we can't trust anyone."

CHAPTER TWENTY-FIVE

A CHATTANOOGA POLICE officer drove the taxi that would take Lausanne from the hotel to Bedell, Inc. headquarters only a few blocks across town. Lt. Desmond and Dom accompanied her on the elevator ride to the lobby.

"You have the sealed letter?" Lt. Desmond asked.

Lausanne patted her chest. She had folded the blank letter the detective had provided for her and slipped it inside her shirt pocket, after the female police officer had "wired" her. She felt ten pounds heavier wearing the concealable bullet-proof vest, although the vest was relatively lightweight.

When they reached the lobby level, Dom hit a button to keep the doors closed, then hauled Lausanne up against him and kissed her. Lt. Desmond looked down at his feet.

"I won't be far away at any time," Dom told her.

"I know." She pulled out of his embrace, hit the open button and marched out of the elevator, leaving Dom and the lieutenant behind, as she was supposed to do. According to the police, none of the suspects, which now included Jeremy Loman, had figured out where Lausanne was, but better to play it safe than to be sorry. There was no need to advertise the fact that she had police backup.

Lausanne walked outside where the taxi waited. The driver got out and opened the door for her. "I'm Officer Anderson," the man told her.

She nodded, then got in the back seat and said, "I'm ready to go."

Lausanne's thick, long hair hid the device planted inside her right ear that allowed her to hear Lt. Desmond.

"Once you arrive at the underground parking deck, I won't make contact unless we know you're in trouble or I feel it necessary to give you information or instructions," he had explained. "But we'll be able to hear everything that's said, so if something goes wrong, we can move in immediately."

"Lausanne." It was Dom's voice, not the lieutenant's she heard in her ear.

"Yes?"

"Are you okay?"

"Yes."

"Look, Desmond's letting me relay info to you for the time being. It seems Patrice Bedell is attending a charity fashion show this evening and Cara Bedell is staying in tonight. Grayson Perkins is still at his office in the Bedell Building."

"What about Jeremy Loman?"

"Loman is driving Edward Bedell's Bentley," Dom said. "He's coming up Broad Street and should arrive at Bedell, Inc. about the same time you do. One of Desmond's men has been tailing him since he pulled the car out of the garage at the Bedell estate."

Dom kept talking to her, shoring up her confidence, reassuring her she'd be safe, that she would be surrounded by Chattanooga's finest. Before she realized it, the taxi took her underground to the parking garage.

"Do you see the Bentley?" Dom asked.

"No, not yet," she said.

"Loman arrived about two minutes ago. Do not get out of the taxi. Wait until you see the Bentley, then have the driver park behind the Bentley and wait for Loman to make the next move."

"I see it," she told Dom. "But I don't see Loman."

"Okay, honey, I'm handing things over to Desmond now."

"Dom?"

"It's going to be all right, honey. When this is all over, you and I have a future to plan."

"What did you—"

"Lausanne," Lt. Desmond said. "Get out of the taxi and wait for Mr. Loman to approach you. We have him under surveillance, but we can't be sure he's not armed. Do you understand?"

"Yes."

The taxi stopped.

"When I hop out, you drive off, right?" she asked Officer Anderson.

"Yes, ma'am."

She opened the door herself, pulled some bills the

lieutenant had stuffed into her coat pocket before she'd left her hotel room, and handed them to the driver. She stood there, stiff as a poker, her heartbeat thumping maddeningly in her chest and watched the taxi drive away and out of the underground garage.

As soon as she was alone, a man emerged from the driver's side of the Bentley. Steeling her nerves, determined to meet danger without buckling, she faced Jeremy Loman, but didn't approach him.

He looked right at her, but it seemed that he was looking through her.

"You're alone?" he asked.

"Yes."

"You brought the letter?"

"Yes."

"I want to see it."

"I want to see my money first," she said.

The Bentley's left side back door opened and a voice from inside said, "Please get in the car, Ms. Raney. I have your money."

Lausanne's heart skipped a beat. Oh shit!

"Was that another voice I heard?" Desmond asked through the device in Lausanne's ear.

"Mr. Bedell, is that you?" Lausanne suddenly felt nauseous.

Edward Bedell leaned forward just enough for Lausanne to see him clearly. Well, this was one scenario none of them had figured on.

"Yes, Ms. Raney. Weren't you expecting me?"

"Ah, not exactly. I thought Mr. Loman was handling

the transaction." *God help me,* Lausanne prayed silently. *I don't know what's going on here. I feel as if I've just stepped in quicksand and I'm sinking fast.*

"I'd prefer to conduct our business out in the open, Mr. Bedell," Lausanne said, doing her best to act as if she knew what was going on.

"Very well. As you wish."

When he emerged from the back of the Bentley, the first thing Lausanne noticed was the gun he held in his hand. Knowing nothing about guns, she had no idea what make or model it was, but her brain registered that it was large and deadly. Was it the same weapon used to kill Audrey and Bobby Jack?

"What would you like to say to me, Ms. Raney?" Edward asked. "Would you like to tell me that Megan Reynolds wrote you a letter telling you that I paid her a small fortune to impersonate my daughter, that I warned her to leave the country and never return? Instead she hired you to impersonate Audrey and then she ran off with my million dollars and wanted more."

Lausanne swallowed the lump of fear in her throat. "That—that's not all she told me in the letter." Brave this out, she told herself. False bravado is better than letting him know you're scared out of your mind, even if you are.

"I have no idea exactly what she told you. But she didn't know anything for certain. She only suspected what had happened because she had known about Audrey's plans to speak to me and when Audrey didn't return to the penthouse…"

Think, Lausanne, think. What could Megan Rey-

nolds have written to incriminate Edward Bedell in his
own daughter's death? Can't go that route. Use another
tactic.

"You killed Bobby Jack Cash," Lausanne said.

"Yes, I did. And I took great pleasure in shooting him
repeatedly, until I was certain he was dead."

"But why did you kill your own daughter?" Lausanne
stared at the gun Edward held in his unsteady hand. *Are
you there, Lieutenant Desmond? Do you have me surrounded with police protection? Can I really count on
you, Dom, to make sure I'm safe?*

"Keep him talking," the voice in her ear said very
softly. The lieutenant's voice.

"It was an accident," Edward said, tears glazing his
eyes. "She and that filthy bastard Cash came to see me
that day. Audrey told me she was divorcing Gray and
marrying Cash, that she loved the man, that they were
leaving Chattanooga together and unless I accepted
Cash into the family, I'd never see her again.

"Cash stood there looking at me, a smirking grin on
his face. I told him I'd never let him have my precious
Audrey and he laughed at me. That's when I took the
gun out of my desk and aimed it at him. When I pulled
the trigger, Audrey stepped between us and…" Edward
broke down and cried.

"Sir, are you all right?" Loman asked. "Is there
anything I can do for you?"

Edward waved his left hand around, all the while
keeping the gun in his right hand aimed at Lausanne.

"Please, come and get in the car, Ms. Raney. I want you to take a ride with me."

"Why should I do that?"

"I would prefer not to kill you here."

"I'd prefer you didn't kill me at all."

"If you don't come with me willingly, I'll be forced to allow Loman to use force."

Loman took a tentative step toward her. She backed up a couple of feet.

"Then Loman's just going to have to use force," Lausanne said. "Because I'm not going anywhere with you. I thought we had a deal. I'd swap you the letter for the five hundred grand. Then I'd keep my mouth shut."

"I had a similar deal with Megan Reynolds," Edward said. "But I don't believe you're anymore trustworthy than she was."

"You didn't mean to kill Audrey." Lausanne said the first thing that came to mind, trying her best to buy some time. "It was an accident, right? Why should you be punished for something you didn't mean to do?"

Okay, guys, where the hell are you? Why haven't you made a move? You're leaving me out here on a cracked branch that's going to break off any minute now.

"Audrey was my life. I wouldn't have harmed a hair on her head," Edward said. "She shouldn't have stepped in front of Cash and taken the bullet that was meant for him."

"When you realized what had happened, that you'd shot Audrey by mistake, then you turned on Bobby Jack and killed him." She jerked her gaze back and forth, from the gun Edward Bedell held, to Jeremy Loman, who kept inching toward her as if he thought by coming at her very slowly, she wouldn't run from him.

Lausanne backed up until her hips encountered the front end of a massive SUV parked behind her. "Your ever faithful servant, Mr. Loman here, cleaned up after you, didn't he? Literally. He disposed of the bodies for you by dumping them into the river and then he cleaned up all the blood in the den or the living room or wherever the shootings took place."

"You're a very smart girl, Ms. Raney," Edward said. "Far too smart for your own good. Megan thought she could outsmart me. She didn't. Neither can you."

"No one ever suspected you, not the grieving father who had all but worshiped his elder daughter."

"I couldn't bear to think of what I'd done. I—I destroyed the one thing that meant more to me than life itself." Edward's big, broad shoulders shook with emotion.

Lausanne turned her gaze on Jeremy Loman. "You're the one who held things together, the one who took care of the details." Her mind created a logical scenario. "The day it happened, you took your employer upstairs to his room, gave him a sedative and put him to bed. Then you went back downstairs and carried the bodies outside and put them in the trunk of—" she pointed directly at the Bentley "—this car, because you knew the police were unlikely to inspect a car used by no one else in the family. Afterward you cleaned up the blood as best you could and tidied the room. Then that night, you took the bodies to the river and dumped them."

"You are very smart," Loman said.

"And so are you," Lausanne told him. "Your devotion to your employer is admirable. I'll bet you're the one who took care of all the other dirty work, like arranging to pay off Megan and maybe even hiring someone to kill her and to kill me."

Loman lunged for Lausanne, who jumped out of his grasp.

When she broke into a run, Edward Bedell shouted, "Catch her!"

"Shoot her, sir," Loman retaliated.

Edward aimed the gun, but before he could fire, a rifle shot rang out, shattering the left back window of the Bentley.

WITHIN SECONDS, the hidden police officers surrounded the Bentley, handcuffed a startled Jeremy Loman and ordered Edward Bedell, who had crawled back inside the car, to surrender.

Dom came racing toward Lausanne, who rushed into his open arms. He swung her off her feet and shoved her behind him, up against the concrete wall near the elevators.

A single shot rang out, as loud as a cannon blast in the quiet of the underground parking garage.

"God damn," Desmond bellowed the curse. "Everyone stay back. That shot came from inside the Bentley."

From where he stood, Dom couldn't see the other side of the parked Bentley all that well, but he was able to see Desmond heading toward the car, his 9mm ready to use if necessary.

Less than a minute later, Desmond called out. "Bedell's dead. He shot himself in the head."

While the police buzzed about the parking garage like a swarm of worker bees, Dom yanked Lausanne around and into his arms. She held on to him for dear life, but sniffling softly as if she didn't want him to know she was crying with relief.

"It's all right, honey. You're safe. It's all over."

Desmond marched over to them, all the while issuing orders to his men. He paused in front of them and said, "Take her home. We've got everything we need for now." When Lausanne raised her head from Dom's chest and looked at the lieutenant, he stared right at her and said, "Thank you, Ms. Raney. You did a great job here tonight."

Dom didn't waste any time getting Lausanne out of the parking garage and away from Bedell, Inc. The officer who had brought Lausanne there in the taxi drove the two of them back to the Chattanoogan Hotel.

When the elevator stopped at the fifth floor, Dom lifted Lausanne in his arms and carried her down the corridor toward their room. The way he felt right this minute, he might not ever let her go. He just might keep the two of them locked up in the hotel room for the next forty or fifty years.

CHAPTER TWENTY-SIX

IN HIS LINE OF WORK, Bain Desmond had been responsible on numerous occasions for informing a family that a loved one had been killed. But in his fifteen years on the Chattanooga police force, he'd never dreaded anything as much as he did telling Cara Bedell that her father had committed suicide, after confessing to murdering his elder daughter and her lover. He had phoned ahead and told her he needed to speak to the family and would appreciate it if she would assemble everyone together before he arrived. Bain had no idea how she'd handle the news or what effect the old bastard's death would have on her life. Maybe she would inherit her daddy's fortune, kick stepmommy dearest out, marry Grayson Perkins and live happily ever after.

When Bain arrived at the Bedell mansion on Lookout Mountain, an area where old money had lived for generations, and rang the bell, Cara Bedell opened the door for him. Her eyes were wide and bright and he realized she sensed that his news was not good.

"Please, come in," she said. "Gray is here. He came straight from work an hour ago and told us that something terrible must have happened at Bedell, Inc., tonight, in the underground parking area. He said that the police wouldn't allow him to get his car and asked him to take a taxi home, but wouldn't tell him what was going on."

"Yes, ma'am, that's correct." Bain entered the two story foyer.

"I did as you requested when you phoned and had Patrice come home from her charity event, but I can't seem to locate Daddy or Jeremy. I've tried reaching them on their cell phones and—"

"Could we join the others, Mr. Perkins and Mrs. Bedell?" Bain requested. "What I have to tell y'all, I'd like to say to all of you at the same time."

"Certainly. They're waiting in the living room." Cara turned and headed toward the closed pocket doors.

She paused at the double doors and glanced over her shoulder at Bain, who stood directly behind her. She looked as if she wanted to say something, but for a good thirty seconds, she simply stared at him, then she opened the doors and walked into the living room.

As soon as she entered, Patrice Bedell shot up off the sofa where she'd been sitting with Grayson Perkins and said, "What's this all about, Lieutenant? If you've dragged me away from—"

"Sit down and shut up," Cara told her stepmother.

"Why, I never," Patrice gasped. "Your manners are deplorable, every bit as bad as your father's."

"What happened in the underground parking deck?" Grayson asked. "When I left, there were police cars and an ambulance and—"

"Yeah, I know. I was there." Bain took a deep breath. "There is no easy way to say this, so I'm just going to say it. Edward Bedell committed suicide. He shot himself in the head. He was in the back seat of his Bentley, parked in the Bedell, Inc. basement parking garage."

Deafening silence.

Patrice slumped down on the sofa, her eyes glazed with shock.

"Poor Edward," Grayson said. "He couldn't bear the thought of living without Audrey. I know just how he feels, but—" He looked up at Cara like a hungry dog begging for a bone. "But he should have thought of Cara, his other daughter, who loves…loved him far more than Audrey ever did."

"Was Jeremy with Daddy when he—?" Cara asked, then clenched her teeth, obviously trying her best not to cry.

"Yes, ma'am," Bain replied.

"Where is Jeremy now?" she asked. "He must be devastated. He loved Daddy like a brother. He'd have done anything for him."

"Mr. Loman has been arrested," Bain said.

"What? Why?" Cara's gaze collided with Bain's.

"Mr. Loman confessed to being an accessory to murder."

"Whose murder?" Grayson asked.

Bain cleared his throat. "Lausanne Raney telephoned the three of you this morning and told each of you that she had received a letter from Megan Reynolds." Bain took his time, speaking carefully, as he explained how

Lausanne had worked with the CPD to set a trap for a killer. "Did any one of you tell someone else about the phone call you received from Ms. Raney?"

"I went straight to the police," Cara said. "I spoke to Sergeant Swain."

Bain nodded.

"I didn't mention it to anyone," Grayson said. "I didn't want anything to do with Ms. Raney and whatever trick she was trying to play on us."

"I told Edward." Patrice glanced from person to person, her gaze questioning them, as if asking, *Did I do anything wrong?* "I thought he should know that the Raney woman was trying to cause trouble."

"Ms. Raney received a call from Mr. Loman this morning, and following his instructions, she met him in the underground parking garage at Bedell, Inc. tonight. Ms. Raney was wired and had police backup." Bain went on to explain about Edward Bedell's confession—that he had accidentally shot his own daughter when she'd stepped in the way of a bullet meant for her lover. Without going into details, he explained how Jeremy Loman had removed the bodies and taken them to the river.

"Dear God, Edward killed Audrey!" Grayson crossed his hands over his chest in a dramatic manner.

"Poor, poor Daddy." Cara gazed off into space, a lost look on her face.

"Later, if you'd like to talk to me about this...about anything, Ms. Bedell, call me." Bain laid his business card on the antique coffee table.

When he walked out of the room, Cara followed and

caught up with him just as he reached the front door. "Lieutenant?"

He turned to face her. "Yes, ma'am?"

"Will you notify me when the police release my sister's body and my father's? I believe it only fitting that they have a double funeral. Daddy would have liked—" Her voice cracked. She tightened her jaw and breathed in through her nose.

Instinctively, Bain took a step toward her. She was trying so desperately to be brave and strong and not fall apart, but he knew she needed somebody to lean on, if only for a little while.

"If there is anything—" He took another hesitant step toward her.

"Thank you, but no," she replied.

He stopped dead still.

"I…uh…should contact our lawyers and see about taking care of Jeremy. He—he tried to take care of Daddy, didn't he, but he went about it all wrong. And then there will be the funeral arrangements to make later and—oh, God, I'll have to make a statement to the press. Bedell, Inc. stock is bound to be affected by this. Gray will be so overwrought that he'll be of little help to me and Patrice will want the will read before breakfast in the morning, the greedy bitch." Cara talked rapidly, as if her mind were whirling out of control with so much to think about, so many plans to make. "I loved him, you know, even if he never loved me."

At first, Bain wasn't sure if Cara meant Edward Bedell or Grayson Perkins, then when she said, "Daddy wanted to love me, but he just couldn't," Bain saw such raw pain in her face that he didn't know whether to turn away or pull her into his arms.

He closed the distance between them and without giving any thought to what he was doing, acting purely on instinct, he wrapped his arms around Cara. She gasped the moment their bodies touched, but when Bain cupped the back of her head, she relaxed against him and rested her head on his shoulder. A few seconds later, she trembled, then began weeping.

"Cara, where are you, darling?" Grayson Perkins called out as he emerged from the living room.

Cara jerked out of Bain's embrace. Their gazes connected for half a second, then she replied to her brother-in-law. "I'll be right there."

Grayson stood on the far side of the foyer, a lost little boy look on his handsome face. He held out his hand. "I'm simply devastated, Cara. However will we survive without Edward?"

"Thank you, Lieutenant." Cara seemed uncertain of what else to say or do.

"Cara!" Grayson lamented.

"You're being summoned," Bain told her.

"Gray needs me." She wiped the tears from her face with her fingertips.

And what do you need, Cara Bedell? "You know how to reach me if…" Bain left his sentence unfinished, then turned and walked out of the Bedell mansion. When he closed the door behind him, he stood there on the ex-

pansive veranda and cursed a blue streak, calling himself
every kind of fool known to mankind.

WHEN LAUSANNE WOKE the next morning, Dom was
sitting across from the bed, his feet propped up on the
edge of the bed and a cup of coffee in his right hand.
He wore his wrinkled slacks from the night before, but
his chest was bare.

"Good morning, sleepyhead," he said.

Stretching, she smiled at him. "What time is it?"

"Nearly ten-thirty."

"I'm hungry." She kicked the covers to the foot of the
bed, revealing her naked body and issuing Dom a seductive invitation.

"I'll order breakfast," he said teasingly.

"I'm not hungry for food."

Dom grinned. "Woman, you're insatiable."

"Are you complaining?"

"No, ma'am. I'm no fool. I know a great thing when
I see it." He appraised her body in a mockingly lecher-
ous fashion. "But twice last night will have to hold you
until later. We have business to discuss."

She crawled out of bed and slinked toward him. He
set his coffee mug on the nightstand. When she snuggled
onto his lap and curled her arms around his neck, he
swatted her playfully on her butt.

"What sort of business do we have to discuss?" She
planted half a dozen kisses over his face as she rubbed
her breasts across his chest.

He grabbed her, shoved her back and said, "Down girl."

Lausanne giggled.

"Come on, honey, let's be serious for a few minutes."

"Okay. I'm serious." She frowned. "Is this serious enough for you?"

With one arm around her waist, he leaned down and grabbed the edge of his discarded shirt from where he'd tossed it on the floor last night. They'd been in a frenzy, ripping off each other's clothes and going at each other like a couple of wild animals. They had been riding the crest of adrenaline highs created by the danger and excitement they'd shared.

"Here, honey, put this on," he told her. "I can't think straight with you naked and wiggling around in my lap."

Lausanne slipped into his shirt, but left it unbuttoned. "Down to serious business. I'm listening."

Dom cleared his throat. "I love you."

She tensed. "What?"

"I love you," he repeated.

"Oh."

"I think this is where you say you love me, too."

"I—I can't."

"Why not? You do love me, don't you?"

"Of course I love you," she said.

"Now that we've got that settled, I have a very important question to ask you."

She averted her gaze, looking everywhere except right at him.

"Lausanne Raney, will you marry me?"

"What did you say?"

"I love you, honey, and I want you be my wife. You

know, love and marriage and kids and happily ever after. The whole nine yards."

She shot up out of his lap, placed her hands on her hips and glared at him. "Are you out of your mind? Just because I'm not a murderer doesn't mean I'm not an ex-con with a horrible track record where men are concerned. What would your family—your sisters—say if you brought a woman like me home and introduced me as your wife?"

"Actually, I'd thought we'd do things up right and have a big Texas wedding back in Green Springs, in the same church where my folks got married. That way my sisters could be your bridesmaids and my dad could be my best man."

"I can't marry you. I'd ruin your life. You know what kind of—"

He yanked her down into his lap and kissed her into silence. When they finally came up for air, he said, "You have to marry me."

"I do?"

"Yes, you do."

"I'm not pregnant, so it's not as if there's a child involved."

"Well, that's not exactly true."

She glared at him. "What do you mean?"

"Well, you see, I'm planning on adopting a little girl named May. She's ten and a half years old and has lived most of her life in foster care. She really needs a mother and father who'll love her and take care of her and appreciate her for the very special child she is."

Lausanne's heart stopped. Then she started breathing again, air rushing out of her mouth in a giant gasp. "Dom?"

"Hmm…?"

"Are you talking about my little girl?"

He nodded.

"Her name is May?"

He nodded again.

"Why has she been in foster care all these years? I was told she would be adopted by a loving couple who desperately wanted a baby."

Lausanne sensed the hesitation in Dom, saw the sorrow in his eyes. Oh, God, no! "Tell me," she said.

"There were several couples who wanted May, but it seems they all wanted a perfect baby, one without any flaws."

"And May was flawed?"

Dom wrapped Lausanne in his arms and held her tightly, as if he was afraid she'd crumble into pieces if he didn't hold her together.

"May was born with a condition known as ONH. Optic Nerve Hypoplasia. ONH is not progressive. It's not inherited and cannot be cured." When Lausanne keened softly, Dom squeezed her fiercely. "There is no known cause for ONH." Dom kissed her temple. "Honey, May is legally blind, although she can see light and shadows."

"My baby girl is blind and I never knew…and because she has this condition, this ONH, nobody wanted to adopt her?" Lausanne trembled, from head to toe.

"As an infant she lived with foster parents who were very good to her and got her all the help she needed, but this couple were in their late sixties. The wife died when May was five and she lived in a couple of other foster homes until she was eight. She's been living with Brenda and Larry Grissom for the past two years. They're good people and are caring for half a dozen children with mental or physical disabilities."

"Oh, Dom. Dear Lord, if only I'd known."

"You know now, honey. Your little girl needs you. She needs us."

Lausanne twisted around on Dom's lap so that they were face to face. "Where is she? Can we go see her?" Tears trickled down Lausanne's cheeks.

"The Grissoms live in a little town less than an hour from here. It's a place called Jasper." He swiped the tears off her cheeks with his open palm. "I spoke to them about an hour ago, while you were still sleeping. They're expecting us this afternoon."

"I'm going to see my daughter this afternoon?"

"Yes, you are," Dom said. "I'm having Daisy, at Dundee's, fax them all the verification they need to prove we're who we say we are. And Berton Oliver has a colleague who is an expert in adoption laws and I've asked him to represent us."

"Us?"

"Us," Dom said. "May's mother and father."

"Oh, Dom." Fresh tears sprang into her eyes. "You really are too good to be true."

WHEN THEY ARRIVED at the Grissoms' large, split-level brick house in Jasper, Larry Grissom met them at the door. He was tall and rotund, with a heavy gray beard and a welcoming smile on his rosy-cheeked face.

"Y'all come on in. Brenda's sister took the other kids over at her house for the afternoon," Larry said. "We thought it would be better if there wasn't so much going on when May meets you folks. She's a real friendly, out-going little girl. Got a fantastic personality. Never meets a stranger and can talk a blue streak. Everybody who knows her adores her."

Larry surveyed Lausanne from head to toe. "I can sure tell you're our little May's mama. She's the spitting image of you. Got that same curly red hair and little button nose. She's a beauty, our May."

"What have you told her about us, about me?" Lausanne asked.

"We just told her that some really nice folks were coming by to visit and y'all were real eager to meet her."

A tall, skinny woman with short black hair and sparkling hazel eyes entered the room. A small, delicate little girl was holding tenaciously to the woman's hand.

"Good afternoon. I'm Brenda Grissom." She eased the child from her side to stand in front of her, keeping her hands gently clasped to the little girl's shoulders. "And this is May."

"Hello, May," Lausanne said, barely managing not to cry. "I'm Lausanne."

"Hi," May said, lowering her head, casting her gaze downward.

"And this is Dom." Lausanne grasped Dom's hand.

"Lausanne and Dom have come here this afternoon to see you, May," Larry said.

May squinted as she lifted her gaze, as if the light hurt her eyes. "Why do you want to see me?"

Dom squeezed Lausanne's hand and when he realized she couldn't speak, he urged her forward, leading her across the room to where May stood in front of her foster mother.

He squatted down in front of May. "I own a ranch out in Texas. I've got a niece about your age and a nephew a little older. They live on a ranch just down the road from mine. We've got horses and cattle and—"

"And dogs?" May asked.

Dom chuckled. "You bet. We've got lots of dogs."

"I like dogs, but Brenda is allergic, so we can't get a dog."

"May, how would you like to visit Lausanne and me, out on our ranch in Texas where you can play with all our dogs?" Dom asked.

May's beautiful little face, which was indeed a miniature of Lausanne's, lit up. She smiled from ear to ear, showing off a set of perfect white teeth. She reached out and ran her fingertips up and down Dom's face, looking him over quite thoroughly.

"I don't know if Brenda and Larry will let me go all the way to Texas," May said. "But I sure would love to play with your dogs."

"What if the first time you visit, Brenda and Larry come along with you?" Dom asked.

"And all the other kids, too?" May pressed her little fingers over Dom's lips.

He clutched her hand in his. "You bet, honey."

May lifted her head, her eyes not quite focusing as she asked, "Can we, Brenda?"

"I think maybe we can," her foster mother replied.

"Lausanne and I are getting married very soon," Dom said. "We'd like all of you to come for the wedding. And if May wants to, we'd like for her to be a flower girl, along with my niece."

"What's a flower girl?" May asked.

Lausanne finally found her voice. "That's a very important job. The flower girls walk down the church aisle in front of the bride and they strow flower petals down for the bride to walk on."

"Oh." May frowned.

Lausanne knelt down beside Dom, reached out and took May's hand. "What's wrong?"

"I probably can't do that," May said. "I don't see very well. I'm not totally blind, but—"

"You wouldn't be walking down the aisle alone," Dom told her. "My niece Maureen would be at your side. You could hold on to her arm. How would that do?"

May's beautiful smile returned. "Yes, I could do that, but I don't understand why you would want me to be a flower girl in your wedding. You don't even know me."

The tears Lausanne had kept under control broke

free and trickled down her cheeks. Unexpectedly, May reached out and touched Lausanne's cheek.

"You're crying," May said. "Are you unhappy?"

"No, darling, I'm crying because I'm so very, very happy."

"Oh, that's good. I'm glad you're happy." May continued studying Lausanne's face with her fingertips, then lifted her hand to Lausanne's hair. "Ooh, your hair feels just like mine. It's thick and curly."

"And it's red just like yours," Dom told her. "And she's pretty, too, just like you."

"Am I pretty?" May asked.

"You're the prettiest little girl in the world." Lausanne barely managed to speak before she started crying again.

"And we want you to be one of the flowers girls in our wedding because we heard how pretty and smart and how very special you are." Dom looked up at May's foster mother. "Isn't that right, Mrs. Grissom?"

"Yes, that's right, Mr. Shea."

Dom put his arm around Lausanne and lifted her to her feet. "We'd better go, but if it's all right with you folks, we'd like to come back tomorrow."

"Absolutely," Larry replied. "Y'all come back as often as you'd like and when you get that wedding planned, we'll come out to Texas and bring you a very special wedding present."

EPILOGUE

THANKSGIVING AT THE SHEA house was a three-ring circus, with kids and dogs and cats and visiting relatives running around in every direction. And that was just inside the sprawling two-story farmhouse that Dom and Lausanne had designed and built during the first year of their marriage. Outside cattle and horses roamed and often four-wheelers roared along the trails cut through the open range. When Dom had retired from Dundee's and they moved to Texas a month before their wedding, which had been an early March event nearly seven years ago, they'd lived in a small trailer that had been set about three hundred yards behind where the present home was erected.

After they first got married, they had flown back to Jasper, Tennessee, to visit May every other weekend during the next three months, letting her get to know them gradually. Before long she had come to Texas for a weekend with them. When they had told her they wanted to adopt her, to make her their little girl forever, she'd hesitated, voicing her doubts about leaving the Grissoms. So Lausanne and Dom had given May all the time and space she needed, extending her monthly visits to Texas from weekends to a week at a time.

Eight months after their wedding, Lausanne discovered she was pregnant. And although she and Dom were ecstatic, they were uncertain how May would react when they told her.

"I think it's wonderful that y'all are going to have a baby of your own," May had said, tears in her blue-green eyes. "I guess it's a good thing you didn't already adopt me or you'd be stuck with me."

Lausanne had wrapped her arms around her daughter and hugged her. Then in very simple terms, she told May a story about herself, about how when she'd been not quite eighteen, she'd given birth to a baby girl and how she'd given her baby away because she'd been told that a wonderful couple wanted to adopt her child.

May had grasped Lausanne's face between her open palms. "I'm really your little girl? I'm that baby?"

"Yes, sweetheart, you're that baby. You're my daughter and I want you to come and live with Dom and me and let us be your parents."

"Dom?" May had called out to him.

He had grasped her little hand. "I'm right here, honey."

"Do you really and truly want to be my daddy?"

"You bet I do."

And from that day forward, Dom had been May's daddy, in every way that counted. When Rafe was born, fat and healthy and his father's spitting image, Dom had continued lavishing as much love and attention on May as he did on their son. Lausanne learned that a man like

Dom had an endless capacity to love. And it was a good thing, since eighteen months after Rafe came howling into the world, black-eyed, red-haired Ronan Shea made his debut.

"Mama," May called out from the kitchen. "The timer just went off. I think the turkey's ready."

"Where's Aunt Pilar?"

"She and Uncle Hart went back to the truck to get more stuff," May replied.

Lausanne finished arranging the flowers in the middle of the dining room table, then shooed three-year-old Ronan and his sidekick Sparkles, the family's golden retriever, from under her feet. "Go see what Daddy and Rafe are doing in the living room."

"I don't want to!" stubborn little Ronan said.

Before Lausanne had a chance to say another word to her younger son, Brandon Shea scooped up his youngest grandchild, held him high in the air and soared him out of the dining room. Ronan giggled with delight.

When Lausanne entered the kitchen, she paused in the doorway and looked at her daughter. May had grown into a strikingly beautiful teenager and already Dom was making fatherly noises about keeping his little girl under lock and key until she was at least thirty.

Standing guard at May's side, her faithful companion, Arlo, the trained seeing-eye Lab they had purchased for May when she came to live with them, lifted his head and stared at Lausanne.

Dom's sister Pilar flung open the back door, a huge box in her arms. Her husband, Hart, brought in an even bigger box. "That's the last of it. Two hams, three pies, a cake and a sweet potato casserole," Pilar said before dumping her box on the kitchen table.

"Where's Maureen and Jonas?" May asked.

"Jonas is coming later and bringing his girlfriend," Pilar said. "I can't believe my son is old enough to date."

"The boy's eighteen," Hart reminded her. "He's been dating for a couple of years."

Pilar sighed. "Maureen's gone down to the stables to see Sunny Girl's new foal. She said to tell you to come meet her and y'all could take a ride before dinner."

"May I, Mama?" May asked.

"Certainly." But please be careful, Lausanne thought. It had taken a long time for her to stop being over-protective where May was concerned. But thanks to Dom showing her how self-reliant their daughter was, despite her disability, Lausanne had gradually stopped hovering over her eldest child.

"Don't smother her," Dom had said the first time he'd put May on a horse alone. "Let her spread her wings and fly." And that's just what she'd done. That had been four years ago, when May was twelve. Now at sixteen she was an excellent horsewoman, far better than Lausanne would ever be.

"If you gals don't need help in here, I think I'll join the men in the living room." Without further ado, Hart left before the women put him to work.

"Any word from Marta?" Lausanne asked her sister-in-law while she pretended not to watch May put on her sweater and head out the back door.

"Marta called last night. She can't make it until Christmas," Pilar said. "But Bianca is driving in from Houston with her new boyfriend in tow."

In the midst of all the hustle and bustle, Lausanne had little time to relax and truly count her blessings that day, but later that evening, when the whirlwind had passed and the children were asleep in their beds upstairs, Lausanne and Dom put on their jackets and went out onto their big front porch. Overhead a three-quarter moon shined down on them and twinkling stars winked at them, high up in the clear nighttime sky. She loved their ranch, Dom's family and the family they had created together. Every day was a blessing.

With Lausanne standing in front of him, Dom wrapped his arms around her and kissed her temple. "Happy, Mrs. Shea?"

"Deliriously happy, Mr. Shea. How about you?"

"Honey, if I were any happier, I couldn't stand it."

"I've been thinking…"

"Uh-oh."

She nudged him in the ribs with her elbow. He grunted, then laughed.

"As I was saying before you so rudely interrupted me—I've been thinking about the fact that I'm nearly thirty-five and if we're going to have more children, we might want to do it sooner rather than later."

Dom turned her around to face him. When she looked up at him and smiled, he clasped her face between his open palms. "Are you pregnant?"

"The stick turned blue," she told him.

Dom let out a joyous whoop. She reached up and covered his mouth with her hand. "Shh... If you wake up those boys, I'll—"

Dom pulled her hand away and then kissed her.

When they came up for air, she laid her head on his chest and wrapped her arms around his waist. The past was a distant memory, a blurry vision of loneliness and misery. Most of the time, it seemed as if all those terrible things had happened to someone else. But not for one single, solitary minute did she ever forget to be thankful for her many blessings, which began and ended with the husband she loved with all her heart.

REQUEST YOUR FREE BOOKS!

2 FREE NOVELS
FROM THE ROMANCE/SUSPENSE
COLLECTION PLUS 2 FREE GIFTS!

YES! Please send me 2 FREE novels from the Romance/Suspense Collection and my 2 FREE gifts. After receiving them, if I don't wish to receive any more books, I can return the shipping statement marked "cancel." If I don't cancel, I will receive 4 brand-new novels every month and be billed just $5.24 per book in the U.S., or $5.74 per book in Canada, plus 25¢ shipping and handling per book plus applicable taxes, if any*. That's a savings of at least 10% off the cover price! I understand that accepting the 2 free books and gifts places me under no obligation to buy anything. I can always return a shipment and cancel at any time. Even if I never buy another book from the Reader Service, the two free books and gifts are mine to keep forever.

185 MDN EF3H 385 MDN EF3J

Name _____ (PLEASE PRINT) _____

Address _____ Apt. # _____

City _____ State/Prov. _____ Zip/Postal Code _____

Signature (if under 18, a parent or guardian must sign)

Mail to The Reader Service:

IN U.S.A.
P.O. Box 1867
Buffalo, NY
14240-1867

IN CANADA
P.O. Box 609
Fort Erie, Ontario
L2A 5X3

Not valid to current subscribers to the Romance Collection,
the Suspense Collection or the Romance/Suspense Collection.

Want to try two free books from another line?
Call 1-800-873-8635 or visit www.morefreebooks.com.

* Terms and prices subject to change without notice. NY residents add applicable sales tax. Canadian residents will be charged applicable provincial taxes and GST. This offer is limited to one order per household. All orders subject to approval. Credit or debit balances in a customer's account(s) may be offset by any other outstanding balance owed by or to the customer. Please allow 4 to 6 weeks for delivery.

BOB206